The Devil Plague
of Naples
Napoleon's Vampire Hunters - 2

BY THE SAME AUTHOR

The Quest of Frankenstein
The Triumph of Frankenstein
Napoleon's Vampire Hunters

The Devil Plague of Naples

Napoleon's Vampire Hunters - 2

by
Frank Schildiner

A Black Coat Press Book

Acknowledgements: Paul Féval and Brian Stableford.

Visit our website at www.blackcoatpress.com

Introduction

One of the chief protagonists of *Napoleon's Vampire Hunters*, the steadfast Jean-Pierre Séverin, is the creation of French writer Paul Féval (1816-1887) and was introduced in his novel *La Vampire*, translated by Brian Stableford under the title *The Vampire Countess*.[1] A detailed overview of Féval's life and career can be found in the introduction to our first volume.

This book also reuses elements drawn from two other Féval novels. The first is *La Ville-Vampire* also translated by Stableford under the title *Vampire City*.[2] It was first published in 1875, although internal evidence suggests that it must have been written eight years earlier, probably for serialization in a newspaper. At the time of its first publication, the horror genre hardly existed, and Féval may be credited with its invention.

Selene, the Vampire City, which vampires call the Sepulchre or Scholomance, is located somewhere "in the barbarous lands around Belgrade" and is normally invisible to mortal eyes. It is a great city of black jasper capped with domes and minarets reaching for the sky, which is eternally in mourning, enveloped by perpetual gloom. Arranged there, in mysterious order, are the sepulchral dwellings of the vampires, that race which the wrath of God has placed in the margins of our world. Their sons, half demon and half phantom, are living and dead at the same time, incapable of reproducing and deprived of the blessing of death. Their womenfolk are ghouls. Some, it is said, have sat on thrones and terrified history…

The second novel is *Les Compagnons du Silence,* translated by Stableford as *The Companions of the Silence*,[3] initial-

---

[1] Black Coat Press (ISBN 978-0-9740711-5-2).

[2] Black Coat Press (ISBN 978-0-9740711-6-9).

[3] Black Coat Press (ISBN 978-1-61227-706-6)

ly published in 1857. *The Companions of the Silence*, which takes place in or around Naples, showcases the moral difficulties in using a hero, Beldemonio, a.k.a. *Il Porporato*, who is a career criminal and a multiple murderer. Although evil circumstances have cast him in that role, even though he makes a habit of trying to right the evils wrought by the law that has proscribed him, Féval doesn't know how to reward him. The prevailing morality of the day, at least as it applied to popular fiction, put severe restrictions on the extent and nature of the triumph that Beldemonio could be permitted to achieve.

The trick used by authors employing morally equivocal heroes was to provide them with adversaries far more evil than they. Enter the Neapolitan chief of police Johann Spurzheim, who not only schemes to bring the hero down, but also everyone he love. It is in the remarkable characterization of Spurzheim that Féval found a new, and arguably unsurpassable, extreme. The astonishing complexity of his evil machinations, coupled with the extremely difficult situation from which he is operating, supplies the novel with its taut narrative tension and complex plot. That charismatic character anticipates the arch-villain of the *Black Coat* series, the decrepit yet seemingly immortal Colonel Bozzo-Corona, aka *Fra Diavolo*, just as the criminal organization of the Black Coats is shadow of the splendid secret society of The Silence.

Féval's ambition took *The Companions of the Silence* into previously-untrodden narrative territory, and made it such an important stepping-stone for other writers of popular fiction. The novel remains very readable today, and it certainly is not lacking in the essential quality of *panache*.

The Devil Plague of Naples is its worthy successor.

Jean-Marc Lofficier

CHAPTER I

Ronato Rotolo giggled as the knife sliced across the palm of his hand. Though the cut was deep and instantly bloody, he tittered away like a child being playfully tickled by a feather. The sensation of pain appeared lost to his drug-addled, alcohol-diseased mind and body. The viscous crimson fluid pooled and fell from his injured extremity in large droplets.

"I can't wait to see what happens next. Give me a kiss, lovely one," Ronato said, his voice an uncontrolled slur with no apparent control of pitch or rhythm.

The object of his drunken affection, the elderly magus Oranto Pirozzi, ignored the foolish warbling of the bleeding fool. A man of medium height with a long, curling, black and gray beard, and a flattened nose with enormous nostrils, he was far from anyone's ideal of "lovely." His sunken, dark eyes and stout form also prevented such a sobriquet—but his nearly hideous aspect was perfect for his work.

Pirozzi was a magus, a dangerous one. His renowned powers were the subject of much discussion throughout the Italian states, with many whispers of his consorting with demons and, worse, foreigners. His patrons included wealthy merchant families and even some minor royalty—each seeking his uncannily accurate horoscopes and powerful potions. Pirozzi was a feared man by those few who knew his reputation. Wisely, he kept himself in the shadows, living as a guest with various powerful patrons.

Grasping Ronato's arm with his gloved hands, Pirozzi aimed the falling blood into a tiny golden, jewel-covered chalice. He studied the quickly filling vessel and nodded his hood-covered head happily. Ronato continued to caper, still seemingly unaware that he was bleeding.

Seconds later, the goblet was nearly filled, resembling a gelatinous wine whose rusty scent wafted over the small assembly of robed figures. Only Ronato was clad in normal, if heavily wine-soiled, clothes. Even his curly, perfumed, blond locks and sparse beard and mustache, exuded a fragrance of spoiled, cheap wine.

Pirozzi nodded towards two of his followers, who immediately moved to Ronato's side and gently propelled him deep into the cavern. The remaining ten hooded men and women followed, walking with lively steps down the sparsely lit, mildew-scented stone corridor. At the rear of the solemn column was Pirozzi, his step slow, his outward manner calm and resolute. One would think, based on his behavior and ritualistic motions, that he was imitating a Roman Catholic Cardinal performing a ceremony in the name of God. Nothing could be further from the truth.

In addition to being an alchemist, astrologer, and ceremonial magician, Pirozzi was a priest of the darkest powers known to mankind. Call that being Satan, Lucifer, the Great Serpent, Beelzebub, Angra Mainyu, or the Prince of Darkness, his mission was simple—spread evil and darkness throughout the world. For the last two decades, in an almost missionary capacity, Pirozzi had created small cults devoted to power of that arch-fiend. This was not difficult—in every large city, there were always the disaffected and foolish among the wealthy. Men and women who were bored with simply purchasing their every desire. Pirozzi sought those to whom baubles and debauchery palled and no longer suffered the ever-encompassing boredom. To those, he offered small, unique seductions while probing for weaknesses. Within a short space of time, these followers were damned—becoming servants of the terrible, cold, darkness of pure evil.

Originally, he had planned to do as he had done in cities throughout Spain, France, Italy and the Holy Roman Empire—set up a coven and leave. There was always some fallen priest that could lead the sad little Satanists, attempting to prove their evil by behaving badly. Pirozzi never cared what happened after he left. He was a missionary of the Morning Star, a magus who spread the corruption of the Father of Lies everywhere he traveled.

At least, that had been the plan before he had come to the Kingdom of Naples.[4] In this large, powerful city of merchants, clergy, and nobles, there was an almost peasant-like suspicion and respect for the mystic arts. Those who were believed to possess the powers of witchcraft, better known locally as *stregheria*, were treated with awe and respect. Even the terrible, terrifying secret police, the infamous Cupbearers, walked softly around one who wove spells and worshipped strange powers.

This changed when Stefano Bove, of the famous spice-trading family, revealed a family secret. After a night of rather dull group sex and murder at the Bove villa on Lake Avernus, the silly, spoiled man-child had led the magus into a copse of trees. Pushing aside a heavily overgrown bush and weeds, Stefano had revealed the mouth of a small cave.

"*Voilà*! According my late grandfather—Satan take his dark soul!—this is cave is the legendary *Porte dell'inferno*, the Gates of Hell. His father said that the demi-god Hercules walked down this cave and into the pit. I explored it and all that's down there is a big stone coffin…" Stefano explained as he then followed the passage into the depths of the Earth.

The find within changed Pirozzi's plans forever. He had been shocked that night—this being as significant a moment in

---

[4] The Kingdom of Naples was a French client state in southern Italy created in 1806 when the Bourbon Ferdinand I sided with the Third Coalition against Napoleon and was in return ousted by a French invasion. Joseph Bonaparte, Napoleon's elder brother, was installed in his stead. The French occupation army was led by then-Colonel Joseph Léopold Sigisbert Hugo (promoted later to the rank of General), the father of Victor Hugo. He was the one who arrested *Fra Diavolo* and had him hung on 10 November 1806. When Joseph became King of Spain in 1808, Napoleon appointed his brother-in-law, Joachim Murat, to take his place. Murat was later deposed by the Congress of Vienna after being defeated at the Battle of Tolentino on 3 May 1815.

his life as the day he had sacrificed his first infant at the Scholomance.

Months of planning passed, almost in an instant, as he prepared for this momentous moment.

Following the line of followers down the cavern, Pirozzi knew he could walk the distance with his eyes closed. He had practically moved into the *Porte dell'inferno*, ignoring the constant drafts and drip, drip, drips of water across the gray stone floor. The ceiling was only slightly higher than their tallest member, Tito Orsini, until one arrived at the room containing the sarcophagus. That chamber was high—over twenty feet in height, free of cold breezes and rising damp. Also, there was a warmth to this room, as if the walls themselves were heated from some hidden furnace.

The room was unadorned, plain, gray, rough stone walls with a sloping roof that rose up like a small dome in a Gothic cathedral. The chamber exuded a wrongness, almost feeling as if the very Earth itself had been scooped out by some unseen, monstrous clawed fist. Every time Pirozzi and his followers entered this chamber, they felt a burdening sense of disquiet that threatened to overwhelm their senses.

The massive stone sarcophagus in the center of the room merely added to the feeling of dread that threatened their minds. The casket was made from a dark stone that appeared to absorb the brazier light rather than reflect it. Almost ten feet long, the coffer appeared to have been exuded from the depths of the Earth into this chamber. There was no means to move the sarcophagus, although the lid yielded through the lightest of pressures.

Revealed within was a corpse, a desiccated, dust-covered assemblage of dried skin and bones with some pale wisps across the skull. None of the coven were certain if those delicate, web-like tendrils were the last traces of hair or an accumulation of pale grime. Pirozzi did not allow anyone to find out, having already identified the occupant of the ancient burial vessel.

Stepping through his followers, Oranto Pirozzi held the chalice of blood before his body like a priest carrying the cross to an altar. He nodded and Tito Orsini and Stefano Bove gently propelled Ronato Rotolo to the magus's side. The drunken nobleman appeared lost and unfocused, no longer laughing and speaking. His dark eyes swam in his head, sliding over the black-robed gathering, the cup filled with his blood, and silver knife in Stefano's beefy hand.

"In the name of the Lord of Earth, Lucifer Morningstar, Prince of the Air, curses upon our enemies. Hail Satan!" Oranto Pirozzi said, his voice sonorous and deep.

For some unknown reason, there was no echo in this chamber, another unexplained oddity of *Porte dell'inferno*.

"Hail Satan!" the coven chorused, each performing a reversed version of the sign of the cross as they spoke.

"In the name of Asmodeus King of Demons, Belial Lord of Pride, Beelzebub Lord of Flies, and Azazel the Black Goat of Darkness, we call on the powers of the Pit! We offer to you the blood of kings!"

Pirozzi slowly poured the collected blood across the dusty grinning skull of the mummified body in the box. That was one of the more difficult parts of this ritual—finding a subject with the blood of kings in their body. Happily, he had found that Ronato's family were blood relations to Henry de Lorraine, 5th Duke of Guise and one-time Doge of Naples. It didn't matter that the House of Guise had ruled the city-state for less than a year—the blood was still present.

"Return to us, Nosos, Lady of Corruption, daughter of the Tenebrae!"

Oranto Pirozzi howled, feeling the dark energy building about the chamber. Somewhere in the distance, a dog howled mournfully. Then, there was a loud crack of thunder that echoed down the tunnel, but died just as it arrived in the underground room that was the *Porte dell'inferno*. A stillness seemed to fill the world, as if all of creation was waiting on a knife's edge for some action.

That was when Pirozzi nodded and Stefano sliced open Ronato's uninjured hand. The drunken nobleman whimpered, a weak squeak reminiscent of a mouse. Otherwise, he did not struggle, allowing Stefano and Tito to place his newly bleeding hand directly over the face of the moldering corpse.

"Look!" Tito Orsini whispered, staring with rapt eyes at the body in the casket.

Pirozzi waved the rest of the coven back and gazed within, his eyes widening in shock. The limbs, formerly mere tatters of crumbling flesh over brown bones, appeared to be reforming. The face, formerly a grinning skull with sharp incisors, was now covered with a papyrus-thin brown layer. A set of nearly non-existent black lips hid the terrible teeth from view as the crimson stream of blood ran in rivulets over the skeletal form.

It was the eyes that held Pirozzi fixed in place. Moments earlier, they had been mere gaping holes, dark empty pits that held no signs of life. Now, sinister pinprick-sized red lights appeared in the empty sockets, giving the impression of some demoniac being rising from abyssal depths. The blasphemous stygian malevolence grew with each passing heartbeat, as if the plutonian depths of outer darkness suddenly expelled a horror from the endless void. Pirozzi, who thought of himself as a sinister being, a demon in human form, felt like one of the squalling infants he happily sacrificed to the Gods of the Netherworld.

Suddenly, there was an explosion of movement and skeletal arms tore Ronato free from the gentle bonds of Stefano and Tito. The desiccated ebony lips latched onto the drunken man's throat and he sighed—releasing a sound of pure ecstasy over the hushed chamber.

Scarlet streams of blood escaped from the tattered mouth, though, with each passing moment, the transformation grew more evident. The emaciated mummy appeared to fill out, grow more life-like. At the same instant, the drunken, though still vital, Ronato appeared to shrink, darken and wither. Within seconds, the body that tumbled to the stone floor was a mere husk—a shriveled collection of dry sticks and papery skin.

The being in the sarcophagus thrust aside the wasted form that had once been Ronato Rotolo. The nobleman's mummified remains shattered and collapsed upon striking the stone floor, shattering like dried twigs across the ground. The red eyes slowly scanned the coven, examining each member in turn, though not lingering on any for more than a heartbeat.

Finally, the crimson orbs settled on Pirozzi. In voice that was a harsh, hoarse, husky croak, the being asked:

"You are the one who summonsed me?"

Pirozzi preened, happy to be recognized by this terrible, powerful being.

"Yes, I am he who summonsed you to service. I am Oranto Pirozzi, a graduate of the Scholomance. You are Nosos, the Lady of Corruption. We have much work for you to do. First, the French control the city and you must kill the new King Joseph…"

Pirozzi's speech was cut off as the decayed hands grasped his head and twisted, filling the air with a loud, meaty crack. The dark magus, the man who had viewed himself as the Dark Angel's favorite magician, died, his head facing the wrong direction.

"Scholomance graduates," the brittle voice rasped, "they never shut up. I do not serve humanity."

The crimson inhuman eyes slowly examined again each member of the coven—the men and women standing frozen in open-mouthed shock. They were used to petty evils, even terrible acts like the rape and murder of children. The swift death of their leader, a sorcerer of inhuman power, had terrified them into inaction.

Now, the frightening, demonic eyes pinned each man and woman into stillness, causing them to feel like insects in a specimen jar. The overwhelming inner power of the undead creature seemed to fill the chamber, causing the weak witches of the dead Pirozzi coven to quake in terror.

"You," Nosos said while pointing a crumbling finger at one cloaked figure. "Stand by my side."

The object of this order was Fortuna Orsini, the young, pretty, impressionable, but otherwise forgettable wife of Tito Orsini. She was a tiny creature with a girlish, round face, a stub nose, long, glossy, straight brown hair, wide innocent eyes, and a surprisingly shapely figure. Fortuna was a gentle creature who participated only minimally in the coven's activities, and even then, with little enthusiasm. Pirozzi and a few others had tried to break her spirit, finding her ultimately an uninteresting object. Other women in the group, like the red-haired, buxom, Baroness Paluzzi, or the sensual, seductive dark-haired Claudine Brazzi, had garnered greater interest, and ultimately greater power and position in the cult. Fortuna was treated as little more than a servant by the members, even her husband.

Fortuna moved with slow steps to the side of the stone casket, her eyes downcast. A few slow smiles crossed the faces of the members, relaxing slightly as the least of their dark circle was brought forth, presumably as the next victim of this undead being. Nosos's red demoniac eyes locked with Fortuna's soft green orbs. The young woman stiffened, trapped under the hellish energy of that piercing gaze.

"Stay right here. Do not move," Nosos said, her voice even rougher than before.

Fortuna nodded, staring at her tiny unshod feet, expecting her imminent demise. The fleshless inhuman head swiveled back to the coven, studying their hidden smug, barely hidden smiles. The thin black lips peeled back, causing the sharp blood-stained teeth to glint and glimmer in the brazier light. A dry cough emerged from the cracked, skeletal throat, one that continued for several seconds. The black lips peeled back even further and all present realized the undead creature was laughing.

Suddenly, there was an explosion of dust and grit and the creature vanished from sight. A shriek of agony filled the air, emerging from the now flayed face of Tito Orsini. Screams of agony rent the chamber, never drifting any further, nor echoing in the slightest. A chorus of wailing cries were each cut off by pulpy, sodden slapping sounds as meaty, sopping carcasses struck the stone floor. The rending sounds of ripping flesh and glutinous lactation assaulted Fortuna's senses as the members of the coven were consumed by the undead entity.

Then all sounds ceased, and the young wife—now widow—realized she was alone with the demoniac being. No signs of life were evident in the room, with only a barely audible occasional dripping sound as viscous blood oozed from the scattered corpses. Fortuna's eyes, staring at her tiny toes, never rose. Her body shivered, gently convulsing like a lost lamb in a rainstorm.

The silence broke as a mucilaginous fleshy percussion ponderously traversed the length of the chamber. A pair of scarlet streaked pale legs halted before Fortuna's downcast face.

"Fortuna," the being before her said in a warm, husky, purr that surrounded and caressed the young woman. "Look at me."

Fortuna shivered and shook as he eyes slowly rose, widening in shock at the sight before her eyes. Her lips opened, but no sound emerged as she stared into the bottomless depths of Nosos's eyes.

"Mine," Nosos whispered and ran and her blood-soaked hand through Fortuna's lovely locks.

Closing her eyes, Fortuna leaned her head against the caressing hand and opened her mouth as a pair of blood-soaked lips covered hers for a hard, passion-filled kiss.

CHAPTER II

"Hold her down you oafs!" Captain Victor Dannel screamed, waving his sword in an arc over his head.

The four French soldiers didn't look up, but pressed their rifles down a little harder. Dannel continued to wave his sword about, though none of the soldiers paid him any mind—they never did, even when he was behaving sanely.

Captain Dannel wasn't much of a soldier, though he did like dressing in the blue coat with red piping uniform of the Garde Impériale. He was especially proud of his long, shiny officer's sword and the tall bearskin cap with the Imperial eagle on the facing. Those were the good points, along with the envious looks he received from the local bumpkins of Naples. The actual fighting and duties as an officer were far less pleasurable. He was a man who regularly failed in life, often without realizing the consequences of his actions. His father, a wine merchant, smuggler, and old friend of Joseph Bonaparte, often despaired at the feckless foolishness of his youngest child. Oscar Dannel, a father of three boys and two girls, was justifiably proud of his other children. His daughters had married important government men, each with bright futures and the possibilities of noble titles in the future. The oldest son, also named Oscar, was a partner in a rising merchant bank and considered one of the great minds of the Empire. The second son, Félix, held a commission as a *Capitaine de vaisseau* in the French Naval forces. Victor was the only child whose actions disappointed the wealthy wine merchant. He had tried to get the lad interested in the business, only to discover he had spawned a child incapable of telling the difference between a Bordeaux and a Burgundy! Happily, none of his colleagues discovered this scandalous and horrific defect in his child—such information could have damage his reputation!

Other attempts to discover Victor's talents were tested over the years, all with results that caused Oscar to internally compare himself to Job from the Bible. For Victor was, no doubt, God's test to determine Oscar's faith. Art and music were fast failures, the boy was simultaneously color-blind and tone-deaf. The mathematics of accounting were also a lost cause and cost Oscar several thousand francs to cover Victor's monstrous errors. Languages, clock-making, the law... each were catastrophes that cost the wine merchant money and years of life in worry. The only talent Victor appeared to possess was an ability to look competent and remain trustworthy to the eyes of observers, even when he clearly was out of his depths. People instinctively trusted the young man's calm, confident face, not realizing he was incapable of recognizing his own lack of abilities. To Victor's mind, failures never occurred. The paints were defective, the violin was a poor instrument, and so on, and so on. It was his brother Antoine who caused Oscar to discover the true path for his wayward child. Antoine owned a business that sewed coats for the Army.

"You are trying too hard," he had told Oscar. "You are trying to push a talentless boy into professions he cannot do, no matter who you hire to teach him the skills."

A swarthy, corpulent man who dressed in expensive clothing, Antoine Dannel was nobody's fool. He held an important government contract and was slowly spreading his business tentacles across the continent.

"I must get him a job," Oscar admitted, as he accepted a glass of his own wine from his brother. "Otherwise, he will never be a man. His mother—God rest her soul!—was too gentle with him, as her youngest."

Antoine nodded and poured himself another glass.

"Agreed, you will find no argument with me. I only add something our father always said when he was deep in his cups. *Do not ask a fish to climb a tree.* The same goes for your Victor. He is a fish and you keep pushing him to fly like a bird. No, *mon frère*, it will not do. Instead, let me call my friend Gilles Lambert. He is a Division General assigned to headquarters..."

Which was how Victor Dannel had found himself a Under-Lieutenant in the Imperial Army and sent into the wars. What Antoine had realized was this—Victor may be a fool, but he was a confident one who could obey the simplest instructions. While most organization would consider that a defect, in the army, this could be a positive trait. They took such men and broke them down, teaching them the exact way to behave under all circumstances. For every military genius like Bonaparte or Murat, they required hundreds, nay, thousands of men capable to obey orders without thought or discussion. Victor Dannel was such a man.

Therefore, since the monstrous attacks had begun in Naples, he knew exactly how to behave. Pin the monsters down with bayonets, wait for the men with axes to chop the creatures into pieces, bag all the pieces, and toss them into the furnace. Simple enough, learned through accidents and men foolish enough to take half-measures. An unbagged arm could still choke you or grab a knife and kill many.

"Caught another one, did you, Captain? Well done, sir!" Johann Spurzheim stated as he alighted from his coach.

A tall man with immensely broad shoulders, a narrow waist, and a head of thinning blond hair, the Chief of the Royal Police of Naples was never far from the scene of danger. The fact that he was Austrian disturbed a few of King Joseph's staff, but only a little. The man was loyal and astonishingly efficient. Also one look from his raptor-like eyes usually caused even the strongest skeptics to dismiss their objections.

"Thank you, Contrôleur Général," Victor replied, lowering and sheathing his sword. "Sergeant Plourde, hold the beast down with your boot, if you please."

Sergeant Plourde, a squat, powerfully-built man in his mid-forties, placed one large boot on the chest of the slobbering woman, preventing the quaking body from rising despite the bayonets piercing her fallen form. She possessed long, ebony hair and might have been beautiful, were it not for her rheumy, unseeing eyes and frothy, babbling jaws.

"This is the fourth this week. The rate of attacks is increasing across the city," Spurzheim mused, rubbing a finger across his luxuriant and carefully waxed mustache.

Dressed in a semi-military uniform made from a pale blue linen fabric, he was an impressive, imperious figure in the bright, summer sunlight. Dannel didn't reply to the police chief's statements; they were irrelevant to his daily orders from Colonel Hugo. Instead, he scanned the vicinity, attempting to see if further monsters lurked about. As of now, the creatures were merely referred to as "partisans," and the blame was placed on the Bourbon insurgents. But nobody in Naples believed this tale—the people, and much of the nobility, were convinced that terrible acts of dark magic was behind the monsters. The French, while not discounting the possibility of dark powers, were more phlegmatic. One did not mention the walking dead in official documents—it was frowned upon by the upper echelons. For one thing, it could cause a panic among the denizens of Naples. Additionally, there may be a natural explanation.

Yet, here they stood, looking down at the struggling body of a bedraggled, foul-smelling woman. She had one musket ball in her head and two in her chest, but none of the gaping wounds bled even a drop of blood. Four large men pierced her shoulders and legs with long, wickedly sharp, bayonets, pinning her to the warm Earth, yet she did not cry out in pain or even acknowledge her terrible injuries. Instead, she writhed, moaned and snapped her teeth, behaving like a trapped wild animal attempting to break free of a cage. They all acted in this frightening manner—which was why the destruction procedures had been precisely designed and enforced by the military.

"Why are the axe men taking so long?" Victor asked, glancing around and not spotting the soldiers assigned to such disgusting duties.

"I countermanded the order," Federigo Gui intoned as he stepped into view.

He was a man of middle height with a bald pate that contained a careful coiffed fringe of black hair, covered from neck to feet in the black robes of the Dominican Order. He possessed deep-set, watchful eyes that gazed upon all with open suspicion. Few were capable of meeting his penetrating gaze, fewer were even willing to try. He was the head of the secret police organization known as the *Cupbearers*, and was probably one of the most feared men in all of Italy. Appointed by Queen Maria Carolina and her prime minister, the Englishman Sir John Acton, he now served King Joseph with equal fervor.

"You have no right," Johann Spurzheim hissed.

He despised the cutthroat Abbot, knowing they were rivals for power. One of them would, in addition to his regular duties, possess the power of deputy minister of the interior. The other would die a traitor's death, this much they both acknowledged.

Federigo Gui's harsh, dark countenance broke into a wide smile of triumph. The expression resembled that of a jungle cat about to pounce and rip and rend its prey. Apparently, this was exactly what he had hoped his enemy would say. Reaching into his heavy sleeve, Gui plucked out a scroll which he unrolled with a snap. King Joseph Bonaparte's seal was visible, even at this distance.

"I think you'll find that I do, my son. His Royal Highness is disturbed by these increasing attacks from Lucifer's minions in his kingdom. This daughter of the Devil shall not be destroyed, but chained and placed in custody." Federigo Gui explained, stepping closing and waving the document in Johann Spurzheim's seething face.

"Are you insane?" Spurzheim exploded, pushing the paper aside. "This undead… thing, cannot be saved! Allow it to remain free and it shall kill us all!"

Federigo Gui shook his head sadly, as if looking at a particularly stupid child.

"We shall do no such thing, my son. The monster shall be chained to a wall and placed in a room with a heavy, stout, locked door. None shall enter the room."

"Then why save the body of this being?"

Johann Spurzheim knew he was playing the part of foolish jester in Gui's little play in the courtyard of the royal palace. Bu, he didn't have a choice. Gui's power was greater than his; his Cupbearers were the terror of Naples. The reason this was still a nearly even battle was because the Dominican Abbot's followers were too hated and feared. This precarious position allowed Spurzheim a chance to build an alternative force of order for the kingdom of Naples.

"I am glad you asked, sir. His Royal Highness and I were discussing these recurring demoniac occurrences over dinner. King Joseph remembered that his brother, the great and God-blessed Emperor Napoleon, is well aware of such otherworldly dangers. To combat such hell-spawned horrors, he employs an expert on the subject—a maestro of the sword and expert in many unique subjects and professions. This man works in concert with one of His Holiness the Supreme Pontiff Pius VII's personal staff."

Gui rolled up the document and tied it closed with a red silk ribbon.

"I assume you are sending a message requesting their assistance. A clever notion, Father Abbot," Spurzheim grudgingly admitted.

He knew they were all out of their depth with these undead creatures. Also, and he was well-aware that his enemy had this thought in mind as well, they could deflect all blame to these so-called "experts."

Gui nodded, smugly triumphant and not hiding his amusement at Johann Spurzheim's discomfort. "Thank you, my son. I expect that we shall meet these men next month. I think it shall be interesting to meet Swordmaster Jean-Pierre Séverin and Exorcist Franz Karnstein."

"I should think so," Spurzheim agreed, memorizing the name. He had two more dossiers to compile now…

CHAPTER III

The *Loire* wallowed in the blue Mediterranean, barely moving from watch to watch as the breeze failed to rise once again. It was day eight of what should have been a three-and-a-half-day journey from Marseilles to Naples. Even the *Loire*, a hulking, stinking tub of a ship known as a "cochon vautré" by the sailors sentenced to work her, were frustrated by the lack of wind.

The *Loire* was originally a 64-gun ship originally designed for commercial purposes towards the end of the reign of King Louis XVI; they were bought into the navy through the clever use of bribery and aggressive commercial tactics from the shipyards. Slow before or by the wind, leaky, and filled with a rapacious collection of rats and other vermin, this class of ship was openly despised by the navy. There was a rumor, one that was well-believed by anyone forced to sail in one of these vessels, that their creation was a clever plan by the British to weaken the French Navy.

In any event, the *Loire* was the last of its class left on the seas. Having lingered for a long stretch of time in the harbor of Toulon, the ship was transferred and made a simple supply vessel from Marseilles to Italy. Never making more than five knots, the *Pig*, as she was openly called by all except her drunken commander, Lieutenant de vaisseau Marcel Le Pen. All knew that service on this craft was a sentence, usually for being just short of completely incompetent. Le Pen was an almost acceptable sailor, good enough to not be cashiered for crashing a corvette into a merchant vessel while on watch, but not enough to stop him from rising further in the navy. The crew was much the same, a collection of layabouts, wastrels, and outright thieves.

The passengers of the *Pig* were no happier than the crew—few having gotten used to the horrific, and rather overwhelming, stench that exuded from the ship's bilges. The passengers numbered ten in all and they were a slightly unusual group for the *Loire*. Six were the common types, commercial men traveling to Naples and other major ports in hope of making important deals with the vast merchant houses scattered about the Italian peninsula. These were types that the sailors knew and understood—sweaty, rotund men with frightened eyes and conversations that usually consisted of business deals they'd made or watch go to ruin. They were easy targets for card games and other games of chance so long as they believed they were getting good value for their wagers. Befriending one could result in a regular source of income for the right officer or warrant rank.

Of the remaining four, one other was easy to comprehend. She was a woman of about thirty, attractive, though far from well-dressed or stylish. The sailors assumed Madame Rosine Gauthier was either a widow or an abandoned woman who was moving back to live with her family in an attempt to rebuild her life. The argument raged among the lower deck until the Quartier-maître de 2ème classe Lucas Rey overheard her conversation with one of the commercial gentlemen, a three-chinned, balding, damp-palmed man named Raphael Petit.

"Her husband was leaving her for the widow of his employer, a firm of wheelwrights. As he was calling her a frigid, stupid, bitch, he stepped into the road and was trampled by a milk wagon. She left him there and proceeded to sell everything he owned, including his dented watch and chain. Now she goes to live with her older sister, hoping to find another husband. Possibly that Petit, though if he lays atop her..."

The petty officer spun an improbable, yet hysterically funny, scenario involving the use of pulleys and cart horses to consummate a marriage between the two passengers.

That left three, and they were all quite outside the range of the *Loire*'s usual passengers. The first was Madame Francesca Policeni. She as tall, heart-stoppingly gorgeous and possessed flowing ebony locks that caused men to weave pathetically poetic comparisons to the night sky. Her large dark eyes seemed to shimmer and cause all she gazed upon to forget to breathe; her figure was like that of a statue by a master sculptor. Why would an astonishingly lovely woman trap herself on a floating disaster like the *Loire*? Based on her dresses, hats, and shoes, she was also very wealthy, as well as the embodiment of Venus in the eyes of the sailors and passengers.

The answer may lay in the second odd figure aboard the *Pig*. This man had the opposite effect on the crew and passengers. Tall, slender, with long hands and fingers, most assumed he was a musician or some kind of artist. This was reinforced by his simple clothing: black jackets, pants, well-used black boots and plain white shirts. Only wealthy artistic types could afford to dress like a dour English Puritan. This belief ended once the sailors observed him practicing fighting on the deck with the third unusual passenger...

Once again, it was the ship's resident gossip, Quartier-maître de 2ème classe Rey, who discovered the answer. In a gathering, deep in the hold, the men who wagered on his information waited with carefully held breath. Partially, this was caused by the fragrance wafting from the bilges, but mostly because the officers and sailors had wagered heavily on each piece of information Rey had obtained.

"He is Austrian," the petty officer stated, watching as coins passed through some hands.

Most had thought that the youngish, handsome, stern man was Prussian, Swiss or Russian. Guzzling a large mug of the cheap wine they kept aboard, one of the benefits of being the arbiter of the wagers on the *Pig*, Rey burped loudly and continued his recitation.

"His name is Franz Karnstein and he's a baron of some kind. Has some position in the Holy Church."

Few coins were exchanged that night, though some debates raged whether he was an actual priest or just one who wished to live like one. This was because the first and second oddities aboard the *Loire* were behaving in a manner that caused gossip among both passengers and crew.

The third oddity was directly connected to the man named Karnstein, possibly as an employer or superior. He was a tall, rangy older man with a calm face and eyes that missed nothing. His light-colored hair and pale, sad eyes caused one to think he might be a missionary, or a physician who'd seen far too much in life. It was the one-legged, foul smelling, cigar smoking ship's cook, Antoine Roche, who supplied a few clues to the identity of the man whose name was Jean-Pierre Séverin.

"He is a swordsman, a teacher of *escrime*," Roche explained as he flicked ashes into the evening soup. "My cousin Milo, the gendarme, met him once. He is friends with someone important and also works in the Paris Morgue."

"That explains the sad eyes," Rey said. "Carrying corpses all day would do that to a man"

The conversation about the third unusual passenger had effectively ended. It didn't matter to the crew that Roche's story was obviously incomplete—a fascinating drama was unfolding between Madame Policeni and Baron Karnstein.

Since the day the passengers had embarked, the lovely Madame Policeni had charmed all aboard. Her bright smile and outgoing manner caused most of the men to fantasize about how her plump red lips would feel, how her voluptuous figure would fit inside their arms. Even Rosine Gauthier appeared to enjoy her company, and they spent their meals together, chatting merrily on a multitude of subjects.

Only Baron Karnstein appeared unmoved—in fact, he appeared completely disinterested in so much as glancing in her direction. Which was even odder since the handsome, if stern, Austrian nobleman, was the object of most of the lovely lady's attention and affection. Despite this, the young Baron Karnstein ignored every flirtatious comment Madame Policeni extended.

A few of the crew suggested he might prefer boys, an affection some of them practiced in secret. This was discarded since the Austrian behaved in this manner to all, even his possible employer, Séverin. Even the garrulous Lucas Rey proved unable to crack the icy exterior of the Austrian baron.

"One look at those eyes… like that of a wolf…" Rey repeated several times to anyone who was willing to listen over a mug of wine.

Which was why more than a few eyes were watching the pair on deck. The beautiful Madame Policeni and Baron Karnstein were seated on a pair of canvas chairs—normally not an interesting event. Yet all eyes were upon both, neither of whom were speaking. The young Austrian was absorbed in a large leather-bound book, his eyes scanning the pages with rapt attention. The attractive dark-haired woman sat nearby, her arms folded across her chest, her shoe tapping the deck with obvious annoyance. This scene continued for a full hour, the only sounds being the gentle leafing of the pages and the insistent tapping of the dainty toes. Finally, Madame Policeni lost this open battle of wills.

"*Coglione! Testa di cazzo vaffanculo! Stronzo coglione!*" she spat out standing with her hands on her hips, before storming down below.

Baron Karnstein looked up and glanced her way as she vanished down below. He then turned back to his book and promptly threw the heavy tome over the rail and into the glassy sea.

"Most people merely abandon a book and allow others to take it," Jean-Pierre Séverin said, sitting down in the chair recently abandoned by Madame Policeni.

"Then those people would be allowing such drivel back out on an unsuspecting populace. I am not in favor of banning literary works, but that waste of paper tested my beliefs." Karnstein replied.

This was the longest speech he had made since coming aboard the *Loire*,-though he did not appear to relax to any great degree.

"That fool Lord Cumberland wrote a long treatise where he holds that vampires are part of distinct bloodlines, each possessing the same distinct powers," continued Karnstein, his face taking on a mask of disgust and making a sound as if he was spitting. "Only a fool would believe such drivel!"

Séverin chuckled for a few seconds and nodded once.

"Yes, I do understand. One of my teachers held that Cumberland and his toady von Meruh were even more dangerous to humanity than all the vampires on the planet. Not sure if I agree with her, but I do appreciate the sentiment."

"Your teacher should read the history of Styria" Karnstein replied. "That pair made the mistake of attempting to battle one of my family. I believe Count Joseph Karnstein threw Cumberland off the parapet of the family castle in Lower Styria. Not sure of his follower."

He then turned his gray blue eyes towards the older swordmaster and inquired:

"You did not sit down to discuss my reading habits."

"Your observation skills do you credit," Séverin replied, not hiding his sarcasm. "Madame Policeni appears to be quite angry at your behavior."

Franz Karnstein rolled his eyes in response.

"I speak acceptable Italian, Maestro. I know precisely the street oaths she directed towards me moments earlier."

Jean-Pierre Séverin settled back in his chair.

"She is a strikingly attractive woman very taken with you and appears quite insulted that the longest statement you directed towards her was, 'please pass the salt.'"

Karnstein shook his head slowly.

"No, incorrect."

"She is not attractive?" said Séverin, lifting one eyebrow quizzically.

Karnstein waved a hand, a cutting gesture.

"Of course, she is beautiful. I do possess fully functional eyes."

"So she is not insulted?" Séverin asked, amused by the flash of annoyance that crossed the younger man's face for an instant.

The emotional response vanished as quickly as it appeared, but this was a crack in the Austrian's fierce armor.

"Maestro," Karnstein said, sounding weary. "You probably speak Italian as well, if not better, than I. We both understood her words, which took eight days on board this rotting, stinking tub before rearing along with her hidden fury. The lady is both exquisite to the eye and enraged by my refusal to participate in her attempted seduction. Do I pass your test?"

Séverin silently clapped his hands in celebration.

"You do, though the trial was not of my making. Madame Policeni chose you on her own, or someone else's, volition. How did you know her intentions were, shall we say, less than honest?"

Karnstein's icy exterior appeared to grow more frigid, though he did not move a muscle. It felt as if the temperature in the air seemed to drop twenty degrees in a heartbeat as he stared out at the vast, unmoving expanse of sea.

"I know such entreaties, having experienced similar attempts since I was a child," he eventually replied, his voice soft, but possessing a chilly edge in tone.

Séverin nodded, having suspected that was one of his pupil's talents. His knowledge of the Austrian noble's history was spotty at best, but he did recall the reason the young man was so determined to maintain control at all times.

As a young man, one not close to his teen years, Franz Karnstein had come into an inheritance. Not his titles and property—that came later. The legacy bequeathed to him came from his terrifying family history. The Karnsteins, one of the oldest and most wide-spread noble clans of Europe, were infamous for the dark deeds of many members of the enormous clan. A startling number of them had chosen paths devoted to the darkest evils—unholy occult wickedness which were legendary throughout the world. To many, hearing the name Karnstein invoked tales, imagined and real, of the more demonic horrors. This would be a weighty legacy indeed, even for an adult. Most would yield to the monstrous evil, especially one embodied in the form of a seductive and lovely woman. This woman, Mircalla Karnstein, was a tall, shapely, flirtatious, blond beauty, who had seduced Franz's mother and had plotted to send him to a dark witchcraft academy known as the Scholomance. It hadn't taken an eight-year-old Franz long to determine that the woman was an ancient vampire—one at least five hundred years old and possessing terrible, dark power. Using this knowledge, at a youthful age, he had destroyed this antediluvian ancestress and been forced to kill his mother, who was also a vampire.

This much Séverin knew, having heard the tale in all its grim, tragic details. His pupil never said anything further of his life, only that he served the Church as a member of the Order of Exorcists and possessed impressive skills in the fight against monsters and other creatures of the night. Otherwise, the man was a mystery, an eager student, but taciturn regarding his murky past.

"Franz," Séverin asked, deciding to take a chance. "Are you a virgin?"

Karnstein did not appear stunned or embarrassed by his personal inquiry. He merely shook his head and ran his index finger down an old scar that marred his handsome face.

"No. I earned this as a result of my interest in ladies. A moment where I ignored my instincts in favor of a woman with the face of a Madonna and a heart as black as the Devil's own. Before you ask, she is dead."

"I understand."

Séverin knew, from long experience with the Austrian Exorcist, that no further explanation would be forthcoming. His noble-born student was capable of ignoring any and all inquiries, no matter the source. This was a skill many ancient families possessed, an almost inborn skill at deflecting conversations away from topics they found distasteful.

"How did you know the lovely Italian lady possessed darker interests in your person?" Séverin asked, suspecting the answer, but wishing to draw out Karnstein.

Karnstein laughed and there was a little amusement mixed with the bitterness.

"She tried too hard to earn my notice. I have encountered seduction attempts by beautiful women in the past. When ignored, as I have done on this trip, they move to another. Usually their reason is because I possess a title and some income. They often wish to be the next baroness, the next mistress of said baron, or obtain material for blackmail. The last ones are often the most persistent. The lovely Madame Policeni tried the hardest and longest of those I've encountered in the past. I will admit my resistance was difficult to maintain at times. Somehow, I did manage to win this battle. I have no doubt she has something else planned for the future."

"I would tend to agree. Have you ever been to Naples? No? I thought as much. I lived there for a time. A lovely city filled with bright, happy people who welcomed King Joseph as their new ruler after the Bourbons' extreme taxation. I say this with honesty, despite being a staunch Republican. We do not visit an occupied city. The French forces were welcomed."

"You say this, why?" Karnstein asked, knowing his teacher was leading up to something.

"There is an element of danger in Naples, one in which I believe you will be acquainted sooner than you would wish. Have you ever heard of the *Camorra*?" Séverin asked, glancing towards the hatchway, recently occupied by the departing form of Francesca Policeni.

Before Franz Karnstein could open his mouth to reply, a fresh breeze, the first in days, caused the *Loire* to creak and groan. Shouts from the rigging indicated that the sailors were aware this freshening wind was their chance to finally make port-only five days late.

"Clear the deck! All civilians down below!" Lieutenant de vaisseau Le Pen barked as he stepped to the worm-ridden wheel.

A short, emaciated man with a large round head and the gravelly voice of a heavy drinker and smoker, he openly despised his ship, the crew, the passengers, and all of life in general. His mood did not improve at the freshening breeze; nothing other than a large jug of cheap wine and a soft bed could penetrate his morose outlook on life. With an oath, Le Pen barked an order, hoping to leave port before dark.

CHAPTER IV

In Naples, the *Loire* was forced to wait six hours for an available pilot. The passengers, having grumbled with increasing volume as they lingered within sight of the glorious city, were elated to find a gangplank in position and their bags being unloaded as they crept out from the stench-ridden hold.

The first to step off was none other than Madame Policeni. A large gilt-covered gold and black coach with a pair of matching white horses awaited her, with a tall, handsome, dissolute fellow enthusiastically waving and exchanging an open kiss with her as she approached. Her bags were snatched up by a pair of immense men, both openly carrying long, wicked-looking daggers with worn handles in their belts. They tossed the vast mountain of baggage on top of the carriage and climbed up. The blunderbusses they took up as they sat down caused many to look away and pretend to find something more interesting anywhere else.

Pulling the shades closed, Ettore Policeni turned towards his wife. He was good-looking at first sight—but a peasant's idea of male beauty—tall, broad-shouldered, narrow-waisted, with twinkling dark eyes, and smooth olive skin. Once one looked closer, the flaws appeared and slowly crept into one's mind. The hair, which was growing thin on top, was too precisely cut and arranged. The olive skin possessed a reddening undertone, evidencing the loosening skin of a heavy drinker. And the clothes were expensive and flashy, the dress of a man who needed to tell the world he was wealthy and important. Ettore's smile vanished the minute they were hidden from view, replaced by a bovine rage that caused his eyes to narrow and his breath to emerge in low snorts.

"Where is the Austrian, *you porca puttana*?" he snarled.

"*Vai a farti fottere, frocio!*" Francesca spat back, her lovely face tightening, her eyes flashing in annoyance.

Ettore raised a hand to strike her, only to feel the needle point of a misericorde under his chin. The tiny, narrow knife could easily slice open his throat or pierce his brain, the weapon was that deadly, and he knew that Francesca was an expert in its use.

"I am not one of your, whores, my dearest husband," Francesca hissed. Lay a finger on me and I shall slice you into strips and serve your flesh to the dogs. Also remember, I do not answer to you."

She watched his face for a reaction. Ettore sighed and looked downcast, but once again yielded to his wife's will. He didn't really have a choice in the matter. Each time he attempted to assert himself over the stunningly beautiful woman, she humiliated him with uncanny ease. As of now, these embarrassments were performed in private, but that could change at any time. He shrugged dramatically, looking more like a naughty boy caught attempting to steal sweets.

"My apologies, my dearest one," he said. "I was anxious since our master is awaiting us both a short distance away."

Francesca removed the dagger and caused the weapon to vanish from sight, but there was little doubt that she could retrieve it, and other devices, instantly should the need arise.

"Of course," she replied and settled back. "Then I shall report to him and you shall hear all… if he consents to your presence."

Ettore sighed and stared at his hands in disgust. He despised his life, even though he was literally living every dream he'd imagined as a boy. Then, he had dreamed of being wealthy and respected, a leader among men and married to one of those beautiful women whom he viewed strolling in their finery after events like the opening of a new opera or a ball at the palace. Ettore had each of those wishes granted, yet he was discontent every day of his life. Possibly the method he had used to achieve these fantasies was the cause of his misery. Spurning the chance to become a cobbler, like his father and grandfather, Ettore Policeni instead had chosen to join his uncle Rogero's *Camorra* clan. This had resulted in his father disowning him and spitting in disgust every time Ettore's name was invoked by the family.

"He chose to join the Devil," Ettore's father, Ignazio Policeni, had declared while spitting on the ground at his son's retreating back. "And to Hell with them both!"

Uncle Rogero's clan was one of the smaller crime brotherhoods in Naples. Founded a generation ago by a distant cousin, their main source of income was stealing flour and wine and selling the same in their own shops. They'd only warred once with the equally undersized Bianchi clan, their battles only resulting in a few injuries and no deaths.

That was a joyous time for Ettore, a period he still recalled with pleasure. The members of the Policeni clan always had more money in their pockets than their hard-working, honest relations, and were able to live life to the fullest. Women, wine, and laughter filled his days—at least in his rose-colored recollections. He chose to ignore the constant one-upmanship you needed to perform to remain one of the men of respect. If your friend bought a new suit, you needed to be seen in a more expensive one soon after. Or you needed to find a means to embarrass your pal because of his purchases—all the while not crossing the line that might result in a blood feud. Ettore also forgot the daily violence, usually directed towards men of his father's age, to earn those coins they jangled in their pockets. Not to mention the time he had spent in prison for the robbery of an important merchant. They hadn't been able to prove he had any connection to the rape and murder of the man's daughter prior to the trial, so he didn't hang.

That was when *HE* had contacted Ettore. It had been a day before his release from the hell that was the prison, when the guards had grabbed him and dragged him to the warden's office. The guards, normally disinterested observers of the casual brutality that filled the prison, had appeared straighter and more determined as they had punched him several times in the stomach before dropping him inside the office. They then had closed the door behind them, fleeing like frightened children.

The man seated behind the long wooden desk was not the warden, a fat, corrupt fool who had earned the job through open bribery and the brutal simplicity of acts. This man was altogether more interesting. He appeared to be in his mid-to-late forties, though Ettore knew looks could be deceiving. Possessing a high, broad forehead, an aquiline nose that resembled that of a bust of a Roman emperor, and heavily lidded glittering eyes that appeared alight with a deep intelligence, Ettore Policeni knew that he needed to be wary around this remarkable person.

"Ettore Policeni," the man said in a sonorous voice that caused the Camorran gangster to stiffen his spine and scramble to his feet.

"I am he. Who are you?" Ettore had asked, confused that he was instinctively recoiling from this man.

If there was one thing he was renowned for in the Neapolitan underworld, it was his courage. Yet, without any threat, this man had had him breaking out in a cold sweat.

"I am Michele Bozzo, but you may call me *Fra Diavolo*. Sit down, we have a great deal to discuss."

Fra Diavolo nodded at the small visitor's chair before the desk.

Years later, Ettore Policeni, the titular *Capo dei capi* of the *Camorra*, wished he had been left to rot in prison, and that someone else had been chosen by the infamous *Fra Diavolo*. Better to be trapped in a stone cell than a prisoner of the Devil himself...

CHAPTER V

"In the name of our Lord, Satan the Dark, I dedicate your soul to the cause of darkness," Hertz Ende stated, handing the chalice of blood to Giorgia Marchesi.

Dipping a finger into its depths, he drew the sign of the reverse cross on her forehead and nodded for her to drink the contents. Giorgia looked frightened, but she leaned forward and began to drink. The crimson fluid fell across her cheeks as she struggled to imbibe the cow's blood. She believed the blood was that of a sacrificed child, a clever bit of trickery on the part of Hertz Ende.

Trickery—that was the real purpose behind all of Ende's actions back since he had been a youngster, back in Elsdorf. The third son of a baker, his father was a man dedicated to his profession above everything else in life. Trentan Ende was a man perpetually on a mission to perfect his craft. Nothing mattered more than details, such as discovering the precise temperature for his ovens, or the exact amount of water to add to the dough. and how long to knead… and so on… and so on…

Unsurprisingly, Trentan's wife had run away with a leather merchant, taking her eldest daughter, but leaving behind her sons, Otto and Hertz. The idea of remaining any longer with a man whose only topic of conversation involved flour, yeast and other details of the baking trade, was close to driving her mad. After an evening of listening to a comparison of the different types of woods and the heat they released, she had realized a simple fact: either she abandoned Trentan, or kill him and be hanged for murder. Her daughter Ida was only six; she would forget her absent father in a short time. The two boys were too old to start a new life; it was best to just leave them to become bakers.

Otto was a duplicate of his father, a tall, rotund, blond man who found the details of the baking craft to be man's highest calling. He had married the dull, not particularly intelligent, Senta Weber, a woman who could listen to tales of flour and dough for weeks without finding it boring. Hertz, in contrast, found the baking profession to be an ancient form of torture, worthy of the Inquisition. His interests were simple: money, women, and spending as little time as possible around bakers. Running away to Bonn, he had worked a few menial jobs before meeting the man who would change his life.

Dr. Bruno Schmidt claimed to be a graduate of the University of Dusseldorf, though he never could produce proof of attendance of this legendary institution. When Hertz met him, Schmidt was slowly dying from a tumor in his stomach—but in his days, he had been something an expert in the esoteric fields of ancient German occult studies. Realizing that this was a means of changing his life, Hertz Ende had made a deal with the dying man. Schmidt had agreed to teach Hertz the basics of the occult world, as well as how to speak and write like a gentleman. In return, the new pupil would supply pain medications from the chemists as well as food and beer.

The arrangement was perfect. For six months, the two men lived the life of teacher and student. Schmidt received regular doses of the drugs that dulled the throbbing, piercing pains in his stomach. Hertz learned to speak with an educated accent, details of the occult, and, most importantly, other languages. One of the keys in becoming a master of the mystic arts was the ability to speak and read multiple languages. Happily, Hertz Ende possessed a gift for this skill and, by the time Schmidt had died, coughing blood and gasping for air, Ende spoke Latin, Greek, Italian, English, and French.

That was when he took to the road, moving from city to city, living the life of a warlock. After a dangerous time in Paris, where Hertz had only escaped an angry mob by fleeing through the sewers, he had learned another important lesson: best to avoid the wealthier classes; they grew angry when they discovered their jewelry gone and their daughters despoiled. No, the best group to work his ways upon were the merchants and lesser bankers. These were often people who sought to improve their standing in the world, looking up at the lofty heights of the wealthy and nobility. Hertz Ende wanted the patronage of hungry, greedy men, grasping women, nearly noble fools, angry at their inability to sit in the seats of power.

In each city, his methods were precise and simple. Gain interest by paying various servants for information and produce a few general predictions to impress the skeptical. Slowly, he would work his way into their confidence and eventually convince them that the best method to ensure their desires was the devote themselves to the path of darkness. The name of their "dark master" changed from place to place—some cities were better suited for the unusual, foreign-sounding demons. For example, the name Lucifer was well-received in Lyons, but Baal was better accepted in Debrecen.

Here in Naples, Hertz Ende had chosen to stick to the simplest of devils—Lucifer and Satan, names based in simple Christianity. He was now slowly building another coven, a Satanic circle more devoted to money and sexual intercourse than anything mystical. This was why one of his earliest recruits had been Giorgia Marchesi. A lovely, intelligent woman, her father was Giovanni Marchesi, a cloth merchant who indulged his only daughter shamefully. Possessing thin blond hair, a large bust, and an innocent face, she would easily entice members who sought a chance to get between her shapely, short legs. Hertz knew that he really was a pimp and confidence man these days, using the veneer of occult knowledge as a means of satisfying his whims. Still, it was better than being a baker.

"Daughter of the Devil, remove your cloak and lay upon the altar. It is time for your final initiation into the Satan's elite," Hertz Ende recited, feeling himself growing hard

The thought of despoiling Giorgia made all his toils worth the effort.

That was when the woman's laughter started, a high-pitched cackle of evil mirth that seemed to shake the small, abandoned church Hertz used as the site of his Satanic circle. Hertz's head swung left and right, seeking the source of the merriment, but saw nothing. Giorgia Marchesi shrank in on her herself, her face even more frightened.

"Over here," a voice said from behind them.

Seated on the altar sat a woman, a vision of loveliness so overwhelming that the false magus and his victim were unable to move. She smiled in their direction and studied them with her incandescent dark eyes.

"Who...? Who...?" Hertz stammered, barely able to form words in the face of such perfection.

"Who am I?" she asked, and laughed musically once again. "I am Nosos, and this is my dearest heart, Fortuna."

A soft white arm came to encircle Giorgia's slim waist, and Fortuna Orsini hugged the pretty blond girl from behind. The former Satanist possessed a kittenish quality that was almost as seductive as the legendary beauty seated on the deconsecrated altar. There was a terrible seductive quality about the wife of the late Tito Orsini. Formerly a quiet, mousey creature, despite her obvious beauty, she had been transformed since becoming the favored lover of the ancient evil being. She combined the two qualities society both approved and despised: Madonna and whore.

Fortuna appeared to be a virginal paragon of womanhood, the perfect wife for any man fortunate enough to win her—until she raised her eyes, smiled and licked her plump lips. Then, she embodied all that society and the Church held as debased and evil. In most situations, these beliefs were ludicrous, the product of ancient traditions and values that weakened the contributions of half of civilization based on birth. In the case of Fortuna Orsini, the supposition was correct. Her transformation by Nosos had taken a gentle, quiet woman and removed all that was decent from her soul. Now, she was a predator who used seduction to feed on men and women without restraint.

"You're pretty," Fortuna cooed, licking Giorgia's neck with a long, crimson tongue.

"What? No, I..." Giorgia attempted to pull away, but froze when her eyes locked with that of Fortuna.

All refusal died on her lips as she stared into the dark, bottomless depths of Fortuna Orsini's eyes. Sighing, Giorgia smiled and opened her arms, accepting the enfolding embrace of the dark-haired vision of loveliness.

Hertz Ende stared with rapt attention, watching as his intended lover moaned and threw aside her robes, laying upon the dusty floor. Her nude body, pink and shining in the lantern light, was even more beautiful than the German occultist had imagined.

"Isn't my Fortuna exquisite?" Nosos stated. "None can resist her when she chooses to make them love her. Sadly, she tires of them quickly. Only I can truly fulfill her every desire. Now, let us talk of you, Hertz Ende—the man who pretends to be a servant of darkness. You possess no powers, use your spotty knowledge of false texts to seduce foolish girls and sell them to lusting old men. You are a lubricious, foolish, stupid, ugly, pathetic little man who would rape a nun if you didn't have enough money to purchase a whore."

Nosos stepped off the altar and turned Hertz's head with one sharp fingernail. He could hear the moans and sighs of ecstasy behind him, but the dagger-like talon on his cheek prevented him from looking behind.

"You... You're a vampire!" Hertz screamed, reaching for a cross he always kept under his shirt.

He flashed the silver symbol in the face of the beautiful monster, knowing that they could not stand before the power of God. But Nosos ripped the holy object from his hand, examined it for a moment, and tossed it aside with a contemptuous flick of her fingers.

"I was born thousands of years before your Christ was killed. Such objects hold no power over one such as I. Nor any of my brothers and sisters of the Tenebrae. Now, try to use that tiny thing you call a mind for something other than your idiotic games."

Hertz was surprised by the failure of his cross, and that this ancient monster appeared more mocking and amused than angered by his attempt to repel her presence. Knowing he had no choice, he asked:

"What do you mean?"

"The correct way to ask such a question is, 'What do you mean, *mistress*?' Nosos explained, her nail pressing a little harder against his face. "Now, speak again."

A slow trickle of blood fell down Hertz's face, a surface cut which was surprisingly painful. He wanted to tell the vampire woman to go to Hell, but found himself overwhelmed by the perfection of her face… her lips… her eyes…

"What do you mean, mistress?" he whispered, without thought.

"Very good. I mean, I have a use for you. If you agree to obey, I will make your life better."

Nosos smiled again, her talon retreating slightly. The sensation was far more pleasant, almost a caress one would use on a favored pet. Hertz Ende was unable to think. He could not resist the sheer perfection that was Nosos. He nodded quickly, ignoring the pain this caused his cheek.

"Yes, mistress. I will obey your every word."

Nosos patted his face and licked the blood off her palm.

"I am happy with you, my slave. You will find a coach outside. Climb aboard and await my further orders."

Bowing deeply, Hertz Ende threw aside his robes and ran for the door. He ignored the nude bodies of Fortuna and Giorgia, though the moans of euphoria did sound muted to his ears.

Nosos gazed down at the bloody, naked body of Giorgia Marchesi and licked her lips. Delicious. Dropping to her knees, she bit down on the girl's exposed left breast and lapped up the blood. Young blood was always a delightful meal.

CHAPTER VI

"Maestro Séverin and Baron Karlstein? Please follow me. A coach awaits, and your bags are already aboard."

Jerôme Després, deputy assistant secretary to the Royal Chamberlain, was a man of average height and build with short, thinning dark hair, red skin from too much time in the sun, and a jaw and chin so massive that they appeared far too large for his body. He spoke in a slow, drawling tone that was the sign of one born to the ancient nobility of France, at least in the mind of Jean-Pierre Séverin.

This assessment by the swordmaster was entirely correct, a truth only one used to the various accents and methods of speech throughout Europe could identify. Jerôme Després was the grandson of Marquis de Merteuil who had fled France at the start of the Revolution. Upon the fall of Jacobins, he had returned and immediately joined the diplomatic service under the protection of an old school friend.

Why was he granted such an excellent position? The reason was simple enough: the Reign of Terror had cost the government men who knew of the social niceties of the nobility. Though Després was not particularly bright or likable, he did possess a regal bearing and an ability to speak and translate multiple languages with a regal sounding accent. This was useful, especially when the Bonaparte family had risen to the purple robes of the Empire.

The difficulty was that Jerome Després wasn't good for anything else. He was incapable of comprehending law, diplomacy, or the politics his positions would normally require. Therefore, he was made the equivalent of a royal herald. His job was to use his voice and nothing else. Just read or repeat what he was told and follow instructions with a religious fervor. This was why he had been sent to the harbor to greet the two visitors sent by the Emperor.

"Yes, I am Jean-Pierre Séverin," the swordmaster confirmed. "Who sent you to fetch us?"

"That would mean you are Baron Karlstein?" Després stated, ignoring Séverin's question and looking at the younger man.

"Karnstein. My family name is Karnstein," Franz corrected.

His voice held no heat or annoyance, he sounded merely resigned at this minor error.

"My paperwork says Karlstein," said Després, glancing again at his papers and reading the words out loud again. "Karlstein."

"The name is Karnstein." Franz corrected again, sighing.

Després examined his paper again and asked:

"Are you sure that is your family's name?"

"Only since Constantine the Great," said Franz, rolling his eyes. "Or possibly Diocletian. The chronicles are unclear."

"I'm sorry?" Després asked, checking his papers once again and reading out the names a third time. "Maestro Séverin and Baron Karlstein?"

"I am Karlstein," said Franz, exhaling, closing his eyes.

"Ah! I thought as much! I assumed you didn't understand what I was saying. Do you speak French?" Després asked in the same language.

Realizing that irony was lost on this man, Franz Karnstein merely stepped aboard the coach and did not bother to reply. He stared out the window and studied Naples as they wound their way through the city towards the palace. Their view of the city was limited to a tour of the more expensive areas. Després chattered away about the delights of Naples, his words demonstrating his superficial knowledge of the region. Séverin refrained from correcting each and every sentence of the glaringly incorrect statements, but made grunts that would put off any other person.

Karnstein, for his part, appeared to be imitating a statue or a deaf man. No amount of questioning or hints broke through his stony reserve. Upon arriving at the palace, he alighted, the first demonstration of life. Turning to Jerome Després, he repeated Séverin's earlier question:

"Who sent you to retrieve us?"

"That would be my humble self," Federigo Gui said, stepping out of the main doorway and giving them both a brief nod. "I am Abbot Gui and I hold a small position within the kingdom."

"Humble? Humble he says?" Johann Spurzheim asked, not bothering to hide his derision and amusement at the attempted self-effacement on the part of the Cupbearer leader. "I also sent for you. My name is Johann Spurzheim and I command the gendarmes of Naples. You would be Jean-Pierre Séverin, also known as Gâteloup—spoiler of wolves. Your companion is Baron Karnstein, a fellow Austrian whose last name is well-known to all in our country."

"Yes, that is quite correct. Shall we conduct this discussion in private, citizens?" Séverin stated, knowing Karnstein would agree. "Our reason for appearing in this kingdom need not become general gossip."

"Agreed," Spurzheim said, turning on his heels. "My office is closer and larger than the good Abbot's. Let us repair there and I shall pour you an excellent white wine I have saved for such an occasion."

"My office affords greater privacy," Gui interjected, taking the lead. "We shall proceed there and learn our ruler's concerns from our honored guests."

Spurzheim fell into step, but secretly, he was seething inside, having once again lost to this monstrous man in even the smallest of contests. Gui appeared determined to not merely defeat Spurzheim, he wished to do so with a smug, satisfied air about him each time.

It would be simplicity itself to whip out my dagger and plunge it in his black heart. The difficulty in doing so is that I would be hanged as a traitor by morning. No, I must win this battle through tactics and strategy, Spurzheim thought.

To get to Gui's office they needed to pass a door with two guards, walk through a room filled with paintings that appeared to watch you no matter where you were, and up a narrow staircase. According to rumors, there were secret passages behind the paintings, each with an armed Cupbearer hiding and watching for intruders. Once up the staircase, there were two more locked doors before stepping into the den of the terrifying master of the secret police.

The room was poorly lit, with only a simple wooden desk and chair for Gui to use. A cloth bell-pull lay just behind his chair and he rang it after sitting down. The others, realizing no other seats were present, were about to speak when a hidden door opened. Five men, dressed in the black hooded robes of the Dominicans, entered and placed three stools before the desk. They left in a silent line, never once looking up or making any sound other than the soft swish of their robes.

"Please be seated," Gui said, not hiding his amusement.

The three men, each perched on the small wooden seats, resembled school children about to receive a lesson from a particularly harsh master. It was Spurzheim who first broke the silence, looking to Séverin with the narrowed, flat, eyes of a serpent.

"Monsieur Séverin—or should I call you Maestro?—your file was started by Armand Chauvelin. One note fascinated me—according to Monsieur Chauvelin, you are a close acquaintance of the Emperor. Yet, you are also an ardent Republican. How is this possible?"

"Obviously it is, at least once in this life," Séverin replied, his sardonic tone causing Spurzheim to stiffen.

"Your file also lists your position as that of the Director of the Paris Morgue. Therefore, since you are part of the police, you shall report to me," said Spurzheim, smiling, his wide mouth and thin lips bringing to rise the image of a poisonous snake.

"I'm afraid I shall not," replied Séverin calmly, with a note of amusement.

He reached into his jacket and removed a document case. Opening it, he handed a carefully preserved letter to the chief of the Neapolitan police.

Spurzheim looked annoyed and confused as he read the letter. Then his light, nearly invisible, eyebrows rose, and he looked over to Séverin with astonishment. He then handed the letter to Gui. The Abbott read the note twice, his normally angry face breaking into a rare smirk of delight.

"According to this document, signed and sealed by the Emperor himself, our friend is no mere coroner; he is an inspector general of all military and police forces in the Empire. It appears that you answer to him, not the other way around. How very droll, no?"

"No," Spurzheim snarled, looking annoyed.

This appointment was truly extra-ordinary, almost unprecedented. Possibly only Joseph Bonaparte and Marshal Murat possessed such influence. Gui turned to Karnstein.

"Lord Karnstein, your file is thinner, but easier to assess. As a member of the minor Order of Exorcists, you are answerable to myself. Archbishop Luigi Ruffo-Scilla was expelled from the city for taking the Bourbons' side against France. As the highest-ranking representative of the Church, you shall report and clear all your work with my office."

"I shall not," was Karnstein's phlegmatic reply, echoing that of Séverin.

Reaching into his vest, he removed an oval disk made from silver and steel. Placing the object on the desk with a dull snap, he pushed it across to Federigo Gui.

"*Sacra Congregatio Romanae et universalis Inquisitionis seu sancti officii,*" Gui read out and all present translated the Latin phrase, visibly flinching. 'The Sacred Congregation of the Inquisition or the Holy Office of Rome and of the universal'.

Spurzheim shook his head in false confusion.

"Forgive me, I do not comprehend the inner workings of the Holy Church. Please explain further."

"It means," Gui snapped, correctly believing his enemy was enjoying the discomfort of this situation, "that your young noble-born countryman is a member of the Holy Office of the Inquisition. He only answers to the Supreme Pontiff and a

Cardinal or three. How is this possible? Who are you, Karnstein?"

Séverin suppressed a laugh, knowing what was about to occur. For all his cold demeanor and puritan image, there was a little bit of the showman in Franz Karnstein. Once given a chance to overwhelm an enemy, he did so in a display worthy of his warlord ancestors.

"Who am I?" Karnstein asked rhetorically. "I am Franz Karl Joseph Vordenburg-Karnstein, Baron Vordenburg, Baron Karnstein, heir to Count Karnstein, Knight of the Sovereign Military Order of Malta, member of the minor Order of Exorcists, member of the Holy Office of the Inquisition, and advisor to His Holiness Pope Pius VII. Why do you ask?"

Gui's eyes widened slightly, but he maintained a placid expression throughout the recitation.

"I ask because your position is very unusual, my lord. My duties are to maintain order in the Kingdom of Naples. You introduce an element of chaos by your presence."

"If I may?" Séverin raised a hand to prevent the growing cold fury from building in his apprentice. Seeing acceptance from Gui and Spurzheim, he nodded. "My thanks. Neither of us possess any interest in creating any difficulties in your city. Our only concern are the supernatural menaces that threaten this land. The sooner we discover the troubles that caused you to request our presence, the sooner we will return to Paris."

Both the master of the Cupbearers and the chief of police entered contemplative silences. Their faces demonstrated their struggles with Séverin's suggestion, finally arriving at acceptance at approximately the same time.

"Very well," Federigo Gui said, standing up. "I will send word ahead. Three days from today, we shall undertake a small journey south."

"I will prepare an escort. Have either of you gentlemen ever visited a prison?" Johann Spurzheim asked, his lips curling in an unpleasant smile.

CHAPTER VII

A tongue of bright red flame licked out from the metal barrel, followed by a small cloud of white smoke. The large man in the center of the room fell to the floor, the sound of the hard slap of the bloody skull striking the dark wooden surface, only slightly muted by the wide chamber. The echo of the explosion slowly drifted away slowly in the distance, a softly diminishing sound that reverberated throughout the massive villa.

The house had once been the property of a lesser member of the Bourbons, a cousin whose job was to laugh at all of King Ferdinand's poor japes. Officially, Count Gennaro was listed as a military advisor to King Ferdinand of Naples and Sicily, holding a rank of Colonel in the King's personal cavalry. What that meant was that Gennaro occasionally walked about in an expensive, well-tailored uniform, and rode in a few parades each year. During the war with France, he was heard complaining that the invasion of Naples was happening at a very inconvenient time.

"My niece was planning a masked ball this weekend! I sent for my costume all the way from Barcelona!" Gennaro was heard to remark before the battle against Joseph Bonaparte and his armies.

Gennaro died from a musket ball to the back of his head. There was some debate by his living relatives whether the shot came from his own men or while fleeing the French during the terrible rout of the Bourbon forces. In any event, his heirs had all fled to Sicily with Ferdinand and the government had seized the property. The villa and land had been bought by a prominent Neapolitan merchant named Policeni and promptly forgotten, except on tax days.

Policeni himself was present, though he did not occupy the large leather chair which was the centerpiece of the room. Instead, he perched on a soft, comfortable divan made of wood, wool, and velvet. At his side was his wife, looking lovely as ever in repose, completely ignoring his presence. A small smile crossed her lips as a pool of bright blood formed around the dead man's shattered skull.

"A perfect shot, Papa," Francesca purred. "It appears the English can do more than sail the ships they steal from France."

"Agreed," Michele Bozzo replied, handing the dueling pistol to the tall man at his side. "Order another set of pistols and one rifle from this man, Manton. Then send word of these purchases to our gunsmith friends in Berlin. If they wish our further interest, they will need to improve their product."

"*Si, Padrone*," the tall man replied, jotting down a few words in a notebook.

A man of above average height and build, he was the second most feared member of the *Camorra*. His name was Giacomo Lando and he was unofficially known as "Piano Piatto" by friends and enemies. This was because his triangular-shaped head appeared, since birth, to flatten at the top of his skull. None were sure whether that was a result of the way he wore his curly dark hair, or if his head was actually deformed. The only time anyone had asked, a drunken capo from the Mosca 'Ndrangheta group of Calabria, the man had vanished days later. All that was ever discovered was his partially decomposed head, missing both eyes and tongue. The dead man's left hand had been severed at the wrist and jammed into the gaping mouth. None of the 'Ndrangheta disputed the killing since it was a true *vendetta* based on an insult. More importantly, nobody wanted to be Lando's next victim.

He was an otherwise handsome man, with a cupid bow mouth, heavily lidded dark eyes and a light tenor-toned voice. He was an excellent singer, preferring German operas over the Italian or French, and regularly donated money to orphanages and other worthy causes. Many in Naples who knew him would have been shocked to learn that he had murdered over four hundred men, women, and children in the course of his duties.

After completing his notes, Lando tossed the corpse over his shoulder and carried him out of the room. None asked where he was taking it, having seen how human remains were disposed of by *Fra Diavolo*'s favored assassin. Giacomo Lando had a simple system—strip down the body, slice it into pieces, and toss the remains into the pigsty. He then burned all clothing and tossed all jewelry or personal objects into the river. Any coins or bank notes were donated to charity in hopes that the good works would counterbalance the blood on his hands in the afterlife.

As Lando carried out his dark disposal deeds, *Fra Diavolo* slowly turned and faced his daughter and son-in-law. His eyes seemed to glitter as he focused on them. Ettore Policeni straightened, and tried to look unconcerned by the attentions of his master. In contrast, Francesca looked languid, disinterested, remaining in repose as she was examined.

"Another failure," *Fra Diavolo* said, shaking his head. "The simplest of assignments—seduction and blackmail of a Karnstein, no less. How could anyone fail?

"I had no involvement, *Padrone*," Ettore said, his words spoken in a rush. "I was in Naples on your behalf the entire time. I also recommended we use a prostitute instead of my dearest wife."

"*Madonna*, you're a baboon-faced fool," Francesca replied, rolling her eye. "Do you even listen to the words that spout out of your mouth? Keep silence and learn something."

Ettore was about to snarl back an insult, when he caught the irritated look on the face of Michele Bozzo. Clamping his lips together, he felt heat across his face as he blushed deep crimson from embarrassment.

"Explain yourself," *Fra Diavolo* stated.

He reloaded the large duel pistol. His movements were quick and practiced and never once did he look down to watch as he worked.

"The Austrian noble Karnstein is not typical of his class," Francesca reported, "let alone his family. Little information was available on him, the majority of his life appears unknown to all, save a few high-ranking members of the Church. He serves them, yet this does not appear to be in conflict with his rights as an Austrian noble. He has no known lovers, debts, or vices, such as gambling or attending the theater. He goes to church almost daily, trains in fencing and other studies under Maestro Jean-Pierre Séverin."

Her words painted a completely detailed picture of their target. She possessed a mind that never forgot a detail or a fact once read or heard. Though he kept other records, *Fra Diavolo* used his daughter's mental gifts as often as possible.

"A boy lover, then. Find a pretty boy that resembles a girl and he shall be ours," Ettore said, smiling in triumph.

"Cretin," spat Francisca, her voice filled with open menace. "If you speak again while I am talking I will spike your tongue to the floor."

"Do continue, my daughter," said *Fra Diavolo*, looking slightly amused by the antics of the married couple.

He'd forced them to wed, using a Bishop and the rule of law to enforce his will. He required a blood tie to the Policeni and possessed only one daughter. She had agreed, despite despising her husband the instant they'd met, and even agreed to consummation with her father and the priest in the next room. What *Fra Diavolo* did not demand was anything even approaching respect or kindness from either husband or wife. It was understood that he might demand a child or two in the future, but not at this time.

"Thank you, Papa," said Francesca, favoring him with a winning smile that he completely ignored. "I threw myself at him and he desired me. Yet, somehow, he knew that my intentions were not in his favor. Despite wishing to bed me, he resisted and ignored my very presence."

"Your conclusions?" *Fra Diavolo* asked, lifting the pistol and examining the flints.

Francesca frowned and considered for a moment.

"I believe, based on the evidence and my experiences, that this man once suffered an attempted seduction that went poorly. Attempting to blackmail him in that manner will fail, nor will bribery hold any power. His ways are closer to that of a priest than a baron. If we wish to use or control this Karnstein, it must be accomplished in a manner that fits his plans. Otherwise he will resist it with all his power."

"There is no man who cannot be bought, bedded, or threatened—other than his Holiness the Pope and our good *Fra Diavolo*," Ettore said, refusing to be ignored. "Everyone possesses a weakness."

"You are incorrect," said *Fra Diavolo*, laying his pistol across his thin lap. "I trust Francesca's view and will add that his teacher, the older gentleman named Séverin, is worse. If you attempt bribery or seduction, Séverin will treat you as a fool. Violence will result in the death of your men. One of my best assassins, whom I called *Mort Séduisante*, attempted to bed and battle him. She failed in the first, and he blinded her in the second. We must not treat this pair the way we do other men. We shall use them while making them believe they control us."

"I will have them watched day and night," said Ettore. "Three teams of three, changing regularly and randomly. May I use *Lama Notturna* if I have need?" he added, invoking the rarely spoken nickname of one of *Fra Diavolo*'s special operatives.

"You may," *Fra Diavolo* replied, waving his son-in-law away.

He watched and nodded as Ettore Policeni bowed deeply to his master and wife and fled the room.

"He's off to one of his whores afterwards," Francesca stated, her voice not hiding her boredom of this news.

"It is a lesser hold we carry over him, a small lever," said *Fra Diavolo* shrugging. "Sometimes a softer approach is necessary to control an underling. Should he anger me or interrupt my plans, I will use my greater power to force him to see reason. It is no bother. He is effective for his position, but easily replaceable. Now, follow me. We have other areas of concern and I have a use for you, my child."

Following her father, Francesca Bozzo-Policeni, re-mained silent as they headed deeper into the villa. The thought of Karnstein and his refusal did prick her vanity, but she knew this was of no true concern. The Austrian was a mere pawn in her father's great game, and he would rise or fall according to *Fra Diavolo*'s whims.

CHAPTER VIII

The procession leading Jean-Pierre Séverin and Franz Karnstein to the infamous Nisida prison was elaborate to say the least. Two full troops of light cavalry surrounded their coach and a pair of wagons full of infantrymen were in evidence. The police chief and the leader of the secret police appeared to be attempting to prove they were vitally important and the Emperor's representatives should be impressed.

Unfortunately for Abbott Federigo Gui and Johann Spurzheim, neither Séverin nor Karnstein appeared especially awed by the military might. Séverin was well-traveled, having viewed elite guard units of men so large that they dwarfed the their escort. Once you've viewed ten thousand Janissaries marching and waving their swords in precise rhythm, a small troop of cavalry were drab and unimpressive in comparison.

As to Karnstein, he never appeared impressed by anything. Séverin, an ardent observer of human behavior, found his lack of interest in even the most beautiful aspects of life to be fascinating. Art, music, military displays, and more, simply resulted in a disinterested reaction from the Austrian Exorcist.

Which is not a good path for any to walk, Séverin mused as he watched his pupil stare out the coach window. *A man who spends all his life searching for evil ends up seeing nothing else in the world. I must find a method of piercing the metaphorical walls Franz has placed around his soul.*

The trip through Naples was silent, only broken by the clip-clop of the cavalry horse's hooves and the grinding sound of the coach wheels through the muck and dirt.

The people moved aside for the procession and appeared disinterested in which dignitary was in the carriage. The French were mostly viewed as a force for good, a fine replacement for the Bourbons who had ruled for centuries. There were those who desired the return of the Spanish kings, or self-rule for the residents of Naples. These appeared to be in the minority, thanks to the treatment the Bonapartist forces demanded for the region. Taxes were lower than under the Bourbons and the residents treated fairly. How long this would last was anyone's guess, but for now King Joseph Bonaparte and his government were hailed by the people of Naples.

"You never answered my question from yesterday. Have you ever been in a prison?" Spurzheim asked Séverin, breaking the silence.

"Yes. I was imprisoned for a time in the Bastille for my Republican beliefs," Séverin answered, closing his eyes and forcing the memory out of his mind.

"Were you freed when your people stormed that prison?" Spurzheim asked, leaning forward, clearly interested.

"No, I was in Calais when that occurred," replied Séverin, shaking his head. "There were only seven prisoners freed that day and I was not among them."

"And you, my lord?" Spurzheim asked the silent Karnstein.

"No," answered the Exorcist, turning away from the window. "I've not suffered that indignity. I've read that spending time in such locations is quite trying upon the soul."

"To say the least," Gui remarked. "A prison is a stone version of Hell. The guilty are sent there, to be held until execution, release, or their death. You are placed in a cell with no company, no books, nothing other than a poor fare of food and water each day. Many go mad from the solitude, preferring death to spending years of their life growing old in silence. Best to be executed rather than suffering in durance vile."

"How does this apply to us?" Karnstein asked, looking slightly interested.

"Just ensuring that you comprehend the fate that awaits all who violate the rule of law in Naples," Gui answered, shrugging and sneering.

"Noted," said Séverin, keeping himself from expressing any disgust or amusement at this power-hungry mocking, beast who believed himself to be a good man.

He was unsurprised by Karnstein's return to inattention; such threats would not even penetrate his pupil's constantly armored mind. This need for power games on the part of the Cupbearer reminded Séverin of another power-seeker. They had only met twice, but that was more than adequate to assess the man's true intentions. Though he had fought monsters in the frozen alleys of Moskva, the ancient majestic greenery of the Black Forest, and even the golden-bejeweled minarets of the Topkapi Palace, that one man possessed a heart blacker than all the creatures he had destroyed. He was the worst type of evil, one who went into a struggle with the idea of doing good for all—but instead became drunk on power, blood, and paranoia.

This man was Maximilien Robespierre, the feared master of the blood-stained Reign of Terror. Though a Republican, Séverin was a man who believed in intelligence and moderation in all areas. Overthrowing the inadequate, foolish, sad, little king was right and just for the proper functioning of society. The days where a fool sat as absolute monarch because he was distantly related to a warlord were passing. The world required men from all classes, whose rise to power occurred by their skills and minds, not their parentage. Napoleon was a perfect example of such genius—his failing was recreating the ways of the old by becoming yet another monarch.

The Revolution against Louis XVI had been right and good. What followed was quite the opposite of what the world needed to progress to true enlightenment. Just when France was on the edge of rising to greater heights, the Jacobins had used the King's pathetic flight to Varennes as an excuse to bathe the country in blood.

Beginning by demanding the execution of the King, Robespierre and his band had ordered death to any whom they viewed as their enemies. Starting with the noble class, they had used the guillotine to fuel the mob's hatred. A river of blood, filled with many who were innocent of crimes other than disagreeing with Robespierre, ran through France. This was best embodied by the man's speech to the National Convention on 5 February 1794, a day Séverin would never forget as proof of Robespierre's madness:

We must smother the internal and external enemies of the Republic or perish with it; now in this situation, the first maxim of your policy ought to be to lead the people by reason and the people's enemies by terror.

Séverin had seen the same mad look in the eyes of many gang leaders and murderers. Robespierre was a man who had moved from a desire to right wrongs, to a monster who could not be satisfied by the death of thousands. He wished to remake the world in his image, become a new Christ, or even a new God, to the people of France. Having created a new religion, the Cult of the Supreme Being, Robespierre—or so most people of France believed—would soon begin a religious crusade as an excuse to murder more enemies. It was the third clause of the dictator's 1794 Decree on this Cult that had caused Séverin to join the opponents of the Jacobins in order to save the lives of thousands. Those words still resonated in his mind as he subtly observed Federigo Gui:

They place in the first rank of these duties to detest bad faith and tyranny, to punish tyrants and traitors, to rescue the unfortunate, to respect the weak, to defend the oppressed, to do to others all the good that one can and not to be unjust toward anyone.

Though the scale was far smaller. Séverin sensed he was facing another Robespierre in Gui. They both appeared to have once gone into their duties with higher intentions. This was sadly replaced by a hunger for greater power and the desire to destroy any who stood in their path. With this understanding, Séverin knew he would continue to observe Gui to learn if his supposition was correct. If so, he would act to prevent the birth of another corpse-strewn city as Paris had become during the Reign of Terror. His Republican ideals demanded no less.

The carriage slowed and they disembarked, walking the short distance to a small, eight carronade naval cutter. The trip was a short one, but Gui and Spurzheim were determined to do so with maximum comfort and protection. With little ceremony, they were soon off, slicing through the waves towards one of the worst places to visit in all of Italy—the political prison of the Kingdom of Naples.

CHAPTER IX

"You, bastard!" Aldo Conti screamed and ripped his knife from his belt. "My brother is dead, and it is all your fault!"

"Yes, I suppose it is my fault." Giulio Nucci replied, his face sad.

He fired the pistol he held under the table. The enraged Aldo shrieked in pain, falling to the ground. He gripped the tattered remains of his groin, screeching in a surprisingly high-pitched wail. Placing the gun gingerly on the table, Giulio stepped to the side of the howling Aldo and knelt down to the man's level. His face, still resembling one of abject misery, took on a slight moue of disappointment.

"Aldo, Aldo, Aldo... One of my oldest friends. Yet you and your brother tried to sell me out to the *Padrone* and his bum-boy Policeni. You think I wouldn't know? You think Giulio Nucci, whom all call *Il Principe*, is a farmer with hay still in his hair? Hmm?"

Giulio tapped the writing man on the nose with the flat side of a long dagger. Without waiting for an answer, he then plunged the dagger through Aldo's nose. The man screamed, a sound that was transformed into a warbling liquid gurgle as the blade plunged into his throat. Giulio thrust his blade over and over in Aldo's dying body, his arm rising and following as blood spattered about like crimson droplets of rain.

Finally, Giulio Nucci stood, his face and body covered with a scarlet film. His right arm, from fingertips to elbow was completely drenched, making him look like a man whose skin had been ripped from his body, leaving only exposed sinews.

Giulio Nucci was a man of average height and build, who moved with a languid slowness that suggested pantherish speed and grace. His skin was swarthy and appeared darker thanks to his prematurely graying wild, curling hair. Giulio was handsome in an animalistic way, his heavy, patchy beard resembling the pelt of a wild beast rather than a man.

"Messy, *Principe* darling," Pia Mele stated, her husky voice sounding bored.

She was a tall woman with a mane of flowing blond hair and sun-kissed golden skin. Possessing large, liquid green eyes and a generous mouth, she was a true beauty that looked very out of place in a farmer's hut in the Naples countryside.

"Messy is all this pig deserves. He cursed me, as he was dying, the bastard cursed my soul. Get me the *stregheria*!"

Giulio's voice rose in volume and pitch. Without a word, a man standing near Pia nodded once and left the room.

Pia picked up a hunk of bread and bit down, pretending she didn't see the terror on the face of her lover. This was one of the great failings of Giulio Nucci's character, his many overwhelming superstitions. For a man who lived entirely by his instincts, Giulio had somehow developed a host of half-remembered taboos and fears that controlled his life. He would never kill a man with red hair, believing they were the children of Cain and would rise as vampires after death. He would never eat a black goat or sheep, believing they were cursed and would grant seven years' bad luck. These were just a few of his many beliefs, and there was no means of discussing their rationality with him. He was as firm in his convictions as a priest was in his faith in the Lord.

Giulio Nucci had been born in the Campania hills to a poor farmer who worked from dawn to dusk to provide for his family. His father, also named Giulio, believed that life was suffering and that the only means of ending the pain was hard work. Giulio Sr had attended church every Sunday, helped his neighbors when they needed another pair of hands, and attended the occasional *fête* or fair as a brief distraction. A simple, normal peasant, as common in Italy and other countries as blades of grass. That he had fathered a son who was his complete opposite in beliefs and manner had been a surprise to the man until the day he died. Giulio Jr, the eldest of two sons and two daughters, hated work, farming, church, school, listening to rules, and eating an equal portion of food in the Nucci home. Beatings, his mother's tears, being locked in the barn, talks with the local priest, all had fallen on deaf ears. Giulio Jr was willful, intentionally disobedient, and a thief. By the time he was thirteen, his father had expelled him from the farm, crossing the boy's name from the family bible and declaring the young demon was "dead to this family."

Giulio Nucci had struggled for a time, roaming and stealing food and clothing throughout the countryside, until he had been caught by Basillio Conte, Aldo and Luigi's father. Basillio, a tall, stout man with a booming laugh and a heavy fist, was a minor *Camorra* leader, possessing a gang of twenty men and boys. Upon catching Giulio attempting to steal one of his pigs, the elder Conte had beat the young rascal bloody. Then he had fed him, unofficially adopting young Giulio into the gang.

Finally, Giulio had found a place where he belonged. The Conte gang were mostly robbers, who pretended to run a small butcher's shop in Naples. They lived the true life of the bandit, roaming the countryside, robbing, stealing, laughing and drinking. An idyllic life for Giulio—quite the opposite to the one endorsed by by his former family, who, as far he knew, were still living on the same tiny farm.

By the time Basillio Conte had died, in bed with a four-teen-year-old whore he had stolen from another gang, Giulio was his obvious replacement. Though uneducated and riddled with taboos, he was as wily as his mentor and the most dangerous man in the clan. Life was good, for a time, but such a perfect life could not last. This time of joy had ended when Policeni and the *Padrone* had brought all the gangs under their control. Others in the past had attempted to unite the many *Camorra* clans, viewing them as a powerful force that could change the face of the Kingdom of Naples. But all previous attempts had failed, the clans being too filled with blood-stained pasts and grudges that went beyond the grave. Giulio, and many other bosses, had laughed when they had listened to the *Padrone*'s proposal. They ignored the kindly worded offers to riches and power, preferring to remain barons in their own tiny fiefdoms. The *Padrone* had expected as much and struck the day after the ignored conference, burning down homes, businesses, and killing men in the streets. Ettore Policeni and his secret master appeared to know every detail of each *Camorra* clan, striking with the precision of a swordmaster and slaying many outright. Soon, all, save the Conte, were forced into obedience, their will sapped by the strategic genius of the *Padrone*.

Now Giulio, and his remaining men, lived the lives of *banditos* rather than *Camorra*. They roamed again, stealing, robbing, and killing any in their path. Five women were now in the Conte clan, lovers and killers in the own right. Pia Mele, a former farm girl whose family had moved from the north to live with relatives after the French stole all their property, was Giulio's lover, his unofficial second-in-command, and the official alpha female of the group. She was the only one able to calm the rampaging spirit of Giulio Nucci.

"Where is the *stregheria*? Where?" Giulio demanded, his face appearing equal parts of rage and terror.

"I am here."

Mama Zullo's voice preceded her as she slowly walked into the hut. A tiny woman, she was dressed all in black and possessed sparse iron gray hair and a deeply lined face that, thanks to the growing shadows in the room, gave her a sinister, ethereal quality. Her long, pointed jaw and wart-shaped nose, combined with the malevolent look in her eyes, caused all in the countryside to acknowledge that she was a witch. Though believers in the word of the Church, the peasants of Campania also acknowledged the power of such ancient wise women. Her potions, charms and knowledge would never be beloved by the residents, but she would be respected as a power one should not anger. Each town or small city possessed at least one elderly woman like Mama Zullo, and Giulio Nucci knew them all. A believer in the ancient magic, he perpetually visited these *stregheria* to get new charms or have them remove perceived curses.

"Lay down on the floor, child."

Mama Zullo's voice was a hoarse crackling whisper. The sound resembled that of rustling leaves at midnight, causing the listener to fear the sound that emerged from her throat, like some terrible nightmarish creature from the depths.

"The rest of you, leave us," Mama Zullo added as she pulled a small wooden plate from the sack she carried over her thin, skeletal, shoulders.

With the infinite slowness of antediluvian ritualistic movements, she poured a measure of oil on the plate and stepped next to the prone form of Giulio Nucci. Neither she, nor the gang leader, appeared cognizant of the shredded corpse of Aldo Conte, mere feet away from where the *stregheria* prepared her spells.

"Close your eyes and repeat after me..." Mama Zullo intoned as the spell commenced.

CHAPTER X

The iron gate of the Nisida Island prison opened with a harsh, high-pitched screech that caused the sea birds to scatter and all present to wince. Granting them just enough space to squeeze in, the imposing gate snapped shut behind the small party allowed within the massive stone walls.

Nisida was an imposing gray stone edifice that resembled a military fort as much as a prison. The walls were high, massive, thick and appeared to loom over a visitor like some massive giant of ancient myth. Light appeared almost muted by these daunting monuments to the punishment meted out by the state. The air about the prison felt heavy, as if the world was pressing down on anyone entering.

Walking through a wide, empty courtyard, the small group stopped before a heavy metal door guarded by a bored-looking fat man with a luxuriant mustache and the scent of cheap wine on his breath. He fingered the worn wooden club hanging from a thong on his wrist as they waited for admission to the interior.

"Four priests? You here to pray for the souls of them inside? Don't bother. Not one of them is worth saving. Only thing they understand is pain. Give them enough, they'll do what you want."

The guard's voice was rough and slurring slightly. He was clearly drunk, but attempting to hide this poorly. Nobody appeared inclined to argue, an unspoken realization that nothing they could say would penetrate this man's obstinate, wine-fueled rage towards the inmates.

The door suddenly swung open, revealing a long, dark corridor made from the same heavy stone used to build the walls. A short, balding man with a sunken chest and a scruffy white beard stood on the threshold. He blinked at the bright sunlight with watery, blue eyes that appeared unfocused.

"F... f... f... follow me," he stammered in a nearly inaudible voice.

He waited as all four men squeezed by him and slowly closed the heavy door. After locking it with a massive copper-colored key, he turned and took them down the hall to another similar door.

"D... d... do... you... h... h... have... any... w... w... w... weapons... on... y... you?" he asked as he unlocked the second door.

Johann Spurzheim, Jean-Pierre Séverin, and Franz Karnstein each admitted they were armed as the door opened. A tall man with thick light brown hair, a thin mustache and a pointed beard awaited them on the other side. He was dressed in a brown smock, matching pants, and high cavalry boots. A worn wooden club, very similar to that of the guard outside, dangled from his left wrist. He smiled at them with a mouth full of tiny, crooked, yellow teeth.

"I heard what you said. If you insist on holding onto your weapon, do not approach any inmates," he stated in a rich, thick Neapolitan voice.

"We are not here to speak to the inmates. Take us to the black door immediately," Spurzheim ordered, stepping closer and looming over the man.

The man blanched, but not at the imposing site of the police chief looming over him now.

"The black door?" he whispered, his voice shaking.

He took a small step backwards and looked as if he was about to flee.

"That is what I said," stated Spurzheim, his voice slow, harsh, filled with unspoken menace. "Take us to the black door. Immediately."

The guard pulled at his beard in a nervous gesture, but finally appeared to relent. He eyed Spurzheim and Gui was unfeigned terror, knowing their bloody reputations. Séverin and Karnstein, he dismissed with a glance, obviously taking them for servants of the two dangerous political figures.

"We will need to walk through the punishment room. The staircase to the black door is on the far side. We use it to scare the prisoners."

The guard's voice was shaky and a little hopeful that the latter might prove an impassable obstacle. But he was disappointed.

"Lead on, my son," Gui said, intervening to reaffirm his own power.

The guard sighed and turned, pointing towards a metal door set in the south wall.

"Follow me. I shall lead you to the black door, but that is as far as I will go. Not even if you make me a prisoner will I pass through that gate again."

"Very well," said Spurzheim, making a cutting gesture with one hand, apparently indifferent to the guard's demands.

"What is the punishment room?" Karnstein asked, stepping through the door at the rear of the group.

"Prisoners who break the rules receive proper chastisement at the hands of the guards. This teaches them that obedience is preferable to rebellion. Rejection of the law is a crime in the eyes of the Lord," Gui explained, adding, "*A righteous man hates falsehood, but a wicked man acts disgustingly and shamefully. Proverbs 13:4.*"

"*If you forgive others the wrongs they have done to you, your Father in Heaven will also forgive you. But if you do not forgive others, then your Father will not forgive the wrongs you have done. Matthew 6:14-15,*" Karnstein replied, his eyes flashing with anger.

"Did you forgive your hell-spawned ancestor, Mircalla Karnstein, after she murdered your father and damned your mother to the eternal flames?" Gui spat back as he whirled towards the young Exorcist, his face an ugly mask of rage and disgust.

"Yes," replied Karnstein, without any anger or sadness. "I pray for their souls every night, in hopes they will one day repent their sins. Saint Timothy wrote something that gives me some hope: *Unbelievers cannot repent without the enabling grace of God. So pray that God would grant them repentance, that this repentance would lead them to a knowledge of the truth. Pray as well that they would come to their senses and that they would escape from the devil's snare.* Kind words for one such as me."

"Lord protect me from the missionaries of the church," said Gui rolling his eyes. "Ones such as you would have us living as paupers by the will of the people."

"Would that be a hardship for you, Father Abbott?" Karnstein asked, looking back at the master of the Cupbearers without any visible expression.

"Enough!" Spurzheim roared, stepping between the two. "We are not here for some clerical debate! Save all this for a better time."

Karnstein appeared ready to snap out an angry retort to the police chief, only to be silenced by a look from Séverin. He subsided and nodded, falling into step behind his teacher.

They passed down two more corridors before approaching an archway twice the height of a man, lined with heavy yellowing stones. The guard unlocked the metal door and pushed it open with obvious reluctance. The hinges released a high-pitched, nerve-jangling screech that caused all present to wince with pain. A harsh, bright light emerged from the room and they were suddenly struck by a harsh, eye-watering wave of new scents. The first was the ammonia tang of urine, a smell recognized universally as an olfactory symbol of fear. This was followed by the earthy aroma of feces, an odor that brought up other childhood humiliations. The rusty scent of blood was also evident, as was a sickly scent that caused even the bloody-minded Gui and Spurzheim to shiver. That smell was the unhidden essence of fear, the inner torment of humanity brought out through acts of savagery too terrible to imagine.

Four men were in the room, three leaning against the walls, looking very unsteady. A pair of wine jugs, both empty, lay on the ground, a thin dark pool staining the floor near their gaping, jagged necks.

The punishment room was at least two stories-high, windowless, and built from the same gray stone that made up the walls. Around the square chamber were racks of whips, ropes, circles of metal, branding irons, and sharp, filthy knives. The floor was speckled with drying dark stains, ranging from small droplets to large pools. Lining the wall, each at least ten paces apart, were heavy chains made from black iron. Each set ended in manacles from the wrist, neck, or legs, and were linked to thick rings set in the stone. These details, they only realized later; another sight caught their vision. A man, bound hand and feet with heavy, coarse ropes, hung suspended from a pulley attached to an arch. He moaned softly, his face black, his eyes crimson, his breathing shallow. Blood leaked from his eyes, nose and mouth, and only barely audible whimpers indicated he was still alive.

"Ignore him," the guard with the pointed beard said, waving a hand. "He's a madman who starts trouble. We'll cut him down at noon, and hopefully he will have learned the error of his ways."

"He will be dead by that time," Séverin stated, examining the hanging prisoner closer. "You must release him immediately."

"If he dies, he dies. It is of no importance. He talked back when ordered to remain silent," the guard explained with a shrug. "He is nothing."

"He is a human being," said Séverin, his voice cold with outrage.

He crossed the room to the pulley. With a carefully deliberated set of moves, he lowered the hanging man gently to the filthy floor. The guard moved to intervene, only to be stopped in his path by Franz Karnstein. The Austrian nobleman did not speak; he merely stood between the guard and the swordmaster. The cold look on his face, the angry glint in his eyes, caused the guard to pause in his protests.

Untying the prisoner's' twisted limbs, Séverin sighed with some relief at the lack of broken bones or dislocated limbs. Looking up at the drunken guards, he ordered:

"Get a litter and take this man to the hospital. Now, if you please."

The sheer weight of his order, spoken in a tone that brooked no disagreement, spurred the others into action. Within a minute, the prisoner was gently placed on a stretcher and carried off to a nearby chamber filled with beds and staffed by a kindly nun. She was a tiny woman with a lovely face and dark, bottomless, wells for eyes.

"I have seen this before," the nun stated after identifying herself as Sister Carlotta. "I will do my best for this poor man, but ultimately, we are all in the Lord's hands. Go with God, child."

"If you are finished with your acts of charity," Gui snarled, sounding aggrieved, "can we return to the reason for our visit to this benighted hellhole? We already tarry far longer than I would have wished."

"Very well," Séverin agreed, falling into step behind Spurzheim.

The guard took them to another heavy metal door, this one possessing a thick layer of dust near the lock. The man's shaking hands caused the keys to jangle and chime like a tiny brass bell. The sound was musical, a gentle tintinnabulation that was quite in opposition to their grim surroundings. He opened the door; it moved easily and soundlessly, but with slow, obvious reluctance. A heavy set of stone steps plunged downward, a weird, eldritch light emanating from small gems set in the walls. This soft light cast pools of shadows about the corners and barely visible ceiling, creating a sensation that they were entering another world—one of darkness, stale air, and unseen demoniac forms lurking just out of sight.

The guard's step was slow, the frightened tread of a terrified child. His head swiveled about, left, right, up and down, as if he was positive the darkness would coalesce into a diabolical form and rip the life from his body.

"What is the source of this light?" Séverin asked.

He'd seen other versions of this glowing gemstones in the past, but these were subtly different from previous incarnations. The guard shrugged broadly and waved his hands about in wild gesticulation.

"We don't know. When the old fort was built by the Greeks, they put these stones in the wall. They're always on, never brighter or darker."

"These walls are not Greek," Spurzheim observed, slapping the uneven, heavy stone blocks with his hand. "I've visited their ruins and they looked different."

None saw fit to argue as they slowly wound their way downward. About ten minutes later, they came to a halt, stopping at a flat landing made from three interlocked stones. This did not hold their attention as they observed what lay mere feet away. It was a rounded arch, seemingly made from a single uncut white stone. It appeared as if this round portal exuded from the very Earth—thrust upwards and settling in this spot. There were no designs on the rock, just a smooth, glassy surface that almost glowed in the shadowy depths. Within it was pure darkness, a plutonian, stygian gloom that appeared part liquid, part obsidian. That crepusculian murk was completely impenetrable, a wall of negative calignosity, as powerful and encompassing as the empty depths of the ether. Just staring in it for a moment caused the viewer an inner dread, a sensation of instinctual terror born in the atavistic depths of the animalistic past of mankind. Its very wrongness evoked the desire to flee from danger, though none took a step to return to the light of life above the Earth.

"The Black Door," the guard stated, taking a large step away. "I go no further. I'll sit on the steps."

"Follow me," Gui said, his voice hushed, his head bowed.

Inhaling deeply and releasing the air in a rush, he stepped into the depths of the black door. At his heels were Spurzheim, Séverin, and Karnstein.

"Sei un cretino, bastardos."

The guard, whose name was Tito Bianchi, walked up four steps and sat down, facing away from the Black Door. He knew he had to wait; he only wished he had something to drink or smoke to pass the time.

Spitting on the floor, Tito tried to think of anything but the curtain of darkness that lay behind his back. He didn't succeed.

CHAPTER XI

"Mistress?" Hertz Ende asked as he carried the dead peasant girl's body to the edge of the lake. "Why are you doing this?"

Nosos, stepping lightly through the woods at his side, looked at her slave with confusion.

"Doing what, slave Hertz? Hertz? I don't like that name. It does not taste good on my lips."

"My surname is Ende. What I mean is, I understand your need to feed on the blood of these peasants. But why do you reanimate them and send them to attack the palace?"

"Ah," Nosos replied, seeing his point.

She smiled, showing her rows of serrated teeth and knowing they glinted like lovely stars in the sunlight.

"That is a good question. A small portion is enjoyment, entertainment in its purest form. The terror the dead cause to the living is a delight to view. My brothers and sisters and I always find that a little fun at the expense of mortals makes the endless years pass by swifter. I like tormenting the rulers of a region, weakening their resolve to remain in control."

"And the other portion?" Hertz asked as he positioned the corpse exactly as instructed.

"Distraction. I have a greater mission in the coming days. This kingdom will become my haven. I need to claim the very heart of the power of the land and people. To do that, I must marshal my powers. I am still not as strong as I must be to become the mistress of all that I survey. Now, shut your mouth, Ende... Ende? No, I don't like it either. I shall give you another name."

Nosos knelt over the corpse of her last meal. Running a long taloned nail across her pale palm, she watched as a thin line of viscous crimson blood leaked from her hand. Sensually she caressed the dead girl's face, smearing the scarlet fluid in an odd pattern across the lips and cheeks. The corpse took on a comical countenance—the too pale skin stained with the red blood causing her to resemble a clown caught in a cloudburst.

That was when she began to sing, the words in clear, distinct, if archaic, Greek:

"Aíma tou aimatós mou akoúo tin kardiá mou perpatíste gia ména ypakoúo sti thélisí mou péraapó ton táfo."

The words were odd to Hertz Ende's ears, sounding half prayer, half commandment. Roughly, they translated to an invocation of the blood and a demand of service beyond death. He might have scoffed at such statements as mere mummery—he had warbled similar nonsense in the past. Yet, he did not, somehow grasping that there was a power in play here that he did not—could not—comprehend.

Then he felt an electrical crackle filling the air, as if a mighty lightning bolt was about to plummet from the sky and strike the land with devastating force. A heavy thrumming of power rang in his mismatched, odd ears, and it felt as if the world itself was holding its collective breath.

The dead girl sat up, her movements jerky and uncontrolled. She stumbled as she stood, her limbs barely in control, dropping to her knees and tripping over a stone as she rose up again. Her eyes were milky white orbs and her mouth moved up and down, filling the air with a light clicking sound that was both unpleasant and unnerving.

The walking corpse was off, pushing through the brush, heading towards the city. Her gait was unsteady, but grew slightly steadier as she vanished from view. Hertz turned away, watching as Nosos's slurped the remaining blood. She led him back to her haven, ignoring the entreaties of her new followers without a second glance their direction.

Hertz Ende noticed one commonality about the men and women that knelt before Nosos' breathtaking beauty. Obviously, none approached their mistress' loveliness, which was inconceivable by mortal standards. Yet the men and women who abased themselves before her perfect feet were stunningly attractive. Their looks were different: tall, short, slender, robust, long-haired, short-haired, thick and thin—each were

72

completely unique and astonishingly attractive. They were all young, the oldest possibly being twenty-five, the youngest, a spoiled fourteen-year-old son of a wealthy baron.

Only Hertz Ende stood apart from this group, but that was no matter. He was the personal slave of his mistress, and the newest residents of Nosos's refuge ignored him in the same manner as they did servants in their homes. In time, perhaps, they would torment him as they had done to so many others in the past. That was their way, the path of the bully and the spoiler. Each, with few exceptions, were men and women who had tormented and teased those less fortunate than themselves. The few that did not behave in this manner in life, now did so in death—or, to be accurate, *undeath*.

Hertz Ende knew that, for all their newly-found power and demonic skills, these were lesser creatures than Nosos. She, unlike her progeny, was not ruled by her cravings. These exquisite creatures were barely human now, more appetite than intelligence. They had periods of lucidity, but in the presence of blood, they reverted to an animalistic state. They were leeches who wore the mask of humanity and, in the face of their food, all pretenses vanished.

Nosos settled herself on a large wooden throne, sitting as regally as any queen of ancient days. She stared at Hertz for a moment; then her wide mouth curved up in an amused smile.

"Sinis," she spoke the word as more of a purr than a statement. "I shall call you Sinis from now on. The name fits your true self. I had considered Epiphagi, but your inner self is more like Sinis."

Hertz, now already thinking of himself as Sinis, frowned, but did not reply. He believed Sinis was the name of a character of Greek mythology, but the details escaped him at the moment. He did like the idea of being named after the legends of that hallowed time.

"Are you not grateful, Sinis?" Nosos asked, a warning tone in her question.

"I am! Thank you so much, O mighty mistress," Sinis replied, dropping to his knees.

Nosos chuckled and clapped her hands together.

"Very good, my slave! Sinis, you shall serve at my side forever and ever. Does that not please you?"

"Oh yes, dark queen of beauty. I am content to stay your slave until the stars fall from the sky and all life vanishes from the Earth," Sinis warbled, his eyes averted from his mistress.

Nosos laughed and nodded.

"I've taught you so very well in such a short time. I am very proud of myself."

With that said, she pointed a long, taloned finger at a muscular male with olive skin and thick dark, curling hair. He stood, a blood-spattered Apollo, and approached with a slow, sinuous step. Nosos pulled the youth down, her teeth sinking deep into his exposed neck as she mounted his engorged member. A moan of ecstasy escaped his lips and he allowed himself to be enfolded in her tentacular grasp.

CHAPTER XII

The curtain of stygian darkness enfolded Jean-Pierre Séverin and Franz Karnstein as they stepped through the Black Door, tossing them into a gloom the defied all sight. It was as if the very illumination of the world had been muted, and all that remained was a cold, formless void. The stillness and silence that surrounded them caused a wave of devastating dread that almost froze the hardy swordmaster and exorcist.

They emerged seconds later in a well-lit black stone hallway whose polished surfaces appeared to shimmer and reflect negative images of all present. Séverin and Karnstein stared back at the Black Door, horrified by the terrible sensation that they had experienced within the infinite void.

"Yes," Gui said, sounding amused by their dismay. "The Black Door always causes one to feel as if one's very soul was imperiled. It is never easier, but at least some awareness is granted that there is an escape, if one does not freeze."

"Before you ask," Spurzheim held up one long, heavily calloused hand to stop the perceived flow of questions, "we do not know who built this the door, or this underground wing of the prison. It was here when the Greeks dwelled in this region, and we never found out how it was created, or why. Just that if we place a servant of the unholy here, they do not attempt to leave. Nor do they appear to need food or water, or whatever they crave to sustain their existence."

The corridor was narrow enough to admit one man at a time, if they were not too stout. The doors were wood and covered with light metal strips in an odd, irregular pattern. They did not have any locks or handles. There was a hush about, a silence as deep and as profound as the inky darkness at their rear.

Gui took the lead and headed down the corridor, which proved to stretch as far as the eye could see. He stopped at the fourth door on the left, and gently pushed the wooden surface.

The door swung inward, revealing a small room, barely high enough for Séverin to stand in, and only slightly wider than the corridor. The walls, floor and ceiling were made of the same black stone, with no scratches apparent.

Laying on a bed made of an unknown metal was a woman. Heavy black iron chains worthy of a naval frigate held her still on the bed. Her head was covered by a steel mask in the shape of leering demon, with huge, heavy lidded eyes, a long oddly-shaped nose and a lolling tongue hanging from its massive maw.

"The Mask of Satan?" Séverin asked, sounding surprised. "I thought such articles had been abandoned centuries ago."

"What is the Mask of Satan?" Karnstein asked, standing in the doorway.

Séverin frowned, his eyes never leaving the form on the bed.

"A Moldavian inquisition torture device. A woman declared to be a witch was bound by the inquisitors. The mask was heated and placed on her face. They hammered it in place with nails. It was a terrible death that was outlawed by Pope Clement XI, if I remember correctly."

"We discovered a small collection in a storage facility on the island," Gui explained, looking very proud of himself. "Many wished to have them destroyed, but I sensed there may be some future use. In this instance, using the mask was appropriate. This woman and others of her ilk are already dead. This is the best means of keeping the damned from harming anyone ever again."

"These walking corpses are a danger to all," Spurzheim added. "We cannot harm them, for they do not bleed or feel pain. We cut them into pieces and destroy the remains by fire. A priest reads last rites over the remains."

"What happens when you cut them to pieces?" Séverin asked, still watching the body on the bed.

"Each piece continues to struggle and attempts to kill any human or animal in reach. I once witnessed a soldier strangled to death by a severed hand," Spurzheim answered, looking annoyed rather than disgusted by the information.

Séverin looked at Karnstein and said:

"This sounds like a form of possession. Can you examine the woman and determine the truth?"

Karnstein nodded and stepped deeper into the tiny room. He stood over the body and prayed softly in Latin for a moment as he made the sign of the cross.

"*In nomine Patris, et Filii, et Spiritus Sancti. Amen.*"

Closing his eyes, his hand raised up and splayed out over the masked head, hovering inches above the cold metal. Minutes passed without any movement from him as he concentrated and barely appeared to breath.

"What…?" Spurzheim started to ask, but was silenced from a look by Séverin.

Gui appeared amused and slightly interested as the young exorcist stood over the undead corpse of a wealthy woman once known as Claudine Brazzi.

Karnstein's eyes opened and they appeared to pulse lightly with a silver energy. His vision shifted, and the world transformed, becoming a world of light and darkness, of strange beings on the edge of his consciousness. This was the true world, the universe beyond the limited vision of mankind. Viewing the cosmos in this manner was dangerous, a path that often led to madness or worse. Sadly, this was the only method of seeing the truth in this instance.

Looking down at the masked, fallen figure, Karnstein spotted the source of her contamination. A gossamer thin wisp of dark energy appeared attached to her, a barely imperceptible strand rising and vanishing into the skein that surrounded them like a massive web of darkness and light. Karnstein narrowed his vision to this miniscule filament, the ebony energy a mere trace leading upwards into the greater cosmos. The filament eluded his scrutiny, shimmering with a depth of darkness as deep and impenetrable as the Black Door. Forcing his mind to relax, he fixated on the object and studied the strand for a moment. The sight he viewed caused him to mentally recoil in disgust and horror. The strand was the embodiment of corruption and blight, a cancerous horror that could spread with the malignancy of a plague. This was evil in its purest form, an energy form of all that was abhorrent in this life and beyond. A wave of nausea filled his very being and it took all the self-control he had learned from a life of horror to prevent him from screaming and fleeing. Summoning his metaphorical mental shields, Karnstein forced himself back into the real world. Gasping for air, having not realized he'd been holding his breath, the Austrian Exorcist was only kept from falling by Séverin's quick, steely grasp.

"What did you see?" the Frenchman asked.

His question was rhetorical, for he had experienced similar situations with the undead in Muscovy and Cornwall.

"A tendril of dark power. A witch... A warlock, or some other being of vast power... They provide a tiny bit of power and keep this... this... thing, from expiring completely. The power is corrupting, evil, though that says so little of the wrongness I viewed."

Karnstein closed his eyes and attempted to slow his rapidly beating heart.

"Can you track it to its source?" Séverin asked.

"No," replied Karnstein, shaking his head. "The trail leads into the web of unlife. I have no way to follow such a tiny sliver of darkness through the greater universe. That would be like attempting to find a single grain of sand on a beach the size of the Earth."

"Then this trip has been for naught. My maid could tell me as much, and I would get her services as well," Gui snapped, looking aggrieved.

"Incorrect, Father Abbot," Séverin corrected. "We now comprehend a bit more of the enemy we face. Now we shall let this being know that we are not so easily frightened. And that their power is not supreme."

"Agreed," said Karnstein. "Please leave the room and close the door. This will only take a moment."

The Austrian straightened, his eyes still on the Mask of Satan. His stern gaze held a tiny degree of pity, but that vanished within a moment.

"What are you planning on doing?" Spurzheim asked, stepping towards the door.

"A form of exorcism," Karnstein replied, never looking up as the men exited the chamber and soundlessly closed the door.

They left the portal open a tiny bit, just enough to peek inside if they wished to spy on the young Austrian Exorcist. Gui whirled on Séverin.

"An exorcism takes a minimum of eight hours and must be approved by the highest-ranking official of the Church. Which, in this case, happens to be me!"

"Does that apply to holy inquisitors?" Spurzheim asked, feigning ignorance, but secretly delighting in his enemy's anger and frustration.

Before Séverin or Gui could answer, the sounds of Karnstein's voice emerged, the words completely incomprehensible. Gui and Spurzheim stepped a little closer, each confused by the sounds.

"*DALKHU TARU SERU ESERU ETUTU INA ETUTI ASBU DARISAM*," Karnstein intoned.

A silver light suddenly flashed, a metallic beam of energy that dazzled the viewers for an instant and disappeared. Karnstein opened the door and stepped out into the hallway.

"It is done. You may bury the remains in holy ground. Please do not leave the Mask on; that woman was a victim. If anyone objects, tell them this is the order of a holy inquisitor."

"What did you do? How did you perform an exorcism in mere seconds?" Gui whispered, his face alternating between anger and fear.

"You have no right to know. If you have any concerns, you may refer them to His Holiness the Pope. Otherwise, I am under seal to not speak of such events," Karnstein replied, his phlegmatic tone causing even greater rage to appear in Gui's narrowed eyes.

Spurzheim looked interested, but also appeared delighted by the Cupbearer master's impotent rage.

Returning through the Black Door was equally unpleasant and they all seemed grateful to be standing on the dark landing. They spied their guard, Tito Bianchi, waiting for them, but not looking their direction. He sat on the steps, his head nodding as he tried to keep from falling asleep.

"On your feet, dog!" Gui roared, kicking the prone guard and snarling as he stubbed his toe.

"My apologies, sir!" Tito Bianchi stumbled to his feet and attempted to bow and salute at the same time.

"Silence! You lazy, useless, unholy creature! You shall lead us back to our ship. Then you shall personally remove the dead prisoner in room four and have her buried in the prison graveyard. Have the mask removed and returned to storage. Then scrub down that room and every other within that wing. If this is not accomplished by morning, the Cupbearers shall visit you and your family. Do you understand me?"

Spittle speckled Gui's beard by the time he had completed his rant. Tito Bianchi attempted to answer, but appeared unable to speak as he tried to salute and bow to the screaming master of the secret police. He led them through the prison and was seen running back towards the interior as they exited.

The remainder of the trip to the mainland was silent, with Gui angrily pacing, Spurzheim appearing amused. Séverin and Karnstein stood away from the other two. The normal sounds of a naval vessel almost appeared muted as they made the short crossing, the sailors sensing that boisterousness might enrage the dangerous monk and his party. As the ship approached the dock, it was Séverin who spoke first.

"I thank you for your solicitousness, gentlemen. My pupil and I learned much from this visit. If you don't object, we shall now leave you, but will return to the palace later."

"So be it," Gui replied.

Spurzheim waved a hand in disinterest.

The silence returned unbroken until the grand carriage of the Cupbearer master departed, his entourage of soldiers leaving in his wake.

As the carriage turned a corner, Karnstein asked:

"You have a destination in mind?"

"I do," Séverin replied, heading west. "The son of my second swordmaster resides in Naples and teaches the art of the blade. Also, his family hunt vampires. I think you will find meeting them quite instructive."

"The last time you told me something would be instructive, I was nearly sacrificed on a dark altar in Paris," Karnstein replied, rolling his pale eyes.

Séverin shrugged, his dour face cracking into a smile.

"It was still instructive, no? You learned how it feels to be the sacrifice in a demonic summonsing from a different perspective. In any event, I think this shall be slightly less lethal. At least, that is my hope."

CHAPTER XIII

Nosos screamed and grabbed her chest, tossing her young lover aside with a contemptuous slap. He skittered away on his hands and knees, resembling a blood-spattered vermin more than a man. The pack of vampires milling in the shadows nearby slid away, retreating from the cave and into the nearby woods. They knew better than to stay anywhere nearby their mistress when she raged.

"Sinis!" she screamed and closed her eyes, trying to control her fury.

Sinis ran to her side, kneeling at his mistress's feet.

"Yes, beloved queen of the night? How may I serve your every need?"

Nosos looked at her slave, her eyes red and narrowed to the point of slits.

"I have been attacked by... an ancient power. Who in the kingdom can invoke such...?" she broke off, unable to complete her statement.

"I do not know, O most beauteous of mistresses. The kingdom is not large, but populated by many people who believe in the ancient powers. People call the witches *stregheria* and threat them with fear and respect. The Church is less powerful than it is was a year ago—the bishop fled the city because of the French," Sinis explained.

In his previous life, he'd hidden away from occult practitioners, knowing they were rivals and possible threats.

"You are useless, Sinis. Do you know that? Useless for all but crawling at my feet," Nosos stated, sighing with disgust.

"Yes, my dark queen. May I make a suggestion?" Sinis asked, kissing her feet.

"Yes, slave. Make your suggestion," said Nosos, sighing again.

"I was a visitor to Naples and hid away from the world. You require the help of someone who has resided in this city for a lifetime. They will know who are powerful and who are false. Perhaps one of your pets? Fortuna or Giorgia?" Sinis suggested, sitting upright and looking at her perfect face.

Frowning, Nosos, shook her head.

"Fortuna is elsewhere. I have need of Giorgia here and her knowledge is limited. The others are nothing, fodder for my future work. I shall look elsewhere, someone who is covered in blood and will learn to obey."

"Genius, as always, dark queen," Sinis applauded. "Shall I fetch the coach?"

"No. I will take a horse, I am an excellent rider," Nosos said, shaking her head. "The scent of death shall lead me about the land until I found the one I require. Until then, provide a new body for the others to feed upon every third day. I shall enflame their lusts and that will occupy their time. Be sure to cleanse the cave daily; I do not wish to return to a sight of an orgy and a vomitorium."

Without waiting for an answer, Nosos walked from the room, exiting the cave. She raised her arms above her head and opened her mouth. A high-pitched cawing sound spat from her lips, an inhuman wail that pierced the sun-dappled forest and caused small animals to flee in fear.

A low rustling filled the air and the brush surrounding the ancient demon suddenly shivered and shook, causing leaves and flower petals to fall at her unshod feet. Slowly, slithering like serpents in the grass, came her vampire slaves. Though lovely of face and body, there was a profane bestial quality to them now. They hissed and snarled and slinked, stopping at the feet of their mistress. Their bodies were piled atop each other, resembling reptiles by their actions.

Nosos's eyes pulsed with an unreal eldritch luminosity, alternating between scarlet and black energy. The light cast an eerie inhuman quality to the setting, one capable of driving the minds of men mad by the sight. Even the insects ceased to chirp and fled the vicinity, sensing the corrupt influence of demoniac horror present.

The primordial being whispered to her followers, her commands piercing their hungers and forcing complete obedience. She spoke for a very long time...

CHAPTER XIV

Séverin led Karnstein through a busy commercial district, filled with small shops and a seemingly endless series of stalls and tented wagons. The loud, brash, chorus emerging from the sellers echoed through the vast bazaar. Men, women, and children appeared to be perpetually jockeying for position. Their voices were boisterous and full of emotions, ranging from the pleasurable to the enraged. The wares varied from the simple to the unusual, each hawked with the same glee.

"Buy my chickens! Nice fat hens, I'll give you a good price," said a thinly-built older man with white whiskers.

"Don't bother with his scrawny birds, two bites and you'll still be starved. Come look at my chickens. The plumpest in Campania!" a heavy-set woman in a muddy brown dress sang out, pushing the smaller man aside.

"Don't listen to her! Her chickens are all feathers, no meat. I'll lower the price since you have a kind face," the older man yelled, elbowing the woman aside.

"A saintly man such as you, good sir, will recognize a liar. He lies and sells stolen, skinny, hens. Come with me and I will show you chickens fit for the plates of a duke, or even a king!"

The woman shoved the older man aside with a hard, calloused hand. The two immediately took to shouting insults at each other, ignoring Séverin and Karnstein as they screamed curses and shook fists in each other's faces.

"That was... disquieting..." Karnstein said, glancing back at the battling pair.

Séverin chuckled and shook his head.

"Average for any true market. You've never visited a bazaar in all your travels?"

"Other than a trip to some of the Parisian book stalls, no," the Austrian said, shaking his head.

"That is not a true market, or as the Arabs call it, a *suk*," said Séverin. "The book-sellers will call out their new items, but little else. A true market is like a living organism. It feeds on the food, which are customers such as ourselves, and either consumes them completely or releases them lessened. In this situation, each time we buy something, the market grows stronger. We, in contrast, possess less money, but possibly something almost as valuable as our coins. Additionally, the weaker parts of this living creature we call a market are also consumed and often expelled. This will result in their either gaining strength and returning, or death. Fascinating, no?"

The swordmaster stepped around a man gesticulating madly and trying to force them into his small, dark, stall.

"Somewhat," replied the Austrian. "Though I believe if I required anything, I should end up paying far more than any item's worth."

Karnstein glanced about, obviously feeling very much the outsider in this location. Séverin barked a laugh and nodded.

"Very wise, my young friend. Do you remember when we first crossed swords?"

"Yes. I knew then I stood no chance."

"Precisely. You correctly identified I was a sword expert and wisely took your defeat as a lesson. Some view such battles and believe their inability to overcome a superior opponent unmans them, reduces them in stature."

Séverin took Karnstein to the other side of the bazaar. The area before them appeared to possess an inordinate number of scantily-dressed ladies. These women were both prostitutes and thieves, living a harsh life and always seeking new victims. Men would be easy prey to their games and end up losing money or getting into a fight with one of the hidden bully boys.

"That is a foolish way of behaving. If you do not know how to perform a skill, how can you be expected to match one who mastered the art form through years of practice?" Karnstein asked, spotting a particularly pretty woman with long red hair, dressed only in a silk shift that appeared almost transparent in the sunlight.

"Agreed," Séverin concluded, "yet some do react in this manner. The men and women who survive for years in a *suk* are masters in their own right. They may be unlearned in other areas, yet they will never fail to earn a small profit from each transaction. The foolish ones wither and die, or become dependents on the stronger ones. Some farmers with no skill at sales, and no family able to fit that role, will sell their goods at a reduced price to one who is expert. The farmer does not lose, yet they will never rise above their current level of poverty. The seller, if they are clever, may end up using their profits to buy an actual shop and gain customers able to spend more money. It is an interesting world that, at times, reminds me of a battlefield."

The swordmaster turned down a side street filled with small, discreet-looking stores. The customers were slightly better dressed, some even bordering on the expensive clothing of the nobility.

"You tell me this because...?" Karnstein asked, glancing back at the market, confused by the change in styles at so short a distance.

"You are about to get another lesson, possibly many. The fencing academy we are about to enter is run by my old classmate, Bartolomeo Dardi. One of his ancestors founded the original school in Bologna approximately three hundred and fifty years ago. Barto, for that is my nickname for him—which you must not us—and his family moved to Naples because they wished to use their skills in another manner."

Séverin stopped before a two-story brick building. The outer facade was cleaner than the neighboring buildings and the sidewalk appeared washed and free of any dust or dirt. Knowing he was meant to ask, Karnstein played his part:

"This business being other than training swordsmen?"

"Yes," Séverin nodded, reaching for the door. "They fight monsters, much like us. His aunt Sylvia was my first teacher."

With that, they walked inside a well-lit front room occupied by a young man behind a small table. He looked as if he
was still in his teens, his long limbs and rash of pimples across
his jawline and nose demonstrating his biological approach to
manhood. He was nursing a small cut on his cheek, but looked
up with clear, dark eyes and long lashes that would, one day,
earn him much praise from the ladies.

"May I help you, signore?" he asked, his voice rising and
falling with each word.

Séverin bowed and favored the youth with a small smile.

"My name is Jean-Pierre Séverin, and this is my pupil. I
believe we are expected by the maestro."

The teen reached for a small, leather-bound journal and
nodded once, his Adam's apple bobbing in time with each
movement of his head.

"Yes, I see you are listed here. The maestro left strict instructions I should announce you first. Please wait here for a
moment."

The youth stood and left the hallway, his movements disjointed and uncoordinated as he vanished from sight. He returned mere seconds later, his face looking sweaty, his eyes
downcast.

"Please head straight inside. The training hall is located…"

"I am aware. I was a student here once myself. My
thanks, signore."

Séverin led Karnstein through the door. The hallway was
well-lit, with many windows along the right wall allowing in
the sunlight. The walls were covered in light wood and the
floor was made entirely of stone. Despite the brilliant rays of
the sun, the building felt cool and comfortable.

Turning into a large archway, Séverin paused to rub his
booted feet on a heavy wool mat. He waved for Karnstein to
follow suit and nodded once the ritual of cleanliness was concluded. The room itself was two stories-high, lit by a series of
carefully placed skylights, with candle holders lining the light

wooden walls. Racks of swords and daggers lined two walls, some sharp, others made of wood for practicing purposes.

The man standing in the center of the room was several heads shorter than Séverin, and possessed a triangular-shaped face framed with a dark beard and mustache. His eyes were wide and appeared to pop from his skull. He was smiling with a wide smile, showing huge, perfect, white teeth. Dressed in a sleeveless brown shirt, matching pants and small, soft boots, he resembled a traveling street acrobat.

"Gâteloup!" he roared, his voice loud, deep and causing the walls to vibrate.

"Barto!" Séverin cried, a rare show of pleasure showing on his face and in his tone.

Bartolomeo Dardi bounded over the five seated youths and scooped Séverin up, whirling him in a circling before dropping him to the ground. They exchanged loud kisses of greeting on each cheek and pounded each other's backs in a manner allowed by old friends.

"Now, you lazy pack of street brawlers," Dardi said while leading Séverin into the training hall, "meet my oldest friend, Maestro Jean-Pierre Séverin, the greatest swordsman I ever met... after me, of course."

A ripple of laughter filled the air and the students rose and bowed greetings. Séverin bowed to all in response and appeared in astonishingly good cheer.

"Allow me to also introduce my own pupil. Standing in the doorway is the young man I wrote you about last year. Maestro Bartolomeo Dardi, allow me to introduce you to Baron Franz Vordenburg Karnstein of the Order of Exorcists."

Séverin watched Karnstein's reaction. Technically, according to the rules of courtesy, he should have reversed the introductions. Franz Karnstein was a baron and the heir to a count, technically the highest-ranking man present. This, however, was quite against Séverin's Republican principles. He held the belief, quite strongly, that a master of an art form should be held in higher regard than one who had just inherited rank.

Fortunately, Karnstein appeared completely disinterested in this apparent breach of protocol. Bowing and clicking his heels in the Austrian fashion, he said:

"Your servant, Maestro. Your academy is very impressive."

Dardi's eyes widened slightly and his smile grew a couple of inches wider.

"I am so very pleased to meet you, your lordship."

Karnstein flapped a hand in a gesture of dismissal.

"No titles for me, please. My Christian or surnames are sufficient."

Dardi looked over at Séverin.

"He is exactly as you described him. I agree with all you suggest."

He turned his attention back to the assembled students.

"Class is over. You may use training halls Marius, Africanis, or Mus if you wish, to train further. *Addio*, my dear wastrels and scoundrels!"

The students laughed and headed out, few even bothering to spare Karnstein a second glance. A few studied Séverin before leaving, searching for something in the normally dour countenance of the French swordmaster.

Once the room was cleared, Séverin returned his gaze to his student.

"Barto and I need to discuss some private affairs for a time. Do you mind?"

Karnstein shook his head, his gaze already traveling along the racks of weapons.

"Of course not."

"If we take too long, I shall send one of my students along with a refreshment," said Dardi. "Please, make use of the training hall. This room we call Caesar, and it is the main teach floor of the academy."

"My thanks," Karnstein replied.

Dardi then clapped Séverin on the back, leading him towards a closed door at the rear of the chamber.

Meanwhile, the Austrian strode over the rack of wooden weapons, marveling at their many sizes and shapes. There were some the size of his forearm, others longer, yet possessing a strange delicacy. One wooden sword rose from the floor to just under his chin level. He had heard of this weapon from his late grandfather on the Vordenburg side of the family. It was called a *Zweihänder* and mercenary companies, known as the *Landsknecht*, used them in battle about three hundred years ago. It was odd to see such a training tool in any fencing school other than a traditional Prussian one.

"Who the hell are you and why are you in my father's training room?" a woman's voice asked, sounding more interested than aggrieved.

Karnstein turned and bowed, clicking his heels as he'd done earlier to Maestro Dardi.

"The Maestro and my teacher went off to speak and asked me to wait here. I am Franz Karnstein."

The woman entering the room was a little shorter than Karnstein and dressed in a slightly more modest and darker version of her father's clothing. Her tight black shirt possessed tiny sleeves that stopped just above her sculpted triceps. Her pants, also black, fell to her ankles and she was shoeless.

"Ah! The pupil of Maestro Séverin. I heard about you and your family. My father and I killed one of your relatives six months ago in a girl's school in Rome. I am Sylvia Dardi, second in command of this school."

She smiled as she approached, moving with the same uncanny grace as her father, though her smile appeared more mocking than happy. Sylvia Dardi was a stunningly beautiful woman. She possessed a rounded face that was dotted with perspiration, full lips, heavy, dark lashes and straight black hair that she wore in a tight queue down her back. Her figure was the classic hourglass, with an astonishingly narrow waist, wide hips and high, full breasts. If she possessed any flaws, it was that she appeared to possess strong, tightly sculpted muscles across her arms and back.

"Let me guess. Was her name Carmilla? Mircalla? Marcilla?" Karnstein asked, sounding resigned.

"Marcilla. How did you know?" Sylvia asked, crossing her arms and looking a little annoyed.

Karnstein rolled his eyes and turned back to the weapons.

"That is a family tradition. The daughters take variants of their mother's or closest aunt's name."

"A family tradition? I thought your family's tradition was following the dark arts," replied Sylvia, stepping up next to him, knowing she was on the edge of his vision.

"For some, not all," Karnstein stated, stepping over to the next rank.

These swords were real, the edges and points glinting in the strong sunlight.

"My father says that you are training to be a monster-hunter. Are you a maestro of the sword?" Sylvia's voice was challenging and she stared at his profile with open hostility.

"No. Nor shall I ever learn such skills," Karnstein replied as he studied a curved Turkish blade.

The weapon was ancient, but well-cared for, and possessed the notches of past use in battle.

"That one is said to be the battlesword of the bodyguard of Oruç Reis, who was also known as Barbarossa, the pirate. A gift from the Bey to one of my family," Sylvia explained, her voice softer for a moment.

"One of the members of a distant line of my family, Comte Leopold Karnstein of Cordoba, fought with the Emperor Charles in the battles against the Reis. He led a force of cavalry under the command of the Marquis de Comares."

Karnstein's statements were in the same disinterested tone he'd used earlier.

"Your family spreads across the world. Some would not say that is a good thing," Sylvia observed, a challenge in her voice.

Karnstein turned his pale eyes her direction.

"Are you attempting to start a quarrel with me, mademoiselle?"

Sylvia smiled, though the look was not friendly.

"I am merely discovering whether my father's closest friend, a man whom I call uncle, is harboring a Karnstein viper in his bosom."

A flash of annoyance crossed Karnstein's face, a brief instance of emotion that vanished as fast as it appeared.

"You believe you are a better judge of character than Monsieur Séverin?"

Sylvia shook her head, her queue dancing with the movement.

"No, but he has a good heart."

"Meaning, you do not?" Karnstein asked.

Sylvia looked annoyed, realizing she'd fallen into that insult.

"I am more cautious. Come, let us train. You do know how to use a sword?"

"A little," Karnstein replied.

He pulled off his jacket. He had known this was inevitable, having been in this situation several times in the past. Removing his neck cloth, he stepped over and pulled free a wooden reproduction of a light cavalry saber.

"Saber? A clumsy weapon for most, though favored by Austrians and Prussians. Very well."

Sylvia selected a matching blade and stepped to the center of the floor. They saluted formally and the duel commenced. Sylvia was faster and skilled, far better than Karnstein with the blade. Within a minute, she scored a killing blow to his chest and accepted his salute with a mocking grin. They started again and she disarmed him within five passes of their blades. With a contemptuous flick of her hand, Sylvia tossed Karnstein back his wooden sword.

"You are slow and unskilled. You will never kill a man, let alone a vampire. Perhaps you can follow your family and take up black magic?" she said, her tone filled with mockery.

Karnstein's face flashed with anger again, though this time, the rage lingered and did not vanish from his eyes.

"I killed my first man when I was age eight. I shot him in the face with a dueling pistol."

He attacked again, his movements faster and harder. Sylvia, though the better swordsman, was hard pressed to keep defending. They both stepped apart, circling, their weapons extended.

"I killed my first woman seconds later with a matching dueling pistol," Karnstein snarled, his attacks still fast and wild, pressing Sylvia back.

He ducked and disengaged when she attacked again, returning to circling. His face was still filled with rage and pain and each word he spoke appeared to come through gritted teeth. Karnstein resumed his crazed attacks, pressing Sylvia back. She appeared stunned by his words and merely defended, never attacking.

"I killed my first vampire a minute or so later," he said. "She was another of the vampire women of my family and had killed my father and my Vordenburg family. The Vordenburgs were the only true family I possessed in this world. Oh, and she also made my mother a vampire, too. My mother was the second vampire I killed. I was only eight years old."

Those final statements froze Sylvia Dardi in place and Franz Karnstein slapped aside her sword and stopped his wooden blade inches from her neck. They stood there, frozen, his pain-wracked face slowly returning to the normally placid expression.

"What is this?" Bartolomeo Dardi asked, sounding outraged. "Sylvia, did you insult this man? He is a guest in my home!"

"Father, I..." Sylvia stammered, her light olive skin blushing crimson.

Karnstein bowed and shook his head.

"Merely a fencing lesson. If you will all excuse me, I missed afternoon prayers and spotted a church at the end of your lane."

With some final statements, spoken in a fast manner to prevent any other discussion, Karnstein collected his belongings and vanished from view. Bartolomeo Dardi looked about to return to his earlier tirade, but was stopped by a raised hand from Séverin.

"Uncle Jean-Pierre, I... his name... I was afraid." Sylvia looked both ashamed and unhappy.

Séverin shook his head and said:

"I understand. I am not angry, quite the opposite. You are the first person my student reacted to with anything close to emotion. This is good. Since you will be working with us..."

"Pardon me?" Sylvia asked.

Dardi and Séverin exchanged an amused look. Dardi chuckled and said:

"There is a great danger to the city of Naples. We shall be working with your uncle and his pupil in this fight against evil."

"A coach shall pick you both up tonight. Have you ever attended a ball at the palace?" Séverin asked, with a smile.

His grin widened when he caught the look of dismay on Sylvia's face.

CHAPTER XV

Jean-Pierre Séverin waited at the rear of the chapel as Franz Karnstein completed his prayers. Though he did not possess the inclination or desire to become a swordmaster, the young Austrian noble did have one quality that was similar to those on that path-steadfastness: he never wavered from his daily prayers and training rituals, his consistency nearly that of Séverin or Dardi.

This was understandable in a swordmaster, one needed to constantly work to improve or one fell victim to age and loss of expertise. From Barto's letter, his Sylvia was much the same. Why Karnstein behaved in this manner was a mystery. Even though he had trained the young Austrian for a year, the man was still very much an enigma.

Séverin fell into step beside the Exorcist, genuflecting briefly as they stepped out into the late afternoon air. The sounds of the market drifted their direction, rising in volume as the sellers sought to empty their stalls and return home by early evening.

"We are being watched. Three groups of individuals," Séverin said, indicating they should walk away from the direction of the market.

"I spotted two groups. One group of three men, all very uncomfortable in clothing. I think they are monks who serve the Cupbearers," Karnstein replied, not looking around.

He'd been taught by Séverin to only use peripheral vision and the objects of the street as a means of observing others.

"And the second group?" Séverin asked, hands clasped behind his back as they strolled.

"Two men, very stiff-backed. Probably soldiers of Spurzheim," Karnstein replied.

"The third group are experts, changing their looks regularly. A man with scar on his right wrist, a woman who wears several articles of clothing and changes them regularly to hid herself, and a young girl with poorly cut brown hair and a dirty dress. They also shadow us," Séverin stated. "Did you hear what Gui said to you when you completed your unusual exorcism?"

"Yes. He revealed he knew more of my history than he originally stated. I was not surprised."

"You should be surprised," Séverin snorted. "The information about your early life is under seal of the Pope. Somehow Federigo Gui managed to violate that rule and discover the name of the vampire you killed. This tells me he is a very dangerous man who has a different agenda."

"Perhaps you are right," Karnstein acknowledged and shook his head. "I apologize for embarrassing you with your comrade."

"You did not. Sylvia insulted you and broke through your self-control. This troubles you, considering you pride yourself on being capable of ignoring all bothersome people. Frankly, I thought Madame Policeni would pierce that armor first. She was truly a lovely woman who threw herself at you with surprising ardor—unless you did not find her attractive?"

Séverin turned them down a busy avenue, full of carts and coaches.

"We discussed this aboard that rotten hulk of a ship. Yes, the lady was lovely to the eye, but she possessed a reason for her ridiculous desire for my body. I am not sure whether it was a game, or as a means of making herself the wife or mistress of a baron. I possess no skill in that area. I merely know when someone wishes to use me under the guise of love or lust."

Karnstein's response sounded phlegmatic, but Séverin knew better and sensed the underlying anger in the young man's tone.

"Understood," the swordmaster replied. "No matter. I doubt we shall see Madame Policeni again in the future. If we do, we can determine her agenda. Sylvia will help; according to Barto, she is an expert at the games women play in Naples and Rome."

"This is your way of informing me we shall be working with them fighting whatever evil menaces the kingdom? Very well," Karnstein sighed. "Do you have any additional surprises?"

"Just one. Did you pack formal dress for court?" Séverin asked, fighting to maintain his dour expression.

Karnstein started and looked confused.

"I do not believe I even own such articles of clothing. I was never publicly presented to the Emperor or His Holiness."

Séverin clapped his pupil on the back and chuckled.

"Then we both have a date with the tailor this afternoon. Happily, I sent word ahead this morning for us both..."

CHAPTER XVI

Ettore Policeni writhed on the floor, his face a mask of agony. His every muscle appeared taut and ready to split from his skin as the seconds passed. Policeni was bent backwards, only his head and toes touching the floor, appearing to be only seconds away from breaking his own back. The cries that emerged from his gaping mouth were the soft mews of an injured kitten rather than the near death throes of a man suffering the torments of the damned.

Francesca Policeni glanced up from her book, smiled, and returned to reading. Seated on a comfortable divan and dressed in a light summer gown of blue silk, she looked the very picture of a wealthy woman of leisure. On a table by her right elbow lay a square of silver that chimed softly, releasing a gentle tune. Two others, one of gold and another of cherry wood, were also on the table, though no sound emerged. Francesca collected *carillons à musique*, owning a collection that filled a small room. Her favorite form of relaxation was listening to the gentle music boxes as she read poetry.

Hearing another whimper of pain, Francesca lowered her book and sighed.

"I will never get a chance to finish *Purgatorio* before the ball if you insisted on moaning like a dying sheep."

Hearing the song end, Francesca touched the gold box and smiled as the new song commenced. Looking down upon her squirming husband, she shook her head.

"I do keep warning you, my dear Ettore. Do not disregard any of my father's orders, or mine. The *Camorra* may think of you as their leader, but you are nothing more than a *Pulcinella* puppet with no Joan. Our stick propping you up is the golden elixir we feed you daily. Each and every time you attempt to increase your position, we must repeat this tedious lesson."

Examining Ettore's face for another moment, she waved a hand languidly in the air. Giacomo Lando stepped into view, a large wooden goblet in hand. Gingerly stepping to Ettore's side. He poured a small libation into the gaping maw of the gangster. Waiting a moment, he poured a little more into the slackening lips and handed the subsiding man the goblet. Ettore gulped down the golden liquid with the greed of a man dying from thirst in the middle of a desert. He collapsed after swallowing every drop, staring up at Francesca with frightened, angry eyes.

"I've warned you three times before, my idiotic husband. Why must we perform this dance each time? You have all you could ask for since you left prison. Yet, you still insist on attempting violate the small set of rules Papa set forth."

Francesca appeared more amused than angry as she spoke.

"What? What did I do?" Ettore asked, his voice more croak than speech.

Francesca sighed and turned to Lando.

"Show him."

Lando smiled, showing no teeth and gently helped Ettore Policeni to his feet. He led the *Camorra* leader out through a back door and into the wide, walled garden. There he pointed to a pair of heavy sacks and waved for Ettore to open the bag on the right. Moving slowly, Ettore opened the sack's untied mouth and gaped. Staring up from the depths of the bag was the head of Bucco Fava, the Roman alchemist. His thin-lipped mouth lay open in a silent, perpetual scream of agony and his sightless eyes seemed to accuse Ettore of bringing about his horrible death. Ettore recoiled, fighting off a wave of nausea and turned his back on the grisly sight.

Following Lando back inside, he stood before Francesca and waited. He tried looking placid, but he remembered the last conversation he had with Fava, a short week ago.

"Have we enough yet?" Ettore asked as he handed the old man the glass vial.

A pair of tiny droplets of the golden liquid lay at the bottom, barely visible in the light cast by the tiny tallows. Bucco Fava did not answer—he merely snatched the vial from the Camorran's outstretched hand. He tilted it slightly while placing a tiny metal tube inside, which he used to remove the golden fluid. He then added the drops into a second vial, this one almost one quarter full. Studying a marker on the side of the second item, he nodded slowly.

"We now have just enough, I believe. I would wish more, but I know you shall not agree to an extension of the collection process. We, the servants of Saint Albertus Magnus, toil away, viewed as criminals by many of the world, our Godly work disparaged by little men who wish to keep all learning for themselves. Did I ever tell you how the Inquisition treated me in Madrid? Had I not fled for my life, they may have done unspeakable things to me! And the time when..." Bucca Fava rambled on, unaware of Ettore Policeni's open boredom.

After rebelling once, and soon realizing that he was a slave to the golden elixir, Ettore Policeni had immediately formulated a plan. The first step, was to find a genius at alchemy who would not talk about his secret task. The answer had come during an assignment in Rome, when he had discovered Bucca Fava hiding from the Inquisition.

"Why do they seek you?" Ettore had asked, drawing the shade on his coach as the driver cracked his whip.

"You heard their spurious charges. They declared I am a warlock who seeks to despoil the dead. I am nothing of the sort, good sir. I am a seeker of truth in this unseeing world. I am a follower of Saint Albertus Magnus, a blessed alchemist who sought to comprehend the natural laws of the universe. The charges from those monsters in Madrid are false, sir, quite false! Alchemy is science, not the simple attempt to transform lead into gold or the dead into living. Let me tell you of the works of..."

Fava spoke for hours, disinterested in whether his audience was paying any attention. When he finally slowed, Ettore spoke again:

"I am enslaved by a terrible potion—one I may not steal. If I bring you a tiny sample, can you discover the ingredients? I will support your work and provide you with a place to live so that you will not be disturbed," Policeni had said, sensing a possible escape from *Fra Diavolo*'s clutches.

"I will provide you with a vial and show you the precise minimum I require for proper study," Fava had replied. "Then I will be able to find the compounds required for its recreation. After some experimentation, I will provide you with a precise duplicate of the elixir you request. If that is acceptable, let us repair to the hovel I now call a home and I will begin packing. I have a great deal of books and…"

Fava once again launched into a speech that lasted until they were on the road to Naples.

Years later, after enduring weekly dissertations from Bucco Fava, the work was truly commencing, but now the alchemist was dead. Ettore was stunned; his one hope for free-dom and revenge was gone. His patience and hard work had all been for naught, *Fra Diavolo*'s tentacles were everywhere.

He now stood like a naughty schoolboy before his wife in her father's home. She ignored him for a full hour, reading her book and periodically activating one of the music boxes. Lando bowed briefly and left, to dispose of Fava's remains.

"You have a question?" Francesca asked, marking her page with a leather strip before placing the book on the table. "Feel free to ask, my darling *stronzo*."

Being called an asshole caused Ettore to flush and blurt out:

"How long have you known? About Fava and… and…"

"And your attempt to recreate the formula? Since you picked him up in Rome, of course. Papa found your actions amusing and decided to see how long would your attempted rebellion take. Your patience did you credit. Papa was proud that you did not waver or become reckless. We killed your silly little man and used your saved elixir as part of what you just consumed," Francesca explained, giggling briefly.

"As to your notes regarding the potion," she continued, "we have everything. All your servant's recorded information and your copies. Papa was very impressed that you discovered one of the ingredients was the venom of the black scorpion. How did you learn that much?"

Tempting as it was for Ettore to curse Francesca out, he knew when he was defeated. There was no purpose in being petulant; *Fra Diavolo* and his daughter had defeated his last hope for freedom.

"I heard the *Padrone* mention it to you in passing once. I wrote the words down, but couldn't find anything further," Ettore stated, shoulders slumping. "What happens now? A trip to the Tiber with Piano Piatto?"

Francesca laughed, a full and rich sound full of mockery and malice.

"Death? *Sei un deficient.* You continue to serve until Papa no longer has any use for you... possibly longer. You are easily replaced, but raising a successor would require a period of retraining. I think this little drama has taught you that it is a waste of time to attempt to escape. No, my dearest *sfigato*, you belong to Papa and me. Attempt something like this a second time and we will withhold the elixir and allow you to suffer again. The only question will be whether you break your own back in pain or your heart explodes."

Ettore nodded, keeping his eyes downcast. He now understood what the priests meant when they discussed selling your soul to the Devil. Ettore Policeni knew he had done just that the minute he had agreed to follow Michele Bozzo's mad plans.

"Good! Now, head back to your rooms. The valets will clean you and get you ready for the ball tonight," Francesca said, picking up her book again, her hand causing the silver music box to tinkle a little tune.

Ettore, finding his courage again, grinned.

"Ah! You're intent on seeing that man you desire, Karnstein?"

Francesca looked up and theatrically rolled her eyes.

"The only desire I have for that cold-blooded hymn singer is to break his spirit. Religious men and women are the most enjoyable to seduce; their lost belief reduce them to slightly above an animal. Do not mistake my anger at failure for any type of interest beyond Papa's orders."

Ettore sighed, defeated again and stalked out of the room. He was angry and knew that he wanted take his frustrations out on someone.

"Maybe that Karnstein," he muttered to himself. "If I kill him, that will spoil the *rompicoglioni*'s plans. She won't be allow to punish me for killing an enemy."

With that thought, Ettore Policeni laughed and clapped his hands softly. This tedious ball had possibilities beyond a chance to be seen in the company of the new Corsican king.

CHAPTER XVII

Pia Mele yawned and climbed out of bed, leaving the snoring Giulio Nucci behind. Usually he was a delightful lover, rough and insatiable, daring and delightful. They usually matched well sexually, Pia preferring someone who could equal her appetites. Giulio was the perfect fit, unless he believed he was cursed. Then he was about as energetic as a stone and not nearly as exciting.

She knew she could seek out one of the other members of the gang, but that would not go well. Some would reject her for fear of Giulio's wrath. Others would take her willingly, but wouldn't be particularly interesting or successful. Pia was in a trap, one she couldn't seem to find a means of escaping.

Stepping outside the small hut, she wrapped herself a little tighter in the blanket and looked up at the dark, starless sky. Pia was not happy with her choices, realizing the shortsighted behavior she demonstrated in running away with Giulio. She had thrown over all of the men in her village for his hot kisses, a life of excitement and few rules as intoxicating as their lovemaking. What Pia hadn't expected were long periods of poverty, living as poorly as her farmer father and the rest of her family. Money ran through Giulio's hands like water in a river--e spent every cent, often on nonsense like *stregheria* or drinks for everybody in a wine shop for a night. It was frustrating to discover that, after a night of drinking and debauchery, they didn't have enough money for food the next day.

"You look sad, my pretty one. Are you sad?" asked a soft voice.

Pia whirled, her knife in hand. She stopped when she saw who was behind her and gaped in shock.

"You won't need that with me, my pretty Pia. I am here to make all your dreams come true. A life of excitement and luxury. No longer sleeping in huts and wondering if you'll eat that night."

The soft voice spoke the words, seeming to embrace her and flow all over her body like a sensual caress.

Pia hesitated, afraid that this was some trap by Giulio to test her loyalty. He was given to that during fits of melancholia, occasionally even threatening her life as part of his games. But this was different from all his other attempts at proving she was going to abandon him. Giulio was many things, but subtle was not part of that list.

"You are afraid of Giulio Nucci? I will provide you with a way to control him completely," the soft voice said. "He will not even realize you are the true leader of his band. All you need to do, is take my hand. One simple gesture, and all your dreams will come true."

A hand appeared, made of shadow rather than flesh.

Pia thought for a moment, afraid yet entranced. The idea of controlling Giulio, preventing him from his foolish actions, was enticing. Not sleeping in farmer's huts and going hungry was an even greater inducement. Hadn't she thrown over three villages filled with boys in favor of a life of excitement with Giulio? Didn't she deserve a life that matched her dreams? If she wanted to starve and scrape, Pia could have married anyone from back home.

The answer was easy for Pia Mele, and if this was a trap, then Giulio was subtler than she realized. With a tentative smile, she extended her hand, shaking and quivering like the rest of her body.

CHAPTER XVIII

"Are you dressed?" Séverin asked, tapping on the door to Karnstein's room.

The palace's chamberlain had assigned them a suite of rooms usually reserved for minor diplomats of little importance. They were about twenty feet square, with vast detailed scrollwork along the walls and a medium-sized painting of Napoleon as First Consul.

"Nearly so, enter if you choose," Karnstein replied.

He sat on a chair near the bed, pulling on a freshly polished Hessian boot. For the first time during their acquaintance, Jean-Pierre Séverin viewed his pupil dressed in clothes that were not merely plain black and white. Thanks to the tailoring skills of Rudolpho Lasparie and his son, the young noble wore a formal suit of black with silver and gold thread. His waistcoat was made from red silk and his hair was pulled back in a short queue. Around Karnstein's neck was a ribbon and medal denoting he was a baron, and he also wore the signet ring of a Knight of Malta.

Séverin, for his part, wore a similar outfit in gray with a pale waistcoat. He, too, wore high Hessian boots rather than hose and court slippers, knowing those adornments were a waste of money. Despite suggestions from both Lasparies, he had also eschewed a wig, knowing they were a symbol of the monarchies of ancient days.

"I am a Republican, sir. I will not seek to embarrass my host, nor will I abandon my beliefs. No, sir, I shall not wear a wig," Séverin had told his old friends.

The Lasparie pair had merely shrugged and gone back to work.

"What do you think of court finery?" Séverin asked, watching as Karnstein buckled on his cavalry saber.

"The clothes are comfortable, but I am uncomfortable with such... vanity..." Karnstein replied, shaking his head.

"I agree with you. Our addition to the ball was, no doubt, through the manipulations of either Federigo Gui or Johann Spurzheim. The King has no interest in our presence and will not receive us… formally or informally. I am not sure why we were invited, but I've found that such occasions are often as dangerous as a battlefield. Be very much on your guard. Neapolitan politics are among the most lethal in all of Europe," Séverin explained as he straightened Karnstein's cravat.

The Austrian did not reply, but joined Séverin in the hallway. A footman in formal livery waited for them and steered them through the labyrinthine corridors of the palace. As they progressed, the décor grew steadily gaudier and more luxuriant. The trappings left behind by the former Bourbon rulers of Naples demonstrated that wealth was necessary, if not completely essential, to their lives. Covering every surface were designs made from expensive woods, paintings of inestimable value, and small items whose sale could have fed a starving family for months.

Instead of creating a sensation of royal majesty, the viewer was left with a feeling of claustrophobic dread. There was an oppressive quality to the gross spectacle, an almost childish need to prove that the owner was greater than any visitor present. Séverin had viewed such luxury in the past and found himself still unmoved, unimpressed, and grateful he ignored such royal foolishness.

Karnstein mumbled under his breath for a moment in German, finally whispering:

"Is the whole palace like…this…?"

"I believe so," Séverin replied. "The former Bourbons were anything but restrained in their tastes."

"This palace makes the Vatican look understated," Karnstein said, looking upon the rococo images with unfeigned distain.

"Sometime I hope you see Versailles. Then you will understand why we French revolted against our kings. Though the Schönbrunn Palace in your own country is even richer. I assume you never visited it the one time you met your ruler?"

"Correct. I was presented at Schloss Hof and while that was excess at times, it was in no way this…display."

Karnstein stared for a moment at a massive mirror filled with elaborate gold work across the face. The edges were covered with chubby-bodied cherubs, their face caught in wide, inhumanly merry grins.

"I visited Schloss Hof when I was younger," said Séverin. "While it is far from Spartan, I do see how this palace would feel disproportionately extravagant. It doesn't matter. We are here because someone wishes to place us in the path of danger. Probably you—my status as a swordmaster is well-known and considered too dangerous by those who seek our lives."

They followed the valet. Music slowly drifted to their ears, growing in volume as they traversed the many hallways leading to the main wing of the palace.

"I shall do my best to avoid difficulties," Karnstein replied, his voice not hiding his growing disinterest.

Séverin chuckled, amused by his pupil's behavior. If there was ever a man who could demonstrate the Teutonic coldness and lack of emotions, it was Franz Karnstein. He reminded Séverin of one of his teachers, a German vampire-hunter named Kronos. He had been a master swordsman with few peers, and an ability to ignore seduction attempts by female vampires. Though Karnstein would never possess Kronos's skills, he appeared to retain the same disposition.

"If you believe you are stepping into a dangerous situation," said Séverin, "evasion is the best solution. Walk away before you are challenged and force the one seeking a quarrel to follow you and make clear their intentions. Naples rules are as fierce and deadly as the streets of Rome, though without the limitations."

They crossed a long courtyard and were ushered into the antechamber just outside the ballroom. The uniformed valet presented a pair of cards to a similarly dressed man several steps from the door. This servant, a tall, thin man with the long, dour face of a Puritan read the paper, sniffed and pointed to a small line of people.

"Wait on the far end of this chamber. Your number is fifty-six. When I say that number, you shall proceed to my side and I will introduce you to the chamberlain. If you do not respond quickly, your names shall be placed at the rear of the line. Do you understand? Good."

The equerry spoke with the nasal intonations of a lifelong functionary in the service of noble masters. Neither Séverin nor Karnstein had any reply to this lofty speech. Instead, they moved to the rear of the assemblage, the disdainful intonations of the man resounding as he repeated his commands to the next set of guests. By the time they reached their indicated location, his voice was a mere murmur in their ears.

"Such men were the next to fall in the Revolution," Séverin remarked. "Just behind the fat nobles who treated the people as lower than barn animals. Almost twenty years ago, that type were also the first to flee when the mobs became fierce. No stomach for more than petty ballroom battles."

His words possessed no heat or anger; they were merely a statement of facts.

"I've dealt with a few over the years, mostly in the Vatican," Karnstein observed. "His Holiness tends to replace them after a time, lest they start believing they control his schedule."

A pair of smartly-dressed soldiers ushered Colonel Hugo, one of the more formidable members of the royal court of Naples. The Colonel was barely visible as he passed, surrounded by a phalanx of honor guard and several officers under his command. An attractive red-haired woman, garbed in a daring yellow dress with a plunging neckline, was at his side, her Neapolitan accent floating above the stomp of the soldier's boots.

"Not his wife, I presume?" Karnstein asked as the entourage passed and entered the ballroom.

"I assume so, given that his wife is French," replied Séverin, shrugging. "Does that disturb you?"

Karnstein shook his head.

"I have enough of my own sins on my soul. I shall not judge others. As it says in *Romans 2:1, You therefore have no excuse, you who pass judgment on another. For on whatever grounds you judge the other, you are condemning yourself, because you who pass judgment do the same things*. I think that is better way of living, though I have been known to forget the words and meaning when confronted with worshippers of darkness."

"Yes, I have witnessed your lack of control under those circumstances. You would be wise to seek a means of preventing that anger from overwhelming your reasoning," Séverin said, remembering their encounter with a powerful satanic cult deep within the depths of the Earth.

The young exorcist had treated these dangerous people with open contempt and had come close to losing his life.

"My struggle, yes," Karnstein admitted, frowning. "I shall not quote the Bible on this failing of mine, I've recited them often in the past. I've never found a way of channeling my rage at such despicable creatures. I know I should forgive, but I do not appear able to."

"As I've stated in the past, there are still many areas of the world where you lack knowledge. Seek new avenues that do not surround the battle of light and dark and perhaps you will find a solution."

Séverin kept his voice even, unwilling to allow his fears for his pupil to be obvious to the young man. This was one of the reasons he had taken the young Austrian as his student, though he had sought to assist in the creation of another warrior on the side of good, one following the heroic traditions of great heroes such as Kronos and Dardi. The world required such men and women to battle vampires and witches who would destroy all life for their dark masters. Equally important was the concern that the hunter of darkness would soon become as much of a plague upon mankind as the creatures they sought. The case in point that Séverin always kept in mind was the terrible witch trials during the English Civil War. A monstrous man named Matthew Hopkins and his dogsbody, a beast named Stearne, had used these uncertain times to condemn the innocent, rape, and murder young women, and steal from the victims. Even worse was a beast named Cumberland and his follower, a nobleman named von Meruh. They didn't even bother to pretend to battle evil; all were guilty in his mind—only he was innocent and worthy of the riches that flowed through his hands. This was the fate that could await Karnstein. The time may come where he viewed all human beings as dreadful sinners, unworthy of his help. Then his deadly skills and talents might destroy the lives of the innocents, and he would become a plague upon mankind as dangerous as a demon. Séverin trained the cold Karnstein in the hopes of preventing such a calamity.

Before Karnstein could reply, they heard the nasal voice of the equerry calling:

"Number fifty-six, please present yourself immediately. Number fifty-six, step forward or you shall wait until the prompt are welcomed within."

"We are Number fifty-six," Séverin stated as a pair of men in the livery of the palace stepped forward.

They quickly whisked both men clean and straightened any clothing even slightly askew. The man on the door sniffed again and nodded slowly.

"You are acceptable, follow me and remain at my rear. You must be announced by the herald of the Court."

Jerome Després stood at attention just outside the massive stone arch that led to the main ballroom. His reddish skin was lightened by a heavy layer of powder and his massive jaw broke into a confused frown.

"My good friends, so pleasurable to see you once again. There appears to be a mistake with your invitation. You, my good sir," he bowed slightly to Séverin, "are correctly listed as Maestro Jean-Pierre Séverin. The difficulty lies in our young Austrian friend here. He is listed as Baron Franz Karnstein, not Karlstein which, as we know, is the correct spelling. The difficulty is the order comes from the Crown, which does not

make mistakes. I am quite overcome by the thought of informing His Royal Highness of the mistake."

"Ah," Séverin said, raising a hand. "As you said, the
Crown does not make mistakes. We shall have to merely pretend that, while in Naples, our young baron's title is that of
Karnstein rather than Karlstein. After all, this is the command
of the King himself, is it not?"

Jerome Després thought for a moment and then nodded
vigorously.

"Maestro, you are right. I believe you are completely
correct in all aspects of the affair. No doubt the far wiser mind
of King Joseph has a distinct reason for this alteration."

"No doubt," Séverin agreed, doing his best maintain a
dour expression.

Turning to Karnstein, the deputy chamberlain bowed.

"I hope this does not discommode you, my lord. We all
must follow the commands of our royal masters. You must,
from now on in Naples, only be referred to as Baron
Karnstein. Is this acceptable?"

"I shall endeavor to remain agreeable on the subject,"
Karnstein replied, his response holding a small tinge of
amusement.

"Oh, thank you, my lord. You do me great service in allowing me to call you by the name Karnstein."

Jerome Després bowed deeply as he spoke.

"You're welcome," Karnstein replied, his eyes on the
ceiling lest he betray his growing amusement.

The deputy grand chamberlain straightened and stepped
forward, hand extended. A teen boy, dressed in a far less
gaudy court costume, stumbled closer and handed Jerome
Després a tall staff with a gilt laden gold ball on the top. The
teen was ungainly, his arms and legs outgrowing his ability to
properly work these extremities. His eyes were downcast and
he appeared to be blushing crimson beneath his rash of acne
across his jaw and neck.

Jerome Després banged the large staff three times on the
ground and noisily cleared his throat.

"Baron Franz Vordenburg Karnstein and Maestro Jean-Pierre Séverin."

Séverin and Karnstein stepped forward, bowed deeply to the distant seated figure of King Joseph Bonaparte. The king did not appear to acknowledge their presence, preferring to continue a conversation he was having with a uniformed man standing on his right. Standing on his left was the robed personage of Federigo Gui. Even from this distance, they could see his bald head swiveling their direction.

Duty completed, Séverin and Karnstein walked down four white marble stairs into the ballroom proper. The chamber was massive, larger than a Paris city block and about as wide too. The walls were highly decorated, covered in brocade, complex rococo designs, and chased with gold leaf. If the hallways were extravagant, this ballroom made the previous sights resemble a farmer's hut in the middle of a muddy field. Even the chairs and small tables along the wall appeared to be made from rare imported woods and the most expensive fabric.

"I would repeat my excoriation of the decor and my Republican leanings, but that would be impolite, I should think," Séverin said, his voice only slightly above that of a whisper. "Additionally, I have little doubt Abbot Gui has his vultures circling as we speak. Watch your words, no matter what anyone says to you."

"I believe you said as much earlier," Karnstein said, bowing as a well-dressed matron passed, a teen girl in tow.

They ignored him, their eyes fixed ahead on a young chinless man chatting with an older man who shared weak facial features.

"Well, this is a wonderful surprise!" Francesca Policeni stated, stepping into view and smiling as she lowered a black fan from her lovely face.

Her dress was made of a shiny green fabric and possessed a plunging neckline of white silk. She wore her hair piled atop her head and curled, causing her long neck to look soft and sensual.

"Baron Karnstein and Maestro Séverin, a pleasure to see you both," she added.

Karnstein looked startled for a moment, then bowed, clicking his heels automatically.

"Madame Policeni."

Séverin too bowed, realizing the danger was present already. Karnstein had properly identified this lovely woman as dangerous, which had to be enhanced in this setting. The difficulty was now how to extract themselves without giving offense. To simply snub her, as Karnstein had done aboard the *Loire*, would be noticed and viewed as boorish. Any man impressed by her beauty could challenge them to a duel.

"Have you ever been to the palace? You simply must see the lovely gardens. After dancing, of course. I am free for this waltz, Lord Karnstein," Francesca stated, practically purring her words.

More than a few men and women stared at her, impressed by the near perfection of her beauty and dress. Karnstein was clearly unable to think of a means of refusing or even replying. Stunned, he opened his mouth but appeared at a loss for an answer. Francesca's smile widened, causing her to resemble a cat toying with a particularly plump and cornered mouse.

"Sadly, you will have to wait your turn. His lordship promised this dance to me," Sylvia Dardi said, stepping next to Karnstein and taking his arm.

She wore a red silk gown with a plunging neckline and medium length sleeves. Her hair was pulled back into a Psyche knot and held back by a sparkling silver comb. While quite different in every way from Madame Policeni, she was not outshined by the wealthy woman.

"Is this true, your lordship?" Francesca challenged, her eyes narrowed and looking daggers at Sylvia.

"Um… ah… ah… yes, of course," Karnstein stammered, clearly shocked by the transformation of the woman he had fought earlier.

Sylvia smiled enigmatically and curtsied to Francesca, waiting as Karnstein bowed before leading him away from discussion. She shot a triumphant look back at the other woman before vanishing from sight in the assembled crowd. Francesca looked as if she was about to spit before turning and flouncing the other direction.

"Your pupil does like to play with fire, Gâteloup. That a true Helen of Troy," Bartolomeo Dardi said, appearing as if out of thin air at the side of Séverin.

Dardi's clothing was a sight to behold, gold, white, and green silk with and a bright blue cravat and a white wig atop his skull. His black beard was carefully groomed, and his yellow hose and black court slippers looked very new. His outfit was remarkable because it had been in fashion… twenty years earlier.

"Barto, you look like your late father, God rest his soul," said Séverin, keeping a straight face as he took in the image of his oldest friend.

"Whose clothing do you think I wear, my friend?" Dardi laughed and pounded his friend's back in open good cheer.

This behavior was very out-of-place in this regal location, but few appeared to pay attention.

"Why do you refer to that woman as Helen of Troy? Because her beauty intoxicates men?" Séverin asked, sensing the answer.

Dardi shook his head and winked one eye in the manner of a street performing trying to catch the eye of a potential customer.

"No, Gâteloup, I called her Helen because she causes the death of anyone who falls under her spell."

"*Camorra*?" Séverin asked, having suspected as much since the *Loire*.

"Her husband, Ettore, is the boss of all the gangs, save one, in the kingdom," Dardi answered, cackling. "She lures men he despises away, and then he challenges them to duels of honor. Ettore does not fight them himself, but uses champions. Why would the *Camorra* seek to harm your pupil?"

Séverin frowned, seeing a man in green appearing to be standing close and pointedly ignoring their conversation. Signaling Dardi, they walked away, placing some distance between them and the possible informant.

"The answer to your question," Séverin said after they found a semi-secluded location, "is that I do not know. Baron Karnstein has never even been to Naples. Yet, aboard our ship, she threw herself at him with the fervor of that dancer you met in Athens."

"A mystery then! How very exciting and enjoyable. Sadly, it must wait. We have far more important business to attend this night," Dardi said, still grinning.

"Oh? Pray tell, what is more important than the *Camorra* attempting to murder my pupil?" Séverin asked, raising one eyebrow.

"The two vampires I spotted just before you arrived. We must seek them out and hope no others are hunting for victims in this grand palace..." Dardi replied.

He led Séverin back towards the main body of the party.

CHAPTER XIX

"You have failed again, my dearest love," Ettore Policeni purred, spotting the enraged look on Francesca's face before she recomposed it into a radiant smile.

"*Li mortacci tua!*" she hissed back, while maintaining a smile. "I had the *bastardo* cornered—he had to either agree to my attention, or publicly snub me in the palace. Then that *puttana* provided him the one means of escaping. Whoever she is, I'm going to slice her peasant face into strips and cover the rest with acid."

"You attempt that, my darling, and the young lady will send you back home with your head under your arm. That is Sylvia Dardi, the daughter of Maestro Dardi. I think you know his name. He is said to be the best swordsman in all of Naples. Some have even suggested he is supreme in Italy, though a few in Rome dispute that title," Ettore explained with amused relish.

"Your point being?" Francesca smiled and curtsied at a passing dignitary, clearly dazzling the man.

The gentleman, a banker of some repute, was pulled away by his wife whose pursed lips suggested a bad time was ahead for him.

"Francesca, you are a lovely and a very deadly woman. Your skills with a sword are impressive, and with a knife even more so. But I merely state that these skills are inadequate compared to that of the lovely lady who stole your Austrian intended," Ettore replied, his smile wide.

He was dressed in an understated court suit in light blue, an exact copy of the clothes worn by one of the palace ministers. Ettore knew he had no eye for color and cut, but he could hire people to fit him in reproductions of outfits worn by the paragons of the Naples kingdom.

"If you are attempting to anger me, my dear husband, you are succeeding. Why would you say such nonsense?"

Francesca accepted a glass of wine from a liveried server but did not take a sip. Ettore shrugged, raising his hands.

"It is a mystery. Like why you throw yourself again at a penniless, Austrian, God-bothering, *pezzo di merda*? The same *stronzo* who keeps eluding your limitless charms."

Francesca appeared to consider for a moment and studied her wine.

"In truth, I agree with you. Stop making that face. I know this is unprecedented in our marriage. The difficulty is that my father issued the order. He either wants the one named Karnstein under his control, or dead. He also informed me that I should do best to not question him on his business. Therefore, I must try again."

Ettore looked thoughtful for a moment, and then nodded. He realized that, in many ways, Francesca was also prisoner of the *Padrone*'s plans. For the first time since she had stabbed him in the leg, the second day of their hurried marriage, Ettore Policeni felt some sympathy for Francesca.

"Then we'd best find a different method of capturing or killing this Karnstein. Where did that *figlio di puttana* wander? Perhaps if we study him and the Dardi woman from a distance, we can understand them better."

Ettore glanced around the room. Francesca smiled, a real smile of gratitude.

"Thank you. This Austrian is the most difficult assignment I've received from my father."

Ettore offered his arm to Francesca, which she took with a small hesitation. They were uncomfortable in each other's company, having spent years fighting. This rare show of consideration on his part was confusing to them both. They strolled silently through the crowd, eyes scanning every face they passed. Despite their discomfort, they were united and determined to make their enemies pay dearly for failing to obey the will of the great Michele Bozzo.

CHAPTER XX

"Thank you for rescuing me, Mademoiselle Dardi," Karnstein said as they moved closer to the King and his court.

He walked very precisely, attempting to appear casual, but there was a stiffness in his movements, an apparent discomfort.

"Consider that my way of offering an apology. My father took me to task for insulting you," Sylvia said, stopping and catching his eyes with hers for a moment.

"Maestro Séverin caused me to realize the natural fear my name brings to those involved in our... shall we call it work?" Karnstein said, looking away and appearing distinctly embarrassed.

"I think the correct word is, calling," Sylvia explained, her voice even but showing some deeper feelings. "Such as those who make the decision to devote themselves to something higher than themselves and their life. My father once took me to see an opera by a man named Mozart. I learned that he was playing before kings as a little child and writing operas at age fourteen. That is a higher calling and you and I chose the same when we were only a little older."

"You suffered too?" Karnstein asked, sensing an untold story.

Sylvia nodded and feigned a smile.

"My mother and aunt. It is a long, sad story for another day. We have something else we must discuss."

"We do?" asked Karnstein, looking confused.

"Yes," Sylvia's smile widened, and she tightened her grip on his arm. "My father spotted two vampires just before you arrived. I located them on the dance floor. We shall dance and try and get closer."

"I... um... do not know how..." Karnstein stammered, hearing the beginning notes of the Viennese Waltz.

Sylvia rolled her eyes.

"You move well enough, if slowly with a sword in hand. Did your teacher not have you mirror his motions to gain greater understanding of the blade?"

"Yes, but..." Karnstein started to say, knowing there was a great difference between following the movements of Jean-Pierre Séverin and dancing with Sylvia Dardi.

"Then we shall consider this another lesson. Despite holding a blade like butcher chasing a bull, you don't move too poorly. I shall lead, and you shall mirror my steps."

Sylvia led him to the edge of the dance floor as she spoke.

"I still defeated you," Karnstein challenged, placing his hand on her back as she indicated.

Their other hands joined in a tight, almost combative grip.

"I stripped you of your blade first. Then you shamed me with your words. Should we face each other with naked steel in the future, you will go home with another scar. Now, do as I say, or you will make me angry. We begin... step, step, step, turn..."

They moved in a small area, slower than most of the dancers, but not looking poorly in comparison. Slowly and surely, Sylvia's quick lessons increased in speed and she stopped speaking. She led Karnstein as they scanned the crowd for the two vampires her father had spotted earlier in the evening. Within a few minutes, neither appeared to realize that they were dancing quite easily and comfortably with each other.

"I do not see any vampires. How were they dressed?" Karnstein asked.

"The woman has black hair and a corset that looks fit to burst. Her dress is light red, and she wears a small false gold tiara. The man is your height, but broader, brawnier with a black beard and mustache."

Karnstein looked over her shoulder and spotted the pair seconds later. The man was handsome, powerful-looking and smiling widely. The woman was voluptuous with dark olive skin and sensual ebony eyes that bewitched any she viewed. They merely appeared to be merely an attractive couple at first glance. After a moment though, their movements betrayed their true origins. Their motions were just a little too fast, a little too smooth and, when they failed to concentrate, possessing an almost reptilian grace.

"I see them," Karnstein hissed.

He released Sylvia's hand and reached for the battered sword strapped to his hip. Sylvia snatched his hand back and held him with a harsh, steely grip.

"*Idiota!* Have you gone insane? You draw that blade and every soldier in this palace will beat you down. Half the men here will challenge you to duels and the other half will demand you cool your hot head in jail. Think!"

"You are correct," replied Karnstein frowning, then nodding.

"Of course I am. Now smile and listen to me. Ah, you have a nice smile, Baron Karnstein."

"I think we can dispense with that nonsense," Karnstein said.

He was grateful that Sylvia had stopped him from one of his rare shows of temper. Vampires were an area of the supernatural world that he could not view in a passive manner. Not after his vampiric ancestor, Mircalla Karnstein, had destroyed his family and attempted to turn him into a follower of darkness.

"Good, good, and you shall call me Sylvia. My father will prefer it and thus, know that you and I have forgiven each other."

Sylvia turned Franz a few steps, so the vampires were now in her view too.

"We need to draw them out of the ballroom," Karnstein said, watching the pair out of the corner of his eye.

"Agreed. I think I have a way. Do you wear a crucifix?" she asked, and snickered softly.

Karnstein looked confused but replied:

"Of course."

"Give it to me, right now," Sylvia ordered, releasing his hand and extending the extremity his direction.

Karnstein, still confused, reached under his medal and pulled free a simple metal cross. The crucifix hung on a simple tong made of leather, as plain an article as one could ever wear.

"Interesting. Most here would wear the holy cross in gold with jewels. Yours could be one owned by a farmer or a blacksmith," Sylvia remarked, taking his hand again while holding the crucifix in her palm.

"And he said to them, *Take care, and be on your guard against all covetousness, for one's life does not consist in the abundance of his possessions. Luke 12:15.* My teachers quoted that often as I grew older," Karnstein replied, feeling Sylvia subtly spin them towards the vampire's direction.

Sylvia cocked her head and studied him.

"Do you often quote the Bible to prevent answering questions?"

Karnstein was startled for a moment and then sighed.

"Yes, probably too often."

"Then stop it, *idiota!* Speak like a person and not a fool whose eyes never rise out of his books!" Sylvia chided, though she was grinning to take the sting out of the rebuke.

"Please stop calling me an idiot," Karnstein replied, surprised he was smiling back.

"Stop acting like one first, Franz Karnstein," Sylvia shrugged.

She then lowered their hands and shifted the cross so that the weapon protruded from their fingers. With a wink, Sylvia led him into a gentle spin, extending their hands a few inches away from their bodies. As they spun, the metal of the cross gently brushed across the handsome male vampire's hand and along his lovely partner's back. The low hiss of sizzling meat drifted to their ears, a soft sound barely audible beneath the music, dancing feet, swishing fabric and light conversation. The odor of spoiled burnt meat flitted through the air, ignored by all save Sylvia and Karnstein.

The handsome vampire and his stunning partner spun quickly, their eyes flashing crimson for an instant. They regained control within a few seconds, staring with naked hatred at the seemingly oblivious Sylvia and Franz.

The song ended seconds later and they, like all on the dance floor, clapped dutifully and moved to make room for others.

"*Mi amore*, take me to the gardens," Sylvia whispered, taking his arm again.

She headed towards the distant doorway leading to the gardens. A short distance at their rear were the vampire pair. Both struggled to maintain control; they were on the hunt and had their prey in sight...

CHAPTER XXI

"Father Abbot," Lorenzo Pinot bowed to the black-cowled master of the Cupbearers.

His voice and movement were shaky, his eyes downcast and fearful as he approached the man he feared most in this world.

"Stand tall, my son," Federigo Gui replied, not hiding his amusement at the later man's terror.

He made the sign of the cross in the air and folded his hands into the depth of his voluminous sleeves. Lorenzo Pinot rose to his full height, a head taller than the secret police leader's average stature. He possessed a lanky build and the long fingers of an artist, short colorless hair, and a narrow, egg-shaped head. Lorenzo's large blue eyes were watery and perpetually looked as if he was about to cry. A very useful tool for Federigo Gui.

"My thanks for your kindness, Father Abbot," Lorenzo replied, unable to meet the Cupbearer master's eyes.

He stared at the ornate gold and ruby encrusted cross that hung from the high, full collar around the man's neck.

"What is it you seek, Lorenzo Pinot? Another model for your latest painting."

Gui smiled a little wider, watching as sweat beaded across the young man's brow. Lorenzo jumped a little at the mention of artist's models.

"No thank you, Father. I merely wish to mention that the two sword lovers are plotting something. They spoke of the *Camorra* and dueling. They then moved away from where I stood, and I was unable to follow."

Gui considered this worm of a man cowering before his gaze with hidden disgust. Lorenzo Pinot was the son of Elia Pinot, a merchant of some note. Elia, formerly the owner of a small fleet of ships, combined his business interests with that of his father-in-law and created Toscano and Pinot, a house that specialized in shipping and insuring shipments of other businesses. Lorenzo, the spoiled oldest son, possessed no interest in business, but did have some skill at painting and sculpture. He had trained in Rome and Venice, returning home to open his own studio and attempted to make a name for himself in the Kingdom of Naples.

Unknown to his doting parents and grandparents, Lorenzo Pinot possessed a dark secret. He liked women, low women of the streets especially. Not sexually—he had never enjoyed the three times he had sexual congress with a whore. What Lorenzo lusted for was their fear and pain. His targets? Starving beggar girls, gaudily painted prostitutes, hardworking shop girls, and the ones who called themselves "artist's models." Promising cash, he used them as subjects for a time until they caused his lust to rise to an uncontrollable height. Then Lorenzo acted, needing to relieve himself of the overpowering need for his subject. He just couldn't allow any woman to have that much control over his mind and body, and there was only one method of relieving the inner pressure.

Drugging and gagging his victim, he tied the unfortunate women up and the torments began. Lorenzo possessed a collection of knives, small scalpels stolen from a doctor, heavy, brutal, rifle bayonets bought from a stall in Florence, and many more terrible instruments of pain and death. His favorite, the pride of his treasure trove, was Roman sica dagger once used as a killing tool by the gangs of the ancient empire. The astonishingly sharp curved blade was ugly, a dark instrument of pain and death, the only purpose of which was to take lives. Lorenzo felt a wave of cold every time he took up this terrible weapon, sensing that the spirit of the blade hungered for blood. Every time he tortured a victim, Lorenzo performed the final kill with the sica.

Four unfortunates had fallen to his dark attentions, forgotten women that few would have missed for long. The last, a once pretty, heavily-poxed seaside prostitute, had died in a glorious orgasmic shower of agony and vitae. Weighting down the body, the pieces of the corpse sunk below the surface of the sea, never to be seen again.

Somehow, in some way, the Cupbearers had learned of Lorenzo's pleasures. After arresting him silently in the middle of the night, the young artist was beaten for hours and left weeping in a pile of his own filth. They had left Lorenzo alone in the dark, a pathetic figure praying for his torment to end soon. That was when Federigo Gui had appeared, a pale, ghostly figure in the gloom. He had stared at the broken artist with unforgiving eyes, his disgust flowing over Lorenzo Pinot and making him feel like an insect or some other lesser creature. Turning away, Lorenzo had waited for this terribly, frightening sentinel of God to pronounce judgment upon him and send him to Hell.

"Do you want to live, my son?" Federigo Gui had whispered, his voice providing a trace of hope in Lorenzo Pinot.

That had been the last moment when his life had been his own. Lorenzo was still a painter and sculptor, allowed to work his art with increasing fervor; he was even allowed to kill the occasional subject, when the master of Cupbearers appeared amused by the artist's "appetites." But that was all the freedom Lorenzo was allowed; his life was otherwise no longer his own. Gui, through a series of disapproving messengers, had forced the murderous artist to attend parties and act as an informant. The Cupbearers were always seeking a means of destroying enemies, or gaining leverage over those who might be useful. Lorenzo had obeyed, knowing his death would surely follow if he in any way displeased Federigo Gui. He lived in fear of so many things now: Gui and his followers, his family discovering his secrets, the people he informed on... the list was long and terrible. Part of him wished he had died back in the dungeons of the Cupbearer's headquarters.

Now in the present, Federigo Gui frowned, not liking the sound of this information.

"Very well. Wander among the party and listen to the people. I expect at least three names of people who spoke ill of the Crown or myself."

"Yes, Father Abbot. Thank you, your excellency," Lorenzo Pinot muttered and backed away.

Federigo Gui watched him go, his face returning to the normal disapproving expression he preferred. He knew he was right, Séverin and his Austrian student were adversaries of Federigo Gui and his interests—which made them enemies of the Kingdom of Naples.

CHAPTER XXII

Johann Spurzheim snorted in disgust at the foolish behavior of Federigo Gui and his lackey. Lorenzo Pinot was a disgusting, murderous little worm, precisely the type of informant that he expected from his enemy. His every report was completely useless—more trivial nonsense. His latest was no different from the dozens of others Pinot had provided.

Spurzheim always found it amusing that Gui met Pinot in public locations, usually in the open air. This was a clear example as to why his enemy was ill-equipped for the duties required for the kingdom. For example, did not Gui realize that Spurzheim was an expert at reading lips?

More importantly, Gui appeared ignorant of basic acoustics and the science of sound. The Cupbearer master, like many in the world, did not realize that sound traveled beyond the ears of the person to whom you are speaking. In the ballroom, there were many locations where, by the concavity of the ceiling and the material of the surrounding area, one could listen in on even a whispered conversation. Most were near the throne, which was probably the intention of the clever builders who had designed this garish chamber.

Spurzheim was wise enough to know every echo location in the palace. This was a weapon he had used to keep from falling victim to the Cupbearer's attempts to throw him out of power. Hopefully, one of these conversations could provide him with the information he required to defeat Gui once and for all. The current discussion between Gui and Pinot was only of limited help. The fact that the Cupbearers were going against the vampire hunters was amusing, to say the least. Did Gui believe he could destroy a pair of men appointed to their secret position by none other than Napoleon?

Musing for a moment, Spurzheim walked over to a patch of gold and marble flooring he knew was free of traveling echoes. There were ways he could use this piece of information to embarrass Gui and weaken his power base. Pursing his lips, Spurzheim considered several courses of action before choosing the safest of the many.

"Captain Dannel, come over to me if you please," Spurzheim said, spotting one of his most obedient men.

Dannel strode to Spurzheim's side and bowed, the preferred salute for formal occasions.

"How may I assist you, Contrôleur Général?"

Spurzheim issued a simple series of orders, knowing Dannel was not capable of anything more complex. He nodded at the bowed response and watched the captain vanish into the crowd. The man would go far—if he lived long enough.

Returning to the royal enclosure, Spurzheim slid into his familiar place near his enemy. Gui ignored him, attempting to resemble a forbidding inquisitor rather than the middle-aged power grasper he was in truth.

They stood together, each unknowingly enjoying the fearful expressions they received from the multitude of men and women who passed their way in hopes of gaining the notice of King Joseph. Neither said a word for the remainder of the ball, their predatory eyes forbidding any from attempting to engage them in anything other than a respectful bow from the people of Naples.

CHAPTER XXIII

"Vampires at the King's ball? How very expected," Séverin stated, keeping his eyes on Dardi.

Bartolomeo Dardi chuckled and nodded.

"Quite true, Gâteloup. It reminds me of when my father took us to Genoa for my uncle's fourth wedding. A simple trip he said, and what did we do instead of dancing with those lovely twins with eyes the color of a clear sky?"

"Chased a priest of Orcus through the alleys in the worst part of town to prevent him from opening a passage to the realm of the dead," replied Séverin, sighing. "I never wore court slippers again after that night."

"Correct!" Dardi threw back his head and laughed long and loud. "This is our lives, my brother. Embrace and enjoy the chase!"

"I shall endeavor to try," Séverin said, pretending to gaze upon a fetching young lady in yellow. "No vampires on this side."

"Nor this one," Dardi said, facing the other direction,

They both stepped aside from each other as if they were about to walk in different directions and examined the area to the rear of the latter. After a moment, Séverin looked away and bowed to a medal-covered Frenchman in an elderly appearing military uniform.

"I see them now—a man and a woman. An attractive pair, which is to be expected," Séverin stated, stepping aside so Dardi could get a view of their targets.

"Ah, yes. Well spotted."

Dardi turned, looking as if Séverin had called him back and looked in his direction in an interested way.

"Precisely the pair I viewed moments before you and your young pupil arrived. Why did you take that one as a student, by the way? He does not appear interested in the fine art of the blade."

"I did tell you what little I knew of his past," Séverin replied, turning his head as Dardi watched the pair. "Does that not explain his commitment to the cause?"

They had performed this trick many times in the past, one watched, the other spoke and looked disinterested. It was an effective skill that allowed them to watch even the most suspicious, if they were careful.

"Commitment, yes," said Dardi. "The difficulty is that he may become one of those who choose the witch-hunter path. My father taught us that training in the art of the sword, in addition to the path of the hunter, is a higher calling. Those who choose the way of the witch-hunter begin to see evil everywhere they look. They become as dark as the demons they hunt. Remember the lists we memorized as we trained?" Dardi asked, appearing to study an odd-looking man whose lower jaw protruded several inches beyond his upper teeth.

"I remember receiving a slap of the cane every time we forgot a name. Your father had very direct, but effective, methods. You occasionally made an error on purpose, did you not?"

Dardi laughed and nodded his head vigorously as they switched roles again.

"That I did, usually when you beat me in some game or got the prettier girl."

"I thought as much… a good plan," Séverin said.

He took a glass of wine from a passing server. He had no interest in drinking it, not when he was on the hunt.

"My pupil Karnstein exorcised a demon in under thirty seconds before my eyes," he added.

Dardi's laugh cut off and he looked gravely at his old friend.

"That is not possible. Unless he holds the blood of beings best never spoken out loud."

Séverin shook his head.

"The reasonable point was made by Karnstein—would His Holiness allow such a one as his personal advisor? Or even in the lesser Order of Exorcists? No, there must be an answer that we did not consider. I shall tell you the details later; here and now are neither the correct time nor location."

"Agreed. We shall continue this conversation in greater privacy. I will continue to urge you to find him a path based in calm and control. Otherwise, we may have to make a sad decision one day..."

Dardi ran a finger across his neck.

"I have some thoughts on that, which I wish us to consider. But..." Séverin said, smiling slightly.

"...this too can wait," they both chorused, using Dardi's father's favorite method of putting off a discussion.

Neither bothered to hide their amusement at the statement, having sworn when they were youngsters to never say that phrase. They'd been aggravated ever time the elder Dardi used this as a means of ending a conversation or a request by Barto or Jean-Pierre. Now, as middle-aged men, they sympathized with their teacher and his desire to teach them a better path in life.

"They are moving," Séverin said, serious once again. "Apparently with some intent. A target for their thirst, do you think?"

Switching again, Dardi nodded.

"Yes, they are headed for the doors outside. We must follow and confront these creatures immediately."

"Then let us tour the grounds for a spell. Those two do not look as if they will be an easy battle," Séverin said, falling into step beside his oldest friend.

"No matter," Dardi shrugged, "they never faced Barto and Gâteloup, the premier blade masters of all Italy."

"I thought we agreed it was Gâteloup and Barto," Séverin said as they walked outside.

"Clearly your mind is aging, my brother," Dardi replied. "There is no beauty or music to that title. No, no, it must be Barto and Gâteloup, masters of the blade..."

Suddenly, he stopped. "This is...unexpected..." he said.

"Troubling would be my assessment, Séverin replied, gazing ahead and frowning.

CHAPTER XXIV

"Lean closer to me, *idiota*. We must look as if we are enraptured with each other," Sylvia hissed, pulling his arm.

"I am trying," Karnstein whispered back, looking annoyed. "And stop calling me an idiot."

"Then stop acting like one. We must lure these creatures away from all sight by pretending to be foolish lovers. Unless you find me ugly. Is that the reason? Do I disgust you?" Sylvia asked, stopping and looking up at Karnstein.

"No, of course not," the Austrian replied, looking confused.

Sylvia cocked her head to the side slightly.

"Then you find me pretty? Am I as beautiful as your *inamorata*, Madame Policeni?"

"She is not my lover. I've never exchanged more than a word or two with the woman," Karnstein replied, looking confused.

Sylvia nodded and smiled slightly.

"Yes, that does fit your frightened look back at the ball."

"Frightened? I was not behaving so... I merely knew that Madame Policeni was not truly interested in me."

Karnstein stopped walking, seeing they were in the center of a clearing.

"Oh, I should say she was very intent on charming you. And your terrified expression told me that she was succeeding."

Sylvia remained close, her dark eyes meeting Karnstein's pale gaze.

"She is attractive, but I do not like her," Karnstein stated, hoping this would be the end of the conversation. "There is something twisted in her eyes."

Sylvia smiled and nodded once.

"That I agree, but I know her by reputation. Still, you did not answer my question. Am I as beautiful as Madame Policeni?"

Karnstein opened his mouth, but appeared unable to formulate a reply. He was about to speak, when they heard the rattle of a heavy footfall in the bushes a short distance away. *Thank you, my savior*, he thought.

Sylvia threw her arms around his waist and leaned in close. Their lips were mere inches apart.

"Is your sword sharp?" she whispered.

Realizing this was no metaphor, but an actual inquiry about his weapon, the Austrian blurted out:

"Yes, I sharpened it myself."

"I am sure you do much by yourself," Sylvia said, not hiding her amusement.

The bushes to their rear suddenly rattled louder and a husky laugh, full of malicious glee, filled the air. This was followed by a bellowing guffaw, the disdainful, cruel sound of one viewing something ridiculous or pathetic. The brush broke apart and the vampiric pair stepped into the moonlight.

"They are so sweet, I could just eat them up. Oh wait, that is what I plan to do," the lovely vampire woman said, her mouth widening as her face slowly transformed.

"I don't like sweet. It makes me hungry," the handsome vampire male snarled, his massive thaws darkening as his mouth expanded to inhuman dimensions.

"Signorina Dardi, can you answer a question for me?" Karnstein asked, his voice cold and mocking.

They were still entwined, their eyes on the undead pair as they transformed.

"Of course, Lord Karnstein. Ask away."

Sylvia's voice also held the same contemptuous tone as she scrutinized the vampires.

"Why do vampires always behave like spoiled children? Every time they are building their courage to attack, we are forced to listen to poorly phrased threats that could not frighten anyone with a drop of sense."

Karnstein watched the vampires out of the corner of his eye. Sylvia rolled her eyes and shook her head.

"I do not know, but at least they are not telling us tales of how long they've lived. If we placed every vampire who has declared that they were at the crucifixion of our Lord, we could fill the Flavian Coliseum and still have many awaiting outside."

"Yes, I have noticed that," Karnstein snorted and smiled. "But not merely vampires. Dark priest often…"

"Enough talk!" the attractive female vampire screamed.

She and her handsome companion opened their inhumanly misshapen maws, causing their faces to split. Their attractive countenances vanished, revealing lamprey-shaped mouths filled with rasping, serrated teeth, and a sharpened tongue with tiny, blackened spikes that appeared to ripple and flow as it lolled and slither as if an independent form of life.

"Hmm, very unique," Karnstein said, inspecting the unusual transmogrification of the two vampires.

"Yes, I do believe these are creatures of a type not seen before. After we dispose of this filth, will you join me in seeking an answer?" Sylvia asked, moving a little closer to the Exorcist.

"Yes, I shall. Thank you. Oh wait, they are about to hiss and attack!" he said, looking rather happy.

As if obeying Karnstein's words, both demoniac beings hissed and flared out their fingers. Huge, horny, hooked spurs slid out from their fingertips. The talons glistened with a viscous venomous exudation that sizzled as it struck the grass. Crouching, they extended their hands and leaped forward.

Sylvia Dardi and Franz Karnstein separated, her hand drawing his sword and winking. He now understood her question: she planned on taking and using his sword in this battle. This made some degree sense to him—she was far better with the weapon than he was, and was not currently armed. Of course, that left him unarmed and forced to rely on his wit. Karnstein guessed that she believed he possessed other weapons and would not miss the blade. Sylvia was clearly a clever, quick-witted woman.

The formerly attractive female vampire turned in his direction, slashing the air with furious, futile, flailing gesticulations. Her motions were lightning-fast, but untrained, causing her to attack with feline ferocity and the rage of an insulted fish wife. Despite her speed, Karnstein eluded her talons and flapping, fanged face with apparent ease.

The massive male, better trained than his once comely companion, moved with greater care. His hand, extended and curled like a trained wrestler, feinted low and reached out to try and get a hold of Sylvia's arm. She danced back and to the left, her sword narrowly missing the titanic wrist. Sylvia spun the sword and laughed, delighted to once again be in a real fight with a worthy opponent.

Karnstein ducked a talon rake meant to rip his eyes and face to ribbons and kicked his leg out. Hitting his enemy's ankle, he swept her feet out from under her, sending the female vampire sprawling onto her face. She exploded upward growling and warbling in an ululational tone that caused small animals and birds in the gardens to suddenly flee in fear. The vampire's spiked slithering tongue lashed out, cracking like a leather whip, seeking Karnstein's neck. He dove to the side and rolled to his feet, stumbling over a rock as he rose. The vampire screeched in triumph as she reached for and lashed out with her lamprey-shaped mouth.

Nearby the huge man jumped backwards, narrowly avoiding the slicing saber. Black fluid slowly leaked from his chest from a nasty slice he had received from getting too close to Sylvia. Reaching down, he ripped a tall sapling up from its roots and flung the wood at his attacker. Surprised, Sylvia barely eluded the tree and found herself tossed to the ground by a backhanded slap from the male vampire. Stunned, she watched as her enemy dropped to his hands and feet and sped towards her, like some massive predatory beast of ancient nightmares.

CHAPTER XXV

The massive wall of vegetation rose up, several heads higher than the tallest man, imposingly wide and forbidding. The passage between the wood and weeds was a gloomy, forbidding tunnel into a deep abyss that appeared to have no end or illumination. A light mist appeared to languidly drift across the path, creating an eldritch atmosphere.

"A hedge maze. Why is there such a ridiculous waste of land here?" Dardi asked, drawing his small sword and sneering at the construction.

"I wish I knew," Séverin replied, drawing his own sword as he spoke.

The blades appeared to be decorative, but were among the most dangerous brawling weapons ever created. The street gangs of Rome and Naples trained in these short swords, knowing they were as effective in crowds and alleys as they were in duels.

Closing their eyes tight, they counted to twenty and opened their eyes slowly. Their eyes adjusted quickly to the murk, allowing them a chance to see where they were walking in the spare moonlight. Together Dardi and Séverin stepped into the hedge maze, standing shoulder to shoulder, and scanning the weed-strewn structure. Based on their limited view, the hedge maze was almost completely abandoned, a remnant of the Bourbon rulership of the kingdom, or earlier.

Spotting some crushed grass, Séverin prodded Dardi with an elbow and headed down the left path. Why the young lovers had chosen to stroll in the dark into a bleak labyrinth was confusing to both men. They knew young lovers often wished to stroll for some privacy—both having done so with their respective late wives in the past—but the choice of a deserted, desolate hedge maze seemed odd, even for the young and stupid nobles of the palace.

"This way," Dardi hissed, spotting a thread of fabric attached to a bush.

The scrap was still moving, only recently being torn from a passing dress. The trail was easy to follow, the heavily overgrown weeds and brush providing them with clear markers as they ventured deeper into the hedge maze. The swordmasters exchanged a look, a silent communication passing between them as they strode ever closer to the center of the vegetative warren.

"Lights ahead," Dardi warned.

Séverin did not respond, but he did slow his pace a step or two and became ever warier. He was grateful Dardi was at his side; he didn't need to worry about the man in a battle with vampires and other monsters. The tiny Italian looked and behaved like a buffoon, but this was merely an act. However fun-loving and genial, Bartolomeo Dardi was one of the coldest, professional swordsmen alive

Turning a corner, he was unsurprised to see four individuals seated on a pair of dirty marble benches. A large lantern illuminated the circular maze center and the two men and women stared at them with smug satisfaction. They were all stunningly attractive young people, exceptional-looking even for the Court.

The women were completely unalike, but startlingly beautiful none-the-less. The taller of the two was willowy, with a long graceful neck, pale, nearly translucent skin, and golden hair that fell in curls framing her classically lovely face. She resembled an ancient statue of a goddess or a muse come to life, and her large green eyes merely added to this ethereal sensation. The second woman was darker of skin and hair, with broad shoulders, a massive bust, a narrow waist and large flaring hips. Her hair was so dark it appeared to melt into the plutonian night. Her eyes were almond-shaped, and gave the impression of being more feline than human. If her companion was the embodiment of an ancient muse, this earthy beauty was like staring into the avatar of a fertility goddess of ancient days.

Their companions, however, could have been molded from the same sculptor. They were both tall, lean, good-looking in a noble, chinless manner, and dressed in the very latest fashions of the Neapolitan Royal Court. Neither appeared to possess any actual character to their faces or style; they were interchangeable escorts, probably second or third sons who did not possess a head for the mercantile life, a mind and political acumen for the Church, or the courage to be soldiers. They were expensive ornaments, probably awaiting the time they would be used by their families for some marital alliance. In time, they would either learn a means of being useful, or they would exist only as expensive appendages, barely tolerated by their noble clans.

"I told you they would follow," the willowy woman said, smiling and clapping her hands softly.

Her lovely feminine companion nodded her head.

"You did at that, my darling. I am very impressed you and Giorgio did not reveal your true nature. Alberto and I did not hide our status as nobles of the night."

"That was easy. Giorgio and I practiced remaining slow and dull. I envied you, being allowed to be free in public. It shall not be long before we will live openly, and all shall bow to our greatness," the willowy vampire explained, taking her companion's hand.

"Oh, I long for that day—is it soon?" the other vampire female asked, smiling and causing her face to slowly transform.

The other nodded her head, also smiling and beginning her transformation.

"Very soon, a mere blink of time."

"Should we come back later? After you've finished your little chat?" Dardi asked, rolling his eyes with exaggerated theatricality.

"No, no, do go on, I always find the braggadocio ramblings of the undead to be most entertaining," Séverin added, surprised by his amused, light-hearted response.

Possibly this was caused by the presence of his old friend, possibly the nature of Naples itself. In any event, he smiled briefly at the annoyed expressions of the two vampiric faces.

"You find entertainment in the oddest place, Gâteloup," Dardi replied, shaking his head.

"Says the man who will cross an entire city to view a puppet show," Séverin said and snorted.

"Enough!" the thinner vampire screeched, her voice a barely human sound. "You mock us, great hunters, yet we lured you here. You are now in the center of an ancient maze and we, the lords and ladies of the dark, shall hunt you both down as you flee for your lives."

"Is that what you truly believe, damned thing?" Dardi asked, laughing again. "Truly?"

"They do," said Séverin. "Shall I explain the truth to them this time?"

Dardi bowed to the Frenchman.

"Of course, it is your honor this time to illuminate these sad, deluded fools to the reality of circumstances."

"What in Lucifer's name are you babbling about, humans?" the lovely, earthy vampire woman asked.

Séverin's merriment changed, the cold professional attitude coming to the foreground.

"Lucifer's name? That reveals some of your origins, vampire. Since you do not understand our meaning, I shall explain to you as simply as possible. Please pay heed, as I do not wish to repeat myself."

"Proud talk for a man about to be torn limb from limb," the thinner vampire replied, her face twisting and transforming as her rage bubbled to the surface.

Séverin raised one finger up and nodded gravely.

"That is why I wish you to listen fully to my words. You have mistaken this situation from the start. While your guise was quite impressive, your choice of battlegrounds caused us both to question the truth. We followed and then you, in your arrogance, made your foolish, fatal, flaw. The lantern at your feet. Why would a pair of young lovers, seeking a private embrace, walk into the center of a desolate hedge maze with a lamp? That is when we knew this was an attempted ruse."

The willowy vampire crossed her arms with evident annoyance and impatience.

"Yet still you came, and we shall kill you both and feast on your souls."

Séverin raised the finger again.

"Now we have arrived at the point of contention. You see, you are not hunting us—we are hunting you and your kind. Your little quartet of deluded undead have not trapped us in the maze with you—you are trapped in here with us. Say your prayers to your dark master, you shall feel his cold embrace shortly."

"Giorgio, Alberto, kill them now!" the willowy vampire shrieked, her face splitting open and causing her to speak through a mouth too comically large for her head.

The two silent male vampires stepped forwards, their mouths splitting open and separating into four flapping segments. The lamprey-shaped maws and rows of serrated teeth flashed in the harsh lantern light—an image straight from the worst nightmares of a gin-soaked, delusional mind.

"My, that is an interesting development," Dardi remarked. "No matter, to arms!"

Séverin stepped forward, his face set, his sword held in a firm grip. Four against two were not good odds... for the vampires!

CHAPTER XXVI

A bizarre grating sound emerged from the abscond face of the male vampire as he rushed towards the fallen form of Sylvia Dardi. This could have been a laugh, though the sound was a strange, gurgling, shrieking, noise that ripped across the nerve endings and brought a cold wave of fear to the intended prey. At least, that appeared to be the idea—a normal person would have been frozen in terror. Fortunately, Sylvia was not a regular woman, not by any standards. Raised by a widower, she was more at home with a blade and in a saddle than in a ballroom. She probably wouldn't know anything about the "womanly arts" had her great-aunt not insisted on teaching her proper deportment and dress.

"Beauty and manners are as dangerous a weapon as sword or a musket," her great-aunt had said after demonstrating why she was considered the most dangerous member of the Dardi clan by defeating her niece and two students at the same time.

This was why Sylvia was unimpressed by the horrific shrieks and rolled to her left when the serpentine barbed tongue slashed downwards towards her chest. She was unable to attack, struggling to keep the unfamiliar sword in hand. She didn't know why the young Baron Karnstein preferred a heavy cavalry saber—the weapon was for horseback and was otherwise clumsy in a duel. Spinning her legs in a circle, she leaped to her feet and pivoted sideways, just missing another strike. She had no choice, knowing that that attack was only a feint and that her foe would soon close the distance between them. His massive hands, each with a huge, wickedly sharp talon reached out, seeking to enfold her into lethal embrace.

Sylvia grinned and dropped into a full split, stabbing the sword up towards the exposed groin. The vampire squealed with fear and threw himself backwards, narrowly missing an attack that would have transformed him into a eunuch. Sylvia, still smiling, popped to her feet and spun the blade in a fast figure eight. Her enemy kept far away, the segmented head swiveling left and right as if seeking a means of escape.

"There is no running away, damned thing. I will slice you to pieces the minute you turn, coward," Sylvia sneered, lowering her blade and looking at the bizarre being with open mockery and disgust.

The male vampire hissed and sliced with his claws, the air whistling with each slash, a nightmarish sound evoking horrors from the depths of the human mind. Even Sylvia, who had fought monsters in the past, shivered with a touch of fear caused by an antediluvian loathing of the monstrous creature. The demoniac being, circling her now-dirty form, preyed upon the living—nothing more. If she let this creature survive, it would feed upon humanity, slowly sucking the life from mankind until nothing remained. Vampires sought to transform humans into herd animals, mindless cattle or pigs, beings only capable of reproducing and eating, and little else. This was the motivation for the entire Dardi family, preventing this apocalyptic future from consuming all life on the planet.

Seeing the vampire's lamprey-shaped maw rear back slightly, Sylvia relaxed. She knew what was coming; the creature was not well-trained in the use of his powers. Every time it acted, its motions changed subtly, a signal all sword experts sought in their opponents. Sylvia's father had taught her to look for those non-verbal clues at all times—information she used to test both enemies and friends.

The prehensile tongue slashed out, seeking Sylvia's neck again. Prepared for this attack, she pivoted to her left and brought the sharp edge of her blade down on the organ. The tongue split, spraying black ichor like a nightmarish fountain. The skull flapped, causing the rows of fangs to rattle, a jangling sound as horrific as any heard this night. The vampire shook and screamed, his mighty mitts balling into huge fists.

Apparently crazed with pain, the vampire charged straight for Sylvia. She again feinted to her left, and sliced off one of the monster's arms at the elbow. The vampire howled and turned in her direction—a big mistake. That left Sylvia enough time to backslash and remove his leg at the knee. The massive male vampire fell to the grassy earth, black blood staining the verdant lawn. The segmented head slapped together and the undead being looked up at her with a disjointed, misproportioned face.

"Please... mercy..." the vampire whimpered, its voice barely human in sound and tone.

Sylvia raised her sword. "Ask it of the Lord," she said as she decapitated her enemy.

Turning around, she watched as Karnstein stabbed downward with a large, sharp tree branch, causing the female vampire to squeal and kick the air before falling still. He sighed loudly, looking weary, but elated at the same time.

"You should have warned me you planned on using my sword," the Exorcist said, looking her direction.

"I did," Sylvia replied, raising an eyebrow. "Why else would have I asked if it were sharp? Did you believe I was going to let you protect me? *Idiota*, I am far better with even this clumsy blade than you."

Karnstein was about to protest, when he realized she was speaking nothing less than the truth. Instead, he snorted and looked down at the vampires they had just defeated. They were melting, transforming into a viscous green and black fetid suppuration with an aroma like burning feces. He recoiled, moving with Sylvia to a short distance upwind from the horrendous discharge.

"*Madonna!* I've seen vampires reduced to dust, skeletons, even rotting corpses, but never have I viewed one melt into a puddle smelling worse than the fish market in summer!"

Sylvia covered her nose with one hand, looking nauseated. Karnstein nodded, watching the two undead creatures deliquesce before their eyes.

"I've been through sewers which were more aromatic."

Sylvia leaned against him for a moment, her eyes locking briefly with that of the Austrian. She returned his sword to his scabbard and said:

"Both of my shoes are lost in that puddle of undead *spazzatura*. I can't go back inside."

"Have you seen the state of your dress and hair?" Karnstein snorted. "If you return to the ball, they will probably place you under arrest."

Sylvia's eyes flashed with annoyance and her face twisted, not hiding her fury.

"Says the man who looks like he dove head first into a swamp!"

Karnstein looked outraged for a moment, then caught the amusement hidden behind Sylvia's false rage. Together, they started to giggle, which soon turned to squeals of hysterical, tear-inducing, laughter. Sylvia remained leaning against Karnstein, her filthy face glowing from the sweat and tears of their exertions. When their mirth slowed, she straightened and frowned.

"I know the servant's entrance on the south side. We can walk to my father's home."

Karnstein shook his head.

"Monsieur Séverin and your father will wonder what became of us."

"*Idiota!*" Sylvia replied, rolling her eyes. "If they do not see us, they will know that we left—and why. If we go to the front for the coaches, we shall be seen by the palace guard, the *polizia*, and every noble in the kingdom! Now, let us go, unless you wish to explain how we look and the damage to the gardens to the guards…"

Karnstein sighed and nodded, taking her hand and allowing her to lead them deeper into the gardens. Finally, he asked:

"Sylvia?"

"Yes, Franz?" she replied, using his Christian name for the first time.

She appeared unconcerned by the dirt covering her feet or the many stones and roots in her path.

"Stop calling me an idiot," Karnstein stated, his voice weary.

"Then stop acting like one," Sylvia replied.

146

CHAPTER XXVII

The pair of vampires hissed and crouched low, clicking their taloned fingers together as their multitude of rippling fangs undulated in their bizarre dissevered skulls. They ran straight for Séverin and Dardi, their prehensile tongues lashing the air as they moved forward at an inhuman rate of speed.

Séverin appeared to step towards his enemy, his small sword flashing. His superior reach allowed him to lunge and pierce the tongue and lamprey mouth of the vampire. The undead reared back, shrieking and wailing as the French swordmaster withdrew the blade and sliced one of the lower flapping segments from the creature's head.

Dardi was laughing and hooting as he danced left and right, his blade flashing through the spare light like a silver bolt of lightning. With each flick, another clawed finger flew through the air, amputated by the Neapolitan swordmaster.

"On three!" Dardi called, grinning madly, eyes nearly popping from his skull. "One, two, three!"

Both maestros lunged at the same moment, their swords piercing the hearts of their vampiric foes, the thin blades slicing through the undead organs and straight through the cold flesh. Simultaneously they withdrew their swords and struck again, their swords penetrating the lamprey-shaped mouths and through to whatever remained of the vampiric brains.

Both monsters slowly fell to the ground, their bodies immediately decomposing into a noxious, foul-smelling ichor. Séverin and Dardi stepped aside, flicking their swords in the exact same arcs. The viscous fluid spattered the dresses of the two seated female vampires, both of whom recoiled in disgust.

"All nonsense aside, who is your master?" Séverin asked, resuming his calm, dour demeanor.

"Giada, my darling," the willowy vampire said to her lovely companion, "destroy these two for me, if you please."

The darker vampire rushed forward, transforming faster than her male companions. Séverin and Dardi killed her at the same instant, the Frenchman's sword piercing her brain while Dardi's destroyed her heart. The vampire dropped to the ground with a wet sucking sound, already beginning to dissolve in the same mucilaginous fluid as her male companions.

The willowy vampire looked frightened, her sneering face falling and replaced by a growing dread. She glanced behind her and to the sides, seeking a means of escaping from the two sword experts. She rose as if to bolt, only to feel the prick of two sword points against her chest and head.

"While you appear to be slightly older than your friends, you're not fast enough to evade us should we attack. Let us begin again… What is your name?" Séverin asked, his voice soft and almost avuncular.

The vampire woman stared up at him with enraged eyes, almost vibrating at the indignity of her situation. Her face slowly undulated, seemingly about to transform into her inhuman form. Both swordmasters pressed the points of their blades slightly deeper into her cold flesh. The slight convulsions ceased, and the willowy woman appeared, if possible, even more outraged.

"I have no master. I am older than you can imagine," the vampire sneered, her voice demonstrating her clear disgust for her attacked. "I was already ancient when your Jesus was nailed to the cross. You don't know what I've seen, mortal. I was worshipped in ancient days as a goddess. The hearts of men and women were sacrificed to me to feed my hunger. I am eternal!"

"You are Matilde Detti, daughter of Manuel Detti of the olive oil concern," Dardi stated, shaking his head. "You were married briefly to Baron Andrea Boni, who died six months ago and left you an old title, a small amount of money, and a villa on the coast. Most thought you'd moved to Rome to seek another noble husband, but it seems you fell in with poor company."

Matilde opened her mouth to fire out an angry reply, only to be cut off by a gesture by Séverin. His stern gaze caused her to hold her tongue and continue to look in his direction with a livid air.

"Before you attempt to lie, do not bother," Séverin said, not bothering to hide his pity for this pathetic creature. "If you wish to call yourself Egeria, the immortal royal consort, that does not interest me. You were, probably within the last few months, infected and transformed into a vampire. Who did this to you?"

"I will not tell you, blood bag! Meat! You are nothing but cattle!" Matilde snarled, her face slowly beginning to split.

Séverin sighed and kicked the vampire woman in the chest. She tumbled backwards, surprised as she crashed to the soft, weed-covered ground. The Frenchman stepped over the bench and stabbed his sword deeply into the shoulder of the vampire, pinning her to the ground. Matilde was about to struggle, when Dardi thrust his weapon through the other shoulder. Gelatinous ebony ichor bubbled out of the wounds and onto the uneven earth.

"Fools! You disarmed yourself! I'll get free and kill you both!" Matilde screamed, trying to stand up despite the agony.

Séverin shook his head and removed a silver flask from his coat.

"You misunderstand us, madame. Swords are merely tools in our hands. We could end your sad undead life with a broom, should the need arise. We were prepared in case a vampire happened to appear at the ball. Your kind always love to live among luxury, even if it is false."

"What are you going to do, mortal? Drink until you possess enough courage to face me?" Matilde snarled, struggling to stand.

Séverin and Dardi placed their feet on her chest, ensuring she was unable to rise. The Frenchman then opened the flask and squeezed out a single drop of clear liquid out of the bottle. He slowly allowed the fluid to fall and strike Matilde on one pale, flailing arm.

The drop struck with a barely audible plopping sound, immediately causing a low sizzle to fill the air. The scent of burning, spoiled, flesh drifted upwards, a fear-inducing scent that filled both swordmasters with a familiar sense of loathing. They spared little pity for those who chose to lead the undead existence of a vampire, to continue to remain in the world and feed off the life of the innocent. Destroying them was as much mercy as they could muster for such horrific beings.

"I'll kill you! I'll tear you apart!" Matilde thrashed and screamed, attempting to pull free.

"Tell us the name of your master," Séverin repeated, releasing another drop onto the vampire's face.

A small black spot marred her perfect features with a curl of gray smoke flowing from the burning wound.

Matilde screamed and howled, her face splitting apart and pulling together with each passing second. The effect was horrific, a nightmarish spectacle that would induce madness on anyone but those possessing a strong, unshakable will. Séverin waited until the fit passed, long minutes of repulsive muscular motions by the vampire. The prehensile tongue lashed the air, unable to hit either maestro, who kept her pinned to the ground.

"What... is... the... name... of... your... master?" Séverin asked again, splashing the liquid with each word.

"No! I... no... stop! Please!" Matilde shrieked, the agony of the fluid finally overwhelming her determination.

"Tell me the name of your master and the pain will cease," Séverin stated, his voice still even.

"I... I... Nosos! She is Nosos the Beautiful!" Matilde moaned, her face a mass of burns and clean white flesh.

"I believe her," Séverin said, lifting his eyes to meet Dardi's grim face.

"As do I," Dardi replied, withdrawing his sword.

He immediately stabbed downward again, destroying the vampire's heart.

Matilde Detti moaned, gasped and collapsed, her body beginning to decompose instantly. Séverin withdrew his blade, immediately, cleaning the metal of the repulsive fluids. Turning away from the melting corpse, he sheathed his sword and said:

"This is far worse than we imagined. Based on the walking corpses, I believed we faced a vampire witch seeking temporal power."

Dardi nodded, also sheathing his blade and straightening his shirt and jacket.

"I would believe the same, had our situations been reversed. Nosos... I believed such tales were mere myths..."

Séverin clapped his oldest friend on the back.

"We should know better than to doubt the stories of our youth. Come, we have a great deal of work to do. Creatures such as Nosos always seek some terrible fate for all of humanity."

Dardi chuckled and clapped his hands.

"We shall be legends, Gâteloup! The first warriors to face one of the Tenebrae in battle since the time of Hercules and the heroes of ages past. Our names shall join them soon enough!"

"If we survive," Séverin replied, shaking his head.

Barto's enthusiasm was infectious, but one of them needed to keep a clear vision of the possible future of this battle.

CHAPTER XXVIII

Unbeknownst to Sylvia Dardi and Franz Karnstein, there had been other eyes watching their battle with the vampires in the palace garden. Ettore and Francesca Policeni had voyeuristically viewed the scene, hidden in the bushes, initially amused at the notion of two young lovers attempting to secure some privacy for their pathetic, yet poetic, lovemaking.

To discover that it all had been a ruse had left them both shocked to the core. The "lovers" had, in fact, attacked others, that proved to be demons! If that were not enough, the ill-bred woman and the pale, pathetic Austrian had destroyed these creatures after a brief battle.

Ettore pulled Francesca away as the other pair limped away. Their voices could be heard, bickering like a pair of squabbling children as they slinked away from the palace.

Walking with calm purpose, the Policenis returned to the party, each taking and downing a glass of wine. They moved towards one of the empty spaces and stood, smiling rather forced smiles.

"That was unexpected and horrifying," Ettore stated. "I thought such creatures were just stories told to frighten children."

He nodded at a passing elderly couple dressed in clothing out-of-date by about twenty years.

"As much as I hate to agree with you, I have to believe you are correct," Francesca replied, a slight moue of annoyance causing her lower lip to protrude like a petulant child. "I still fail to see why Papa wishes Karnstein under his control. That fat Dardi girl demonstrated greater skill at fighting. However, I doubt either of them would be much of a difficulty for Piano Piatto or Lama Notturna."

"I do not know," Ettore said, smiling at Francesca., "but we will watch them closely. If necessary I will use Lama Notturna to place him in our power. Then, after you get your revenge on the Austrian for his behavior, we can discover what's so special about him. And placing that Karnstein under your control will impress the *Padrone* more than waiting for him to seek our help."

"*Merda!* Taking that step is too dangerous, and Papa does not take disobedience kindly. For now, let's just observe his behavior and that of his cow-faced *puttana*. If you wish us to work together, we must not exceed our position in Papa's organization. To do so would cause him to view us as trying to challenge his leadership. And we both know what that would mean…"

Francesca opened her fan and moved the ivory item vigorously. Ettore shuddered and nodded.

"Piano Piatto—if we were lucky…"

"Doctor Dolore if we were not…" said Francesca, looking ill behind her fan.

They shared a look of understanding. They then composed themselves and returned to watching the crowd, spotting no one of interest within their reach.

"We watch for a time," Ettore said. "We have the right to use Lama Notturna. Karnstein and the Dardi woman will never know they are being shadowed."

Francesca thought for a moment and nodded.

"I agree. Best to wait for our moment and learn more of what Papa wishes from the *stronzo* and his *puttana*. Can you believe he chose that cow over me? Incredible!"

"Karnstein is a fool and the woman belongs on a farm," Ettore stated, knowing better than to admit that he found Sylvia Dardi attractive.

She was a little too robust for his tastes, possessing strong muscles and expertise with a sword. He had enough of that with Francesca and didn't need another dangerous woman in his life. His affairs were always with shy, weaker-willed women he could buy and toss aside without concern. Ettore knew better than to admire Sylvia Dardi except in a distant, clinical manner. Francesca would know if he lusted after the swordswoman.

Francesca watched him for a moment and smiled quickly.

"Come, let us dance. Once we are done, we shall go home and you may join me in my room for the night."

Ettore kissed her hand and led his wife towards the dance floor. A night with Francesca was always delight, true erotic pleasure for an evening alone. When she was sated, usually after some hours, he was expected to leave quietly and stay away in the morning. By afternoon tomorrow, she would resume her cold, dangerous demeanor and Ettore knew better than to try and approach her until evening at the soonest.

That aside, Ettore took Francesca into his arms and they began to move with the music. A night of pleasure was worth a day of danger, at least in his opinion.

CHAPTER XXIX

T was near morning when Séverin and Dardi returned to his academy. Having gone back to the ball, they stayed in public and waited to see if anyone discovered the liquefied remains of the four vampires. Nothing strange occurred, but they could not find Sylvia or Franz for the rest of the night.

"They will have returned to your home," Séverin stated after checking the Austrian's room in the palace.

"That is odd. They were clearly enamored, so why go to my home where I may grow enraged if this Austrian takes advantage of my dearest child?" Dardi said as his hired coach left the ball.

"Takes advantage? Barto, your dearest child would castrate any man attempting to lay a hand upon her without permission," Séverin replied, hiding his amusement at his friend's annoyance and discomfort. "Also, I have difficulty seeing Franz Karnstein behaving like a stallion in heat. They had a reason for their actions."

Dardi frowned and thought, finally bursting out in snorts of laughter.

"Yes, yes, Gâteloup, you are right. My Sylvia is not one to allow a man to believe he is her master. My students learn that, to their infinite regret, when they believe she, as a mere girl, should fall at their feet when they make their interest apparent."

"Why is she not married? She is what, eighteen now?" Séverin asked, hoping he was not opening a wound.

Dardi continued to laugh.

"Twenty-one! Can you believe it? I had the son of a wealthy banker asking for her hand at age fourteen. She would not even consider the match. In fact, Sylvia ran away to a Carmelite nunnery when her aunt and I pressed the suit. She made me swear a holy oath that she could choose her own husband. I despaired, but finally agreed... What else could I do? She is my only child and the Dardi blood must not end with me!"

Séverin nodded, comprehending the dilemma. His own son was dead and his name would die, but that was not of any particular concern in his mind. To Séverin, the loss of his son meant the loss of true joy in this life. All moments in the light were mere glimpses of the greater happiness he once felt. Though Jean-Pierre Séverin enjoyed his work and his pupil, he found the happiness to be a true diminution of what he had experienced in the past, like comparing a single candle to the sun.

"It shall not, Barto. Sylvia is merely a strong-willed woman, like her aunt and grandmother. Even your sainted father could not change the mind of your mother when she was determined, God rest their souls."

Séverin joined Dardi in making the sign of the cross. Dardi nodded, his head bobbing up and down like a comic puppet.

"You speak the truth, Gâteloup. Father could be quite the orca, a truly giant monster who looked as if he ate babies for snacks when angry. But mother... she would make the Furies flee in terror when someone broke her rules. Do you remember her wooden spoon?"

"I still have a small scar on the back of my hand from that spoon," Séverin replied, rolling his eyes. "You can see it in bright light or when I grip my sword too hard with my left hand."

The carriage stopped before the academy just as the light of dawn appeared in the distance. This was false dawn, a radiance from the coming sun, a reflection of the fiery orb that lit the heavens. The two swordmasters entered moments later, their keen noses picking up a series of unusual scents.

"Blood and dirt," Séverin said, drawing his word.

Dardi nodded, also drawing his blade.

"Also that repulsive aroma that these vampires release when their undead lives are snuffed out. I think we must put these two to the question."

156

"Agreed," Séverin said

He and Dardi started a slow search of the building. The first floor proved empty, though traces of dirt were visible near door approaching the back staircase.

Heading upstairs, Dardi pushed open a door and looked confused. He waved Séverin over and pointed to a torn, soiled garment that appeared to have been Sylvia's gown. The large bed at the other end of the chamber was unused, as prim and proper as if the maid just placed the linen covers in place.

Closing the door, they repeated the room check four times, only discovering a pile of men's soiled clothing in a small room reserved for students. Neither Sylvia nor Karnstein were evident in any of the chambers and there were no additional sounds in the house.

Dardi's face suddenly took on a grim, angry cast and he headed up to the third floor, his personal area of the house. With an angry shove, he opened the door to his room, gripping his sword tightly as he stepped inside. Despite his fears, his daughter and the Austrian exorcist were not in evidence—there was no hint anyone entered these rooms in a day.

Seeing his friend's confusion, Séverin raised an eyebrow and pointed at the two other doors visible on the floor. Dardi stepped over to one, revealing a small closet filled with cleaning supplies and a large brass telescope pointed at a shaded window.

The second room proved to be Dardi's personal library, study and office. Started by his great grandfather, there were approximately one thousand volumes lining the walls. The subjects ranged from the deepest philosophical tracts to lurid penny dreadful tales sent by friend in London. Two entire walls of shelves were devoted to the study of supernatural creatures, with volumes as old as those that could be found in the Vatican archives.

This was where they found both young people, asleep in different areas of the room. Sylvia sat at Dardi's heavy wooden desk, a series of papers scattered across the surface. Her head slumped forward, her face not visible behind the curtain of her damp, ebony hair. Karnstein sat in a simple wooden chair, a heavy book in his lap. His head was on his chest and he breathed softly, barely audible as he slept. Both wore clean tunics, training clothes used by students of the academy.

Dardi sighed silently, stepping next to his daughter. He was about to stroke her long hair fondly when a page protruding from the stack caught his eye. Pulling the paper free, he studied the design for a moment and grew serious once again. Without a word he held the page out for Séverin to view.

Etched with simple, yet clearly defined lines were two figures, a muscular male and a shapely female. Their faces were split open, revealing the starfish shaped maws of the vampires from the ball. The rows of horrific teeth were in evidence as were the dark talons. Though quickly drawn, the figures were unmistakably the creatures the two swordmasters had faced that night.

"Do you think...?" Dardi whispered, nodding towards the paper.

"Yes. I think they faced these creatures and prevailed. Think of the smell."

Dardi frowned, his eyes widening.

"With only one sword between them! We must hear this tale!"

Séverin sheathed his sword and clapped his hands together twice. The sound was similar to that of a piece of green wood snapping in the wind. Sylvia and Karnstein both started, the latter catching the book in his lap before the leather-bound tome crashed to the floor.

"Have a nice nap? Perhaps you can explain your disappearance and this..." Dardi said, sounding more amused as he flashed the etching of the vampires.

"Sylvia...excuse me, Miss Dardi, told me that you spotted a pair of vampires," said Karnstein, reddening slightly when he realized his mistake of speaking familiarly about Sylvia Dardi. "We found them while on the dance floor."

Sylvia did not appear to have noticed the social slipup and continued Karnstein's explanation.

"We lured them into the gardens and destroyed them both. Our clothes were ruined and so we walked home."

"Miss Dardi and I used the bathhouses, changed into these tunics and she drew the creatures. It took many attempts to get the details correct," Karnstein added, looking Sylvia's direction with an annoyed expression.

Sylvia's face also changed, not hiding her anger.

"*Idiota!* You were concentrating too much on the unimportant details. Who cares which direction the left upper flaps teeth point?"

"The direction could be critical should there be another type of vampire or demon that resembles these monsters! And stop calling me an idiot!" Karnstein shot back, closing his book stepping to the other side of the desk.

"Then stop acting like one! We both know that there may be finite differences between these vampires, so it is more important to focus on the larger details," Sylvia snapped, standing and leaning across the desktop.

Karnstein and Sylvia continued to squabble, not noticing the amused looks from Séverin and Dardi. These two resembled a married couple from a *Commedia dell'arte*, screaming insults and fighting side by side against all comers.

"Enough!" Dardi yelled. "Listening to you two makes me grateful I never remarried. How did you defeat two vampires with only one sword and no holy water?"

Giving each other an annoyed look, they told of their battles against the pair of vampires in the garden. The sniping resumed through the story, especially when Sylvia and Franz got to the part where she took his sword and left him unarmed. Eventually, they completed by returning to their walk home.

A silence overtook the study as Séverin and Dardi exchanged incredulous looks. The Frenchman knew there were no lies or shaded truth, but these two did not appear to realize the full import of their actions. Sylvia was a young woman of twenty-one who had never fought a monster without the guidance and assistance of her father. Franz was a little older, but he had managed to kill his foe without a musket, blade, or that odd ability to exorcise demons. Séverin did not hide his elation and could see Dardi felt the same way.

"You both did very well, for young, barely-trained children," Dardi said, laughing and hugging his daughter while giving Karnstein a nod.

"Agreed," added Séverin. "I do believe we must find you another weapon as your primary means of attack. I shall think on the subject, after a few hours' sleep."

"Yes! Both of you, to your rooms and sleep," said Dardi. "Then we shall all meet for a late breakfast and plan. For now, *Andiamo!*"

CHAPTER XXX

"Sinis, where are you my faithful pet?" Nosos called out as she entered the cave.

Sinis ran in from the rear of the cave, dropping to his knees and kissing the vampire queen's feet.

"Oh, my lovely mistress," he said, "you were gone so long! Life without you was terrible. I missed your beauty and perfect voice. Please do not leave your slave behind you again for so long!"

Nosos rolled her eyes and stepped past her prone servant.

"Enough, pathetic one. I felt ripples in my web of power. What occurred while I was away?"

Keeping his eyes lowered, Sinis said in a hushed voice:

"I helped the six you allowed to venture to the royal ball, obtaining coaches and restating your commands. They were to meet me at the hour of the wolf. None appeared, and I waited until just before sunrise."

"They are destroyed. There are two hunters at the palace, summonsed by the French king of this land," Nosos said, sighing with the sadness only an immortal being was capable of feeling.

"Only two, mistress?" Sinis asked, still staring at his beloved owner's feet. "But Matilde was nearly as old as Fortuna and capable of defeating Giorgia in a duel. The others were young, but they were stronger than any mere mortal."

"I see your point, pathetic one," replied Nosos, frowning. "Two humans should be easily overcome by six of my children. I shall have my new servant observe and report. Perhaps they are not humans... that would explain much..."

"New servant? Are you replacing me, mistress? Oh please, do not abandon me! Life without your perfection would be torture!" Sinis whined looking up at his owner.

Nosos laughed and patted her slave on the shoulder.

"No, no, my dear wretch. You shall remain my slave for all time. I require a being who has no thoughts other than my needs, my desires. The stars shall vanish into dust before I release you from my service."

"Oh, thank you, beloved one! This pitiable slave lives only for you; you are the very air I breathe."

Sinis kissed Nosos's foot once again, his eyes still not daring to look up.

"My new servant is a tool, a weapon to use against my enemies. I shall send one of my pretty toys to help. These two hunters must not thwart my plans for this kingdom."

Nosos spoke more to herself than Sinis, almost ignoring the groveling creature who knelt at her feet.

Allowing his mistress an hour to think, Sinis finally spoke up, having much to tell her and being unable to wait any longer.

"Cherished and perfect Goddess, I do have a gift for you. May I get it?"

Splaying her fingers, Nosos dismissed her slave without bothering to look his direction. Sinis backed away, bowing and mumbling prayers of thanks, before vanishing from view. He returned moment later with a wide clothbound ledger, a battered dusty item that resembled the type used by government offices or counting houses.

"What is this?" Nosos looked surprised as she took the odd item, an unusual present for one such as she to receive.

"You once mentioned an interest in discovering a source of corpses for your wondrous magic. I wished to make you happy and remembered that Alberto's father was in charge of surveying the city. He is a very organized man who Alberto said made the government employees actually work for the first times in their lives. Look at what they produced!"

Sinis practically shook with fear and elation as he pointed at the words of the cover. Nosos read the hastily scrawled information twice, her eyes widening. Quickly she leafed through the thin volume, scanning the top line on each yellowing page. She started at the words on the second to last page, her mouth forming a large "O" shape in her shock. Nosos slowly read each line, three times, memorizing the information, her smile of triumph growing wider with each passing second. Lowering the book, she looked down at her slave fondly.

"Sinis, you are truly my favorite slave. I am glad I chose to let you live and transform you into something useful. This book will ensure the kingdom shall be mine, a foothold to bring about a new world. A world where my people rule supreme and humans are our food and playthings. You are a good slave, Sinis. You may kiss my other foot as I read."

Crawling forward on his belly, Sinis rose to a kneeling position and kissed and licked his owner's foot. Above him, Nosos read the poorly drawn script a fourth time, her sharp toothed smile twinkling in the oil lamp.

"The Catacombs of San Gennaro," she read a fifth time and laughed.

Her sinister mirth caused even her fanatical vampiric followers to scurry away and hide elsewhere. Nosos's terrible screams of evil delight chilled the undead beings, causing them to wonder if they misunderstood their terrible goddess and her plans for the future.

Eventually, she stopped cackling and placed the book aside. She needed to explore the underworld of this kingdom once again There were ancient passages, deep beneath the Earth, formed by the Tenebrae and their slaves. Many of these tunnels had been destroyed by the humans and earthquakes, but a number still existed, and even the disused ones could be excavated and put into temporary use. They had seventeen days, eighteen if they stretched the work to complete this plan. This idea contained less risk, and added a layer of protection for Nosos's ends. If that meant to sacrifice all of her followers, then, so be it. There were always more humans she could turn into appendages.

"Sinis," Nosos said, not looking her servant's direction, "send René to me now. Then assemble the rest of my servants. We have much work to do in the coming days."

Sinis bowed deeply and cried:

"At once, my Queen! Thank you for the gift of your gaze!"

Watching Sinis back from the room, Nosos continued to smile. Yes, she liked this new plan much better...

CHAPTER XXXI

"Up, Giulio! Wake up! We have much to do!" Pia Mele said, shaking her lover and praying that this new way worked.

If this was some odd trick, Giulio Nucci would blacken both her eyes again.

Giulio's opened quickly and he rose in bed, a confused look crossing his strong features. His graying hair was a mass of tangles that caused his head to look too large for his body, a freakish image in the morning light.

"What is it? What is wrong?" he asked, staring her direction with hooded, angry eyes.

Pia tensed and pressed forward, trusting that he would now obey her will. The trick, she was told, was to make him believe that her orders were all his idea originally.

"You told me to wake you so that you will have time to prepare for your raid. We must be on the road before noon so that we may prepare the ambush. Is that not what you said?" Pia asked, holding her breath after the last word.

Giulio was no fool; if the promised ability to influence his actions failed, she would receive a fist to the face seconds from this moment.

Giulio looked muddled for a few seconds, then his face broke out into a wide, happy smile.

"Yes! The raid tonight... I forgot all of it. Where are my plans? My maps!"

"Over here, *Principe*, darling."

Pia handed him a roll of paper that held the objective.

"I am very surprised you plan on attacking the French," she said. "Will they not be armed with rifles? Are the guns and bullets you steal worth the risk?"

Giulio unrolled the map and laughed, his inner madness evident once again.

"Of course it is worth it, woman! We can take the best guns and sell the rest. Soon *Il Principe* and his band will be the only power in all of Naples. I shall be a king, not a prince! Now, make me breakfast. I have much to do!"

Pia smiled and went about her business, grateful she now controlled Giulio Nucci. He possessed the potential to be a great, if mad, leader of men. When the time was right, she would formally marry him in a church and they would live like the kings of ancient days. She, Pia Mele, would be a queen and would live in a house with a bath and possess many dresses and servants. Others would cook what she wanted and she would ride through her town in a fine coach and smile down at those who believed her to be a wicked woman. A glorious dream that would soon be a reality.

Queen Pia of the Kingdom of Naples? No, that is too weak, Pia thought as she prepared the morning meal. *Queen Pia of the Two Sicilies? Better, but still not good enough. Empress Pia the First of Italy! That is much better, like one of those ladies who had statues made of them in Rome!*

Smiling to herself, she heard her lover barking orders at his men, waking them from the beds. Giulio roared down any protests, overwhelming the band of criminals and bandits.

"We will be in the saddle within one hour! Get food in your bellies and make sure your powder is dry!" he snarled.

Pia heard a yelp of pain from one of the men.

"Why did you kick me?" a young voice called out, sounding aggrieved.

"Because you move as slow as my crippled, blind, nonna! Get up and get ready! If you are not on your horse by the time I come back, I shall remove your head, empty your skull and use it as my saddlebag! Do you hear me? Do you?" Giulio asked, his voice dropping to a dangerous near whisper.

"Yes, *Principe*! I am sorry!" the young voice replied.

The sounds of shuffling feet drifted Pia's direction. She smiled as she finished the fast breakfast. She grabbed Giulio's canteen and headed to the well to fill this for his travels. Everything in life was wonderful and would only get better!

CHAPTER XXXII

"Ah, good!" Séverin stated as a refreshed Franz Karnstein entered the training hall.

The Frenchman wore the same finery from the night before. None of the academy clothing was long enough for his tall frame. Karnstein wore the same tunic, having abandoned his clothing as useful only as fuel for a fire. He had rescued his boots, family crest medal, ring, and crucifix from the pyre.

"Good?" he asked, looking confused.

"Yes. I hoped you would be prompt, as you always are to all appointments. Dardi knows I wished to speak to you alone. He planned to do the same with Sylvia."

"Did we do something wrong?" Karnstein asked, his tone wary.

Séverin shook his head. '

"Quite the opposite. Barto and I were very happy with your performances against such dangerous enemies. I was especially interested in your skills without weapons. Did you use the wrestling and foot fighting skills I taught you?"

"Yes. I only possessed some rudimentary wrestling teachings when I was younger. One of my father's servants showed me a trick or two."

"Let us test your skills then," Séverin said after studying Karnstein for a moment.

Drawing a wooden small sword from the racks lining the training chamber, he nodded once after testing the balance. Without warning, he then lunged forward, aiming for Karnstein's heart. The Austrian exorcist stepped aside, reaching to grasp one of Séverin's wrists. The French swordmaster withdrew, turning and slashing for his student's arm. The attack missed by inches and Séverin was forced to duck a hard punch to his head. He slashed the sword and racked across Karnstein's torso, a clean, perfect strike. Karnstein stepped back and shrugged ruefully.

"I lose again. A not unexpected state of my training."

Séverin shook his head and returned the practice weapon to the rack.

"Not so, you had me on the defensive for a moment. That is impressive for an untrained student, which I consider you in unarmed combat. I shall alter your training to reflect this previously unknown preference."

Karnstein looked skeptical.

"What good is unarmed training if I cannot protect myself against a sword stroke? To say nothing of a vampire, who are faster and stronger than a simple mortal such as myself."

"Ah!" Séverin said, with a nod such as that teachers provide for students who finally demonstrate some much needed insight. "There are means of fighting that you do not comprehend yet. The gangs of Palermo, Rome, and Naples rarely use swords in a fight, viewing the weapon as slow and unwieldy. They developed fighting arts that are lethal and frequently result in the severe injury or death of their opponents. The system is based on small arms, daggers, short swords, clubs and street weapons. Formal steps of dueling are considered, by these criminals, to be a waste of time. For them, life and death are all that matters."

"I see," Karnstein still appeared uncertain. "And vampires? That appears a less certain method of fighting such creatures."

Séverin plucked another wooden weapon from the brackets and tossed the item to Karnstein. The wooden blade was about twelve inches long, including the handle, and narrowed to a dull point.

"This is a mere practice weapon, a means of teaching students how to fight and protect themselves against short blades," Séverin explained. "But if such a weapon was made of a strong, treated wood, you would have your means of battling vampires."

He put the weapon back on the rack.

"Interesting," Karnstein replied. "Has anyone ever fought vampires with wooden blades and short weapons as their preferred method?"

Séverin shook his head.

"Not as far as I have read or learned in my years. Yet this matters little. Once it was believed only holy crusaders should fight creatures of darkness. Then a man, an English Puritan no less, proved that faith and a strong arm was enough to hold back the darkness. Dardi's people and other families have trained in the art of the sword and studied the many vampires that have emerged throughout the world. My teacher, after Barto's father, was a man named Kronos, who had refined these skills even further and added a level of professionalism by working in concert with an academic. The point I make is this: our fight against vampires and other horrors must change with the times. If you had a choice in a duel of a knife or a pistol, which would you choose?"

"The gun, of course," Karnstein replied, frowning. "I used to be accused of being less manly by the Swiss Guard for such a choice."

This was news to Séverin, never having heard a word about Karnstein's service to the Pope.

"You were called out to duel?"

"Yes, twice. The first was a Swiss Guard officer whose sister was killed by a member of my family. I avoided the issue for a time, but he would not relent. As injured party, I chose pistols. I lived, he did not."

"And the other duel?" Séverin asked.

Karnstein sighed and shook his head.

"A foolish boy. He was in love with a beautiful Roman woman, the daughter of a count. There was an understanding between them, but she was fickle and transferred her interest to me. He demanded satisfaction and I chose pistols. He fired his while my back was turned, missing me completely."

"You killed him?"

Séverin's stomach flipped at the thought of such a duel. He'd seen many of that type in the past-young fools trying to be brave, completely unprepared for the reality of a battle to the death. Often they died, and that was an unfortunate loss of life. But Karnstein shook his head, a look of disgust crossing his face for a moment.

"No, I had no desire for his blood. He was just a young idiot, in love with a woman who was not worthy of his attentions. I grazed him across the cheek with my musket ball. That satisfied all demands for honor since I spared his life. He ended up marrying the girl in question and she cuckolded him with his own cousin the day after their wedding."

"Interesting and very proper according to the code duello. Also, my point exactly. To try and make you into a swordmaster was never my intention. I told you so when you came to train with me. The difficulty was discovering your strengths while compensating for your weaknesses. To you, a sword is not an art form, but a tool, *n'est-ce-pas*?"

Karnstein raised a hand to signal his agreement. This was old ground for them both, having discussed this after some of their training sessions during the last year.

"This was why I stressed little on any specific style for long. You are competent with all I taught you, uninspired to seek perfection in any specific weapon. After your battle without weapons, I see the reason with clearer eyes. In a real sense, you are closer to being a soldier rather than a hunter. This is good; a soldier uses a different approach to so battle than a swordmaster or a witch-hunter. The latter is what I feared; you remember the letters I had you read regarding the Englishman named Matthew Hopkins?"

Karnstein face transformed into a look of extreme loathing and disgust.

"A rapist and murderer who used the false title of witch finder general to satiate his lusts."

"Just so—and what of Jindřich František Boblig of Edelstadt?" Séverin asked, having taught his pupil the history of all inquisitors and their actions in days long past.

"A monster, a crazed beast with no understanding of that which he faced. He also did not realize a Karnstein was the one who encouraged his excesses. Count Leopold Karnstein used the killings as a part of a ritual in honor of his dark patron. May they both burn for all eternity in Lucifer's furnace!"

Séverin noted again how unwilling his pupil was to hide his family's dark origins. Many would try and distance themselves from such terrible tales, but his student viewed that as a sin nearly as great as the acts committed by his family.

"We spoke of the actions of Cumberland and von Meruh, too. Do you see the pattern?" Séverin asked. "The witchhunter often falls and becomes a being as monstrous as the ones they originally chose to battle. This was my fear for you, since your determination to fight is as fierce as I've ever seen. Happily, we have found a different path now, and your training will take on different dimensions. I may enlist other experts to assist me in certain areas."

He lifted a sword bayonet from the rack and examining the ugly weapon for a moment. Karnstein's face clouded with apparent confusion.

"First, you spoke of street gang weapons; now you tell of soldiers. Forgive me, maestro, but I am confused by your discourse."

Séverin clapped the younger man on the shoulder.

"Good! That is the beginning of wisdom. Just know that I have a clearer method of preparing you for the future. You may continue learning to use your beloved saber, but that will be a small part. Your days of relaxation are over."

Karnstein blinked, looking unsure as to whether the maestro was making a joke. He was rescued by the appearance of Sylvia and her father, the latter bounding into the room with a happy laugh.

"Why is everyone so serious?" Dardi asked. "We are alive, the sun is shining and breakfast is on the table. We shall eat and then our work begins! Did you tell him of his duties?"

The swordmaster waved them towards the dining room, bit Séverin shook his head.

"Not yet. We have other matters to consider. Have you done so with Sylvia?"

Dardi shook his head and chuckled.

"I shall put it to her now. We seek information on vanishings low and high…"

Séverin continued the thought:

"Barto and I shall approach from the top, discovering who is missing among the wealthier segment of society. The woman we defeated, Matilde Detti, was amongst that group. We shall determine who else is missing and, if possible, why."

"That sounds like a nearly impossible task," Karnstein remarked. "A kingdom's worth of people to sort and determine their position. How shall you proceed?"

"We have already some thoughts about the matter. You two will have your own work that will take up your time," Séverin said.

They entered the dining room just as the cook placed a large tray upon the wide, wooden table.

"I do not like the sound of that statement, uncle. What work?" Sylvia asked, frowning.

"I doubt you shall like it, my child," replied Dardi, chuckling. "You and the *barone* shall consult every spiritualist and witch you can find and determine if any are knowledgeable about the current events. I suggest you both arm yourselves and wear comfortable shoes…"

CHAPTER XXXIII

A monk with a handsome face and a well-trimmed blond beard ushered Johann Spurzheim into the office of Federigo Gui. The master of the Cupbearers sat before a large, highly decorative Bible that Spurzheim believed was the personal property of the last king of Naples. Gui held up one stubby finger, hushing any potential statement as well as controlling the meeting from the start. He continued reading for a full minute before placing a strip of silk between the pages. He then closed the heavy tome with a contented sigh and said:

"I always find such contentment when I read the words of Saint Jude. Do you know the passage where he tells of the angels who disobeyed the Word?"

Spurzheim shook his head, already bored with this obvious and ridiculous attempt to frighten.

"No, I do not recall."

Gui smiled, his ugly face looking even more predatory.

"I remember the quote exactly, *And the angels which kept not their first estate, but left their own habitation, he has reserved in everlasting chains under darkness to the judgment of the great day. Jude 1:6,* a very memorable statement, do you not think?"

"I should think all passages by one of the Apostles qualify as important and memorable, Father Abbot," Spurzheim replied, amused to see the smile on Gui's face slip slightly.

"Quite true, my son,' Gui nodded vigorously. "Now, to temporal matters that must be addressed. I believe the pair of hunters sent by the sainted Emperor Napoleon are working without providing us with information as to their actions."

Spurzheim shrugged, grateful his response ended Gui's latest attempt to prove his power.

"I am sure they are doing exactly as you suggest. Both men were clear in their disinclination to obey our commands."

Gui waved that aside with a cutting gesture.

"That is so, but they did not tell us of their actions in the very gardens of this palace! Do you know this, or are your spies working as inefficiently as ever?"

Spurzheim rolled his eyes and opened a small leather book he held in his top pocket.

"Maestro Jean-Pierre Séverin and his friend, Maestro Bartolomeo Dardi left the party and followed four people into the abandoned hedge maze. The sounds of a brawl occurred and only Séverin and Dardi emerged. In the center of the maze—which I did demand destroyed but was overruled by your office—were pools of an acidic discharge. Said fluids burned the fool who dared to touch the disgusting mess with his bare hand. The area was cleansed and the ground beneath was gray, as if volcanic ash lay on the site."

Gui's face flushed and turned crimson with embarrassment at the police chief's detailed information. He finally spluttered:

"What of the Austrian?"

Spurzheim smiled a little wider and continued reading in the same bored tone of voice.

"Baron Franz Karnstein and Signorina Sylvia Dardi strolled outside and were followed by four others. Two of those following returned to the party, the other two did not. Two more pools of the same foul fluid lay upon the grass and, as before, the ground beneath was scorched and rendered lifeless. I ordered the gardeners to dig up both areas until the ground is clean again. The filth was tossed into the sea and new dirt and stones now hide the unholy contamination."

"You let them go? You did not demand an explanation?" Gui screamed and hammered a fist on his desk top.

Spurzheim closed the book and returned the item to his pocket.

"I am not interested in their falsehoods or half-truths. They are being watched and I will learn of their actions within minutes. Then, if they are guilty of any form of treachery towards the kingdom, they will be arrested and confronted with facts. Before you insist you have methods to wring the truth from their bodies, I shall remind you of two facts: first, Monsieur Séverin is here by personal appointment from Emperor Napoleon Bonaparte, brother of our good King Joseph. Second, Baron Karnstein is part of the personal staff of His Holiness the Supreme Pontiff. Do you wish to anger either of their patrons? That would be, in my humble and simpleminded view, a risky proposition. However, if that is your choice, you are welcome to make the attempt…"

"Enough!" Gui snarled.

He lifted the gold and silver bell on his desk and shouted: "Brother René, to me at once!"

The handsome young monk appeared at his master's side an instant later. He made no sound, but bowed deeply and waited, hands folded deeply into the sleeves of his black robes.

"Escort our visitor out of my sight and then bring me the file in the red cover I handed you this morning," Gui stated through clenched teeth, waving Spurzheim towards the door.

Spurzheim rose, smiled once in muted triumph, and followed Brother René out of the Cupbearer's sanctuary. It had been a minor victory, but a telling one. In his opinion, his enemy was losing his grip on basic reality and beginning to behave in a troubled manner. This could be to his advantage, if he did not fall prey to the same insanity. Any type of crazed behavior could, and would, become dangerous in the coming days, this much was certain. The possible outcome was pleasing—the end of Federigo Gui and his Cupbearers, and the rise of Johann Spurzheim to rank of head of police, secret and public for all of Naples.

CHAPTER XXXIV

The bored guards followed the line of wagons as they wound through the narrow lanes leading to the main road to Naples. The weather was hot, the duty dull, and no girls of any kind appeared on the roads. It was close to mid-day and heat was rising to nearly unbearable levels, causing them to sweat profusely in their dark, army uniforms.

"At least there are no flies," one grizzled old soldier re-marked, causing more than a couple of men to make the sign of the evil eye against such a thought.

This was not normal duty for the regiment; they were used to field actions. The difficulty lay in the English, more specifically the English navy. Their ships harassed the brave French forces and took all-important cargoes such as guns and powder. Therefore, clever ways were needed to bring the much-needed weapons to the kingdom of Naples. Someone in Paris had suggested the old method, a caravan of wagons carrying the goods over carefully chosen routes.

This was their fourth assignment, a grueling duty that weakened their morale each time. They wished to be part of the next campaign for the Emperor, battling the Austrians, Russians, or Prussians. That way they could earn some loot once the fighting was completed. All in the regiment had been part of the glorious war against the Bourbons in Naples and most had earned a nice reward for their troubles.

The only positive part of this dull duty was the final des-tination—Naples, capital of the kingdom. The people, on the whole, welcomed them and treated them fairly. The girls were pretty and it was nicer than being stuck on the frozen wastes of Austria or Germany.

As this was their fourth journey, the regiment's normally military trained behavior had turned lax. They didn't march in columns and the Major in command, a drunken fool named Lefebvre, never bothered to send scouts ahead to check for possible partisan actions. Instead he contented himself with a jug of cheap wine and a space in one of the covered wagons, leaving the work to his junior, inexperienced officers. A small betting pool had started, wagering when he would pass out or begin singing a naughty song about goblins.

The reverie and hopeful prayers against flies ceased when a medium-size tree fell across the road. The column halted, with the horses almost grateful to stop pulling the heavy loads in the hot sun. The regiment was momentarily paralyzed, looking back to the wagon where the Major supposedly sat in command.

"All men! Get over there and move that tree. Now!" a twenty-year-old, untrained lieutenant said.

His voice did not crack and he tried to hide his pride as the soldiers ambled over to the fallen tree, placing their guns in easy to reach triangular groups. The sergeants immediately organized the men along the length of the tree—the closest to military precision the regiment had been in weeks.

"Sergeant?" the same older, grizzled corporal who mentioned flies piped up. "This tree is wet… and smells strange."

The sergeant in question was about to bark out a sarcastic rejoinder, when the wood suddenly ignited. Flames, some higher than the top of the wagons, exploded from the tree and engulfed most of the men. A loud series of guffaws filled the air and the sounds of sporadic gunfire added to the screams of burning men. The air smelled of burning flesh, blood, frightened horses, and gunpowder. These were the last thoughts of the scorched sergeant before a musket ball caused his heart to explode in his chest.

The only survivor of the debacle was the drunken Major Lefebvre, asleep in the same wagon. Giulio Nucci and his men dragged the man aside, causing his head to strike the ground several times.

"Spare him," Giulio stated as one of his men pulled his knife out and leaned over the unconscious form. "It is bad luck to kill a drunk who is sleeping. Take all the guns, leave the men their clothes only… but no boots. It is bad luck to leave a dead man with his boots on when you leave behind his corpse."

The gang obeyed, knowing better than to question their leader's odd superstitions. Despite his beliefs in good and bad luck, he had led them through some difficult times. Now, Giulio had managed to destroy an entire army regiment without a drop of their blood spilled. The nagging question of how the French might react to this attack was unspoken, for the moment. They trusted their leader, sensing he had a plan in mind.

For his part, Giulio was a contented man. Pia waited in the mansion they had appropriated that morning—a nearly abandoned ten-room villa that overlooked a lake. Life was good and was going to get only better.

As to the lone survivor, Major Lefebvre received a promotion and a position back in Paris where he served as a minor bureaucrat for the rest of his days. When Major General Lefebvre died at his desk at age seventy-three, all Paris mourned the loss of a great hero who had only sought to serve the state and promote business for new vineyards in his beloved wine market. He was survived by four children, eight grandchildren, two great-grandchildren, and seven vintages of red wine named in his honor.

CHAPTER XXXV

"I have a question for you," Sylvia Dardi said as they strode across a busy, bustling street full of carts laden with goods of all types.

She wore a riding outfit, a light dress that allowed her to mount a steed without showing too much leg to anyone. The hat atop her head was a tricorn, a far outdated fashion that she somehow appeared to make charming.

"Only one? How refreshing," Karnstein commented, his tone acidic.

Day four of their search and so far they had found nothing for their efforts. Both also realized that they were capable of arguing over any subject under the sun or moon.

"*Idiota*, you know what I mean. Here is my question: why do you dress like a *imprenditore di pompe funebri*?" Sylvia asked, ignoring a passing whistle from a man leading a pair of horses.

Karnstein took a moment to translate the meaning, not having heard that phrase before now.

"A conductor of funerals? An undertaker?"

"Yes," Sylvia nodded and smiled, taking his arm again.

She often did that when they spoke, and Karnstein never objected, despite their squabbles.

"I do not dress like one of those people," he replied, looking down at his plain, simple clothing.

"Ah, but you do. Black and white, nothing else. No colors of any type, no adornments other than the plain cross you wear at all times. If you wore a black hat, you would be mistaken for a *imprenditore di pompe funebri* rather than a *barone*. What is the reason?"

Karnstein shrugged, wishing their latest destination were closer. He was not comfortable with such conversations, not that his feelings on the matter interested Sylvia. She appeared oblivious to his disinterest in discussing personal matters.

"I have no interest in luxuries or vanity," he said. "I dress as simply as I am able without wearing rags."

Sylvia smiled and shook her head.

"That is a response you planned in advance. You developed it where... Rome? When you served *Il Papa*?"

Karnstein nodded and sighed. Somehow this woman appeared to understand each time he armored himself against a discussion. It was very annoying, yet here they were again speaking of his life and ways.

"Yes. Why do you wish to master the sword? That is uncommon for a woman."

"Do not turn the conversation back on me, Franz Vordenburg Karnstein," replied Sylvia, shaking her head. "I asked you a question."

"And I answered it. Now I ask you one. Answer, please," Karnstein said, repeating their old formula for an argument.

She asked a question, he answered it without details and responded with a question of his own.

"You did not answer me; you just admitted I was correct," Sylvia said, releasing his arm and beginning to walk with angry steps. "There is a reason for your *imprenditore di pompe funebri* style of clothing."

"It was deemed adequate when I met the Holy Roman Emperor himself. And the Pope. And the Emperor Napoleon," Karnstein replied, matching her step for step. "Now, why do you want to be a swordmaster? You know this will cause many to view training with you poorly. By your age, most women are married."

"Madonna, you're as bad as my father! *Why are you not married and giving me grandchildren?* I answer you and all, I marry when I choose and not before," Sylvia snarled, not looking his direction.

"I did not ask you about marriage and children. I asked you about being a maestro of the blade," Karnstein shot back.

"*Idiota!* The answer is the same!" Sylvia yelled, stopping and placing both of her fists on her hips.

"Stop calling me an idiot!" Karnstein said, stopping and dropping his fists to his sides.

"Then stop acting like one!" Sylvia said.

She glanced around and, in a softer voice, added:

"We've arrived at our latest magician's. We shall use the second story since everyone on the street can hear you yelling like an old man at children on his doorstep."

"And you screaming like a fish peddler on a hot day," Karnstein replied.

"*Idiota*," she said, taking his arm and leading him towards a red painted door.

"Stop calling me..."

Karnstein was cut off by a tight squeeze of her hand on his arm.

"Hush," she whispered, just as the door opened.

A tall, thin man in loose fitting gentle's garb opened the door and stared at them with large, owlish eyes. He was a handsome man, roguish looking, and possessed a thin mustache that appeared freshly curled and waxed. He studied them for a moment, his look predatory. Spotting Karnstein's expensive boots, small sword, and pale looks, his look changed to one of gentle amiability.

"You have come to meet Countessa Angelica?" he asked, his voice more of a purr than actually spoken words.

"Yes, sir. It is very important. We heard she is an expert on all matters of the heart," Sylvia responded, her voice more cultured than her normal Neapolitan tones.

"Yes," the man said, smiling broadly.

The look on his face was delighted, but the affable attitude was not reflected in his eyes. They stared at Sylvia and Franz with the hungry expression of a cat about to consume a fat mouse.

"The Countess has saved many young marriages and was even asked advice from... Well, I should not say... But he is very high-ranking in the Court..."

"How did you know we were married?" Franz asked, playing his part and looking very surprised.

The handsome man's face twisted into a knowing grin, almost a sneer.

"Why, the Countess told me this morning. Please, come in and sit down. I shall see if the Countess deems the spirits ready to answer your questions."

The followed their guide down a cramped, dimly lit hallway and into a small square room probably intended as a large closet. A pair of new, cheaply-made but falsely impressive-looking wooden chairs rested on one wall. A squat table covered with circular stains and poorly hidden scuff marks.

"A glass of wine perhaps?" the man asked in the same insinuating purr. "Oh, do forgive me, I am Anton, the Countess's assistant."

Sylvia politely rejected the drinks and Anton vanished from sight. She looked at Karnstein and rolled her eyes. This was the second spiritualist they'd visited today and the nonsensical behavior of these charlatans was wearing on her spirit. Still, they had a duty to perform.

"I think this Countess shall have our answers, *mi amore*," Sylvia said, taking his hand and clutching it with a well-practiced fervor.

"I hope so. My parents write daily, demanding word of a grandchild," Franz replied, using the story they determined would impress the mountebanks best.

This was a true test of these spiritualists, *stregheria*, warlocks, and dark priests. In truth, Karnstein's father had died when he was eight years old at the hands of Mircalla, the ancient vampire who had also infected his mother and turned her into one of the undead. Though this was a fresh wound in Franz's mind, he did believe that it was also the perfect test. If these so-called mistresses and masters of the mystic arts spoke of his parents, then their falsehood was revealed. The one "dark priest" who had determined Karnstein's parents were dead, had spoken of them missing their son and other platitudes.

"My mother," Franz had explained to Sylvia after having slapped the deceitful mystic across the mouth and stormed out, "was a cold, nasty woman whose only interest was being admired. She loved mirrors, new dresses, and her favorite carpet. I was expelled to my own wing of the castle and not allowed to approach her at any time. Except each Sunday when we traveled to church and she pretended to be a loving mother."

"What of your father?" Sylvia had asked, forcing him to sit at a fountain so they could speak quietly.

"I barely knew the man, shrugged Karnstein. "He spent his time as a member of the Emperor's Court, a military advisor. The few times we met, he treated me like a puppy who might piss on the floor. He sent me gifts he earned by gambling. They were adult objects, like dueling pistols, a book of French etchings that one of the priests said was pornography, and a sword."

Only someone truly connected to the universe would know the truth of Karnstein's sad life, a truth which, outside of Styria, was only known to Jean-Pierre Séverin, and now, Sylvia Dardi.

Anton returned a moment later, his sneering smile still in place.

"The Countess will see you now," he said.

Still holding hands like they were unable to release each other, Sylvia and Franz followed the man into a larger rectangular room that seemed to have been originally intended to serve as a dining room. The walls were plain wood and covered with ancient-looking bas-reliefs of gods and demons. These were cheaply made fakes, available in the marketplace in every city in Italy and Greece, though slightly better made than most on the market.

The windows were covered with a gauzy scarlet fabric that cast an ethereal light. A single lit taper on a silver candlestick rested on a small round wooden table surrounded by three chairs. The chair closest to the far wall was larger, designed to resemble a throne, and possessed a series of poorly carved mystic carvings across its surface.

A woman entered the room a few seconds later, her body covered in a loose-fitting gown made of green silk. Her hennaed hair was shoulder-length and curled. She possessed a narrow face with a long, pointed chin. She stared at them with large gray-green eyes and huge, luxuriant, dark lashes.

"Good afternoon, young people. I am Countessa Angelica Carfulena and I heard your plea through the power of the Heavens. You wish to know when you will have a child, do you not?"

She spoke in a quivery sounding voice that appeared full of knowledge and foresight. The style was familiar to anyone used to Greek theater—this was the standard speaking style of the chorus as they predicted the downfall of the unwary.

"How did you know that?" Sylvia asked, her eyes wide.

She raised her free hand to her lips, her expression shocked and a little frightened. The Countessa settled herself slowly into her throne-like chair and waved Sylvia and Franz into the seats opposite. Her face creased in a knowing smile, a look that denoted knowledge beyond that of normal men.

"I speak to the angels. They tell me of those who would seek my knowledge. They sent me a vision of your travails. You wish a child, one that will make your parents content?"

Countess Angelica still spoke in the same whispery tone, as if sharing a secret.

"Yes," Sylvia said, pretending to look at her companion. "George's parents will not grant him..."

"Maria," Karnstein said, his tone chiding. "Let the Countessa tells us what the angels have to say."

Angelica looked briefly content and then nodded sagely.

"You speak wisely, young George. Place your hands on the table. You too, Maria."

"How did you know our names?" Sylvia asked, pretending to appear surprised.

This was her favorite test of the spiritualist's veracity—a true believer never failed to remind her that the names had been spoken mere seconds earlier.

"The angels told me of your coming, this morning, my dear. Your names, your marital strife, your desire for a child, the inheritance George will receive from his parents once you have a baby. The angels in Heaven know all and will tell you what you must do to appease their anger. For the angels are unhappy and you must turn them away from their wrath."

Angelica leaned forward and blew out the single candle.

As the false spiritualist composed herself, Karnstein looked at Sylvia and rolled his eyes. This pair was as ridiculous any they experienced so far. Time to find a way of ending this nonsense so they could move to the next mountebank on their list.

"Do not speak," Angelica whispered, "just allow your minds to concentrate on the name Gabriel, greatest of all the angels."

Sylvia looked amused, close to giggling or simply roaring with laughter. She found amusement in the antics of these false prophets and their ridiculous games. To her, they appeared to be a kind of theater, harmless silliness until they started demanding money or services for their "assistance from Heaven."

Lacking the light of the candle, the room took on a strange, eerie air, as if they had entered a new world of red light and deep shadows. The false ancient idols appeared to stare down at them, their weird, wizened expressions appearing to disapprove of the presence of mere humans in their eldritch sanctuary. As expected, Angelica moaned and rolled her head like she was falling asleep. She opened her eyes and only the whites of her eyes were visible. Then the table shook and rose a few inches from the ground. The table, which had seemed substantial at first glance, now appeared quite light, shaking and floating before their eyes. The Countessa continued to wail, her hands pressed flat on its surface.

That was when Franz kicked the underside of the table and knocked the floating furniture to the floor. Angelica shrieked and tumbled with the table—the wires attached to her wrists and shoes still locking her in place. This was an old mummers' trick—a set of hidden wires attached secretly to the table allowing the false spiritualist to float the object without appearing to move.

"I wonder if the angel Gabriel would approve of such falsehoods?" Karnstein asked, shaking his head with open disgust.

Anton appeared a second later, his face twisted with fury.

"You bastards!" he roared, reaching for Sylvia.

Sylvia did not pause; her hand grasped the small sword on Franz's belt. With a smooth motion, she drew the blade and placed the tip against the handsome mountebank's chest.

"You were saying?" she asked, slowly rising and looking amused.

Anton stopped, but then suddenly smiled as the table flew like a massive arrow, hitting the lovely swordswoman and tossing her backwards.

Sylvia's weapon flew from her grasp while Angelica rose from the ground, her face slowly transforming.

Anton's mouth split open and his prehensile tongue lashed out, latching onto Karnstein's arm. The sharp barbs dug deep into the exposed flesh and the young Austrian gasped in pain.

With a yank, he crashed to the floor, his arm feeling as if it was on fire, his body unable to breathe as the agony rose with each heartbeat.

"Food," Countessa Angelica whispered as her face split open, revealing rows of teeth in an inhuman head. "We shall feed on your blood!"

CHAPTER XXXVI

"We are too late, again," Bartolomeo Dardi said as they stepped into the lady's bedroom.

Matilde Detti's rooms were in shambles, every drawer open, clothes and small items tossed on the floor from some previous search. There were a great many papers thrown about in the library, mostly records from her father's former duties. The rest appeared to be detritus, nothing of interest.

"I doubt that, Barto," Jean-Pierre Séverin said, kneeling by a pile of clothing. "This is a search by an angry or desperate man. He will have overlooked many things while looking for something he considered important. No, my friend, there is more to find in this home."

"All I have learned is that Matilde Detti was interested in clothing and silly baubles," Dardi said, pushing aside a pile of shoes as he looked in the dusty closet.

"In that, you are correct. There is more, a secret we are not finding. It is here, all we need to do is...aha!"

Séverin snatched up a pile of pamphlets and shook them above his head triumphantly. Dardi looked up and asked:

"I assume that means you are correct for once."

"I am always correct in the end, my friend," Séverin snorted. "But to answer your question, yes. This is the first clue in days."

Dardi dropped the abandoned blue dress and stepped up to his taller friend. Glancing at the papers, he smiled.

"Small books on magic and raising the dead. She was a secret lover of the supernatural. This led her to fall into the hands of the demon."

"I doubt it would be so simple as that, but yes. Now, let's begin searching for secret hiding location. These papers are long abandoned; she would have others, or possibly even a *Libre Maleficium*."

Séverin began tapping the side of the dresser in search of secret compartments. Dardi returned to the closet, running his hands over the walls.

"How would a twit like Matilde Detti get her hands on a Luciferian bible?" asked the Italian. "Such items are not easily available, even for gold."

"I very much doubt her version would be a true tome, written in blood and printed on human skin," Séverin explained as he ran his hands over the legs of the furniture. "There are lesser versions used by dark priests as a means of enslaving their followers to greater powers. According to legend, one was secretly created on the same printing press Gutenberg used to create his version of the Bible."

"I assume you learned that from your pupil," Dardi grunted. "That sounds like something his witch-hunter's mind would remember."

"Correct," Séverin confirmed, moving to a dressing table. "And he is not a witch-hunter."

"Yes, yes, your new direction. A soldier of the light rather than a swordmaster. The difficulty with such notions is they are untested and prone to fail. Then we have produced a well-trained witch-hunter."

Dardi pulled over a chair and started tapping the small ceiling of the closet with the handle of his knife.

"Then we'd best hope your Sylvia assists me in preventing such an occurrence. You do realize she's decided on Franz as her future husband, don't you?" Séverin asked, standing straight and frowning.

He needed to think like Matilde Detti, not a clever person who would hide secrets with innate intelligence. The young woman was a wealthy pleasure-seeker, a woman who sought naughtiness, not true evil.

"Know it? Gâteloup, my daughter is so enamored with that cold-blood Austrian, she speaks of nothing else. Oh, she hides it beneath complaints and anger, but she does not allow him away from her sight for long. Have you ever heard the Sicilian term *colpo di fulmine*? The thunderbolt?" Dardi asked, hopping off the chair and surveying the room with his wide, bulging eyes.

"Yes," Séverin nodded, "your grandmother used to tell us to beware the thunderbolt when we left the house. I assumed she was warning us about the weather."

Dardi laughed and shook his head.

"No, she meant the moment where a man and a woman meet and are instantly enamored. It sounds wonderful, but often becomes messy and dangerous. Fortunately, your pupil is unaware. Ah, the pleasures of being young and stupid!"

Séverin nodded, but was only listening with half an ear. The majority of his attention was scanning the room and considering the destroyed vampire once known as Matilde Detti. He knew, as did all who battle for their lives, that humans were creatures of habit. This innate truth allowed the observant swordmaster to recognize strengths, weaknesses and habits in their opponents. If you understood your enemy, you had a greater chance of comprehending, or even possibly anticipating, their actions. He needed to treat Matilde Detti in the same manner.

"Are you listening to me?" Dardi said, stepping before Séverin's unseeing eyes.

"One moment, please."

The Frenchman turned all of his attention to the consideration of the now completely dead Matilde Detti. He had only known her for a brief time and, sadly, she had behaved with the same arrogance as most vampires. She believed that, as a member of the undead, she was better than any human. However, this did not appear to be the simple bravado of the newly-risen vampire. Matilde Detti behaved in a manner that allowed her to control her three undead companions. This meant that conducting herself in an imperious manner was a second nature. She was used to issuing orders and being obeyed. Partly, this was due to her wealthy upbringing and, as Dardi had indicated, her noble husband. The rest was because she had believed none could resist her beauty and demands. The destroyed vampire, both before her undead existence and after, was a spoiled, haughty, narcissistic, overweening, malodorous creature, whose only virtue was a pretty face and glorious golden hair.

Understanding his enemy, Séverin walked over to the large mirror and sat down on the small chair placed before the glass. He reached forward with both hands and felt the wooden edge, immediately discovering an indentation covered by a piece of soft cloth. Gently pushing his fingers forward, he felt a piece of leather and a squared edge. With a nod, he gently pulled the book from the hiding spot and held the item up for Dardi to see.

"*Voilà!*" Séverin said, opening the cover.

A page of poorly drawn script greeted his eyes. He knew exactly what he had just discovered and squinted in an attempt to try and decipher the terrible handwriting.

"Her diary, I believe. This will be difficult to read. I've seen better handwriting from near illiterates."

"Allow me," Dardi said, taking the book.

He read for a moment and continued:

"It's far from the worst I've viewed. I believe government men write with their feet while drinking poor Austrian wine."

"That was oddly specific, Barto. You must explain the full tale when we have a moment," Séverin said, as his friend shooed him from the chair and sat down, reading.

"Of course, now be quiet!" Dardi said, scanning the pages slowly. "I must concentrate; this woman's spelling is terrible."

"*Was* terrible," Séverin replied, continuing to poke around.

He doubted there would be anything of interest; the other searcher had been thorough and hadn't bothered to hide his actions.

An hour later, Dardi sighed and looked up.

"I need a large glass of wine! That was exhausting, and not in a pleasant manner."

Séverin, who was leafing through the magical pamphlets raised an eyebrow.

"I assume that means you discovered our next direction... after your drink?"

Dardi laughed and leaped to his foot.

"That I did, Gâteloup! When this silly woman decided to be bad, she fell in with several sorcerers and witches. One appeared to teach her the most, until she bored of his attentions. A German named Hertz Ende..."

CHAPTER XXXVII

Sylvia Dardi immediately rolled to her left, barely avoiding a thrown candlestick. The metal cracked against the wall, sending shards of wax across the floor.

The Countessa Angelina stepped over Franz Karnstein's fallen body, her horrific tongue lashing the air as she strode towards Sylvia's fallen form.

"Blood," she rasped, her voice sounding as if it came from the depths of that terrible, fang-filled throat.

Sylvia looked around, searching for her missing sword. The weapon wasn't visible, and she didn't have any time to look. Grabbing the candlestick, she threw the dented item at the spike-filled tongue, then crawled towards the splintered table. The edge of the terrible tongue sliced across her leg, brushing across her calf, causing her to wince in pain. Having been cut by swords in the past, Sylvia knew she was bleeding and would have a hard time moving with anything close to alacrity.

Across the room, Karnstein bit back a yell of pain as the tiny barbs slid deeper into his hand and arm. Surprisingly, there was no blood flowing from the dozens of tiny wounds. It felt almost as if the needle-shaped teeth were slowly consuming the precious *vitae* as it leaked from his body.

With infinite care and precise motions, Anton's terrible tongue drew Karnstein towards his fang-filled maw. The gaping, leech-shaped face shimmied and shook as a bestial, demoniac moan of ecstasy emerged from the horrific exposed throat. The barbs sunk a little deeper and a very human sounding giggle filled the air. The pain increased and Franz found his body slowly, inexorably, weakening with each passing second.

Nearby, Sylvia pushed herself up to her knees, watching her vampiric enemy while scanning with the corner of her eye for her sword. She spotted the familiar blade under the tossed table and threw herself towards the weapon. The blood-stained spot where she had just knelt exploded in a wave of wooden splinters as the horrific tongue lashed at her location. With a serpentine grace, Angelica recoiled her favored weapon and moved to face Sylvia.

"I shall feast on your flesh!" she screamed, pulling her head back to strike.

Snatching up her small sword and lunging at the same time, Sylvia pierced the heart of the being known as Countessa Angelica.

The vampire shrieked in agony, a sound cut off as the small sword sliced through her brain.

"Sorry," Sylvia replied as the vampire collapsed, "I am spoken for already."

Karnstein pulled back on the tongue, feeling a wave of nausea fill his body. But the maneuver did provide him with a precious moment, allowing him to reach into his jacket. Removing a tiny stone bottle, he pulled the stopper free with his teeth. Then, spitting out the stopper, he said:

"*In nomine Patris, et Filii, et Spiritus Sancti. Amen!*"

He poured a clear liquid across the taut tongue. He and Sylvia were better prepared now, carrying tiny bottles of blessed water from the Cathedral of Naples, in case they did meet a vampire.

The effect was instantaneous and appalling to witness. The elongated spiny muscle turned black and started to smoke and crack as if a fire was burning the offending object from within. The vampire Anton screeched and wailed as the inhuman organ crumbled into black soot, falling to the floor in a small heap. He turned to run, his movements a shambling, stumbling, simian lope rather than a human gait.

Karnstein kicked a foot out, catching the retreating vampire behind the knee and causing the creature to fall face first upon the wooden floor. In an instant, he leaped on the vampire's exposed back and drew his dagger. Without a word, the Exorcist plunged the blade deep into the vampire's neck, pinning the monster to the floor. With two hands, he pushed a little harder, ensuring the knife sliced deep into the wood.

"*Idiota!* That will not kill the vampire!" Sylvia said, pausing to rip a length of cloth from Anton's pant leg as a temporary bandage.

"I don't want to kill this thing. And stop calling me an idiot," Karnstein replied, taking her sword and repeating the actions, this time near the lower back.

"Then stop acting like one! What are you doing? If you say torturing this pathetic, fallen thing, I shall grow angry with you, Franz Karnstein!" Sylvia warned, dropping into the Countessa's chair and carefully cleaning her wound with a matching bottle of holy water.

"Torture? No, I do not torture. I need a vampire so that I can attempt to discover the power that created such creatures," Karnstein replied, pulling out his plain metal crucifix.

He whispered a quick prayer, made the sign of the cross and returned the object to his shirt.

"How do you plan to discover such knowledge?" Sylvia asked as she completed the bandaging of her leg.

"I have my ways. Please, do not speak until I am done. No sounds."

Karnstein closed his eyes. He went still, his breathing so shallow that it appeared almost suspended in that time. Then, slowly, his eyes opened. They glowed with a silver light, an inner luminosity that appeared to pierce the back of the fallen, helpless vampire. He began to speak, his voice deeper and echoing with inhuman depths that could not be comprehended. The words sounded like gibberish, but there was a definite pattern to the syllables.

"*Anshargal Ati Me Peta Babka Nisme Annu Isten! Usmi Annu Isten Ina Akhkharu Ma Ina Maskim Xul, Ina Kashshaptu, Ina Lilit, Su'ati Mursu In Matum!*"

A silver sigil appeared before his body. For a brief instant, a five-pointed star in a circle, surrounded by odd ancient appearing characters, pulsed before Karnstein's body.

Within five seconds, the eldritch image grew brighter and dropped like a falling star into the back of the vampire Anton.

Anton wailed softly and fell silent as the Exorcist's pulsing eyes stared about the room without appearing to see anything. His head stopped swiveling, focusing a few feet above Sylvia's head. His entire body stiffened and his energized eyes appeared to open even wider and his mouth dropped in shock.

"Oh dear Lord above," Karnstein whispered, his face losing all color.

"What?" Sylvia asked, ignoring his previous warning of silence. "What are you seeing?"

"The end of everything…" Karnstein replied, still staring above her head. "No… no… Stay back… no…no…!"

CHAPTER XXXVIII

"Answer me this, Gâteloup: why do all dark magical types choose to live in abandoned churches?" Dardi asked as he opened the lock with a set of metal wires. "There is no truth in the notion that this provides them a closer connection to the Devil."

"I am sure it is part of their desire to prove they are truly demonic to their wealthier patrons," replied Séverin, shrugging. "My pupil insists it is because such men and women behave like spoiled children, determined to prove their naughtiness."

The lock opened with a low snap and Dardi put away his tools while drawing his sword.

"I believe you both are correct. Charlatans who wish to prove they are bad, evil people."

Séverin didn't reply; he merely pushed the door open and peered inside. The church was a dilapidated ruin, a wooden box in need of months of repair work, or a tear down followed by a new structure. As the sunlight slowly flowed through the door into the chamber, the sounds of scurrying feet drifted in their direction. The sound was familiar: mice, rats, and cockroaches. The red roaches of Naples were notorious for their massive size and bold behavior—a pest rivaling that of the rats in the poorer parts of the city. Once, during a house fire, Séverin had watched in horror and disgust as a veritable crimson tide of insects flowed from the depths of the inferno, seeking new vistas to infest.

Sniffing the air, Séverin stated:

"Not abandoned. The air is too fresh."

"Yet, there is some dust on the mockery of an altar," Dardi nodded, frowning. "The melted candles look as if something gnawed on them recently."

Séverin walked across the room, scanning the chamber. The walls were free of any adornments, with even the stained glass windows replaced by cheap wooden planks that appeared warped and crumbling from the elements. An upside down cross rest against a nearby wall, the image of Jesus Christ stained with dried blood, filthy and even more dust.

"Abandoned for ceremonial use, I believe. However, I believe the owner still makes use of the building," he remarked as he knelt and picked up a metal goblet.

The cup was painted gold and adorned with gaudy false jewels that sparkled in the sunlight. The tip of the vessel and the interior appeared covered with a dried brown substance whose stench caused him to recoil in revulsion.

"Blood," Séverin stated, dropping the offending article back on the altar. "Probably not human. It smelled like spoiled animal blood of some type."

"Huh. Typical," Dardi sneered, nodding towards an open door that led to the sacristy.

The sacristy had been converted into a small bedroom, with a small plank bed, an old bureau, and a simple table, with a matching stool. Séverin poked through the dresser, finding a collection of old and new clothes—nothing of interest. The furniture was simple, possessing no space for hiding spots and looked similar to dozens of others he had seen over the years. Just to be safe, he felt behind the backing near the wall, but discovering nothing.

"Ah, here we find something interesting," Dardi said, looking beneath the bed.

With a quick shove, he pushed the cot aside and pointed at the ring set into the floor.

"A basement—all churches have a basement. It is where they hid anything thieves may wish to steal."

Without waiting for a response, Dardi pulled open the trap door, revealing a stone staircase. Walking back into the church, he returned with the partially melted, gnawed candle which he lit a moment later. Sword in hand, he headed down, Séverin a few steps behind him.

The minute Dardi's foot touched the soft dirt that made up the basement floor, the weeping began. The sound was soft, but growing in intensity and volume with each passing second.

"A woman," Dardi whispered.

He turned in a slow circle with the candle. The low light revealed a heavy wooden door, held in place by a rust-pitted iron bolt. With a frown and a slow nod from Séverin, he seized the metal and pulled open the door.

A woman, her thin frame barely covered by a shapeless gray pile of rags, cowered back from the light. She whimpered and seemed to shrink away, pressing herself against the stone wall.

"No, please! No more! Please let me go! I won't tell!" she wailed, her voice a rough, husky tone.

"We are not here to hurt you, Signorina," Dardi said, stepping into the room and sheathing his sword.

The girl lifted her face slight, one dark eye visible beneath her veil of filthy, mud colored hair. She held up a pair of manacled wrists attached to a chain on the wall.

"You will free me? Will you?" she asked.

"Of course!"

Dardi produced his lock picks while examining the metal binding. Séverin exploded forward, grabbing his smaller friend by the collar and pulling him backwards.

"Barto! No!" he shouted.

Dardi stumbled and nearly dropped his picks, his deft fingers snatching them from the air before they dropped. He looked quizzically at his fellow swordmaster, but held his tongue. Séverin pulled Dardi back another step.

"Barto, her chains never made a sound… and her crying did not start until you were nearby."

"No!" the girl shrieked, her voice rising and echoing in the small space. "Free me! Free me now!"

Séverin reached into a pouch at his belt and scooped out an item. He threw a fine mist of powder at the cowering woman and said:

"I pray I am wrong."

The woman screamed and rose up, thrashing the air madly. The chains on her wrists never made a sound and her hands turned black from the powder. The air roiled, as if a tiny tornado had appeared in the small basement room, tossing the powder aside and throwing a layer of dust into the air.

"Free me, free me, free me, free me, free me, free me, free me!" she howled, her voice becoming rougher and less human with each passing second.

"What did you throw at that woman?" Dardi asked, pocketing his picks and redrawing his sword.

"Salt," Séverin said, his face set in stone. "And that is no woman. That is a ghost—one who seeks to consume our souls!"

The spectral woman stepped their direction, the cloud of her hair parting, revealing a face ravaged by disease and the putrescence that comes after death. Her one good eye stared in their direction while her curtain of hair parted and unveiled the other eye was little more than a tattered, scarred ruin. Her feet never touched the ground as she slowly floated towards them, her words no longer recognizable as speech.

"Interesting," Dardi said, stepping out of the room and slamming the door shut. "How do you kill a ghost?"

Séverin shook his head as they ran up the stairs. He glanced over his shoulder in time to see the ghost woman's ethereal form slither through the time-ravaged door. Her emaciated hands appeared to be bones stretched over mottled skin and her fingers looked as sharp as daggers. The human mask they had viewed seconds earlier was slipping away with each passing second. Soon this creature would resemble a nightmare given form, the living embodiment of fear and rage.

"That is the difficulty, Barto," Séverin replied, slamming the trap door closed and shoving the bed back in place. "You cannot kill a ghost since they are already dead."

Dardi ran for the door as a mist floated through the bed, beginning to form into something approaching human shape.

"The only exorcism I know," said Dardi, "will take eight hours to complete. I doubt she will accommodate us and wait so long."

"Possibly not," Séverin replied.

He looked to the partially open door. He cursed inwardly at the twilight he viewed through the gap. The only other way he knew to destroy a ghost was to force the creature into the sunlight. Sadly, that was not an option any longer.

The door suddenly slammed shut and a moan of anger and pain rose up, shaking the abandoned church to the very rafters.

Séverin and Dardi whirled, spotting the skeletal wraith, the tendrils of her hair floating like an inky curtain about her cadaverous countenance. Her ruined lips peeled back, exposing sharp, twisted, black teeth in a mouth too big for a human head. A loud shriek filled the air, emerging from the ghost as she extended her hands and floated their direction.

"Time for one of your plans, Gâteloup. What shall we do?" Dardi asked, tugging vainly at the door.

"I was hoping you would tell me," Séverin said as the air around them dropped several degrees and the walls started to shake. "I'm open to suggestions…"

CHAPTER XXXIX

Franz Karnstein stared up; the twisted skein of life unveiled before his naked eyes. It was difficult to view the world in this manner—man was not meant to see such images. The weight of the world pressed down on him, the sheer overwhelming image of life in this world could tax even the greatest mind. Yet he had to press on and examine this vampire-learn the creature's terrible secrets if possible.

This was only the third time he had performed such a ritual since he had taken on his role in the world. He had been warned against such actions by his teacher, the most knowledgeable person he had ever known.

"Vampires," his teacher had intoned, "are many, varied creatures. Many are merely undead shells inhabited by a minor demonic being. They take on the mind and some of the personality of their host. Slowly they become more bestial and only humans with very strong personalities can refrain from becoming little more than appetites with a semi-human face. The point I make is, staring into such evil is an assault on your mind, body, and soul. You, of course, remember your vampiric ancestor Mircalla?"

Karnstein, then still in his teens, hadn't hid his loathing and bitterness.

"The monster who killed my Vordenburg family as well as my parents? Yes, that is a creature I will not forget until my dying day."

"Had you viewed her lovely face through true eyes, your loathing would have overwhelmed your unprotected mind. To view such evil is a risk that you might not survive with your mind intact. The reason why so many practitioners of witchcraft go mad is because they view evil in its purest form for too long. Their minds shatter and they become lost in destructive dreams."

Despite this warning, Karnstein had viewed a vampire warlock, a graduate of the evil school of magic known as the Scholomance. The result was as his teacher had predicted—disgust and horror, a feeling that he was drowning in a sea of corpses caused by that evil creature. He had ended the vampire's undead life an instant later, stabbing him through the heart with a wooden stake and destroying the body with fire.

The second time was a sadder affair, a desperate desire to save someone special. He had vainly hoped to be wrong, that she had been spared when he had executed the lead vampire of the region. The old tales said that if you killed the main vampire, all of the newly-transformed would return to being human. Like many legends, that story was a fantasy, wishful thinking on the part of someone who had hoped to save their fallen loved one. Karnstein had staked the first woman he had ever loved that day, vowing to never again look into the true inner nature of a vampire.

Until this day—until he and Sylvia faced monstrosities with segmented heads full of fangs. The sheer inhumanity of these creatures had shocked him to his core, shaken his spirit. Though he never would have admitted it, especially to Sylvia, these demoniac beings had appalled him in ways he didn't think possible. Karnstein had faced fiends from Hell with less fear than he had felt from these unusual vampires.

For that reason alone, because no fighter on the side of evil should allow terror to rule their choice, Karnstein had chosen to use his inner power once again. The Sumerian phrases tripped off his tongue as easily as his native German, invoking that which lay hidden within his soul. The nature of this power was fully known only to himself, with His Holiness the Supreme Pontiff comprehending some of the implications.

Which was why he had flinched when he had stared at the pinned form of the vampire named Anton. Unlike his previous viewings of vampires, this undead being was not inhabited by a demon or other such entity. Instead, a tendril of power flowed into the creature, granting a form of inhuman life to its body. The mind was a barely functional object, a trace of the previous inhabitant of this shell. Some of the personality and memories remained, though both could be consumed in an instant by the dark force allowing this artificial form of life.

Concentrating on the ebon strand of energy, Karnstein immediately felt a wave of cold fear fill his mind and body. Though he had beheld the very fabric of unlife that was a demon from Hell, he had never perceived a force as terrible as this thread of power. The essence was an abhorrent, corrupting force, a negative energy in opposition to all life. This was an eldritch transgression, a terrible assault on the very fabric of the universe... and this was a mere filament emerging from a greater power...

Following the thread from the vampire, he watched as its power interlocked with other similar fibers in the great skein of life. The corrupt energy followed a long path, though short in actual physical distance, towards a source deep within the depths of the Earth. There, the master of this vampire squatted like a monstrous massive, bloated, demoniac beast. This creature was pure horror, an organism created by a mad mind exhibiting no characteristic of life in this universe.

The being observed Karnstein, spotted his radiant living form whose makeup was the opposing force to the contaminated disease that was the fiend. Yet, for all the power he possessed, Karnstein was a minuscule wisp of silver energy. He felt like a tiny, flickering candle attempting to plunge the very depths of the abyssal, stygian cosmic void. That was when tendrils of plutonian power flowed through the strand connected to Anton, seeking to envelop the Exorcist. He recoiled in terror, the loathing and terror this demon inspired causing his abilities to weaken and fail. There was no escape, no means of fleeing this malignant horror,

"Oh dear Lord above," Karnstein whispered, his face losing all color.

He spotted the secret this creature was seeking to conceal. It planned on spreading its contaminating influence throughout the whole world. All that would remain would be darkness, an entire world of diseased unlife. Every form of life on Earth would be corrupted, from the humans to the birds in the sky, to the insects whose lifespans are measured in mere hours. All would be consumed and become an extension of this ancient inhuman horror.

"What?" Sylvia's voice floated through the depths, an echo in his ears.

"The end of everything..." Franz said, seeing the terrible, ebon power pressing towards him, seeking to infect him and turn him into another of these puppets that believed they were vampires. No... no... Stay back... no...no...!"

Then the thread connected to Anton vanished and there was a roar of fury that shook the ethereal plane. Throughout the whole world, every form of life, from human to single-cell organisms, unseen and unknown to all, experienced an instant of horror and disgust. The experience took less than a heartbeat; it was a flash that was ignored by all beings a second later. Yet a few throughout the world knew something terrible and fiendish was roused and enraged at being thwarted.

Karnstein fell backwards, his vision clearing, his body shaking like a leaf in a hurricane. He stared about the room with eyes that were unable to focus—a face wild with undisguised terror. A rank odor filled the air and his head swiveled with mad motions, resembling a puppet whose master was unable to control the myriad strings.

Suddenly, Sylvia squatted across his legs, pinning him in place. Her calloused hands seized his face, her powerful arms struggling to defy his attempts at moving away. She moved her face left, right, up and down, attempting to stay in the crazily dancing eyes that seemed to be moving independently.

"Franz! Franz Karnstein! Look at me! Look at me now!" she said, repeating herself as sweat pooled across her face and arms.

Minutes passed, but finally she was able to catch both eyes and forced them to keep her own face in view. Karnstein's body slowed, the convulsions ceasing, his eyes coming into focus. A few minutes later, he slumped, his body unable to move.

"Franz? Do you hear me?" Sylvia asked, sighing and grateful to see life in those exhausted, pale eyes.

"Yes, Sylvia. Did you... how did you...?" Karnstein seemed unable to fully form sentences as his shattered mind slowly reassembled.

"Stop whatever you viewed? I assumed it had something to do with the vampire we captured. Since you were being attacked, I destroyed the vampire. Did it work?" Sylvia asked, dropping her hands to his shoulders.

"Yes," Karnstein replied, closing his eyes and attempting to rebuild his mental defenses. "That may be the only reason I'm not infected and one of those... things... thank you..."

Sylvia rolled her eyes and smiled.

"Shut up, you great *idiota*."

The corner of Franz Karnstein's mouth lifted in a partial smile.

"Stop calling me an idiot."

"Then stop acting like one," Sylvia replied.

They hugged each other tightly. They stayed in that position for several minutes before she added:

"Can we continue this discussion elsewhere? We are currently sitting in a growing pool of melting vampire and the stench is worse than a charnel house."

Karnstein hiccupped, bordering on either laughing maniacally or weeping. Sylvia's arms tightened around him- providing much needed comforting support and the near fit subsided as quickly as it had arrived. He nodded and they rose, their clothing torn, tattered, and stained by the liquid remains of Anton.

"They're not really vampires," he said, allowing her to lead him out of the room and through the doorway from which Angelica had emerged earlier. This was a kitchen, with an unused wood burning stove and a pump for fresh water. A second open door revealed a small bedroom with piles of male and female clothing.

"We will talk of vampires and demons and such later. First, you will go outside and find the wood pile. Get enough wood for the rest of the day and stack it near the stove. I will fill a pot of water and find us suitable clothes to leave here when night falls. We must be clean and find a way to look presentable."

"But…" Karnstein started to say, but he was cut off by a sharp look from Sylvia.

"*Idiota*! You are wasting time and we are covered in that contamination! Go!"

Sylvia pointed a finger at the doorway leading to the back. Karnstein knew when he couldn't win a battle, he merely said, "Stop calling me an idiot," and left.

"Then stop acting like one," Sylvia replied, watching him as he left.

She then smiled to herself, remembering the words of her aunt whose name she shared. The older woman, a former agent for the Pope and the first teacher of Jean-Pierre Séverin, had instructed Sylvia privately when she had coaxed the young girl out of the nunnery.

"You must seek a husband who is strong, dangerous, and good. You will grow bored with anything else. A weakling who allows you to win every battle will bore you to death—or worse, into the arms of a pretty, but unsuitable fool of a man. One who fights back is better, though not one who argues day and night. My third husband was a clerk of the law who debated day and night. By the time a werewolf ate his face, I was almost grateful he was no longer talking."

"That sound quite impossible," Sylvia, then an astonishingly pretty, if argumentative, teenager had replied, frowning and reconsidering the nunnery again.

"Not so, it is merely difficult. Being selective might have spared me five incompatible *idiotas*," explained Aunt Sylvia. "I married in fits of insanity. The final test is to see if they can lose gracefully. When you are speaking sense and they know to give you your way this time, even though they fight you other moments, then you have the right man. I found him once, but he chose to marry a slip of a French girl and run away to Africa. If you find such a one, do not let him go."

Aunt Sylvia had regret in her eyes as she remembered her lost love.

Watching Karnstein leave and search for the wood pile, Sylvia nodded and started to search through the discarded clothing. Yes, the young Austrian baron would be the right choice for a husband. She'd already managed to break through his armor and see his true self. Now to make him realize his own feelings... the most frightening part for her...

CHAPTER XL

Nosos screamed and fell to the hard packed earth beneath her feet. Something had cut her off, destroying two more of her vessels! An ancient and terrible power, one in total opposition to herself and the Tenebrae, stood between Nosos and total victory. That power was said to be lost in time; yet she had just seen the man, viewed his spirit and... almost consumed him...

"No!" she whispered emphatically.

Her earlier assessment was wrong, far too hasty a reaction. That One stood against her and her kind. Yet, he was weak, new to his inner force. He might be dangerous to the possessed and the lesser creatures of the dark. To them, he had to be a terror as great as any they had encountered. But Nosos knew she had been a mere moment away from sending her power into his spirit and snuffing him out forever. That man would have become another receptacle for her power—and still would! Just like those pathetic creatures who toiled digging day and night beneath her feet.

"You bellowed, mighty mistress?" Sinis asked, bowing and scraping before her prone form.

"Two of my creatures were destroyed—the false spiritualists calling themselves Countessa Angelica and Anton," Nosos replied, pushing herself up into a sitting position.

"Their job was minor, great queen," said Sinis, frowning. "They were to start fires. We can find others for such duties."

"It is not the loss of their service that disturbs me, pathetic one. Their nightly feedings served me, helped me regain much of who I once was before I slept," Nosos admitted. "Once I was a power that shook the fabric of all creation. Now I am little more than a shell of my former self."

Sinis looked confused, forgetting his momentary toadying.

"That cannot be true! You have a plan to control all of the kingdom. You told me so yourself!"

Nosos laughed, a terrible evil sound filled with mockery and disgust.

"I lied, fool! I slept for centuries; I'm little more than a pile of dust and bones. When a simpleton from the Scholomance found a means of reviving me, I fed. But do you imagine that a few hundred lives are enough to grant me my true power back? With each alembic I fill, I grow stronger and become closer to the true Nosos who was once feared throughout the Earth."

"Then why do you have your vampires digging day and night, finding old tunnels?" Sinis asked, watching his mistress with open confusion.

"Who am I, Sinis? Who am I truly? Not the nonsensical titles given to me by the slaves below us and yourself. Who am I?" Nosos asked, tapping her raw chest without a finger.

"You are Nosos of the Tenebrae, daughter of Nyx, the embodiment of darkness, and of her mate Erebus, a member of the dark fates whom the Greek called the Keres. You are Nosos the Corruptor," Sinis replied, remembering words of Hesiod's Theogony.

"Partly right, partly wrong," Nosos said, chuckling. "I am Nosos of the Tenebrae and we were also called the Keres by some in the world. My mother never used the name Nyx. That word, like that of Erebus, are titles, not identities. My mother's name was Pandora, and I do not know who fathered myself and my brothers and sisters."

"Pandora? Who released evil into the world by opening a magic box?" Sinis asked.

Nosos stared at Sinis for a moment and then shrieked with laughter for several minutes. Finally, she subsided and said:

"Is that the tale mankind tells? Pandora's box of evil? Oh my, humanity is an endless joy to witness!"

"I don't understand, mistress. What do you mean?" asked Sinis, taking a step back, frightened by the ancient being's reaction.

"Pandora's box, Sinis? Pandora's box? The term is a euphemism, wretch. The only box of evil is the one between her legs! She bore all of us, the entire Tenebrae. Each of us were a different horror to visit upon the Earth. And now, we come to where you were quite wrong. You called me, Nosos the Corruptor, didn't you?"

"Yes, mistress," Sinis answered, bowing before her again.

"The title Corruptor is a misinterpretation of my true self. Corruption emerges from the Latin word *corruptus*, meaning blight. Do you know what a blight is, my pathetic little worm?"

"A plague?" Sinis whispered, remembering the tales of the Black Death destroying nearly all life in the world.

Nosos laughed again and clapped her hands.

"Yes, worm. Disease! For that is my power. Those pathetic pretty toys below are not vampires. They, and the eight I lost, are extensions of my will, of my power, nothing more. I play with them and cast them aside in favor of the next toy."

"None matter?" Sinis asked, his voice hollow.

"Fortuna is my handmaiden, possibly Giorgia too, as her replacement. You are my slave. The others are only vessels for my power. You may as well ask if one cares about a strand of hair or a fingernail," Nosos explained, staring at the small tunnel dug by the hardened hands of her vampiric servants.

"Then why do you not create more, mistress? If they make you stronger, I should think you would wish to infect an army of such humans," Sinis asked, seeing this as a fairly obvious question.

"For the same reason I only saved Fortuna out of her entire dark coven—few humans are capable of becoming one of my true followers. You would not, but you are the perfect slave. You will stay at my side forever, as I promised. As shall

Fortuna. This is why the loss of eight in the last few days enrages me."

Nosos reached out to one of her vessels operating in Naples. He would be of some use for now. Closing her eyes, she spoke to his mind, her instructions being a means of confronting the new danger threatening her plans.

"Mistress, I have something else to report. The vampires below crave blood and lives. They are feeding on rats. Shall I bring them humans to consume?" Sinis asked, glancing down the hole and shuddering.

"No," Nosos said, coming out of her brief trance. "Let them feast on as many rats as they can catch."

"I only mention their feeding because the rat blood and meat... it is changing them..." Sinis stammered, glancing again at the hole and looking ill.

Nosos smiled, her black fangs too massive for her human shaped mouth.

"I know, my pathetic little insect. That was my plan since you showed me the tunnels beneath Naples. Now, go and prepare my coach. I wish to sleep in a human bed and Giorgia awaits me in her family home."

Sinis knelt and kissed his mistress's feet, loping away at a veritable run. He still didn't know why Nosos had the undead creatures digging more tunnels beneath Naples, but he would find out. Though his mistress had changed him using her dark powers, she hadn't removed his curiosity and self-interest.

CHAPTER XLI

"I have an idea!" Dardi whispered, edging away from Séverin. "Can you keep the ghost's attention for several minutes? I have a notion that might send it back to the grave forever!"

"I suppose I have no choice," Jean-Pierre Séverin replied, moving away from the door.

He was on an opposite course from Dardi, one that would take him closer to the ravening specter. As he hoped, the ghost's empty eye sockets swiveled in his direction. Dardi ducked behind a small wooden pillar, dropping low to avoid easy detection. The ghost screeched again and launched its misty form towards the fleeing Séverin. The skeletal form appeared even larger, though less substantial, as the ethereal being slid through the abandoned altar and reached for the swordmaster's heart.

That was when an idea came to Séverin, one from the earliest days of his training under Kronos and his academic partner, a hunchback named Grost, who was one of the great experts in the field of vampires and the undead. One of his lessons, all but forgotten by Séverin until this moment, was upon the subject of ghosts and other dead beings.

"Ghosts," Grost had said as he lifted a glass flask and examined the contents, "are not undead. They are fully dead. Which means the methods we use of combating the undead are rendered useless, no?"

A young Séverin hadn't liked that idea and shaken his head.

"There must be some means of destroying a spirit. They're monsters!"

Grost looked over his spectacles, his wise eyes almost sad as he viewed his student.

"Can you destroy anger? Can you destroy betrayal?"

Séverin looked confused, his flow of anger momentarily checked.

"What does that mean, Professor?"

"You have so much to learn, young Jean-Pierre," sighed Grost. "I think you believe a specter is the soul of a dead human dwelling on Earth?"

Séverin nodded, unsurprised by his teacher's perspicacity. For all his twisted body, Professor Hieronymus Grost was one of the wisest, kindest, men one could ever meet. Grost shook his head again, his face sad.

"That is a mistake, young man. The soul is not an item one can abandon like a dropped coin. That which the Lord gave to all living beings heads either to Paradise or the Pit of Eternal Darkness. Though there is some belief in a stopping place between called Purgatory... In truth, I believe that is but a fictional construct by romantic writers. The soul does not wander about the land like a tinker seeking knives to sharpen."

Séverin frowned, understanding the point.

"Then what is a ghost? Are they real?"

"To answer your second question first, yes, they are truly real. As to what is the substance of a specter? I have theories, nothing further. In my experience, a ghost is a trace of a person left behind because of some tragic event. Strong emotions are a form of power—many warlocks seek the fear and pain of their victims as a force for their evil enchantments. My theory, which is shared by many eminent scholars, is that this state of extreme energy releases a tiny sliver of the self into to ether. This echo of that dead person either dissipates or remains and gains energy of a similar dark nature."

Séverin inhaled slowly and thought for a moment.

"Then to confront a ghost is like fighting pure anger," he said, "or fear, or sadness? Then nothing could stop them if they are attacking..."

"Do not be so hasty or extreme, Jean-Pierre," replied Grost, shaking his head. "A ghost is a creature of energy and energy can be dispersed. Salt absorbs their essence and blessed objects burn them. The sun dispels their power and, according to a Danish monster-hunter I know, cold iron is as lethal as a sword. An exorcism will work in the same manner as for a demon. The difficulty is that none of these solutions demonstrate God's forgiveness, and they are unpalatable. A kinder method is always a better choice, though I know not what method that would be, sadly. Did not the Bible tell us *Judge not, and you shall not be judged. Condemn not, and you shall not be condemned. Forgive, and you will be forgiven*?"

Now, in the present day, Séverin's dire situation did give him a notion regarding the ghost. If successful, this may provide his late teacher's soul with a bit of solace. If it failed, he would be dead and possibly a ghost haunting this ruined church along with this sad woman.

As Dardi ducked into sacristy, Séverin pulled out a bit of salt and tossed it at the ghost while secretly apologizing under his breath. The ghost shrieked and thrashed as black spots covered the creature's hands and skull. Séverin then pulled out his flask of blessed water and walked in a circle around the ghost. Pouring the water, he said a brief prayer and hoped this would work. He then stepped back and waited as the specter focused on him once again. The creature moaned and floated forward, stopping when its misty form touched the holy water.

"Nonononononononono!" it screamed, its last vestiges of humanity dropping away as the frustration rose.

"I'm sorry," Séverin said and sat down on the floor. "You deserve better treatment than I gave you this day."

The ghost screamed and raged, the murky haze flowing and abutting the circle of blessed fluids and receiving the eerie burns. The inhuman countenance stared at Séverin and howled, the wood beneath the creature's unseen feet cracking.

"I'm sorry," Séverin repeated. "I wish I could help you get some peace. I would even help you get revenge, if that is what you seek."

"Free me! Free me! Free me! Free me! Free me!" the specter cried and moaned as it struck the holy water barrier.

"You are free, Mademoiselle. You no longer can be hurt. Who did this to you? Who hurt you?" Séverin asked again, hoping he could reach this trace of a dead woman.

"You killed me! Youyouyouyouyouyouyouyouyou youyou!" the ghost continued to scrape at the invisible barrier, receiving black marks each time.

"No, I did not," Séverin said, shaking his head slowly. "You never saw me before I opened the door. I am sorry you were treated terribly. Who hurt you?"

The ghost appeared to freeze, the empty sockets focusing on Jean-Pierre Séverin's face.

"You...you...are sorry?" it said.

Séverin straightened and nodded.

"If you tell me your name, I will pray for you and light a candle for you each time I visit a church."

The ghost floated in place, no sounds emerging from the ruined lips. Dardi appeared at the far end of the room, his face full of delight. He stopped in the doorway, raising a piece of metal in his hands. The item was a rusted iron door bolt from the basement door, an item that might injure or even destroy the ghost. But Séverin did not wish that, unless he failed. Raising his hand, he sent a subtle signal to his old friend, and again addressed the ghost:

"You were imprisoned and murdered. Who did this to you? Please, I want to help you."

"I... was... Alessia," was the whispering reply, and the face began to resume a normal shape. "Alessia... Ricci... I... I... men... used me... money... food..."

"I am sorry you had such a difficult life, Alessia Ricci," said Séverin, bowing his head. "I promise you I shall pray for you every night and light a candle in your name. Who murdered you? I will make them pay for their crimes against you in life."

The ghost stared at him for several minutes, her semi-human face blank and unmoving. The spectral body was partially visible now, but no emotional response was evident. That was when Séverin decided on a new course of action—a risky proposition at best. Standing, he stepped over to the circle and scuffed out the line of liquid. Kicking over a layer of dust, he stepped back and opened his arms.

"There," he said. "I do not hold you against your will. If you decide to kill me, I shall not fight you, Alessia Ricci. I only hope you will spare my life so that I may pray for your deliverance and grant you peace."

The ghost floated mere inches away, her nearly human face still unmoving and spectral. Finally, she spoke, her words sounding closer to human speech for the first time since he first viewed her in the basement:

"Her name was Nosos... she... she... hurt me... make her pay... pray for me..."

The ghost of Alessia Ricci slowly turned insubstantial, fading away into nothingness. In less than a minute, nothing remained, no trace of the specter other than the twisted splinters of the floor where the inhuman being once stood.

"Gâteloup, what did you do?" Dardi asked, tossing the shaft of rusted metal over his shoulder. '

It struck with a loud clatter, which the Neapolitan swordmaster ignored. Séverin made the sign of the cross and replied:

"I provided peace to the poor, murdered woman. It is a theory one of my teachers held about ghosts. He wished a kinder method of dealing with such victims. Come, I need to visit a church and fulfill a promise. I shall explain as we walk..."

CHAPTER XLII

"Now," Sylvia said as she straightened Karnstein's collar, "you promised to answer my questions."

The Exorcist frowned and shook his head.

"I do not believe I promised such. I don't think that was ever discussed."

Sylvia snorted and rolled her eyes.

"Then your memory is faulty. What language did you speak? I speak Italian, French, Latin, English, Hebrew, and Arabic. Nothing you said sounded like any of those speech."

Karnstein blinked, surprised by her statement.

"Who taught you so many languages?"

Sylvia smiled and raised her hands.

"Who else? My father and my aunt. How many do you speak?"

"Many," Karnstein replied, but looked down. "I was forced to learn them when I was growing up."

"And which did you used when you knelt over Anton?" Sylvia asked, raising an eyebrow.

Karnstein sighed, already sensing another defeat. Sylvia possessed an annoying ability to see through his methods of avoiding a conversation.

"Sumerian. It is the oldest language in the world."

"Which you used to cast a magic spell," Sylvia replied, frowning.

Karnstein shook his head, having had this discussion with others in the past.

"No, not magic. I am skilled in an ancient form of exorcism. The Pope would not allow a wizard to serve in the holy orders, even a lesser one."

"I think you are telling me only a small part of the truth," said Sylvia, her eyes narrowing. "For now, I will allow that to pass, but we shall return to this subject in the future. I want to know what you viewed when your eyes glowed silver? No lies! Your mind almost broke and I must know what we face."

Karnstein shuddered and closed his eyes. He performed a quick meditative exercise based on the Spiritual Exercises of Ignatius of Loyola. The Saint, a former soldier, understood the difficulties of outside forces and how they can affect one's actions. Saint Ignatius wrote that his Exercises, *have as their purpose the conquest of self and the regulation of one's life in such a way that no decision is made under the influence of any inordinate attachment.*

Opening his eyes, Karnstein nodded and knew he was in better control of his mind and body. Somehow, he was holding Sylvia's hand tightly, though that didn't feel strange. Inhaling and exhaling slowly, he said:

"When I look… though looking is not the right word… when I see the world that way, I see the truth of all life. It is like seeing the inner person… but not… I'm sorry, I do not know how to explain what I see…"

"You are doing well enough," Sylvia said, smiling. "Please, continue and I shall ask questions for what does not make sense."

Karnstein nodded, but felt troubled inside. His Holiness and Cardinal Della Genga suggested in the strongest terms that he not expose anyone to his "abilities".

I may be exposing Sylvia to a whole world of danger. But wait! She's already fought monsters, he thought and decided to tell what he could to this impressive woman. She was also so very pretty…

"When I looked at Anton, he was just the same as the undead woman in the prison. There was the same strand of dark power flowing into him and that walking dead woman in the prison. The power is what kept them… sorry the word *alive* does not fit…" he explained, looking at Sylvia and feeling a little foolish.

"Animated?" she suggested.

"Yes, thank you," said Karnstein, nodding. "The dark energy keeps them animated. The walking dead woman was mindless, a bare thread a power. Anton's power was easier to follow… that was when I saw it… and it saw me… it was horrible… like gazing into a void… it was so evil, worse than any demon… I felt stained… dirty… it saw me and then… and then…"

Without realizing it, Karnstein started to shake, his whole body shivering, though not from fear. This was the shudder of revulsion one experiences in the face of the truly demoniac beings that exist beyond the knowledge of mortal man. He had faced demons straight from the sulphur-scented depths of Hell, vampires whose unholy appetite caused the deaths of legions, and even greater horrors. Yet this creature, this profane curse on all life, filled Franz Karnstein with a deeper loathing than any fiend he had fought in his days. Sylvia leaned her shoulder against his side and entwined her fingers in his other hand.

"It came for you?" she asked.

Karnstein nodded quickly, eyes downcast.

"I tried to stop it… but it was like trying to push back the ocean… an ocean of pain…"

"You fought demons before? Possessed men and women?" Sylvia asked, leaning back slightly so their eyes met.

"Yes," Karnstein replied, his shivering slowly ceasing as he focused on a different topic. "I exorcised my first one when I was thirteen."

"With your ancient power?" Sylvia asked, raising an eyebrow.

"Yes. If I have a few seconds time to concentrate, I can send them back to Perdition in seconds."

"And every one of them was in a body? A living or a dead body?" Sylvia asked, smiling slightly.

Looking confused, Karnstein thought for a moment before replying:

"Yes. Though living people possessed by a creature was more common. Why?"

Sylvia smiled triumphantly at him.

"Because, *idiota*, you do not think" she said. "You see a lesser version of a devil from Hell when they possess a body. This time, you viewed one of those creatures in their true form. That is a sight not meant for mortal eyes, even ones such as yours."

"How do you know?" Karnstein asked, too thoughtful to even object to being called an idiot this time.

Part of him thought the idea was ridiculous, another easy explanation for a something too big for simple words. The other half of him could see the sense of Sylvia's words. She rolled her eyes and replied:

"Because, my dear *idiota*, I read and listen to my betters on such subjects. All, even Albertus Magnus's unpublished notes, indicate that such beings are powers that would overwhelm the minds of even the strongest human. You viewed a demon, or something similar, and you wonder why you were unable to face it alone? *Idiota!*"

"That is sound reasoning and stop calling me an idiot," Karnstein said, looking at Sylvia with greater respect.

"Then stop acting like one," Sylvia said, standing up as she spoke, forcing Franz to also stand since their hands were linked. "Now we will walk home and you will tell me more of how you were able to defeat creatures in less time than the men in the Holy Church need to unpack their vestments."

Karnstein sighed and followed Sylvia through the house. He did not seem able to evade her inquiries short of outright refusal. He might have to resort to that choice soon, as they were about to enter areas of information that could not be disclosed to anyone, not even Jean-Pierre Séverin.

Sylvia took his arm, and they strolled slowly, appearing to be a happy young couple out for a walk through the closing marketplace. Their conversation was light and insubstantial, the easiest disguise to keep them from being detected by inquiring eyes. They just turned a corner, when Karnstein stiffened at the sounds that drifted to his ears.

"We're surrounded," he said in the same matter-of-fact tone.

"*Idiota*, I know. I grew up in these streets. We will have to fight our way out," Sylvia said, her hand drifting down towards his sword.

"No," Karnstein replied, stopping her.

Séverin had taught him about street gangs, kidnapping and assassins. This group appeared armed, but the carriage slowing down the street suggested that this was not a lethal assault by intention. Karnstein then knew the best way of getting Sylvia away safely.

"Only one man is in that side alley. When I say go, we run and take them by surprise. Ready? Go."

Sylvia released Franz's arm, pulled up her skirt and dashed for the alley. A man stepped in her path, a well-dressed fop with a rapier in hand and a sneering smile across his face. He swung the sword before his body to frighten her away—a very big mistake. Sylvia charged forward, grabbed the man's wrist as her other hand raked across his eyes. The fop yelped and then screamed as she twisted his arm and snapped his wrist. Kicking her attacker in the groin, she snatched up his sword and realized she was alone.

Spinning around, she spotted Karnstein, standing only a few feet away. Two men lay at his feet and he was holding off three more with the small sword and dagger. Another four were charging from the far end of the street and the grinding sound of a carriage rose with each passing second.

Sylvia wanted to run to his side, but knew that was as foolish as his actions. He had given her a means of escape, trusting that she would help him against whomever was trying to capture them both. That didn't make her happy, but she knew it was the best chance they would both survive.

Fighting back tears, Sylvia ran down the alley and turned into the main avenue. She needed to arm herself and get her father. Them, they would find Karnstein and kill anyone in their path.

"*Idiota*," she thought, shaking her head as the tears came despite herself.

CHAPTER XLIII

The blow that dropped Franz Karnstein to his knees wasn't from one of the clubs attempting to split his skull, nor was it from the various swords, each incorrectly handled by their wielders. The strike came from below, specifically from the man Karnstein had thrown to the ground and stunned with a kick to the chin. Somehow, that particular enemy had regained enough sense to grab a dropped club and hit the Austrian exorcist behind the knee.

Falling forward, Karnstein punched an exposed groin and swept another man to the ground. He tried to rise when a loud voice broke through the grunts and moans.

"Jump on him! All of you now! Do not let him rise!" the harsh voice snarled.

The voice was familiar, but Karnstein did not have time to consider the speaker. That was when he was enveloped in human bodies from all sides. Strong hands and heavy forms covered him from above, below and all sides. There was nothing he could do; the sheer weight alone forced him flat to the Earth and unable to stand. A few choice blows to the ribs knocked any ability he had to fight back and soon his hands were tied behind his back. Someone pulled a dark cloth hood over his head and, a moment later, he was lifted and tossed into the of the carriage.

"Where is the girl?" asked the grating voice.

By the sound and echo, Karnstein believed he was at the feet of this man, his identity still elusive.

"Got away, the bitch," replied a second voice, one more polished and aristocratic-sounding in tones. "She kicked Tonio in the balls and almost ripped out his eyeballs. By the time the idiot let us know, the slut was gone. I sent Matteo and two others to her home. They'll bring her along once she arrives."

At their feet, already feeling better, if slightly uncomfortable, Karnstein smiled. Sylvia got away and they only sent three men to tackle her. They didn't know his Sylvia, she would make all of them regret they were even alive. Just then he realized what he'd thought.

I thought of her as my Sylvia. What is wrong with me? I've known her a short time and we do nothing but fight. It must be such silly attraction... she is so very... no, don't even think about her skin and her hair and... oh Lord in Heaven, this is ridiculous. I decided years ago that I would avoid entanglements because I do not live a normal life. No, this will not happen, he resolved as the streets changed from stone to dirt.

"You, Karnstein. Do you hear me?" the grating voice asked, a toe prodding his side.

The Austrian considered pretending to be unconscious, but had a feeling that would not go well for him this time. Once, after being kidnapped by a warlock and his sister/lover in the Black Forrest, shamming unconsciousness almost resulted in his losing a hand. Best to accept his state and wait, listening to what happened.

"Yes," Karnstein replied, still trying to place the voice of his kidnapper.

"We are traveling about the city and other places for a time. If you sit quietly, you shall be left alone. If you make so much as a sound..." a heavy object tapped Karnstein's shoulder and arm, "...you shall hurt in ways you cannot begin to imagine. Agreed?"

"Yes," Karnstein replied and closed his eyes.

As his ears listened to the sounds of the streets and the wheels, he prayed silently:

"*Anima Christi, sanctifica me. Corpus Christi, salve me. Sanguis Christi, inebria me. Aqua lateris Christi, lava me. Passio Christi, conforta me. O bone Iesu, exaudi me. Intra tua vulnera absconde me. Ne permittas me separari a te. Ab hoste maligno defende me. In hora mortis meae voca me. Et iube me venire ad te, ut cum Sanctis tuis laudem te in saecula saeculorum. Amen.*"

Then, he lay back and listened to the changing sounds beneath the wheels. From the dirt tracks, they returned to a stone road, although one with pits and holes. The smell of baking bread drifted to his nostrils. He recognized that smell, having experienced it a day ago when Sylvia had taken him through the western end of the city to the small home of a *stregheria*. That old lady was just a folk witch, simple wisdom and herbs, nothing evil or mystical. To get to her, they had crossed an area filled with bakeries, each competing for the right to be viewed as the best in all of Naples.

Sylvia said most bakers were here and we then got into a fight over the woman who looked my direction. I didn't smile at her... Sylvia got jealous...? But why? No, best think only on the current problem. I can't get free, whoever tied the knots knew how to do so effectively. Possibly a sailor? If a sailor, then we may be heading to the harbor... There, a ship can go anywhere in the world. However, Maestro Séverin taught me that principle by William of Occam: Plurality is not to be posited without necessity. *The simplest explanation is that I will soon find myself, if I am on a ship, headed for the prison...* Karnstein thought as the scent of salt water slowly grew stronger.

Therefore, he was unsurprised when they stopped and he was tossed into a small ship. The trip across the heavily rocking sea was, as expected, short and slightly nauseating from his prone position. A pair of strong hands forced him to walk blindly for a time, the sandy ground soon replaced by concrete or stone.

Karnstein knew that he was in the prison they had visited the day before—the terrible scent was just too distinctive and terrible. The odor of blood and human waste almost overwhelmed him as his captor dragged him through a series of tunnels. Closing his eyes, Franz he himself to ignore the familiar scents, the ones he knew from his last visit. They were the embodiment of fear, which was the last emotion he could allow right now.

Then, after hearing the sound of a heavy door bolted behind him, the iron grip on Karnstein's arm loosened and the hood was yanked away.

Slowly opening his eyes, he found himself exactly where he had expected to be: the torture room. The face peering in his direction was the only surprise.

"*You?*" he asked, confused.

Something was very wrong…

CHAPTER XLIV

"Stop where you are, lady," Matteo Bruno stated, smiling as he fingered his favorite stiletto.

A tall, plain-looking man with a blocky build that always appeared to border on fat, he was well-dressed and resembled a rising merchant. What he was, in fact, was a sadist. His job was to appear prosperous and then perform acts of dreadful cruelty to specific victims.

The unwanted fifth child of a carpenter, Matteo's father, Angelo Bruno, had been a brutal, angry man who had despised his life and everyone in it. His wife, Sofia, had been even worse—a bitter, accusatory emotional vampire who had tortured her children with a poisonous tongue. By the time Matteo had arrived, the marriage had been a battle zone, filled with angry, harsh words and heavy blows. The children, three boys and two girls, had all turned out exactly as their mother had predicted—evil, nasty, and bad. When they had died, Angelo and Sofia Bruno had managed to spawn two professional robbers, a paid killer, an arsonist, and a carpenter who had created homes that were deadly to anyone unfortunate enough to reside in one when the wind blew from the south.

Licking his lips, Matteo slowly looked Sylvia up and down, his eyes lingering on her chest.

"Drop the sword and we can have a little fun," he sneered.

Sylvia raised the rapier and snapped back:

"*Mangia merde e morte! Fanculo figlio di puttana!* Where did you take him?"

Matteo was stunned by the flow of harsh, guttural curses emerging from the woman's lovely lips. Flushing, he snapped back,:

"*Porca Madonna!* You want your man back? Spread your legs for me, *puttana!*"

"*Succhiacazzi!*" Sylvia snarled, as her rapier slashed out at the gangster.

Matteo screamed in pain and clutched his face. His two helpers, hiding to the left and right of Sylvia, stepped into view. The larger, stupider of the pair, a round bully named Nicola, started to laugh.

"What is so funny?" Matteo screeched. "The *puttana* nearly cut off my face!"

Sylvia snorted and flicked the blood off the blade with a flourish.

"Don't be silly. If I wanted to remove your face, you would be picking up the pieces from the street."

"Don't kill her, but make her hurt," Matteo snarled, nodding his head towards Sylvia.

Nicola roared and ran forward, his blood-stained club held high above his head. Just as suddenly, the howl was replaced by a gurgle and a moan as the thin rapier blade pierced the large man's throat, causing him to fall to the ground. His neck was a bloody, ripped, vestige of flesh, stained crimson as the vitae fell onto the street and formed viscous pools of fluid.

"*Cagna!*" Tomas yelled, slashing the air with his cutlass.

He aimed for Sylvia's head, but missed her by mere inches. A moan then escaped his lips as the lovely swordswoman lunged forward and impaled his heart with her blade.

Matteo, eyes wide, shook his head and turned to run. He caught the glimpse of a dour face before finding himself crashing face first onto the street, senseless. Strong hands stripped him of his weapons and shirt. A moment later his hands were tied behind his back.

"Sylvia, my dearest girl, what is this?" Dardi asked, gesticulating wildly at the fallen men. "And where is your Austrian?"

Sylvia, pausing to kick Matteo twice in the ribs, looked up at her father.

"We were attacked by men. The *idiota* pretended to run with me and fought them so that I may get away. These *bastardos* beat me here and attempted to do the same to me…

When I get my hands on that arrogant, Austrian *idiota*, I'll kill him myself!"

Dardi hugged his daughter, pretending he did not see the tear streaks across her face.

"Yes, yes, I understand. Come inside, we must change clothing to get ready to perform a rescue of the *idiota*."

Sylvia pulled away and snapped, "Do not call him that, Papa!"

Dardi bowed his head to hide his grin.

"My apologies," he said.

He watched as Sylvia stormed into the training school and turned to Séverin:

"Gâteloup, let us bring this one inside. We will wring all the truth from his tender body and rescue your pupil."

"Then who shall save him from your daughter?" Séverin replied, shaking his head.

"Perhaps we shall say a prayer for the young man's soul. He will be either engaged to my daughter, or dead. I am not sure which fate is less dangerous," Dardi said, laughing as he closed the academy door.

As the door closed, a dark figure detached itself from the shadows and walked around a corner. A small horse stood placidly waiting, the dark eyes staring at a rat as it scurried across the lane.

The skeletal form leaped on the horse and rode into the darkness, vanishing in mere seconds. These events would be of interest...

CHAPTER XLV

"I do believe you are surprised," Federigo Gui said, smiling and folding his stubby hands into his high-collared robe. "You are not nearly as clever as you believe, young man."

"And you are a fool, Gui. Do you think His Holiness will stand for your actions? Or the Holy Inquisition?" Karnstein snarled, only held in place by the powerful grip of the man holding his arms.

Gui chuckled and shook his head.

"They shall not be in a position to question my choices. Perhaps I shall be the next Pope, or the king of all Italy."

Karnstein regarded the Abbot and shook his head.

"I was wrong, you're not a fool, you're a madman. Do you actually think Napoleon will allow you to replace His Holiness or his own brother? He'll put you down like a mad dog."

Gui continued to laugh softly for a moment before he said:

"René? Place his lordship in restraints. But leave his mouth unbound, he has much to say and explain."

Karnstein struggled to free himself, but to no avail. The powerful hands of the man named René moved him along as if he was as light as a child. Within a few minutes, Karnstein lay upon a metal frame, heavy chains binding his arms, legs, and torso in place. René proved to be a very handsome man, about his height, with broad shoulders and a blank look on his sculpted features.

"Ah, very nice," Gui purred, patting the Exorcist's cheek with false affection. "Time to introduce you to the one who will pose a series of important questions you will answer."

"I will not," Karnstein replied, echoing the statement he had made earlier in this man's office.

René immediately punched him in the stomach—a hard strike that immediately caused a wave of nausea to fill his body.

The henchman raised a fist to strike again, but was stopped by a gesture from Gui.

"René, stop that right now," Gui said, waving his assistant back. "He must answer questions. If he is beaten to death, this shall not be possible."

Karnstein coughed a few times and looked up at Gui with naked hatred in his eyes.

"You are supposed to be a man of God!" he spat out.

Gui laughed in a loud, braying tone with René joining in the merriment a few seconds later.

"Man of God? What a pretty, and meaningless, phrase! I will tell you a truth known to anyone with enough common sense, Herr Baron. I never believed in God and the word of the Bible. I joined the Church because I was not born with royal blood. That shall change soon enough. Like that Corsican peasant, Bonaparte, I shall establish a new dynasty as a king."

Karnstein sighed and rolled his eyes.

"If you are about to start informing me that soon you shall rule the world, I would prefer that the torture begin immediately."

Gui looked as if he wanted to bark back a rejoinder, but the soft sounds of footsteps caught his attention. Glancing over his shoulder for a moment, he turned back to Karnstein, smiling again.

"I think we shall accommodate your wishes," Gui said, his voice returning to the same purr used earlier. "Allow me to introduce you to Sister Fortuna. She will be the one asking you the questions I mentioned earlier."

Sister Fortuna proved to be the nun that Karnstein and the others had met earlier, her pretty face evident under the wimple. She was smiling, her girlish round face studying him with wide dark eyes. Karnstein examined her back, trying to use the observation techniques he learned from Séverin. This time, he noticed something quite unusual and looked at Gui with an accusatory look.

"A nun who does not wear the crucifix? Merciful God in Heaven, why?"

"What do you mean?" Gui asked.

Karnstein's face shifted into a mask of fury and disgust.

"You sold out humanity to that demon! Why? Why would you sell your soul for a promise of fading glory?"

Gui chuckled and shook his head.

"I had no idea exorcists were so poetic. Sold my soul? I agreed to that when I forged the Abbot's signature naming me his successor and poisoned that pious pathetic priest. Until the Bonaparte usurper arrived, I was the most powerful man in the kingdom. Under the great goddess Nosos, I shall be so much more. She will rule the world and I shall serve as one of her favored satraps."

"No," Karnstein said, his voice hushed. "I shall send you to Lucifer's side very soon."

Gui snorted, shook his head and turned away.

"I doubt we shall ever meet again. Sister Fortuna is very... enthusiastic... about her work. Farewell, Baron Karnstein."

With that, Gui and his servant swept out of the room. Karnstein was now alone with Sister Fortuna, whom he doubted was a nun or anything even slightly connected to anything holy. She appeared at his side, pulling the wimple from her head, revealing a head of thick, glossy, straight brown hair that fell past her shoulders. She was pretty, not beautiful, but striking in a doll-like way, though with a large bust.

"You are a Karnstein," she said, her voice a husky growl. "I've heard much about your family. You must be the oddity, taking the side of the false Messiah. Didn't one of your ancestors attend the Scholomance and return as a vampire?"

"I believe the last count was that eleven members of my family graduated from the academy."

The Austrian disliked talking about the dark mystics in his bloodline, but he knew it was easier to indulge in than his future torture. Fortuna frowned as she pulled a lever next to his head. The metal frame shifted, causing Karnstein to lay prone and look up into her puzzled eyes.

"Eleven?" she said. "Then you would be allowed to join and learn the true path. I read in Simon de Montfort's *Black Bible* that the family of a Scholomance are automatically admitted as students."

"They would not want me," Karnstein replied, trying to hide his amusement.

Fortuna leaned closer, obviously believing she was able to charm him with her more attractive qualities.

"Why?" she asked.

"Possibly because I've destroyed five Karnstein vampires and sent a host of demons back to Hell. Oh, and just for your information—the *Black Bible*? Said to be written in the blood of infants by Simon de Montfort when he ruled England? It's a forgery. The true author was a printer in the employ of an English criminal named Jonathan Wild. The English hanged him approximately one hundred years as a thief. The blood in the original was red ink and a man named Macheath wrote the tracts as a joke."

Karnstein didn't hide his amusement as he watched Fortuna's face transform from sensual come-hither to horrified realization.

"You… you… destroyed vampires?" she whispered, recoiling from contact with his skin.

"I killed my first vampire when I was eight years-old. She was a Karnstein, believed to be five hundred years-old. My second was my own mother, converted by my ancestor to become a blood-drinking plague on all mankind. Since that time, three more Karnsteins who had sold their soul to Satan fell beneath my sword. Not to mention many warlocks and witches who sought to become vampires or other fiends."

Karnstein's words were flat and almost bored-sounding. This was an act, designed decades earlier as he sat on a set of steps, waiting for his priest to come back to the castle.

The memory of that moment came back, a flash of an eight year-old Franz Karnstein, his blood-spattered face blank and staring. Over him loomed the massive Father Sandor, the powerful priest who had brought Count Karnstein and the bishop's men to the castle. Though a child, Karnstein had learned the truth about his "cousin" Mircalla. The memory was always the same, in stark relief every time he discussed his past.

"What happened here, boy?" Father Sandor had asked as the bishop's people examined the bones and whispered the word *vampire* under their breath.

"Cousin Mircalla was a vampire. She made mother into a vampire. I... sent them... away... they're gone... were already gone," Karnstein had mumbled.

Then, he seemed to pull his shattered spirit together and looked at Father Sandor and the bishop's representative and spoke in a more even tone.

"I killed my mama. She was a vampire too."

And then he burst into tears.

That was the last time Karnstein had cried, other than when tears came to his eyes caused by pain. He had built an armor around his emotions, rarely allowing himself to experience anything other than anger. Until recently of course...

Fortuna stepped back and reached for another lever. Her face was twisted, almost inhuman as her rage rose. With a snap, she pulled the lever and Karnstein was turned so that his back was fully exposed.

"I think we shall start with the claws of pain. The English call this device the cat o' nine tails, which sounds gentle to my ears. Do you know the claws of pain, murderer?" she asked, though her question was rhetorical.

Raising the whip, she slashed the nine leather cords across his naked back. The pain was horrific, a searing, burning sensation that caused his whole frame to shake in agony. He bit back a moan, knowing he would cry out eventually, but not immediately. The pain grew with each stroke, ceasing after what felt like several hours, but was in fact mere minutes.

The frame suddenly shifted and Karnstein opened his eyes to see Fortuna staring down at his sweating, drawn face. She looked happy and caressed his cheek for a moment. Then the whippings resumed, the leather straps slicing through the flesh across his torso and legs. The pain took the air from his lungs and soon he felt the occasional strap striking his face and spoiling his vision.

"You did not cry out," she said, and giggled like a merry child. "I find that stimulating... arousing. A man or a woman who can accept pain and not give in immediately are the best lovers, I find."

"If you say so," Karnstein managed to gasp, his face feeling tight.

Fortuna smiled and patted his back, causing the pain to return in greater force.

She then licked her bloody hand, her face slowly transforming as he watched. After a moment, she stopped, seeming to regain control of herself, and dropped her hands to her sides.

"Enough pleasure, time for questions. How did you see my cherished queen Nosos in her true form?" Fortuna asked, her look vacillating between interest and anger. "That should not be possible for a meager human such as yourself. I am mighty Nosos's personal handmaiden and I may only glimpse at her greatness."

"Greatness?" Karnstein spat back, not hiding his disgust. "Your Nosos is a demoniac fiend, an evil disease who seeks to transform this world into a lifeless canker."

"What did you say?" Fortuna whispered, her face twisting with fury.

"You heard me, slave of darkness," he replied, allowing his disgust to flow freely from his tongue. "You call yourself her handmaiden? You're nothing but a piece of her with delusions of individuality. She consumed you and all your individuality along with the rest of her walking corpses. All she needs to do is concentrate and you'll be nothing more than another mouth she can use to feed her bloated, inhuman, corpse of a body."

Fortuna's lovely face froze and the look in her eyes became deeper, darker, and ancient. Then she began to speak, though her voice was rougher, sounding similar to an aged crone than a young, lovely, lady.

"You know too much, little exorcist," Nosos said, speaking through Fortuna. "I no longer care about the source of your powers. My dearest little Fortuna shall torture you to death, sending you to the afterlife in agony. Perhaps I shall use your corpse as a plaything."

"Am I meant to be horrified? I've been listening to the ravings of demons since I was a child. Go back to your pit, fiend, you bore me!" Karnstein replied, looking away.

In truth, he was frightened of this creature, but he knew better than to show his terror. Like predators in the forest, demons fed on your fears.

"My dear Nosos gave me permission to enjoy your pain," Fortuna said, her normal voice returning.

She reached out and pulled his face back so that their eyes met.

"I think we shall start now. First I shall remove and eat your lying tongue."

"*In nomine Patris, et Filii, et Spiritus Sancti. Amen,*" Karnstein replied, saying a brief prayer as Fortuna revealed a long, wicked looking knife.

The blade's handle was encrusted with dried blood, the brown stains releasing an odiferous stench of rot and corruption. This was a knife well-used for torture and murder, an instrument of pain and death. Fortuna held the weapon with terrifying familiarity as she slithered closer.

"Once I am done with your tongue, I shall cut off your nose and eat that next. Then your manhood... that shall be a true pleasure for us both, until it is not for you of course," Fortuna crooned, running a small hand across his chest and down to Franz's groin.

She caressed him and then looked confused when he displayed no response to her touch.

"Sorry," Karnstein croaked. "I do not find necrophilia arousing. Also your breath is quite rank."

"You bastard!" Fortuna shrieked, raising the knife. "Say your last prayer, if you like. Not even God will save you from my special attention!"

That was when the distant door flew open with a slam and Fortuna's head exploded in a shower of black blood, bone, and gore. She tumbled forward, her corpse slowly rolling off Karnstein's battered body. He was blinded by the revolting vitae covering his face and chest as well as his injuries. The sound of someone approaching drifted his direction and he felt soft hands cleaning his face and chest with a cloth that smelled like vinegar.

"Ssshhh, don't worry," A soft, female voice whispered. "We will clean you up and get you healed soon."

"Sylvia?" Franz asked, his vision still clouded by viscous fluids.

"Sylvia? *SYLVIA?*" the husky female voice screeched.

A harsh hand rubbed the cloth roughly over his eyes as the flow of Italian oaths exploded into his ears.

"*Testa di cazzo! Coglione! Mangia merde e morte!*"

A moment later, the cloth was pulled away from his face and he looked up at a beautiful, irate countenance. The woman was familiar and the enraged glint in her eyes was almost frightening. Dressed in a riding habit, her lovely dark hair flowing freely about her shoulders, she was stunning even to the Exorcist's eyes.

"You dare mention that *puttana* to me?" Francesca Policeni snarled. "After I saved your miserable life! You *finocchio*! I should cut off your manhood and feed it to the wolves!"

"Eh, *sgualdrina*! Step away from my man!" Sylvia said, stepping into the room with a confident stride.

Dressed in a black jacket, riding pants, Prussian boots, and an old tricorn hat, she resembled the arrogant young woman Karnstein had met a few weeks back. This time her steely anger was directed entirely toward the well-armed woman standing at the Austrian's side.

"Who are you to call me that, *puttana*?" Francesca snapped back, stepping away from Karnstein and raising the blade in her hand.

Sylvia raised the musket in her hand and said:

"My name is Sylvia Dardi and you will keep your paws away from my *fidanzato*."

Francesca threw back her head and laughed in open mockery.

"Brave girl, waving a gun about and screeching threats like a fishwife. What will you do if I don't agree? Shoot me in cold blood? You haven't got the spine for that, *puttana*!"

Sylvia chuckled and tossed the pistol aside. She drew the dagger from her belt and spun the blade in her hand.

"I discharged the shot in the body of one of your sailors two minutes ago."

Francesca smiled and stepped forward.

"I've been wanting to mark your peasant face since the ball."

"You can try," Sylvia replied.

And they started to circle each other, blades moving in slow silver arcs.

CHAPTER XLVI

Nosos screamed, a sound of deep despair and agony which caused the cave walls to shake and shards of rock and dust to crash to the Earth.

Sinis rushed into the room, his horrific face frightened by the howls that emerged from his mistress. Dropping to his knees, he waited as she raged, shattering the few measly sticks of furniture, including her throne styled chair.

Time passed, and the storm in the cave continued until finally Nosos collapsed in an exhausted heap on the sandy floor. She wept, black tears staining the floor as she softly sobbed. Finally, she slowed and repeated one word over and over in her anguish.

"Fortuna," she continued to whisper, her voice cracking.

Sinis realized that his mistress's favorite consort had somehow been destroyed. Realizing there was one way that might salve her pain, he ran from the cave and coached a short distance at full, reckless, speed.

Within five minutes he returned, an unconscious body in his arms, a lovely woman at his side.

"Go to her, she suffers, and you must help her," he whispered to Giorgia.

The young former Satanist pupil of Hertz Ende had flourished since her transformation. Her formerly thin blonde hair was now a thick, mane of gold—an enticement she used to lure men to their doom. Giorgia supplied the steady stream of victims as food for Nosos and was her favorite after Fortuna. Laying the unconscious body of the boy Giorgia had provided this night, Sinis fled from the chamber and waited in the niche assigned as his home. Moans of ecstasy drifted his direction followed by shrieks of agony as the boy was consumed by Nosos.

This was everything Sinis had hoped for this night. Soon his mistress would call him to her side and he would have the honor of collecting the remains and placing them in the pile with the others. He wanted to bury the remains, the stench was terrible and the rats and other animals were constantly feeding on the moldering corpses.

A short time passed, and Sinis suddenly knew he was needed. His mistress had the power, rarely exercised, to summons him from any location. Placing his face in the dust, he waited to be acknowledged.

"Rise, worm," Nosos finally said. "You pleased me this day. Bring me and my new consort two more bodies. Then you will take her to that island prison to assume Fortuna's power and position."

"Dark Queen, why would you send away your new handmaiden so soon?" Sinis asked, afraid of a recurrence of Nosos's dark despair.

Nosos tittered, followed a few seconds later by Giorgia's laughter.

"Sinis, you are quite amusing. My consort is more than my favored sexual partner, wretch. She exists as a fount for a portion of my power. Fortuna collected many more slaves for my army and they are now uncontrolled. Giorgia shall do the same once she arrives and exercises the new gifts I gave her this night."

"Thank you, my Queen," Giorgia replied, snuggling closer to Nosos.

Nosos's clawed hands stroked the girl's damp, gore-stained hair.

"You are welcome, my pretty one. Now, kiss me and we shall consider who shall serve you as you did for my poor Fortuna. Perhaps Anise or Vincenzo?"

Sinis backed away as the sounds of love-making resumed. Finding two more bodies at this hour would not be easy. Hopefully a peddler or a prostitute would still be wandering about the area. If not, Sinis knew of a cottage a short distance from the lake with two small children...

CHAPTER XLVII

Francesca Policeni slashed out first, her attack fast and aimed for Sylvia's lead leg. Sadly for her, Sylvia Dardi was already out of range, her motions slow and methodical. Francesca whirled and grabbed a bucket near her feet, hurling its contents at her opponent.

Sylvia danced out of the way, a little water striking her boots. She released a brief laugh and then stepped in close. She punched Francesca in the stomach while blocking a blade strike to her chest. She then ducked a grabbing hand and sent the wealthy, gangster woman sprawling on her back.

Francesca immediately spun and swung her blade at Sylvia's ankles. The latter leaped over the blade, back flipped like an acrobat, and landed several feet away with a smile. Francesca scrambled to her feet, her expression ugly.

"Madonna! You are outmatched, *puttana*!" Sylvia said, her eyes narrowing.

Francesca sneered and reached down, pulling out Karnstein's small sword. The weapon, previously on his belt, lay on the floor near the frame where he lay in paroxysms of pain.

"*Vaffanculo*! I'm going to slice your face off and wear it as a mask during Carnivale!"

Sylvia rolled her eyes and drew her own small sword.

"Shall we then?"

Francesca lunged, demonstrating some training in fencing. Sylvia parried without any visible effort, her stance calm and relaxed. Francesca attacked three more times, each move easily blocked by Sylvia's blade.

"You are holding the sword too loose," said Sylvia. "Remember, always hold the blade like you held a little bird in your palm. Too loose and…"

Sylvia parried another lunge and sliced open Francesca's other arm. She then struck the sword once, sending it spiraling into the air. She caught the sword by the handle and added in the same lecturing tone:

"...the bird flies away."

She tossed the sword back to Francesca. The Policeni woman snarled and feinted a lunge. She hacked through the air, trying to slice open Sylvia's throat. For her part, Sylvia appeared amused, merely stepping back a few inches and allowing the point to whistle past her in a fast arc.

"Now you're holding the sword too tight," she said. "Remember the little bird, *puttana*. Hold the little bird too tight and..."

Sylvia parried Francesca's sword at a very precise angle. The Austrian's small sword snapped on the impact and the pieces dropped to the floor. Sylvia placed the tip on Francesca's left breast, just above the heart as she concluded her instruction:

"...it dies. Any last words, *sgualdrina*?"

"*Li mortacci tua*," Francesca spat back, dropping the snapped sword from her nerveless grip.

"Forgive me for interrupting, my dearest Sylvia, but you must not kill her. No matter how much she deserves it," Jean-Pierre Séverin said, stepping into the torture chamber.

His favorite rapier was in one hand and a large pistol in the other.

"Why?" Sylvia snarled, her eyes still on Francesca.

The daughter of the infamous Michele Bozzo, the *Padrone* of all the Neapolitan *Camorra*, visibly wilted in fear at what she viewed in that enraged gaze.

"We need every able, or even slightly able, body moving and able to fight. You see, this prison is—" Séverin broke off as the door to the infirmary flew open.

A guard, his face half-missing, stumbled into view. He moaned and shambled forward, his hands extended, his ruined countenance staring at Sylvia and Francesca.

Séverin fired his pistol, causing the remains of the creature's head to explode back into the infirmary. The walking dead man collapsed in a heap, no longer moaning or moving.

"…as I was saying," Séverin continued, glancing down at the liquefying remains of Fortuna, "…this prison is filled with the undead, and something has woken them from their slumber. If we are to survive, Madame Policeni must assist us. It is in her best interest."

"Francesca shot her… the vampire… though they're not really vampires…" Karnstein managed to mumble.

Sylvia looked furious, but the point of her blade fell away from Francesca's chest. She stepped over to the Austrian's prone, chained form and kissed him quickly on the lips. She then cupped his chin.

"*Idiota!* You call her Madame Policeni if you speak to her at all. Understood?"

"Understood and stop calling me an idiot," Karnstein replied, trying to smile, but not succeeding in making anything more than a rictus.

"Then stop acting like one!" she replied, kissing him quickly again and unfastening his bonds.

Francesca moved to the other side, assisting and shrugged at Sylvia's black look.

"We do not have time to waste, if the Maestro is to be taken at his word. I won't bother your *fidanzato* any further."

"Fine, this time," Sylvia snapped back. "But I will be watching you."

"What does *fidanzato* mean? I don't know that word," Karnstein asked as the frame was righted.

Sylvia helped him step off. He was naked, his clothes piled in a heap near where he lay. His step was faltering; the harm caused by the whipping was painful, but not crippling.

Francesca giggled, causing Sylvia to blush and fire another look of smoldering anger her direction.

"I shall remain silent, for now," said Francesca. "Maestro Séverin, we have a truce until I get to safety, and then I shall owe you, and you alone, one favor. Agreed?"

"Agreed," Séverin replied, reloading his revolver.

Nodding towards the weapons, he added:

"Find a weapon you trust. Nothing too heavy, we have a lot of fighting ahead. Sylvia, take care of Franz and dress his wounds. I shall join you in a moment."

Sylvia shot Francesca another dark look and hissed:

"A *fanabla*!"

She then helped the Austrian towards the small hospital.

"Should you not close that door?" Francesca asked, pointing at the opening from which Séverin had emerged.

She picked up a light cavalry saber and testing the balance.

"No," Séverin replied, pulling out a second gun and loading it with careful movements. "Maestro Dardi is scouting out our various escape routes. There are more than two hundred prisoners in this location alone. I know not how many guards. All are walking dead, attacking and killing any living being they spot. If they attack, strike for the skull. The heart works too, but is difficult to strike."

"Thank you," Francesca replied, tossing aside the sword and picking up a similar blade.

"Follow my directions and you may survive," Séverin continued, as he attached the revolver to his belt. "However, if you attempt to harm or hinder Signorina Dardi, I shall feed you to the marauding dead on this island myself, is that understood?"

"Completely," Francesca said, settling on the third light cavalry blade. "He was an assignment. Oh, my vanity was pricked that he spoke her name when I rescued him, but I had no true interest in him. I just dislike losing."

Séverin nodded once and said:

"Watch the door. If anyone comes, call for help."

Séverin turned toward his student.

"*Idiota*! Stand still, and let me finish!" Sylvia yelled as Séverin approached.

She had Franz seated on a chair and was swabbing his back with vinegar and water.

"You already washed that area!" Karnstein yelled back. "And stop calling me an idiot!"

"Then stop acting like one!" she replied, reaching for the bandage.

Séverin remained composed, but secretly felt both amused and grateful. These two would bark and snarl at each other until the heavens fell—but the Lord help any man or woman who tried to pry them apart. The Maestro knew that if anyone ever called Franz Karnstein an idiot, they would face the wrath of Sylvia Dardi. Likewise, if anyone spoke ill of Sylvia in the hearing of Franz Karnstein.

This, combined with the new training regime he had been designing might be the means of keeping Karnstein from following the dark path of the witch-hunter. This was a new age for mankind, one based in greater freedom of thought and deed. The only chance it had to succeed was by abandoning the horrors of the past. Witch-hunters were relics of bygone days, products of ignorance and fear.

Unless creatures like Nosos triumph... Séverin thought.

"Maestro, someone approaches," Francesca called out as Séverin assisted Sylvia.

"Go, I shall complete this and we will join you soon," Sylvia said, tying off the bandage with expert hands.

Séverin stepped out, just in time to see Dardi pop into the room. He was not smiling and the cutlass he held looked soaked with a variety of fluids. Additionally, the whole torture chamber reeked from the melting remains of the creature once known as Fortuna Orsini.

"Gâteloup, it is worse than we imagined," Dardi said, slamming the door closed and throwing the bolts. "Nothing lives on this cursed island and they seek more lives."

"But that was our only way out!" Francesca cried, reaching for the door.

Just then the sounds of heavy blows struck the metal. The number of strikes increased and the door vibrated with each assault.

"There are at least a hundred on the other side of the door, seeking to enter. It will not be long before they succeed," Dardi explained, his stride taking him deeper into the chamber.

"Then we must go deeper into the prison and find another means of escape," Séverin said. "No prison has a single point of exit."

Sylvia and Franz appeared in the doorway.

"How would you know that?" Francesca demanded, looking rebellious.

Séverin turned his pale eyes on her, his look hard, his manner flinty. Waving for the group to follow him, he headed for the far door.

"When I was a prisoner in the Bastille, I learned all I could of my place of confinement. Had they ordered my execution, I had three means of escape. Happily, I was released and those methods remained known only to myself. Since that time, I have made it a point of learning about prison design and structure. It provided me some solace should I ever be imprisoned again. As we walk, we must talk. Have you ever heard the name Nosos in the past?"

"No," Sylvia and Francesca replied at the same instant.

They both looked annoyed and looked away as they followed Séverin from the room and deeper into the prison.

"Yes," Karnstein and Dardi replied.

"How did you learn that name?" Séverin asked, surprised by his pupil's response.

Dardi was no surprise, of course. The man had been raised to fight monsters. But Franz Karnstein, in contrast, had never explained the source of his odd bits of knowledge on a variety of subjects. However, his ignorance on the most basic facets of life was also equally puzzling. He could explain for an hour the dangers of facing a practitioner of magic from the Deep School versus that of Scholomance; yet, ask him to name a composer, artist, politician, or popular writer and he would be hard pressed to state one. An odd individual, though one Séverin liked a great deal.

"*Oedipus* by Seneca the Younger. There's a long quote I was forced to remember that reads, *Wherefore speedily expel ye the king from out your borders, in exile drive him to any place so-ever with his baleful step. Let him leave the land; then, blooming with flowers of spring, shall it renew its verdure, the life-giving air shall give pure breath again, and their beauty shall come back to the woods; Letum and Nosos, Mors, Labor, Tabes and Dolor, fit company for him, shall all depart together. And he himself with hastening steps shall long to flee our kingdom, but I will set wearisome delays before his feet and hold him back. He shall creep, uncertain of his way, with the staff of age groping out his gloomy way. Rob ye him of the earth; his father will take from him the sky.*"

Séverin nodded and waved a hand to stop the group.

"Nosos is one of group called the Keres, also known as the Tenebrae. They are the Dark Fates, the spreader of horror in the world. Barto and I once faced Mors, the demon woman of doom."

"She wanted to consume all life on Earth. We stopped her," Dardi added, cocking his head. "They are through the door to the torture chamber."

"And ahead at that far door," Séverin said, pointing.

The sounds of hammer fists rose with each second. He pointed at another large door on the left and aid:

"We must turn here; it should lead to the south wing."

"That creature is no ordinary demon," Karnstein managed to say as Dardi closed and bolted the door behind the group.

They now stood in a long corridor with a door at the far end and a staircase leading into the depths below the prison.

Karnstein, with Sylvia's interjections, explained the events of their confrontation with Countessa Angelica and Anton. Then, with halting words, he told them of his glimpse into the source of the power behind these creatures.

"That sounds like a demon to me," Francesca said as they headed down the corridor.

"*Taci*!" Sylvia snapped. "If he said that is no ordinary demon, it is no ordinary demon. *Capisci*?"

Francesca didn't look annoyed; she merely rolled her eyes and chuckled.

"Madonna! I did not realize I was facing the thunder-bolt."

Sylvia looked ready to snarl back, when she was stopped by a gesture from Séverin. He looked at his student, knowing Karnstein possessed insights that few understood—including himself it seemed.

"Explain your meaning. Remember, Barto and I faced one of this creature's fellow Tenebrae before. That day, we two, and a more experienced expert, faced a being of terrible power that was a demon."

Séverin turned sideways so he could keep an eye on the door ahead and Karnstein.

"Please make this quick," Dardi murmured. "I can hear the undead attacking the next door."

"We shall. Franz, if you please?" Séverin replied.

Karnstein sighed and appeared to move a little closer to Sylvia.

"If you fought one this fiend's brethren, then you only viewed the barest piece of the whole creature. I have personally expelled many demons; I've looked at their inner darkness. They are terrible, unclean, creatures, and I pray daily to keep the darkness from touching my soul."

"Very poetic," Francesca sneered and smiled at Sylvia's furious expression.

Karnstein continued as if Francesca was not even present.

"The presence I observed in the skein of all life was greater… more monstrous than any demon or vampire or loup-garou. Just looking at that… It was like swimming in an ocean of horrors… That stain on the world is so much more than a mere demon…"

"When I killed the vampire," Sylvia shushed Karnstein before he objected to the term vampire again, "Franz came out of that place, his mind almost broken. His eyes—they were looking in different directions and he shook for a long time."

Séverin frowned and nodded.

"That explains much of why this monster's actions appear so random. We will talk more on this after we leave this place."

He stepped over to the door, which opened at a touch revealing a rectangular chamber with a series of wooden cots. A table with dice and an overturned wine jug were in view as were scattered clubs and random pieces of clothing.

A single wooden door suddenly flew open and men, each dressed in the slovenly jerkins of the prison guards, stumbled into the chamber. At the same instant, the door at their rear shook as numerous hands assaulted the closed portal.

"Now we are truly caught between Charybdis and Scylla," Dardi said, grinning. "Let us slice through these undead guards and find the exit! *Andiamo*!"

CHAPTER XLVIII

"René," Federigo Gui said, settling into his favorite chair, "find me the arrest warrant papers. We have a great many to fill out this night. Tomorrow morning, we take the kingdom for our mistress. Oh, and tell that idiot chamberlain that I need an immediate audience with the soon-to-be-slave King Joseph. We shall make this last act of government legal and proper."

"The king left for Rome yesterday, Father Abbot," René said, his voice flat. "You asked me to monitor his movements."

Gui frowned and thought for a moment.

"When does he return?"

"Two days from now for a meeting with the military advisor, Colonel Hugo, and a dignitary council," René replied, adding, "He then leaves for a week to visit several villas in Capri."

"No doubt to pick a new royal mistress since his queen prefers to live elsewhere," Gui mused, tapping his teeth with a fingernail.

His temptation was to force the keeper of the royal seals to allow him use of the king's personal stamp. That was a risk, especially as he planned on riding himself of Johann Spurzheim. The chief of police was not one of Joseph Bonaparte's favored followers, but he did possess some power in the kingdom. Also, attacking one of Napoleon's advisors without actual royal backing could result in difficult times.

"Then we shall wait."

Gui closed the file with arrest warrants for Spurzheim, Séverin, and Dardi, among others. He stopped at the final warrant, that for Sylvia Dardi. An idea struck him, one that filled him with a wave of amusement.

"Send for Lorenzo Pinot, immediately. If he is not standing before me in one hour, I will have the messengers whipped until they possess no skin left."

Gui settled back in his chair as René left the office. Tenting his fingers, he smiled at the thought of the disgusting little murderous monster assaulting and destroying the Dardi girl. Pinot was garbage, a fiend with a blade in hand, a coward under all other circumstances. He was also a mildly talented painter and sculptor, though Gui sensed his true art was the way he despoiled women. The master of the Cupbearers appreciated this talent since women deserved nothing more, nothing less. This was not to say that Gui hated women—that was too simplistic. He despised all females, but that was not because he preferred men. No, the Abbott found every man, woman, and child to be a hateful being who deserved pain and horror.

Take his father, a good man in the eyes of most people, a family man who worked hard, followed the Church, and was kind to the poor. All true, though they missed the man's habit of seducing the young maids in the hone and forcing them to receive abortions from Mama Coltello before he sent them to work for one of his friends. The hypocrisy had bothered young Federigo, though that was merely one example he found in every person he ever encountered. An observant child, he always found the flaw in each person. Take the village beauty, Aurora Rossi, a tall, stunning, dark-haired, emerald-eyed goddess whose husky voice had enflamed his lust. Watching her one day, he had noticed something she had tried to hide from all people—she was only happy when she played one lover against another. Gui subtly spread that information around and soon Aurora was hissed at in the streets and treated as if she had been a leper. Horrified, she had ran away and died of starvation in the streets of Rome. All because Federigo Gui didn't like the idea of anyone possessing a hold over him, even unknowingly.

The rest of his life had followed that path, outward control, inward observation for weaknesses. Then, once a chance arrived, he would destroy anyone standing his way. Whether it was through words, rumors, or poison, Federigo Gui received a modicum of pleasure squashing enemies like bugs under foot.

"Lorenzo Pinot, Father Abbot," René stated, pushing the frightened murderous artist into the office of the Cupbearer's master.

"Ah, very good," Gui said and smiled, enjoying the way sweat beaded on Pinot's upper lip. "I have a service for you, little Lorenzo…"

CHAPTER XLIX

Bartolomeo Dardi pressed two revolvers into Karnstein's chest as he slammed the door close.

"You two, guard the rear. Do not let anything enter this room."

"Father, you cannot mean it! Why that...?" Sylvia said and was cut off by a chopping gesture from her father.

"Your baron is badly injured; you will not allow any creature near him. Also, we must not be assaulted from behind. Do as I say, dear daughter."

Dardi leaped forward with a laugh.

"He's not wrong," Karnstein said, still wincing at the impact of the two guns against him flesh.

"My father is often..."

"I am injured. If I try to swing a sword, I will not do well," said Karnstein.

He noticed her face and looked confused.

"What did you think I meant?"

"Nothing! Nothing!" Sylvia said and pulled him back near the door.

The flood of walking dead guards fouled each other in the small doorway, their stumbling, shambling forms slowing what would be an overwhelming tide of cold flesh. The first two fell to Jean-Pierre Séverin's sword, falling as their brains spattered out of the back of their skulls.

Francesca Policeni lunged forward, her technique that of one who spent time in a training hall. It was lovely, precise, exactly as presented in fencing manuals, and tickled the undead guard's chest.

Dardi pushed her aside and lashed out, his short arm extending the blade and piercing the skull. The guard collapsed and two more stepped in place, both of which he dispatched with a pair of simple lunges.

"Madame Policeni," Séverin said, kicking an approaching undead man into another and watching them stumble over each other. "We are not in a training hall. Either attack with full power or allow Sylvia to take your place. She will not fail."

Francesca muttered an oath, her face looking ugly as she kicked the next attacker and split the creature's skull. She attacked a second and cried, "*Morire bastardo!*"

Dardi danced about, laughing and destroying the attackers.

"Signora, you can't kill these men; they're already dead!"

"Concentrate! I believe we are almost done with these monsters," Séverin said.

His movements were never wasted, his every attack a demonstration of calm accuracy and excellence. His word proved correct; a moment later Dardi dispatched the last guard, leaving the floor littered with the putrefying dead. The stench was abominable, rising as they fell by the blades of the two swordmasters and the criminal leader.

"The outer door shattered a moment ago," Karnstein said, slowly moving forward with Sylvia's help. "The walking corpses shall be upon us in seconds."

His words proved prophetic as the door they had entered moments earlier shuddered and cracked. Without prompting, the group exited, though there was no means of locking this door. They ran down a short corridor that led to a second one built exactly as the others. The halls were dark, dusty, and filled with the scents of rot and mold—odors often associated with an abandoned location.

"I believe we are in the administrative wing of the prison," Séverin explained, heading down a new corridor. "The doors will lead to storage and offices. We must not enter any for fear there are no exits."

"Gâteloup, the undead broke through the final door, they will be flooding into this wing now," Dardi said, glancing over his shoulder.

Séverin opened his mouth to reply, when a loud splintering sound filled the air. Looking around the corner, he spotted a series of doors, each breaking apart as hands and legs thrust through the portals. Pulling back, he shook his head and pointed the direction of the breaking doors.

"Our only means of escape is that direction. We must move single file quickly. A staircase is at the end of the hallway, leading down below the prison."

Karnstein and Sylvia reluctantly parted. He forced her to step ahead of him, his stony face ignoring her silent entreaties.

"Baron Karnstein cannot move faster than a slow walk. We should leave him..." Francesca started to say.

The words caught in her mouth as a dagger touched her throat. Sylvia's face was unearthly calm as she said:

"Oh, do go on. Finish that sentence."

"Sylvia!" Dardi yelled. "We do not have time for this nonsense. Nobody will be left behind."

"And I will force myself to keep pace," Karnstein said.

Sylvia paused a few seconds and stepped back.

"*Andiamo*," she said.

With that, they started to run down the hall, despite the inhuman snarls filling the air and the clawed hands reaching for their arms and legs...

CHAPTER L

"Do not fire until I give the word," Giulio Nucci stated, caressing his new rifle with loving hands.

The new French arms were wonderful, truly powerful and loaded faster than any gun they owned in the past. He heard, from one of the men in the wine shop they had stopped in, that the French could fire their muskets three times in one minute. Giulio was the fastest in the gang at two per minute, but that would change as they practiced.

Sending two of the men forward, he watched as they killed the pair of guards with their long knives. They dragged the dead men out of sight, depositing the still bleeding corpses behind a pair of flowering bushes not far from the gate. Opening the gate wide enough to admit the gang, Giulio ran in a low crouch until they reached the barracks. Checking the door, he smiled as it proved to be unlocked and opened silently.

"Bring them in," he whispered and watched as four men ran away, returning seconds later struggling with a barrel and a lit lantern.

Pocking a pair of holes in the side, Giulio nodded, and the men threw open the door. They kicked the barrel inside and backed away. Shouts of surprise sounded inside and one of the gang tossed the lantern inside a second later. They turned and ran just as a wave of flame exploded through the door and nearby windows. Giulio laughed as the shrieks of the French soldiers filled the air.

"Fire if any of those bastards tries to escape!" he yelled. "Watch the windows!"

A few of the soldiers attempted to crawl out the windows, only to be gunned down by the gang. They laughed as the soldiers tried to beg for mercy, but dying seconds later.

"You three," Giulio pointed at a small pack in the rear. "Move to the left and kill anyone you see. Gio, take two more

255

off to the right. Nobody lives. Understood? Good! The rest of you, with me."

Giulio reloaded his rifle as they headed into the temporary headquarters of the French army in Napoli. Soldiers ran out, weapons in hand, officers drawing swords, and a few scantily-clad ladies screaming in fear. Giulio and his men killed them all, women included. They set to blaze every room, with only the slim, imperious-looking officer spared and brought outside. The man's name was Adam Le Meunier and he struggled in vain against his captors. A plain-looking, hard-working individual, Le Meunier was a soldier whom the higher-ranking members of the military prized. He was intelligent and brave with tactical skills and just enough ruthlessness to be useful in a newly kingdom. His goal was to be like his hero, the great Lazare Hoche.

"You are the man who rules over this part of my homeland, eh Frenchman?" Giulio said as he drew his new sword bayonet and slid next the shivering captive. "That shall not do. We shall send a message to your masters… let them know they are not welcome in our country!"

An hour later, the gang left, jubilant but a little confused as well. They were wealthier by a small pile gold coins and some ammunition for their guns. Yet in doing so they had murdered almost one hundred French soldiers, set fire to their buildings and watched as Giulio Nucci had tortured a man to death. While they liked the idea of greater funds, this action did seem out-of-character for their leader.

"Are we guerrillas now?" more than a few asked in various forms that evening and in the subsequent days.

The money was far better, but they were attacking the French army—the same army that had conquered Naples with ease. Giulio, in contrast to his men, was happier than he had been in years. His new ideas were brilliant and successful; he was rapidly becoming a legend. He, the great *Camorra* boss Giulio Nucci, was now the very devil to his enemies. No longer was he called *Il Principe*; now Giulio Nucci was *Fra Diavolo*, the devil to all French invaders.

CHAPTER LI

The moans and screams rose as the doors continued to snap and shatter under the weight of the unliving. Their hands waved and grabbed the air and the wood continued to buckle under their unyielding pressure.

"We move at a trot, not a run," Séverin said. "If you are grabbed by a hand or teeth, call out and we shall extract you. Do not pull away, even if it hurts."

Turning, he set the pace while stepping over a thin, emaciated claw of a hand that had scrabbled towards his ankle. A loud scratching sound drifted to their ears, only partially muffled by the snapping of cheap, old wood.

"Ahhh! They have me!" Francesca shrieked as a large fist caught her arm in a tight grasp.

She struggled, pulling backwards and dropped to one knee. Sylvia snorted, not hiding her amusement, and sliced the hand off at the wrist. She yanked Francesca back to her feet and propelled her forward with a hard shove between the shoulder blades.

"That one thinks she is my rival?" she muttered, sounding amused.

She grinned and added a falsely chirpy, "You're welcome!" to Francesca's flushed, furious face.

"We continue," Séverin said, resuming his pace.

The doors shattered every second, the wood sending splinters littering across the path. Just as they stepped clear of the hallway, the other end of the corridor filled with the shambling, ambulatory undead they had barely avoided moments earlier. Their torn and tattered flesh failed to slow these creatures as they moaned and gibbered, screeched, and snarled, as they loped towards their living targets.

"Let us slow them a few steps," Dardi said, pouring a line of gunpowder behind him as he followed the others.

Then, striking the flint of his musket on the stone, he set fire to the powder, which immediately ignited. A veritable wall of flames exploded behind his fleeing form, the heat becoming a wall of force that appeared to explode in every direction.

"Downstairs! Quickly! That flame will vanish in seconds," Séverin ordered.

He pulled a huge steel door open. A gloomily lit staircase lay within and a small series of lights were visible in the distance. Ushering everyone inside, the Frenchman slammed the door and threw a heavy bolt to lock it from within. Sighing with open relief, the tall swordmaster resumed his position at the head of the column and started down the narrow, stone steps.

"That door will hold them far longer. It is made of heavy iron, including the frame," he explained. "Usually that is the weak point. That's how the dead tore through the doors at our rear. But this one will take them days to destroy."

"Are we planning on staying down here for that long?" Karnstein asked, wincing as he followed the rest down the steps.

"No," replied Séverin, shaking his head. "There are means of escape below. Water and waste must flow, or else this entire prison, prisoners and guards alike, would be dead from the bloody flux. We may confront some random undead, but the majority are on the floors above our heads."

They reached the bottom of the stairs and faced a straight corridor that headed to the left and right. Séverin sniffed the air and frowned, then stepped towards the right, when he was suddenly stopped by Karnstein's hand.

"No, not that direction" the Austrian said. "Unless your intent is to head us into the Black Room."

"What is the black room?" Sylvia asked, stepping to his side.

"A rip in the world. A piece of the void," Karnstein explained, ignoring Francesca's rolling eyes and snort of derision.

"If you say it is in that direction, we shall not pass that way," Séverin said, silencing the questioning looks from Dardi and Sylvia with a gesture. "I have no desire to pass through that again."

The trek through the underground of the infamous Nisida Prison was positively dull in comparison with the horrors they had witnessed earlier. Two shambling corpses, each more skeletal than the other, were dispatched by Séverin and Dardi with almost bored motions. The search continued; each door opened onto either storage rooms, empty, filthy chambers possessing no signs of life, or further corridors.

"Is the plan to have us die of thirst rather than being torn to pieces by the monsters above?" Francesca demanded as the passed through yet another door leading to a new corridor. "And if Herr Baron Karnstein can exorcise demons, why does he not do so to the ones above?"

"I can destroy these creatures one at a time, but it is faster to use a revolver or a blade," Karnstein replied, his hand against the wall to prevent him from swaying as he stood.

He was steadily weakening and appeared to be operating by sheer will alone.

"It matters not," Séverin interjected. "I found what we sought. A sewer tunnel…"

He pointed at a door ahead. The stench of human waste filled the air, a putrescent cloud that was noxious and nauseating.

An hour later, a small fishing scow offloaded five figures whose scent was so foul that the horses in the nearby carriage appeared to shy away and shake their heads. Ettore Policeni stepped out of the carriage and stared in shock at his filth-stained wife as she brushed him aside.

"Madonna, you stink! What happened? And why is your…?" he started to ask, only to be stopped by a look from Francesca.

The murderous glint in his eyes caused him to recoil instantly. He was grateful for some distance between himself and his wife and took an additional step backwards.

"Get in here, *bastardo*. We have much to tell Papa," Francesca hissed.

She then disappeared into the depths of the carriage.

Ettore made the sign of the cross and stepped into the coach, trying to keep from retching. This would be a long trip home...

CHAPTER LII

"We have a visitor," Dardi said to Séverin as they practiced advanced rapier work the next morning. "Shall I fetch…?"

Séverin shook his head, lowering his blade.

"Karnstein needs his sleep and Sylvia would react poorly if we tried to make her leave his side."

This much was the stark truth. By the time they had returned to the academy, Karnstein had succumbed to his wounds and passed out. The injuries he had received at the hands of the vampire woman named Fortuna were terrible, but with rest, he would heal in a short time. Since then, Sylvia had only left the room to get food for them both.

Johann Spurzheim stepped into the room, his stern face possessing little of the disdainful humor that he had demonstrated during their previous encounters.

"You are mere days away from being arrested," he said. "Both of you and your followers are the targets of the Cupbearers. They only wait for the return of King Joseph sometime tomorrow night. Then Gui will demand your arrest and likely succeed."

"No doubt yours as well, Monsieur Spurzheim," Séverin mused aloud. "How did you find out?"

"The walls of his headquarters possess a heat vent based on the Roman hypocaust. He demanded those chambers and relegated myself and my people to the windowless cells at the far end of the palace. What he failed to realize is that the hypocaust are an open space in the walls and floor. To state simply, gentlemen, I listened in and learned his plans. I will even go so far as agree with you, Maestro Séverin. I am to be arrested as well, and my offices merged with his Cupbearers."

"Continue talking, Commissario," Dardi crossed his arms across his chest. "You have more information to tell."

Spurzheim released a lungful of air and frowned.

"I also learned that Gui serves a demon and that his new secretary, René, is a vampire."

"They are not vampires," Karnstein said as he and Sylvia stepped into the training hall together.

"You thought to leave us out?" Sylvia asked, smiling with open amusement.

"You insist on that distinction every time we use the word vampires, Franz," Séverin said. "I think it is time you explain fully. Allow Herr Spurzheim to hear as well."

Karnstein looked to Sylvia and an unspoken conversation appeared to pass between the two. Finally, he nodded and said:

"Very well. The difficulty will not lay in your comprehension of what I say, but in my difficulty in explaining what I witnessed."

"Just do your best," Séverin prompted, returning his practice rapier to the rack.

Karnstein's eyes appeared to take on a distant quality, as if he was viewing an object at a great distance. His words, when they came a moment later, were carefully controlled and reminiscent of the cold personality he presented to the world.

"When I examine a being," he said, "I see the energy within the shell we call our bodies. A person, good or evil in their intentions or actions, glow with life energy. Vampires and demons are dark creatures who inhabit a human body. To look into their soul... no, that is the wrong word... A demon uses a human body the way we do a suit of clothing. A vampire is a mindless creature that joins with the dying human. The monster takes on most of the memories and personality of the now-dead human. Their insane appetite and the demonic lusts rise and they either become nothing more than feeders in the dark or fiends capable of terrible evil."

"This much we always suspected," Dardi said, pursing his lips and nodding his head. "Books and monster hunters always suggested that was the reason why vampires exist."

"I'm grateful my words are making some degree of sense," Karnstein replied, still looking distant. "When I study

262

the world through my altered eyes, there are threads of light that head up and out into the world. It's like a giant spider web. My teacher in this art form referred to this as the skein of life. I used this skill on the body of the undead man named Anton, and saw that he he was different. He wasn't real... there was no him in there..."

"What is he saying? This makes no sense. Skein of life? A person who is not real? What was he, a puppet?" Spurzheim demanded, his face not hiding his derision.

"Shut up!" Sylvia said, her face not hiding her annoyance.

She subsided after a motion from her father, and went back to listening to Karnstein.

"Anton was consumed by a darkness, a power that was like nothing I'd ever seen in the past" said the Exorcist. "It was like gazing into a void, a living but not living void. There was no Anton in there, not even a trace... the dark power filled his body and it was the only thing within... he was nothing more than a tentacle or a thread of something greater... I followed the thread of black energy from his body and into the skein... then I saw it..."

Karnstein's voice was a hushed croak, only slightly above a whisper. He didn't seem to notice that Sylvia had taken his hand, but it was clear he was reliving the terrible events of that day.

"What did you see?" Séverin asked.

Karnstein shuddered and he looked up into his teacher's eyes.

"A living darkness full of disease, hatred and destruction. This creature was terrible... It was like staring into a star made entire of black energy. It only sought to consume and control the entirety of all life... It was so powerful, just looking at that... that... I was drowning... nothing I could do... I would not be me if Sylvia hadn't... but it is still out there..."

Sylvia stepped in front of Franz and took his face in her hands. She didn't speak, but forced his staring eyes to meet hers, moving slightly to make sure he could not see anything but her face. She held him for several minutes, patiently watching him without appearing to breathe. Eventually, he nodded, and she released his face with apparent reluctance. Their fingers entwined, and she stepped to his side. Her position and stance were protective, possibly threatening to any nearby. Karnstein looked back at Séverin.

"I have seen the truth within witches, warlocks, vampires, werewolves, and demons. That creature was more than any of them... More powerful than all the vampires I've ever fought if they were mixed into one being like a chemist's potion. This was a nightmare and I thought I was going to be consumed by it like that pathetic creature we captured."

"I think this man should be locked in a cell with other mad men," Spurzheim sneered, shaking his head. "Everyone knows the Karnstein family are a pack of madmen."

Sylvia was about to reply, when the Exorcist held up his free hand. She closed her mouth, but her eyes looked at Spurzheim with angry intent.

"If you believe I am one of the black Karnsteins, then leave," said the Exorcist. "You are not being held here against your will, Signor. The exit lays behind you and none shall block your passage."

"And if I choose to stay, Herr Baron?" Spurzheim asked, a note of challenge in his tone.

"Then kindly shut your mouth and leave the discussion to others who comprehend the subject at hand," Karnstein spat back, causing Spurzheim to step back a pace at the furious look on the young Austrian's face.

"I believe I comprehend the meaning of your words," Séverin stated, analyzing the information. "The power you observed consumes the victims from which it feeds. Those it decided to keep become puppets, a false version of their true self. This demon, for lack of a better term, uses its victims as its tentacles of power."

"What about the shambling, attacking dead men we witnessed on the island?" Dardi asked.

"Pawns, weapons, and slaves," Séverin replied, running a hand over his chin in thought. "It explains also why this creature's actions are random and inexplicable. You used a word that describes Nosos exactly... disease. This monster is unique and terrible, but also limited. A disease must spread, must take form so that the sickness spreads from creature to creature."

Séverin began to pace the training hall.

"This is a very interesting theory, but how does it help us battle this monster?" Spurzheim asked.

Dardi snapped his fingers and laughed.

"If we can destroy the tentacles and the power, the creature can be destroyed!"

"No," Karnstein replied, shaking his head quickly. "No mortal weapon can destroy this monster. It is not like anything we've ever seen."

"It does not matter" Séverin stated, stopping before his pupil. "We have avenues of attack and a means of compensating afterwards. What we must do is find out the monster's complete plan. For that, we require you to act again, Franz. You must examine the creature and find out its intentions."

"No! That beast almost destroyed him last time!" Sylvia yelled, stepping between Séverin and Karnstein.

"Nevertheless, it must be attempted," Séverin said, his voice calm. "Otherwise, we will continue to flail blindly against this monster—and it will win."

Karnstein looked down and nodded.

"Yes, I will do it."

He looked at Sylvia who was about to protest, but his face remained implacable.

"I must do it. Come, I need to go to the church and pray."

Sylvia didn't reply, but shot an angry look over her shoulder as they left the room. A few seconds later, the front door banged closed and a silence entered the training hall.

"If the baron dies in this attempt, that girl will make it her life's mission to kill you, Maestro Séverin," Spurzheim said, snorting with laughter and shaking his head.

"We were aware of that some time ago, Spurzheim," Dardi said, joining the laughter. "Still, your pupil is taking a terrible risk, Gâteloup."

"I know," Séverin replied, his face remaining as impassive as ever. "It is unfortunate that we have no other means. I believe that, based on the Contrôleur Général's information, Nosos's attack on the kingdom will take place very soon."

"I said nothing of the kind! You cannot believe I am in league with these… things!" Spurzheim spluttered.

Séverin shook his head.

"Of course not. I merely extrapolated based on Abbot Gui's determination to arrest all of us as fast as he can. He is not desperate yet, given his willingness to await the King's return, so we have some time. Yet, the arrest does mean that they are preparing for the monster's major attack. Therefore, we must attempt to discover the details of the enemy's plans. Also, I have an idea how to break Karnstein's away from the fiend, should the need arise."

"Gâteloup," Dardi said, still grinning, "you have that glint in your eyes that means we are about to walk into danger."

Séverin raised an eyebrow.

"Does that mean you plan on fleeing?"

Dardi threw back his head and howled with laughter.

"Never! Together we shall once again face down the hordes of Hell, armed only with a pair of swords and our wits!"

"Then we're doomed," Spurzheim said, shaking his head.

CHAPTER LIII

The woman was as enticing as Father Gui had indicated—a lovely creature who was just common-looking enough to fit his needs.

Lorenzo Pinot watched Sylvia Dardi, his lust rising in his breast, sweat appearing across his brow. It had been three weeks since he had last created another work of art upon the canvas of a woman's flesh. Already he was wondering what her body would look like if he removed her nose and ears, but left her large breasts only lightly sliced.

The difficulty lay in that she wasn't alone. To take a woman off the street, even in daylight, Lorenzo needed a small degree of privacy. Even in a busy street, he knew how to disarm a crowd with a few choice words and a little prodding in the bitch's back with his blade. But his chosen subjects had to be on their own, preventing anyone from objecting or remembering who took off their friend, daughter, or lover.

Waiting outside the small church, Lorenzo patted the *sica* blade thrust in his pants and observed the lines of the building. As an artist, he enjoyed the wonderful architecture of Naples and often used the flowing lines as inspiration for his own artistry. His artwork, the paintings and sculptures often, used such images as a means of transforming the simplistic into the divine. As for the bodies of his victim, that was an art form only he truly comprehended. Lorenzo wished there was a means of sculpting human flesh the same way he did stone or clay. That would result in art that would make Da Vinci and Michelangelo look like children sketching in the street with chalk. Imagine a woman, a living breathing female, whose parts were in a more pleasing order. The thought was truly inspired by the fires of creation.

Lorenzo's reverie broke when Sylvia's shapely form appeared in the doorway of the church. Her ebony hair shimmered in the sunlight though the riding clothing she wore did nothing to sexually arouse Lorenzo's lusts. He knew that when she would be tied up in his studio, shredding her clothing with his knives would establish who was in command. Then this Sylvia Dardi would be where she belonged, in the power of Lorenzo Pinot.

Stepping over with delighted anticipation, Lorenzo looked as if he was about to enter the church. Sylvia paid him no mind, which offended the artist of human flesh even more than her improper clothing. Breathing heavily, Lorenzo yanked out the *sica* and raised it before her wide eyes.

"Do not make a sound," he hissed, slowly extending his arm to bring the edge towards her face. "If you scream…"

That was the last Lorenzo could say before Sylvia grabbed his wrist and twisted. The thin bones snapped, causing the dagger to fall from the artist's now crippled fingers. He yelped, a high-pitched yowl that caused him to sound more like an injured kitten than an adult male. Sylvia shoved him back and stooped to pick up the *sica*. She examined the weapon with a contemptuous eye before using the cobble stones to bend the blade in half.

"Go away, little man," she said.

Despite the stabbing pain in his arm, Lorenzo pulled out his other blade. This was a heavy bayonet, his second favorite armament after his now destroyed *sica*.

"*Putanna*! I kill you!" he shrieked, raising his knife above his head and stabbing downward

Sylvia stepped to the side and caught her attacker's arm. She winked as he struggled to free himself from her grasp. Seeing his shocked look and feeling the momentarily slackened muscled, she thrust the arm downward. The blade bit deep into her assailant's leg and Lorenzo was too shocked to even scream. He pulled the blade free, watching as his trouser turned crimson in an instant. With a contemptuous kick, Sylvia propelled him down the street, where he stumbled and fell onto the hard-packed Earth. A low moan emerged from his lips as the world slowly grew dark.

"My son, are you injured?" a deacon asked, spotting the collapsing form.

Seeing the growing pool of blood, he nodded and called back to his cousin, a fellow priest in training.

"Get over here! We have another stabbed man. Help me carry him to the doctor!"

In the front of the church, Sylvia kicked the bayonet into a sewer grate. Karnstein emerged a moment later, his look quizzical as spotted her near the sewer.

"Someone dropped a piece of metal. It might hurt a horse or a child," Sylvia explained, telling a version of truth that prevented any further discussions.

Karnstein nodded, already apparently disinterested.

"We'd best return. I have to do this, Sylvia."

Sylvia took his hand and squeezed it tight.

"I know," was all she managed to say as they strolled back to the fencing academy.

They were quiet the rest of the walk.

CHAPTER LIV

"Do you need a special space or location to do you... What is it that you do, Karnstein?" Dardi asked as Sylvia and the Exorcist returned to the academy.

Karnstein didn't answer for a moment, his thoughts on Séverin's request. He wasn't given to using these skills often, knowing they weighed heavily upon his mind. Even a momentarily glance into the skein caused him to see how unimportant anyone person was in this world. As humans, it was easy to ignore the volume of living creatures that existed, even in a small location. Which meant the more of the skein you examined, the greater you realized your own relative unimportance. Still, this was the best chance of discovering this... fiend's identity and plans. They had a name, Nosos, and a possible identity from ancient literature. That could mean everything or nothing—there was no way of knowing. The only truth was that, if this monster infected him, death would be preferable than existing as a shell, a tentacle of that ancient evil. Realizing everyone was staring at him, Karnstein bowed and clicked his heels.

"No, Maestro. I just need a place to sit and some quiet to help me concentrate on the invocation," he replied.

"What happens if we interrupt you when you are casting your spells? Death to us all?" Spurzheim asked.

"I do not cast spells. This is a form of examination and exorcism that predates our Lord's birth. But to answer your question, it means I must start over and regain my calm and control. Unless you are demon, what I perform is of no matter to any present."

"Then let us move to Barto's personal study," Séverin said, ushering everyone up the stairs. "That will allow us a chance to sit in comfort while you perform your work."

Dardi took a seat behind his desk, while the others stood, looking uncomfortably at Karnstein. The young baron shrugged and moved to sit in a wooden chair, but was stopped by a gesture from Séverin.

"No," Séverin said and pointed at the divan. "I told you I have a notion of how to assist you. Mademoiselle Dardi shall sit at your side and take your hand while you are gazing into this other world. She will anchor you and you will listen for her voice."

"It is not another world that I study, but the…"

Karnstein's explanation was stopped by Sylvia's hand across his mouth.

"*Idiota*! We do not need one of your lectures on the holy power you use. Simply nod and get to work!" Sylvia snapped and removed her hand.

"Stop calling me an idiot," Karnstein replied, some heat in his words.

"Then stop acting like one!" Sylvia replied and smiled.

The corner of Karnstein's mouth twitched in a partial smile and he sat down at her side on the divan. Spurzheim rolled his eyes and appeared to mutter something about the horrors of youth, but he was ignored.

"Very well," Karnstein said, moving a few inches away from Sylvia. "I will begin. Please remain silent until the working is complete. Then you may do as you wish. My answers may be a bit slow and this will take some time. Possibly hours, maybe even days."

"Why so long? You found this Nosos creature with ease last time," Spurzheim asked, not hiding his skepticism.

"Last time I had the body of one of the fiend's tentacles to use as a link. This time I have nothing. I search through the entire universe for the plutonian void that is Nosos. I have no means of knowing how long it shall take to scan the skein."

"Let the man work, Spurzheim," Dardi said, leaning on his desk, his bulging eyes looking at the police chief with open hostility. "Ask your questions later!"

"If there is nothing more?" Karnstein asked and looked at the others.

He then nodded at the ensuing silence and closed his eyes.

"Very well, I begin."

Clasping his hands together, he performed a quick silent prayer. Opening his hands, he then began to speak, the sounds causing Dardi and Spurzheim to gape in shock.

"*Anshargal Ati Me Peta Babka Nisme Annu Isten! Usmi Annu Isten Ina Akhkharu Ma Ina Maskim Xul, Ina Kashshaptu, Ina Lilit, Su'ati Mursu In Matum!*"

A silver sigil appeared before his body for an instant. His eyes slowly opened and the silver illumination covering his orbs caused Barto and Spurzheim to stare in open-mouthed shock. Both appeared unable to speak for an instant, before exploding into a flood of words.

"*Gott im Himmel!*" Spurzheim breathed.

"Witchcraft!" Dardi said, standing and staring at Karnstein's shimmering eyes.

"Only if you believe *il Papa* hires warlocks, Father," Sylvia replied, her voice full of acid.

Dardi opened his mouth to reply, but his words were lost as Karnstein reared back, his face a mask of terror.

The Exorcist's head was pointed downward towards the floor, yet he gazed about in every direction.

"The darkness… it spreads… all below us… it is like a flood and will drown us all in disease and death! Death! Death to all life!"

CHAPTER LV

Pia Mele read the note a third time, confused by the request. Why did her patron want her Giulio Nucci to attack and kill a minor court official as he toured the countryside? The last targets made sense, robberies of weapons, food, gold, and the death of many French occupiers—these were a means of gaining power. The chamberlain of the royal court was just a servant, a nobody in truth.

No matter, Pia would follow the directive. In all things, her patron had proved correct, so why question her now? Returning to her bedroom, she spotted the snoring Giulio, head back, sweat drying on his naked chest. Their lovemaking was frequent and, if possible, more intense, these days. Another improvement in her life, thanks to her benefactor.

Reaching into the bag of personal items by the bed, she removed a small wooden box. Within the shallow depths of the container was a fine brown powder, the granules possessing a sandy consistency. Removing a tiny pinch between her fingers, she returned the box to her hiding place and climbed into bed with Giulio. With a quick blow, the powder flew into the sleeping man's face, vanishing in seconds.

"Giulio? Giulio Nucci, can you hear me?" Pia whispered, moving closer to her lover.

"Yes," he mumbled, his eyes never opening.

"You will lead the men on a special job. You want nothing more than to butcher the pig who is the chamberlain of the French king, Joseph. Once he is dead, you will be happy and will return here to your Pia. You want nothing else. Do you understand?"

"Kill the pig of a chamberlain. Return to Pia. I understand," Giulio mumbled in reply.

Smiling, Pia left the bed and stepped out onto the balcony overlooking the large expanse of property. This was the life she had always sought, one without a care for the world. They had enough money to pay the locals to clean and cook, leaving Pia time to walk and buy new dresses and continue to look pretty. What more could she possibly need?

A swat on her pert bottom told her that Giulio was awake. He stood behind her, naked, tumescent, and grinning broadly.

"Good morning, my little Venus!"

She turned, grinning and responded:

"It is afternoon, *Fra Diavolo*."

"Morning, afternoon, night? What does it matter? I have a pig to kill today and my musket needs polishing," Giulio said and laughed.

"Musket? Looks more like a cannon to me," Pia replied, dropping to her knees.

An hour later, Giulio strode out of the villa, his good humor still present.

"My friends, we have a special duty today! Today we kill a French dog and all his men."

"Why? Where is the profit?" Nino Nucci, a distant cousin of Giulio's asked.

He was a young man, still in his teens, with a long, sallow face and an inability to grow anything approaching a beard. Smarter than most of the gang, Nino was the only one willing to openly ask questions of their leader these days.

Giulio patted his cousin on the face fondly.

"Nino, Nino, Nino, not everything is about profit. This is about blood and revenge. This *bastardo* will pay for what he did to me."

That ended the discussion, even for the skeptical Nino. In the *Camorra*, the vendetta was an accepted ritual that would not, could not, be questioned.

Within an hour, they were off, none even considering how this grudge between their leader and the French friend of the king emerged. Such was the way of the *Camorra*…

CHAPTER LVI

Sylvia didn't wait for a cue from Séverin or her father; she was already straddling Karnstein's legs, grabbing both of his arms and shouting:

"Franz! Franz! Listen to me, do you hear me? Franz!"

Karnstein struggled for a moment before hearing the voice. It drifted to him from a great distance, more of an intrusive echo than anything actively connected to him and the skein of all life.

"Sylvia?" he whispered.

"Yes, you hear me. Listen to my voice. I am turning your head, look only at me," Sylvia's voice seemed to say.

His vision shifted and Karnstein spotted her in the skein. Her bright energy was mere inches from his eyes, blinding him from the ebon void that was encompassing the world.

"I see you," he whispered, a sense of calm beginning to relax his taut, terrified, body.

"Good," Sylvia said. "Now, we will look again at this darkness. I am with you this time. I will stay with you the whole time."

Karnstein shuddered at the thought, but he did allow his eyes to drift downward. The tide of darkness shuddered and quaked, a vast oceanic tide of disease and horror that caused him to recoil again.

"No, Franz! Do not be afraid," Sylvia said. "I am still here. Can you see me?"

Glancing up, Karnstein spotted her light at his side, mere inches where his shell resided.

"Yes," he replied.

"Then we will now look at this horror. What is it? Is this Nosos the size of the city now?" Sylvia asked.

Karnstein studied the gloom, moving his mind closer waves of horrors he witnessed. As he approached, he realized that this was not a wave, but closer to a rainstorm. What appeared to be a single mass of black, diseased energy was thousands, no, millions, of tiny creatures. They moved under their own power, their connection to the greater power an uncountable number of infinitesimal threads.

"It is not one creature, but millions... tiny. Some are so small... none man-sized... they move every direction... underground... some not... millions of them!"

Karnstein suddenly felt overwhelmed by the sight, the sheer volume of creatures under Nosos's control.

"I am still here, amore. Look at me again," Sylvia said, her voice piercing his rising panic.

Seeing she hadn't left his side, Karnstein turned back to the creatures. Their life energies were all gone, consumed by the darkness. Examining the almost microscopic threads, he realized they all connected to a vast void in the distance.

Moving his mind closer, he spotted one other strand, a thicker cord of negative power that connected to one being... a human-sized tentacle that one possessed hundreds of small strands in a vast web.

Viewing this information from a distance, he realized what he was viewing. It all made sense, though the others might be able to interpret it better.

Pulling away, he said a brief prayer of thanks out loud:

"*Gloria patri, et Filio, et Spiritui Sancto. Sicut erat in principio, et nunc, et semper, et in saecula saeculorum. Amen.*"

Karnstein removed himself from the skein of life. That was when he realized that Sylvia was seated astride his body, her strong hands resting lightly across his shoulders. Her father, one of the most dangerous swordsmen in Europe, watched with a bemused expression, as did the dour Jean-Pierre Séverin, and the sneering Johann Spurzheim. The young Austrian flushed, his pale skin turning crimson at the scene before his pale eyes.

"If that is a holy ritual, I could see myself suddenly becoming religious," Spurzheim said, rolling his eyes.

"What did you see, Franz?" Séverin asked, stepping between the police chief and Sylvia.

Karnstein looked at his teacher over Sylvia's shoulder.

"Below the ground and above, Nosos is spreading her power. She is doing it using tiny creatures, some smaller than my fingernails, others larger, but none the size of a man. Also, one of her tentacles receives a great flow of dark power. From that creature, there are hundreds of smaller vessels."

"That is meant to tell us something?" Spurzheim asked, shaking his head. "You sound like one of those witch women who promise to tell your future for a silver coin."

"No, it makes perfect sense," Séverin said, his eyes distant. "Nosos is a disease and one of the greatest plagues to ever assault mankind, intending to spread through the world, starting in Naples. This fiend means to destroy all life in the kingdom by flooding the land using the oldest method."

"Rats and mice!" Dardi said, his fists crashing on the desk.

"Correct," said Séverin, nodding gravely. "The city, all cities, are infected with the plague of these creatures. The Black Death nearly destroyed the world. Imagine if the mind of a monster was behind that assault upon life?"

"Then we are doomed," Spurzheim snarled. "I can muster possibly one regiment of soldiers and an equal number of gendarmes. That is not nearly enough to combat millions of rodents infesting the kingdom."

"Those will be of use, but there are others we can bring into this battle," Dardi said, smiling.

His eyes met Séverin's and a silent communication passed between the two men. They nodded, instantly comprehending the full scope of the possible plan.

"Monsieur Spurzheim, you and I must speak in detail," Séverin said. "Barto, can you recruit the others?"

Dardi clapped and rubbed his hands together.

"Easy enough, my friend. First, Sylvia? Can you do me a simple service?"

"Of course, Papa. What do you need?"

Dardi rolled his eyes.

"Climb off the young Baron Karnstein's lap. I find it very difficult to concentrate when you are seated in that location."

CHAPTER LVII

"O magnificent Queen of the Night?" Sinis asked, kneeling before his now-fed mistress.

The corpse of an old man lay on the sandy ground, his body shrunken and resembling a bumble of dried sticks more than a once semi-vital being.

"Sinis, you are becoming a source of irritation with your constant questioning. I know it is your nature, but it is also a failing. Allow me to answer before your tiny mind formulates the question that disturbs your pea-sized brain. You wish to know why I used my pretty slaves to dig a tunnel into the Earth, correct?"

Nosos opened her rheumy eyes and looked down at her kneeling slave

"Yes, o beautiful dark one. If you please," Sinis said, eyes downcast. "It confuses me. I thought you planned on using them to spread throughout the world."

"This is so, worm. However, your little book of graves reminded me of ancient days. You know that Naples is an ancient city. You believe it was first settled by the Greeks, no?" Nosos asked, chuckling softly.

"Yes, mistress," Sinis answered.

"The Greeks built their city on the ruins of an outpost of a people known as the Hyperboreans. Those people may have succeeded the Serpent-Men, former rulers of this part of the world. Or possibly the Dragon-Kings. I do not remember. I am still trying to return to being the complete Nosos…"

She frowned.

"The complete Nosos? But you are Nosos, the Daughter of Darkness, sister of the Tenebrae, lady of disease and corruption, mistress of…"

Sinis suddenly found he was unable to speak, his jaw frozen.

"Yes, yes, I know my titles. Your voice begins to grate on my nerves, Sinis. I am not fully come to my power. Does disease flourish across the lands? Are all beings in the Kingdom my slaves? No. Soon, when nothing but death and dying reside in this land, I shall be Nosos again. My power shall be that of a Goddess and, as I did once, I shall spread my plagues throughout the world..."

She paused and added:

"You may speak again."

"Is that why you keep sending walking corpses to assault Naples, mistress?" Sinis asked. "Because you are not fully Nosos yet?"

He remembered asking this question in the past, but receiving an answer that was unsatisfactory.

"Something like that, yes. I was playing, enjoying myself with my new lover's lives, my returning powers. Fear can be a disease too, slave. Do you fear me, Sinis?"

"I do, might queen. I fear you, hate you, love you, and worship you," Sinis replied, knowing complete honesty was needed now.

"Good, wretch. That is how a slave should feel about his better. You give me power through your inner conflict. But let us return to your question—why dig a tunnel? As I said, the city of Naples is ancient. The people who lived here numbered in the thousands and they were, for the time, intelligent. For religious reasons, they placed the temples of one of their gods deep within the bowels of the Earth. When you showed me the plans of the underground crypt, I knew a better method of spreading my power through the land. Digging a tunnel, I had my pretty slaves connect the crypt and the sewers to that ancient temple. This provided me with a means of spreading myself faster. Remember when you told me that my lovely vampire slaves were consuming rats for food?"

"Yes, mistress," Sinis replied, suddenly realizing how small he was in the plans of his owner. "You appeared unconcerned—almost happy even."

"That is because they did so at my orders. All their actions are mere echoes of their former selves to greater and lesser degrees. I ordered them all to feed on the rats. This allowed me to take control of the vermin and send them out into the population of such creatures. Each rat then attacked another and those attacked more...I belief the growth is known as exponential." Nosos replied, licking her cracked lips.

Sinis looked up, his face not hiding his shock. "Then you must control thousands of rats by now, great queen!"

"Yes, worm. And to answer your next question before you ask it, I keep them in the ancient temple because it is easier. When I begin my reclamation of Naples, I shall send my disease-ridden vermin to every corner of the land. Until then, keeping the little pests in one location allows me to focus on other areas. Like deciding when to have Giorgia bring her army of the dead to attack the city. No matter, soon the Kingdom of Naples shall be mine. Then we shall spread to Rome, Florence, and beyond the borders. Wonderful, is it not, pathetic one?"

"Yes, mistress," Sinis said, grateful for his place at her side

CHAPTER LVIII

"You asked to see me?" Ettore Policeni said, sitting himself behind the rococo-styled wooden desk.

He wore a comfortable blue suit, elegant yet understated, and carried a light wooden cane with a silver ball on top.

"No," Séverin said, his resolute face only demonstrating a slight hint of boredom.

Ettore looked nonplussed for a moment and then smiled.

"You wished to do business, Maestro Séverin? Therefore, you must speak to me. My wife, though a lovely intelligent woman, is not a man. She does not have any role in business affairs."

"I seek to speak to the head of the *Camorra*," Séverin stated, his voice not hiding his boredom.

"You said that earlier and, as a rare honor, I agreed to meet you personally. In saving my dear wife, I believe I owe you a debt. Now, state your business or leave. I am a busy man with many affairs to conduct."

Ettore slapped a flat hand on his desktop.

"You are the titular leader of the *Camorra*, Monsieur Policeni. But I seek the puppet master, not the little wooden man," Séverin replied, still speaking with open disinterest.

"You dare...?" Ettore exclaimed, his face turning red with rage.

Séverin held up a large hand to cut off the coming flow of threats and fury.

"Before you say another word, remember a few simple points, Monsieur. First, if you threaten me, I shall face you in a duel and slay you in three moves or less. Second, if you attempt to name a champion, I shall ensure that you are mocked mercilessly throughout the city before I kill your hired duelist. Third, your threats do not frighten me—nor does the silent man with the knife who lingers at the rear of the room. If he advances so much as a step, I shall end your life and then his

282

as well. Now, please bring me to the head of the *Camorra*. This discussion is becoming wearisome."

Ettore continued to turn red throughout the calm recitation of facts. Finally, he reached into the desk's top drawer and scrambled for his musket pistol.

Séverin appeared at his side, his movements a blur, his actions instantaneous. He slammed the drawer closed on Ettore's hand, causing the man to yelp in pain. Opening the drawer a second later, he snatched the revolver out and pointed the weapon at Ettore's head.

At the far end of the room, Lama Notturna stopped moving, dropping his hands to his side. He was a tiny man, almost dwarfish in height, with a thin, nearly emaciated body, and astonishingly long arms. His face was handsome, classic male beauty that one would expect to see on a statue of a Greek deity. The handsome countenance was jarring, in direct opposition of the strange body.

"This farce has gone on long enough," Francesca said, sweeping into the room in a gown made from red silk. "Ettore, you are making an ass of yourself."

"I... but..." Ettore spluttered, vacillating between fury and embarrassment.

"Shut up," Francesca said, though there was no heat in her words. "Lama Notturna, thank you. You may leave. Speak to Giacomo, he will explain your duties."

Francesca watched as the oddly-shaped man exited the chamber.

"That man, his name is Night Blade?" Séverin asked, interested despite himself.

"It is the only one he uses or allows anyone to say. He is the best silent killer in all of Italy, or so I have been told. Now, you wish to speak to the head of the *Camorra*?"

"Yes," Séverin said, his look hardening imperceptibly. "Are you about to insist you are the leader of the criminal underworld, Madame Policeni?"

Francesca laughed, her lovely face looking even more attractive in her merriment.

"No, not at all. We both know I admitted to receiving my interest in Baron Karnstein as an assignment. To say now that I am the mistress of all would be insulting your intelligence. No, please follow me. Leave behind the weapon. Ettore shall not touch it again today. Shall you, Ettore?"

Ettore shook his head, now looking embarrassed and downcast.

"No, I shall not."

Séverin returned the revolver to the drawer and nodded in Francesca's direction. He was unsurprised to hear the slide open and the sound of the weapon being cocked slowly.

"*Bastardo*!" Ettore screamed.

"Ettore! Put that gun away!" Francesca snarled, pulling a knife from her sleeve.

Séverin appeared disinterested as he raised one hand, splaying out his fingers. A musket ball lay between the forefinger and thumb. He glanced over his shoulder and said:

"You were saying?"

Ettore stood drop-mouthed for a moment, before shrieking in pain as Francesca plunged her knife through his hand. Pinned to the desktop, he moaned and looked with terrified eyes at his furious wife.

"Giacomo!" she yelled.

A moment later the large bodied, flat-headed man appeared in the doorway.

"Take Ettore to have his hand bandaged. Then lock him in his room for four hours."

"No!" Ettore screamed, his eyes widening in terror. "Please, Francesca! Not four hours!"

"One more word and I shall make it five," Francesca replied.

She turned back to Séverin and smiled brilliantly, suddenly becoming a different person.

"Maestro? Please follow me and all you require shall be provided. Do you wish a drink or some food?"

"No, thank you," Séverin replied

He followed the lovely, deadly lady from the chamber. She took his arm and steered him down a short corridor and into what appeared to be a ballroom. The room was long, square, and possessed a mosaic marble floor that appeared highly polished and well worn. Positioned in the center of the dance floor were three simple wooden chairs, the type found in kitchens across the continent. A far door opened and in stepped a man, possibly in his late forties, dressed in a simple brown coat and matching suit. He looked as if he was a bookkeeper or the lesser employee of a merchant bank, a nobody in the greater society of Naples.

That was the first impression, until his eyes locked upon a target. These luminous orbs stared out with a power and wisdom that was unnerving and caused many a brave man to quake with terror. The inner power of Michele Bozzo was a physical force that overwhelmed most the instant they were in his presence.

Séverin appeared unmoved, the wave of the newcomer's personality washing over him and falling away as if it had never existed. He stood before this terrible man, an unmovable object in opposition to the overwhelming force—equal, yet apparently disinterested in pursuing a conflict. They stood poised, their eyes meeting, instant recognition of the elements in question—neither willing to test the limits of this intellectual, metaphysical struggle.

"Maestro Séverin," Bozzo said, sitting down. "Unknowingly you inconvenienced me when you blinded one of my favorite assassins. The woman was mad, but very beautiful and excellent at eliminating enemies. Did you have to slice out her eyes?"

"Possibly not," Séverin said. "I could have killed her when she demanded we duel. What I did was crueler, but proper."

"I understand," Bozzo replied, pointing at the chair opposite. "I do not believe you are here to do business. Unless this is a discussion about my attempt to suborn the young exorcist Karnstein? Is that the reason for your visit?"

Séverin shook his head.

"No. Madame Policeni no doubt explained his disinterest in her obvious yet impressive charms. She could no more entice him than I could lure him away from Sylvia Dardi—and vice versa concerning Mademoiselle Dardi. Merely out of academic interest, why did you seek Karnstein's seduction?"

Bozzo chuckled and raised a hand in open amusement.

"That should be obvious, Monsieur Séverin. The man is a baron, eventually to be a count. He will inherit nearly as much property and power as the Emperor of that land. Controlling him through my daughter would enrich my organization greatly. Young Karnstein has influence in the Court of the current Pope, which is a power I should like to possess, in time. Lastly, his skills as a destroyer of demons is a form of protection that may benefit myself and my organization in future days."

Thinking for a moment, Séverin slowly nodded.

"I can promise you one of those areas of concern. Should a demon arise or a vampire appear in your future endeavors, Franz Karnstein will provide service to expel the fiend."

"In return, I leave him and the charming Signorina Dardi to their own future? Done—a fair enough trade. Is that why you are here?" the mastermind of the Naples underworld asked, his voice sounding slightly disappointed.

"Of course not," Séverin said. "Allow me to ask Madame Policeni a question. Did you tell your father all of what occurred on the island prison?"

"I did; what of it?" Francesca replied. "He had some difficulty believing the full scope of the event."

"You spoke of undead women and walking corpses," Bozzo said. "My skeptical reaction was proper, I should think. I do believe she was not lying or modifying the truth in any way. Why?"

Leaning back in the chair, Séverin explained the full implications and discoveries since his parting with Francesca Policeni. He did not hide how they had discovered the truth of

Nosos, or the probable outcome if her plans came to full frui-
tion.

"I think you also realize that such a creature would not
be satisfied with this small kingdom," Séverin concluded.

Michele Bozzo stared at Jean-Pierre Séverin for several
minutes, his eyes never appearing to even blink as the full
focus of his mind and personality bore down on the older
swordmaster. Finally, he broke the silence with a slow nod
and said:

"Yes, I do believe you, Monsieur Séverin. You do present an untenable threat for myself and my interests. I doubt
you are exaggerating in any manner. Therefore, you desire my
assistance, and that of my people in some foolish plan to defeat this ancient monster. Yes?"

"Yes," Séverin replied. "Are you willing to join our efforts in stopping this demon?"

"I should think I have no choice. Though I do notice you
did not say help or assist. You apparently do not consider
yourself my commanding officer—to use a term found in the
military."

"I do not believe you would allow yourself to be under
anyone's command, Monsieur. I will tell you what I require of
your organization and followers. I believe we shall be able to
work separately, yet together with the same goal in mind. No
doubt, you will also use this as a means of enriching yourself
and your organization."

"Let us sit in the dining room and you shall tell me your
ideas" Bozzo said, standing up. "There we shall finalize the
full details and correct anything you missed or misunderstood.
You were right in one respect—I would not have agreed to
follow you as if you were my Colonel."

They stood, and the leader of the *Camorra* led them
deeper into the grand villa. The sounds of shrieks from the
throat of the distant Ettore Policeni was only slightly jarring,
muted by the planning session that occurred over a pleasant
lunch of eggs and peppers.

CHAPTER LIX

Just as Jean-Pierre Séverin, Michele Bozzo, and Francesca Policeni were about to sit down for a meal, albeit one punctuated by the shrieks of agony from Ettore Policeni, Pia Mele read the note in her hand. It had arrived in the basket of an elderly woman who came in every day to clean the rooms. The old woman, whose name Pia had never bothered to learn, handed her the paper, her pudgy, sausage-shaped fingers releasing the paper quickly and with open relief. No words were exchanged, with the old woman who had quickly hobbled off out-of-sight.

Pia reread the note and smiled, knowing this duty would be a true pleasure for her Giulio. He'd been vigorous last night, enflamed with passion after butchering the chamberlain of the royal court. This job would probably have him so horny that he would half-cripple her for a day. That would be fine; life was far better now that his direction was fixed elsewhere.

On soft, cat-like footsteps, Pia returned to their bedroom. She was unsurprised to find Giulio on his back and snoring softly. Their lovemaking had been frequent lately; he slept a great deal to keep up with their mutual needs. Reaching into her small pile of clothes, she pulled out the container and removed a pinch of the wondrous powder. Blowing it his direction, she sighed as it fell short of his face and landed on his sweaty, hairy, chest.

Annoyed, Pia frowned and turned away to grab some more and try again. She just pulled the small box out, when a massive, mighty fist clamped down hard on her wrist. Pia cried out in shock, terror, and pain as her hand opened and Giulio snatched the box out of her grasp.

"What is this? What is this? You are casting spells on me?" Giulio screamed, shaking her and throwing the box against the far wall.

His eyes were wide, wild with rage and the innate fear of the dark powers.

"No, Giulio! No!" Pia moaned as her head snapped back and forth in his terrible grip.

Spotting the paper in her other hand, he ripped it from her grasp and read the simple lines. The orders were clear: Giulio and his men were to attack the home of Colonel Hugo, the personal military advisor to King Joseph Bonaparte. Hugo and all his men and servants were to be butchered and the house was to be burned to the ground.

"You!" Giulio whispered as he crumpled the paper and dropped it to the ground. "You are the reason I keep attacking the French, even when I do not make money each time. You cast spells on me, Giulio Nucci, *Fra Diavolo*!"

Pia tried to pull free, but he was too strong. His other hand closed around her long, slim neck and the fingers slowly squeezed, the force increasing painfully with each passing second. Pia gagged and gasped, trying to breathe. Her small hand wrenched at the wrist, but she could not free her neck from the mighty clasp whose pressure mounted steadily. Darkness entered her vision and her legs shook, causing Pia to fall backwards onto the bed she recently shared with Giulio.

Giulio's other hand encircled the other side of Pia's neck and he felt soft flesh yield beneath his powerful hand. An appalling crackling and crunch filled the air as his lover's neck crumbled and splintered, becoming little more than a fleshy sack of bloody ruin.

His face a mask of rage and sorrow, Giulio continued to strangle the dead body of his lover for several more minutes. Realizing she was gone, dead and forever unable to manipulate his life, he dropped her onto their bed. Then, still nude, Giulio stepped out onto the balcony.

"Nino! Get everyone together, pack everything! We leave in an hour!" he barked, spotting his cousin a short distance away.

"Where are heading?" Nino asked.

"North! I need to find Mama Zullo and a new place to live! This one is haunted!" Giulio spat back and strode inside.

Despite the sudden change, members of the gang weren't unhappy with this revelation. The old Giulio, the one who consulted *stregheria* and the like, was easier to understand than this one who attacked the French.

When they left the villa, taking all their spoils and items, a few wondered what befell the lovely Pia Mele. None would dare ask, suspecting the answer was the reason the gang was headed back for another session with the ancient, and quite frightening, Mama Zullo.

CHAPTER LX

Victor Dannel never understood his superiors, not since the day he had joined the army. Their orders never seemed to make sense, even more so since the walking dead had started attacking Naples. These were particularly bizarre, ones he knew could not be true based on the past.

"We now know the source of the plague of the walking dead, Captain," Johann Spurzheim had said, his voice calm and commanding. "They are based in the prison island of Nisida. You and all your men will travel across and attack when you receive my signal. Leave no walking corpse behind and do not go into the Black Boom. Those details will be explained to you soon."

Though no genius like the Emperor or his Marshals, Victor could sense a lie when spoken on a military subject. He knew the walking dead were not based in the prison for two simple reasons. First, he and his men had transported one corpse to the prison and saw the guards and the inmates. All were alive and behaving like living, breathing, if highly oppressed, people. Second, all the shambling corpses he had destroyed were dry; none smelling like fish or salt water. Had even one walked out of the depths of the sea, there would have been some evidence of that passage.

Despite these lies, Victor knew better than to question the Naples police commander. If he and his men discovered there were no walking dead, then he would demand answers from the somewhat terrifying Spurzheim. But he sensed this would not be so, which was why he immediately issued orders to prepare his men.

"One final point, Captain," Spurzheim said, raising one long finger in the air. "There may be one or more men or women who can walk and talk like anyone else. They must be killed as ruthlessly as any you destroy on Nisida. Those people are the source of the plague that threatens the kingdom. You must be ruthless, none of these unholy monstrosities must be allowed to exist another moment."

Victor had some doubts that the Police Chief had any interest in areas pertaining to religion, but wisely kept such thoughts to himself. Like any in the upper officer class, Spurzheim said what needed to be spoken under such circumstances. Whether Victor believed it or not was unimportant, duty came first. The truth as to why Victor and his men were attacking a prison of walking dead was easy to understand. That they would also be killing regular people was confusing and bizarre—but orders were orders.

This was why, at four o'clock in the morning, Victor Dannel and his men sat in the chill wind from the sea in a series of small boats. The sailors were equally bored, a few looking as if there were a few dozen places they'd rather be than the strip of water between the city and the island prison.

A signal flag went up over the port, the first message that the attack was imminent. The sailors, sighing with annoyance to a man, moved to their duties and soon the crafts were underway. It wasn't long before the soldiers lined the cove, their ranks straight, their weapons in hand.

"Sergeant Plourde," Victor said, his next order directly from the manual of arms. "Check all weapons and powder. When we attack, we will be entering as if it was a breech."

The good Sergeant saluted and made an inaudible reply, having already ordered the other non-commissioned officers to do exactly that a moment earlier. Plourde also gave Private Perrin, the Captain's orderly, a look that indicated the same. It would not do to have their officer killed in the opening engagement because his powder was wet or his weapons were unprepared.

Perrin gave a quick salute and a wave of the hand that told the whole story to the top NCO of the unit. The orderly had already checked the powder, flints and edge of the officer's blade, but he would now do so again. Such was the way of old campaigners, no need for a lot of wasteful talk.

292

Moments passed, then half an hour, without any word. Just as the first rays of sun were starting to slide over the horizon, a loud explosion seemed to rock the entire city. Even across the bay, flames, some shooting as high as the top of the buildings, flared up and added a terrifying illumination to the land.

"The city is being attacked!" one of the soldiers cried.

"No," Victor Dannel said, shaking his head. "That is our signal. Prepare to advance!"

CHAPTER LXI

As Victor Dannel sat and tried to look like a proper officer in a gently rocking boat, the city of Naples was a veritable beehive of activity. Or possibly an ant's nest, since workers moved about the city in groups, their loads far too great for a single man. Since midnight, or possibly earlier, the furious, precise, actions had occurred, the workers moving to assigned stations and performing their tasks. The work was odd, but simple, emptying buckets and barrels of oil into various sewer openings, cisterns and other places about Naples.

Enlisted for this task were two sets of people—each quite distinct from each other. The first were city employees, men and women tasked with ensuring the proper running of the kingdom. Neapolitan by birth, they were hard-working, if somewhat oppressed, by their situation. The Bourbons were corrupt and overtaxing, even going so far as to promote an Englishman to the position of Prime Minister! The French Bonapartists filled the upper ranks with Frenchmen and were mistrustful of the bureaucrats. The difference between the two was that the French lowered the taxes and appeared interested in allowing some citizens a chance to rise to higher ranks.

"This is secret work," the police chief, Johann Spurzheim, had emphasized. "If word gets out that you are acting as I ordered, a panic may spread across the city."

"Why?" a minor and famously complaining member of the public works department named Beneventi had demanded.

"We work to prevent infections and diseases. If people believed there was even a chance of such existing beneath their feet, a riot would break out. Possibly many riots. Do you wish that, Signor Beneventi?" Spurzheim asked, his tone mild.

Beneventi's eyes widened at the thought and he made the sign of the cross.

"Holy Mary, no! The last riot cost the city…"

"Yes," Spurzheim replied, cutting off the flow of talk. "No one, not even your families, must know what you're going to be doing. If all goes well and everyone performs their duties properly, a bonus of two weeks' salary will be granted. A pleasant gift for a night's work and your silence. If your families ask questions, just tell them you are working through the night to prepare a special event for the King."

The bonus was an easy promise, one suggested by Spurzheim himself in the planning meeting. The funds would flow back to the crown soon enough. The Feast of San Genaro was a few short weeks away and spending was always free during the festival. The lies were close to the truth anyway; the King was returning shortly and plans for another ball were underway. Nobody knew what this party was for, and no one cared.

"Do not miss any assignments," Spurzheim added. "You will be watched and anyone who does not complete their duties will prevent everyone else from earning the money from the crown."

This had also been his suggestion—self-policing was a very effective way of ensuring everyone worked hard and nobody attempted to avoid the hard work.

The second group of individuals were as unalike the first as possible. They were hard, dangerous-looking men, armed with knives. Some were women, worn by time and ill-treatment, bitter-eyed harridans, young crones in the making, and many bedraggled children whose hungry eyes stared out at the world with the dull gaze of soulless, ancient beings. These men, women, and children were criminals, beggars, and prostitutes, the underclass that reside in every city on Earth. They were enlisted to service by the terrible ruler of the *Camorra*, a handsome, brutal bastard named Ettore Policeni.

Ettore strode into the warehouse meeting hall, dressed like a member do the royal court.

"Good evening, my friends," he said.

He drew a knife and, without a word of warning, plunged the blade into the neck of Gino Onio, a known rapist and thief.

"Good," Ettore said, cleaning his stiletto with a handkerchief. "I think we are all better off without that *stronzo* in our company. Now, we are cleansing the sewers and all the underground. This will help our work, and all will make money from it."

Just then, a cry sounded from the middle of the room and the crowd parted. Lama Nottura stood, a woman dead at his feet, a garrote in his hands. The woman was young, pretty and dressed in a red cotton dress that showed her spectacular figure.

"Ah, yes," Ettore said, smiling. "Poor little thing, she was an informant to the police. Her lover died at Giacomo Lando's hands before the meeting. I expect he shall be found one day. At least, a piece or two of him should wash ashore eventually."

The rest was easy, assign the locations to each group, have a second group check all was completed and issue a few threats. The few times the enlisted criminals spotted the government employees toiling away, they shrugged. They knew that their *Padrone*, Ettore Policeni, possessed a far reach of power. Seeing government people performing his work just proved that point.

As to the government employees, they chose to ignore the poorly-dressed men and women as they poured the viscous fluids down the drains of Naples. The work, thanks to the swarms of hard-working, and sometimes frightened, men, women, and children, ended at about three o'clock in the morning.

When the explosions commenced, the city was rocked by rocketing flames and at least ten fires. The loss of life was later calculated to be fourteen dead.

For days, the city and land nearby smelled like burnt cooking oil, but that, too, faded in just under a week. Stories abounded as to the source of the explosions, but some government worker or criminal whispered that it was to prevent a coming plague… or attacking English… The tale changed in the telling, becoming wilder and more preposterous in a short period. The oddest exaggeration was, from a few early arriving market merchants, that they had heard a great scream of agony, followed by a deep wail of loss. Silly stuff, of course, but a few swore it had seemed to fill the air.

The only question that remained a mystery was, who had started the fire that had ignited all the sewers and underground passages of Naples?

CHAPTER LXII

"What was that?" Federigo Gui roared as the city of Naples shook. "Has the volcano erupted?"

Seated in his office, he had woken early and read through his files to find more people worthy of arrest. These he could hand over to René, who would transport them to their mistress's side as food. A gift for Nosos and a means of clearing up the few possible sources of resistance left in Naples. That would pave the way for Federigo Gui to become the new Emperor of Naples and Sicily. Then he could turn his eyes on Rome, Venice and the rest of Italy. The new Roman Empire whose only God would be the Dark Mistress, Nosos. A wonderful future… for Federigo Gui at least.

Gui stood in his chair and ran to the window at the far end of his chamber. Fires leaped high throughout the city, as if the legendary Hell beneath the Earth had suddenly erupted and became one with the city of Naples. Stepping back, Gui turned to yell for René, when the door exploded inward.

Shards of wood and stone blasted into the office, sending Gui sprawling to the ground, his face and hands burning with a searing pain. He sat up slowly, his eyes blurry as René shot into the room from one of the secret passageways. His underling's face split, beginning to transform as he ran towards the gaping hole that had once been the protected entrance to the master of the Cupbearer's sanctum.

Gui's vampiric assistant howled and then stopped in his tracks as he stared at what greeted him within the doorway. Before he could make another sound, a series of enormous explosion shook the office followed by three large puffs of heavy, dark, choking smoke. René sailed backwards, striking the far wall, his limbs detaching from his hurdling body.

Johann Spurzheim stepped into the room, a massive blunderbuss in his hands. A stream of men, all dressed in the uniforms of the Naples police force, spread out through the chamber. Some ran to the desk and files, loading them in a large wooden crate. Others, armed like soldiers, charged through the doors, their war cries and shots echoing through the palace.

"What...? What...?" Gui managed to mumble through his ruined, torn lips.

Spurzheim nodded to two of his men, who lifted the battered Abbot up in their arms. He moaned in pain, the splinters from the explosion having entered in his legs as well as other body parts.

"Federigo, Federigo, Federigo," Spurzheim said, shaking his head. "Did you truly believe I would permit you to arrest me and other worthy citizens of the kingdom? That I would sit by and let you hand over everything to demon from the pits of Hell?"

"She... is... not... a... demon..." Gui managed to whisper. "She... is... a.... Goddess..."

"Isn't he a holy man?" one of the police officers asked. "Isn't the first commandment, *Thou shalt have no other gods before me*?"

"How did you know that? I've known you five years and you've never even walked in a church," the other police officer asked his fellow.

"My mother was a prostitute and one of her customers was a priest. He used to tell me stuff while he was waiting for his turn," the first officer replied.

"You are correct, that is one of the first commandments," Spurzheim said, handing his expended blunderbuss to another police officer. "However, I believe our friend Abbot Gui never truly believed in God, the Devil, or anything other than his own right of personal power."

"You... you... won't..." Gui mumbled, trying to look at his rival with defiance.

Spurzheim rolled his eyes and pulled a soiled handkerchief from his jerkin. Shoving it in Gui's mouth, he said:

"Please, I have no interest in listening to your rambles and threats. Your power is broken, your followers, and the monsters you served shall all perish in flame this night. You have no place in Naples anymore, Gui. In fact, you have no place on Earth anymore."

Without another word, the Police Chief of the Kingdom of Naples, drew his belt knife and cut the throat of Federigo Gui.

The master of the now-destroyed Cupbearers died, his end ignominious and ultimately forgotten in time. His body, and that of his human followers, received pauper's burials, a common grave and a worthy end for a terrible man who wished to sell the lives of all living creatures for a tiny bit of temporal power.

CHAPTER LXIII

"It begins," Karnstein said, watching the flames leap from a sewer grate.

The light of dawn was barely beginning, when the whole city of Naples was illuminated by the vast explosion from beneath the Earth.

"Really? I had not noticed," Sylvia said, grinning and blowing him a kiss.

The young Austrian ignored her reply, watching across the city as the gouts of flame exploded from the many sewers and ancient cisterns.

"I still wonder if the oil fell deep enough to ignite the dwelling of the plague rats," he mused.

"It does not matter, Franz," Séverin said. "Think carefully of every time you visited a sewer to assault evil. What did you smell?"

"Rat droppings," Karnstein replied, still fascinated by the flames, more appearing in the distance, others dying away in an instant.

Séverin, Dardi, and Sylvia laughed, realizing the young Austrian exorcist was not attempting to be humorous. His statement was completely true, if slightly ridiculous.

"Yes, true, and probably waste from a thousand other beings," said Séverin. "What I was referring to were the many gasses. Remember how I told you that carrying a lamp could cause explosions? Imagine how dangerous the sewers became when we poured thousands of gallons of oil into the depths. I doubt much fell to the greatest depths, but that did not matter. The fires spread; we only see the upper levels as the flames burst into the air. Now, you must determine if the plan worked."

With a frown, Karnstein nodded and headed towards the partially enclosed tent. Sylvia took his hand, her face showing a trace of annoyance that he hadn't taken hers first. They shared a quiet moment, before he sat and said a brief prayer. Then he closed his eyes and the Sumerian words flew from his lips, a jarring sound that grated on the few listening ears.

"*Anshargal Ati Me Peta Babka Nisme Annu Isten! Usmi Annu Isten Ina Akhkharu Ma Ina Maskim Xul, Ina Kashshaptu, Ina Lilit, Su'ati Mursu In Matum!*"

The sigil once again appeared before his body before vanishing without a sound. Then he opened his eyes, once again filled with a brilliant silver illumination. His head moved left, right, up and down. He appeared to start and his face denoted surprise, shock, but not a trace of fear.

"What do you see, Franz? Tell me, *amore!*" Sylvia asked, not touching him this time.

"The void... the darkness beneath the Earth... it... it... it..." the Exorcist stammered, his eyes widening.

"It what?" Sylvia looked as if she wanted to strangle him or hug him close.

Karnstein continued to stare, gazing and not believing his eyes. There, beneath the Earth, was the void once again. Yet this terrible disease, filled with gloom and horror, was vanishing, burning away. With each passing second, the vast inhuman cloud diminished, its power and pain being purged from the Earth. The sight was beautiful, as if the light of Heaven was shining down upon the horrors that had so terrified him earlier. This time the monstrous power from the pits of plutonian evil had fallen away forever.

"It burns away... Sylvia... the void is falling away..." Karnstein whispered, barely able to believe his eyes.

Sylvia looked over her shoulder at her father, who nodded once. The lovely woman frowned, but nodded back.

"Franz, *amore*? Do you hear me?"

Karnstein's gaze did not shift as he watched the transformation of the world. It was like watching a human body being purged of the unclean ravages of disease.

"Yes, Sylvia, I hear you."

"I need you to keep looking. Find where the power is coming from..."

302

She paused, her face showing concern and fear.

"Look for that demon you saw last time... the source of the evil..."

Karnstein did not respond, but he shifted his vision along the ground, following the vanishing threads of power. They all sailed into the skein, each puffing from existence before he could follow them to their source. Yet he continued to search, his mind and spirit rising and surveying the myriad of souls that filled the land.

Then he spotted the creature, a stygian stain that appeared to infect the very universe by its terrible presence. The horror sat in the center of a vast dark web of negative power, a terrible bloated black spider that squatted and consumed the lives of every soul nearby.

As he studied the vast negative lattice, Karnstein realized the myriad of disease spreading strands subtly vanished before his eyes. The dark web appeared weakened, slowly disappearing, shrinking inward towards the terrible demoniac atramentous fiend.

"I see it... the power... the dark vitality that infected everything... it... it's...vanishing..." Karnstein whispered.

CHAPTER LXIV

"Squad two, take the lead position!" Victor Dannel ordered, switching the soldiers who had led the assault with another unit who were awaiting their turn.

The grounds outside and within the prison walls had been cleansed, the shambling corpses sliced to pieces as each had appeared. Now the true danger was ahead. Hundreds of these walking corpses still lay within the walls, according to Contrôleur Général Spurzheim's information.

Sergeant Plourde, standing with the first ranks, entered the main doorway leading to the prison proper. He waited for his eyes to adjust to the gloom and waved the unit forward. Dannel followed with the next squad, his sword in one hand, a pistol in the other. Perrin was a step behind, his Captain's rifle over one shoulder and a variety of other weapons and other items stuffed in his many pockets and large pack.

"Stop here, form ranks!" Dannel ordered. "Let's draw some of the beasts out to us."

He watched as the first rank fell prone. The second rank kneeled and raised their rifles, while the third rank remained standing.

"Why are we doing this, Captain?" Plourde asked. "Gunfire only slows them down; they're already dead."

"We will cut their numbers down by firing all shots at the creatures' legs," Dannel answered. "The more that we prevent from standing, the easier it will be to slice them into pieces. We don't have time to fully destroy all the corpses. We shall bag them and create a series of large bonfires once the building is clear. Allow me to start."

Pointing his gun down the long hallway, Dannel fired one, throwing open the massive iron door. A series of loud moans filled the air and the doorway suddenly filled with the torn bodies of the shambling dead.

"First rank, fire!" Dannel ordered

The hallway soon shook with the reverberation of the musket fire. The bodies fell backwards, knocking over other shadowy figures at their rear. But, within a heartbeat, other forms filled the entrance, their moans echoing as the sounds of the rifle fire died down.

"A little further, I want them to be just inside the door," Dannel said, remembering that the Italians had tried to do that to his unit when they had breeched their walls.

The undead shuffled forward, three emerging from the doorway and into the corridor. They stepped forward, their hands outstretched, their ruined mouths opening and closing like deranged, frightening marionettes.

"Second rank, fire!" Dannel ordered and took his rifle from Perrin.

The undead fell, their legs ripped apart by the musket balls. Five more appeared at their rear, their bodies torn by the third rank's fire. As they fell, the first rank fired at the next stumbling corpses. Four more full volleys fired, with all the ranks shredding the undead with systematic ease.

"Fourth and fifth squad," Dannel said, his voice choked from the powder-his ears ringing from firing the guns in an enclosed space. "Advance with fixed sword bayonets and hand axes. Slice all limbs free and place them in the bags. Stack the bags three feet apart in the prison yard."

With calm efficiency brought about by the regular practice of destroying these monsters, there were few small injuries: two corporals bruised by kicking legs and a private receiving a black eye from a flailing fist, but otherwise the remains ended up bagged and placed out of the way.

Replacing the squads, they repelled two more attacks with the same results. The bodies, thirty-eight in all, each ended up in bags in the yard. Dannel considered the situation, realizing their positional attack was too slow. They would have to remain in this location for months to clear the prison. They needed to enter and force the creatures to attack en masse.

"Advance," Dannel ordered and the regiment strode into a large room.

At a first glance, the chamber was filled with inexplicable objects—metal frames, ropes, and chains. Soon it became apparent that this was a torture chamber, a location where the prisoners were beaten and harmed at the whims of the prison guards.

"Sergeant Plourde," Dannel said, "when we leave, please have the men cast these disgusting objects into the sea. Thank you. Now, we shall advance as a regiment. Scouts shall move in advance and we shall attempt to force an engagement with small numbers of these creatures. We shall then…"

"Captain, Captain!" Corporal Oscar Perrin, Private Perrin's nephew, called out, running forward.

He was a younger duplicate of his uncle, a ranker who had only risen to his rank because he didn't appear to feel the need to drink heavily the moment he was off-duty.

"Yes, Perrin?" Dannel asked, his voice calm, his demeanor unruffled.

He sensed something bad was about to occur, but the manual always said an officer must not appear frightened.

"They're coming! Hundreds of the *fils de putes* are pouring from both hallways!" Oscar moaned, his eyes wild.

"Calm yourself, Corporal. They are no match for our regiment," Dannel replied.

He looked at his top NCO.

"Sergeant, the doors appear destroyed. We shall form a half circle at the rear of the room. Have all men with grenades ready. We shall use them on this engagement to destroy most of these abominations. Rank fire and keep the second rank not shooting, but fending off any walking corpses that get too close."

The men ran into their assigned locations, sensing this was about to be a life or death struggle. They were all used to danger, but fighting dead men and women who stumbled, grabbed, bit, moaned, and attempted to tear out your brain was a frightening concept.

Then the monsters came, a near tidal wave of undead monstrosities, each of whom sought the lives of the soldiers. The ranks of muskets raised up to the many shoulders, awaiting the order to fire.

"Even ranks, fire!" Dannel ordered and fired his musket at charging horde of monsters.

The explosive retort was deafening, amplified exponentially by the enclosed stone chamber. The charging undead exploded into bits as a cloud of heavy smoke wafted over the area. Handing off his weapon to Private Perrin, Dannel accepted the second weapon. His orderly immediately started the procedure of reloading the musket. Raising his other musket, he barked out:

"Odd Ranks, fire!"

The muskets roared, and another line of the shambling horrors vanished, shredded by the powerful lead balls. Dannel issued another set of orders and a continuous flow of fire followed, the odd and even troopers each blasting away at the Emperor-approved rate of three shots per minute. The undead were barely visible in the heavy cloud of choking gunpowder fumes, a cloud that seemed to thicken with each passing second.

"Cease fire!" Dannel ordered.

All gunnery ceased. The Captain knew that he and the rest were nearly deafened by the musket fire, but the result was evident. Heavy mounds of twitching, twisted, torn, undead lay in mounds before the regiment.

As the smoke slowly dissipated, the ringing of the soldier's ears prevented any talk or banter. A low tittering emerged from the ranks, a high-pitched titter that spread to through the ranks.

"Quiet down!" Sergeant Plourde barked, casting a harsh look on the privates still quietly cackling.

Suddenly, a woman in a blue gown strode into view, her long blonde hair twisted and tangled about her head, resembling tentacles more than lovely locks. Her face split open and she screamed, revealing rows of teeth and a long, lolling tongue.

"You shall die and serve great Nosos!" she yelled. "All of you shall serve as my slaves and I will make you pay for…"

"What in all that's holy is that?" Private Perrin asked, eyes wide.

Dannel did not hesitate, having received orders on this subject. Drawing his musket pistol, he fired the gun straight into the woman's chest.

"That," he said, handing off the gun to his orderly, "is the creature controlling these monsters. Her death is essential to complete this duty. Sergeant, send the third squad to that hut at the rear of the yard. There are barrels of lamp oil within. Let's use a bit of oil and fire to cleanse these creatures. By the time the fire dies down, we can search the rest of the prison and ensure our duty is complete."

"Yes, Captain!" Sergeant Plourde replied, saluting and issuing the orders to the men.

"Well done, boys!" he added as third squad ran off to get the oil.

CHAPTER LXV

Beneath the earth, in one of the outlying sewers, Jacopo Bianchi and five rats ran as fast as their legs could carry them through the muck and mire. The flames had not reached them and all shared the same thoughts. They needed to run for their lives and survive the inferno that threatened their queen's plans.

Once a handsome man with strong muscles and an uncanny skill at wooing any man or woman who caught his sexual interest, Jacopo had been transformed since his time digging beneath the Earth. Now, his body was shrunken, possessing the pale, mucus-laden skin of a worm or other dirt-dwelling creature. His shoulders appeared rounded and his stride was closer to the sub-human lope of a gorilla than that of a man. His hands and feet were longer, bonier, and possessed ragged black claws that could tear through flesh, stone, and possibly even metal.

The worse changes were to Jacopo's skull. His head, formerly possessing a thick mane of dark, wavy tresses, was no devoid of a trace of hair. His cadaverous, ashen aspect resembled that of a disease-ridden corpse than that of a man who once aspired to live a life like that of Don Giovanni. Jacopo's once striking face now possessed elongated, canine quality, complete with serrated brown and ivory incisors that protruded from his closed, rubbery, black lips. His yellow and red eyes were sunken, shrunken, appearing more insectile than mammalian.

Though he had wailed and gnashed his teeth as his hair had fallen in vast, bloody clumps, he hadn't been alone. All his fellow vampires suffered the same as they toiled in their dark queen's service. Only the rats, first food, then friends, had transformed more than he and the other vampires. Once small and large creatures with matted brown, black, or gray fur, these tiny sewer-dwellers had became the stuff of nightmares. He still remembered the first time he had spotted one of the twisted terrors of the deep as it had risen before his eyes and joined the digging.

"What in Lucifer's name is that?" Jacopo had cried, staring and pointing.

The beast was a foot long, hairless, with massive, oversized teeth, and wicked black talons that ripped through the rock surface of the cavern.

"Our mistress's slaves," one of the others had explained. "Every rat we eat comes back as one of her pets. When they don't help us dig, they're out converting more."

Within a few days, the tunnels had been swarmed with these large, horrific, phantasms. They had flooded the tunnels, an immense undead, pale, skittering, and twittering horde that tore through the thick rock; thus, they had joined the tunnels to a mighty, stench-laden cavern beneath the city itself.

Then they all had waited, servants of mighty Nosos together. The vampires had squatted in the dark, like twisted, pallid toads, barely moving in the stygian gloom. The rats had squeaked and squealed as they ran and climbed over every surface. Their movements had been frantic, both frightened and elated, their unliving, rodent minds energized by the thought of spreading their disease to all living beings upon the surface.

The time in the dark had seemed endless, but Jacopo had not minded. He had felt the cold caresses of Nosos and she had promised more in the future. He had moved to a far corner, spotting a small sub-tunnel that could lead him to the wharf district.

Then it came... A vast squall of heat and fire. A loud, high-pitched series of squeals from the rats had filled the air and Jacopo had felt himself thrown back by a blast of incandescent heat. The very air was aflame and a choking, explosive cloud appeared to spread with each second.

"Nosos! Nosos, save me!" one of the vampires had screamed as her phlegm-covered, bald body had ignited.

She had been a pretty girl, a favorite of Fortuna's, but within seconds, she was little more than a pile of ash.

Jacopo and his rat brothers had fled through the sewers, not hiding their terror. They had sensed they were all that remained from the millions of creatures once in the service of great Nosos. But they would survive, they would flourish and Nosos's plans would happen soon enough!

Reaching the end of the tunnel, Jacopo looked up and spotted a small metal grate with hints of the dawn's light peeking through the bars. Smiling, he grabbed the stone wall and climbed upward, his rat friends at his side.

"I owe you a gold coin, Lama Nottura," a soft, gentle male voice said. "This is where the rats, small and large, will try to escape."

Jacopo looked up and spotted a man standing near the grate. His features were difficult to discern in the growing light, but he did appear to possess a triangular-shaped head with a flat-topped skull.

Just then another figure, smaller than the first, stepped into view. He poured a bucket of liquid through the grate, covering Jacopo and all five rats in a heavy, viscous fluid.

Jacopo sputtered and spit out the liquid, beginning to transform into his more dangerous aspect. Then the scent filled his nostrils and his inhuman eyes widened.

"Oil? Oh no!" he shrieked.

"Oh yes, you ugly *stronzo*," Giacomo Lando replied, dropping a lit candle on the body of the retreating creature.

Jacopo Bianchi and his five rat friends, the last of Nosos's underground followers, ignited in flames in an instant. All six died screaming, transformed into dust before the eyes of Michele Bozo's two most dangerous acolytes.

CHAPTER LXVI

Nosos shrieked, crushing her chair's arms and flinging the wooden shards aside.

"Giorgia! René! Giorgia! My Giorgia is gone! René is gone too! What is happening?"

Sinis crawled inside the large cavern chamber, his eyes lifted despite his preference for keeping them lowered. His mistress's screams rose, shaking the walls and echoing throughout the small cave. He watched as she fell to the ground and beat the sandy earth with her mottled fists, the very picture of a child throwing a tantrum.

"Fear not, dark queen of beauty" he said, standing up. "I shall go to the underground and retrieve another handmaiden. Thérèse was pretty before she started consuming rats. You can change her back and create a new handmaiden."

Nosos looked up, her rheumy eyes staring at him with naked disgust.

"She is gone, you stupid, ugly, wretch. All of them, my vampires, my rats, even the few walking corpses I controlled. All are gone!"

"Then we must flee, lovely one! I shall get the coach and we will be out of the Naples in the hour. We can travel anywhere and start anew!" Sinis said, reaching for his mistress and pulling her back into her ruined throne.

Nosos backhanded Sinis, sending him sailing across the room and crashing into the distant stone wall.

"We shall not flee, worm. Whoever did this shall come to me. I feel this in my bones. You shall hold them back in my name. And I shall greet them should they get past your pathetic form."

"But what if they kill me, O darkness of my soul?" Sinis asked, rising to his knees.

He was uninjured by the attack; his mistress had recreated him into a being far stronger and nearly impossible to injure.

Nosos laughed, spitting aside a vast ball of green phlegm.

"You cannot die, Sinis. You are mine; only I may end your existence."

Sinis bowed and backed out, grateful to learn he was immortal now. His Goddess Nosos had made him one of her angels—or devils. It mattered not one wit to Sinis, formerly Hertz Ende. He was where he belonged, obeying her every whim.

Shuffling out to the cave mouth, he squatted down and waited. Sinis could wait for a thousand years if necessary.

Hearing approaching footfalls, he rubbed his hand together in anticipation. The only thing in life nearly as wonderful as serving Nosos was killing in her name.

CHAPTER LXVII

The trek to the lake overlooking the cave used by Nosos was not easy, yet far from dangerous. Though Franz Karnstein did have a clear location on the creature, he was merely able to point the direction the being lay. The ethereal world he viewed did not account for streets, buildings, traffic from carts coming to market, or even an abandoned building that was now engulfed in fire.

"No! You're going the wrong way!" Karnstein yelled, pointing north as their wagon turned east. "That way!"

"*Idiota*!" Sylvia said, at his side. "We cannot drive through walls!"

Karnstein didn't appear to hear her, pointing north.

"That way, turn that way."

"Are you listening to me?" Sylvia demanded, moving in front of his glowing eyes.

"Yes," Karnstein replied, his face never wavering. "You're still going the wrong way. Oh, wait, that's right. Keep going that direction. No! Sop turning!"

This continued for two hours, Karnstein resolutely demanding one direction, Sylvia yelling at him, Séverin and Dardi ignoring them both with amusement. The French Maestro read a map as they traversed the city, their covered cart easily navigating the flourishing city.

"Based on his direction, I believe we are heading towards Lake Avernus," he stated, tapping the page.

The map was an up-to-date French surveyor's graphic, presented to them by Spurzheim during the planning process.

"Yes, it would be there," Dardi said and snorted. "The *Porte dell'inferno* is said to be located near the lake. The name alone attracts the foolish worshippers of darkness."

"The entryway to the underworld in mythology is near Naples? I'm surprised I never learned of this in the past," Séverin mused.

"That is because it is not true," Dardi replied. "There are caverns near the lake, none particularly large and important. A few attract devil worshippers and other easily lured *idiotas*. What are you planning to do with my daughter, by the way? I know she will leave with her baron."

Séverin was unsurprised by the question, knowing it was lingering in the air for some time.

"If they come with me, I shall lodge her nearby until they are married. And I shall train her to become another maestro of the sword. That is her other desire and, I believe she possesses the skills to earn such a title."

"No man shall accept her as their teacher," Dardi stated, glancing at his friend. "And few women possess an interest in sword combat. Why would you bother?"

"Knowledge for knowledge's sake is never wasted, Barto," Séverin said. "She shall not want for money, I believe. Franz is owner and heir to a great many properties throughout Europe. Who knows what the future holds for those two? I will not stand in the way of their paths to happiness."

Dardi grunted and checked the bickering pair in the back. Karnstein's hand still pointed the same direction and that did appear to be the Lake Avernus area. The rattle of the cart and he clip-clop of the horse's hooves drowned out Sylvia and his voice for another hour.

"Stop!" Karnstein yelled, his voice rising above all other sounds. "There! It is there!"

"Come out of the skein, *amore*. Please, do it now," Sylvia said, her voice lower. "I need you to see the real world again."

Karnstein's face looked rebellious for a moment, and then he nodded and said a brief prayer:

"*Ave Maria, gratia plena, Dominus tecum. Benedicta tu in mulieribus, et benedictus fructus ventris tui, Iesus. Sancta Maria, Mater Domini nostri, ora pro nobis peccatoribus, nunc, et in hora mortis nostrae. Amen.*"

He opened his eyes to find Sylvia inches from his face, a stiletto in her grasp. The point of the blade was less than an inch from his jugular vein.

"What is this?" he asked, shock written across his face.

"Prove to me you are my Franz—not infected by that monster from Hell," Sylvia whispered, her eyes watery.

"How may I do that, Sylvia?" he asked.

"Tell me something only Franz would know. Quickly, do not think."

"You called me your fiancée when you rescued me from the clutches of an angry Francesca Policeni," Karnstein said, smiling as she blushed.

Lowering the dagger, Sylvia replied:

"I was just…it was just…"

The young Austrian chuckled and removed the signet ring from his finger. He placed it on hers and said:

"I accepted."

Sylvia's cheeks blushed even deeper crimson and she answered:

"*Idiota*! You are supposed to ask me!"

"Very well. And stop calling me an idiot," Karnstein replied, half-smiling and reaching for the ring.

"Then stop acting like one," replied Sylvia, pulling her hand away.

"Would you just kiss her and seal the bargain? We do have important work to do such as saving the world from a terrible fate," Dardi said, leaning into the back of the wagon.

His odd face was smiling broadly, and his bulging eyes looked ready to burst from his head.

"Father! We were having a private moment!" Sylvia's color further deepened, and she looked away.

Séverin leaned inside and said:

"Nothing you two do is private. Get on with it; we are wasting time."

Sylvia Dardi and Franz Karnstein sighed at the same time, turned to each other and looked resigned, annoyed, and amused. Then they leaned forward and kissed, just a simple touch of the lips. Yet at that moment, the world appeared to stop for them both. Their eyes closed and slowly their arms encircled each other, their grips fierce, their bodies pressed hard together. The embrace continued for several minutes before their faces slowly separated, though their arms did not release each other.

"Why didn't we do that before?" Karnstein panted, his pale face flushed.

Sylvia grinned slightly.

"We were not engaged before now, *idiota*."

"Before this continues," Dardi said, rolling his eyes, "move apart! We have much to do and little time. Move, I say!"

With open reluctance, the young lovers released their grip, though their hands remained linked as they slid a few inches away from each other. Both swordmasters looked amused but nodded at each other in a silent discussion.

"Franz," Séverin said, breaking the silence. "The chest to your right possesses all we shall require this day. Open it, please, and pass out the objects within."

Releasing Sylvia's hands with great reluctance, Karnstein crawled to the rear of the wagon and opened the large wooden chest. The trunk was full of objects and he handed each back to the others.

Assembling next to the cart, the two swordmasters and their pupils checked their weapons one final time. Checklists complete, Dardi stepped towards the closest path and said:

"Sylvia, you are with me. Franz, you and Gâteloup will circle through a different path."

"Father!" Sylvia protested, looking at Franz.

"I thought we would…?" Karnstein started to say, stopping at a gesture from Séverin.

"You and Miss Dardi are very much in love, a beautiful result in this battle against a terrible evil. This also means you are unable to think clearly and dispassionately when the other is near. Until that time arises, you must work separately when hunting or battling evil. Is this understood?"

Séverin's voice possessed an unmistakable note of command. Karnstein frowned, but nodded once, soon followed by the same gesture from Sylvia. She clapped an old, battered tricorn hat on her head and gave Karnstein a meaningful look before following her father into the woods.

Karnstein watched her leave, turning away when the path turned, and Sylvia and her father vanished from sight. He looked back at Séverin, who had studied his face with searching eyes.

"Are you capable of focusing on the battle we face? It is no shame to say no. I remember being young and in love with my late wife. There were times all I could consider was her hair or neck or... well, you do comprehend my meaning."

Séverin's dour face studied the Austrian exorcist's stony countenance. Karnstein nodded, resembling the cold, harsh inquisitor of past days.

"I shall endeavor to keep my thoughts entirely on the battle. Do you anticipate any more of the walking dead?"

Séverin nodded and started walking down a different path.

"I do. From what you viewed, we destroyed much of Nosos's power. That still leaves a very dangerous demoniac being capable of terrible evil. She was known as one of the Dark Fates of legend."

"I do..."

Karnstein's statement was cut off by three shambling dead, a pair of withered elderly women and a shrunken man whose face was a mottled ruin. Raising the blunderbuss in his hands, he fired at all three. The explosion was powerful, a cannon shot, though in miniature. The shot tore the legs asunder of all three undead creatures, tossing them back and filling the air with a heavy, acrid fog. Séverin scanned the small forest, his eyes seeking movement, his ears keenly aware of distant shots fired.

"Reload, if you please. We can only use this weapon until we reach the caves. Once inside, such a device could injure friend and foe."

"Ricochets are quite dangerous," Karnstein agreed as he prepared the blunderbuss.

"My greater concern is stone splinters from the walls and roof. Like wooden ones in shipboard combat, they're capable of shredding the flesh from your bones in an instant."

"You've served aboard a ship?" Karnstein asked, falling into step at his teacher's side.

"One year in a privateer along the French and Spanish coast. I owed a favor to an old friend and that was my method of repayment. Ah! Here comes a larger number. I think Nosos seeks to drown us in shambling corpses while she works some other form of deviltry."

Séverin saw six or seven of the undead creatures shuffling through the tree line. Their moans and gnashing teeth were a terrible, inhuman chorus that would drive a normal mind to the breaking point.

"That will not do," Karnstein said, stepping forward. "I shall engage these creatures. You circle around and get to the cave. I'll join you as soon as I can break away. If I keep destroying Nosos's undead minions, the fiend will believe her plan is working."

Séverin looked ready to argue for a moment, but the plan won out. Pulling free one of his musket pistols, he handed the weapon to his student.

"Do not linger. Do as you need to these creatures and possibly another set. Then find a way around them and join me in the cave. Just to the east of the large villa."

"Understood," Karnstein replied.

He fired the huge, short-range gun. The undead fell, bowled over by the force of heavy metal. Two remained standing and the Austrian exorcist dropped the heavy weapon and pulled out a pair of pistols-firing just as Séverin ducked from sight. The gunshots echoed from all sides as the Maestro blazed his own path through the underbrush. This was the best solution to the dilemma, but he did not have to like that his student was taking the risk.

CHAPTER LXVIII

Across the forest, approaching from the other direction of the cave, Bartolomeo Dardi and his daughter Sylvia held the same discussion. Dardi, blasting a line of the lumbering corpses with the other blunderbuss, had said:

"Do not make me order this, daughter. I will stay here and keep these bastardos busy for a time. Go!"

"Papa, no! I won't leave you!" Sylvia replied, drawing her cutlass and looking defiant.

She disliked the weapon, but agreed to carry it on this occasion. Cutting weapons were the best attacking on these undead beasts and the cutlass, a heavy tool, was even more effective than the saber on occasion.

"You must," Dardi replied, placing aside the blunderbuss and drawing a cutlass in one hand and a musket pistol in the other. "One of us must keep the illusion of resistance while the other seeks out the cave. Go! I shall join you before too long."

Sylvia frowned, but nodded a second later. Kissing his bearded cheek, she said:

"Join me soon."

Dardi nodded and laughed as he sliced the legs out from an undead creature while pistoling the next in the head. He was still roaring and yelling as Sylvia vanished into the woods, the sounds of her passage lost in the laughter and woops of Maestro Dardi's attacks on the shambling undead creatures.

Sylvia said a brief prayer of thanks that these woods were not the harsh, untamed tangles of the ancient Forest of Massimina. There were parts of that land that would repel her as easily as a wall—such was the thickness and powerful antediluvian majesty of that primeval forest. This section of woods was tame, almost a garden in comparison. The brambles were low and weak, and the trees were spaced at an almost mathematically precise distance.

Hearing the rising sounds of moans and groans as well as dragging limbs, Sylvia dropped into a crouch behind a bush.

A section of the path was barely visible, and she watched a dozen of the walking corpses lurched past her location. Had they been creatures with more than a base intelligence, they might have spied her form as they passed. Fortunately for her, they were little more than appetites with legs, horrific weapons capable of killing and destroying, but not thinking past their mistress's base commands.

Waiting a minute or two, Sylvia heard no other creatures coming in her direction. Staying off the path, she increased her speed as she moved towards the distant cave.

A second party of shambling corpses appeared a short time later, their numbers at least twenty this time.

I should join father and keep him from getting killed by these monsters. But he did demand that I go ahead and swore he would join me soon, Sylvia thought as the monsters passed her nearby hiding spot, their groans and growls drowning out the sounds of the woods.

I could attack them from behind... but he said he would stay safe. He never lied to me in the past... I must go on. I just don't like it, Sylvia thought and ran ahead.

She didn't like this choice, but knew that this was the predicament often faced by monster-hunters.

Fifteen minutes later Sylvia stepped out of the woods. She soon spotted a small entrance to the hillock that held the legendary, infamous *Porte dell'inferno*. Despite the name, there was nothing particularly sinister about the cavern mouth. The opening was slightly higher than her head and shaped in an irregular oval. A distant light from deeper within glimmered and shimmered, occasionally appearing irregularly as her angle changed with each step.

"Oh, how delightful!" a giggling voice said. "My mistress will love having you. You will make a lovely handmaiden for the Dark Queen of Corruption!"

Stepping out into the light, Sinis smiled and added:

"Come with me, pretty one, and all your dreams shall come true."

Sylvia's eyes widened and she extended a hand…

CHAPTER LXIX

Jean-Pierre Séverin stepped into the cavern, surprised by the lights that illuminated the passage. He had a phosphorescent rock in his belt, the only type of illumination he trusted under such circumstances. Having battled vampires and other dark creatures underground as often as above, he knew the dangers of gases in such tunnels. This time, it appeared, his preparations were not required.

Passing a vast, gaudy, golden candelabrum filled with melting tallows, Séverin sniffed the air experimentally. Besides the burning wax, the air possessed the scents of rotting vitae, past sexual congress, and corruption. The sandy ground appeared covered with spilled fluids, slowly being absorbed into the Earth, There were unknown stains covering the walls, like bizarre and disgusting paintings from a particularly demented artist. Altogether, the *Porte dell'inferno* was a horrifying place, though not a location from the deepest circles of the Hell.

"Jean-Pierre Séverin," a rough, phlegmy feminine voice rasped from the inner cave. "Welcome. You are a famous man and I look forward to your friendship."

Turning the corner, Séverin was dumbstruck by the woman before his eyes. She was tall, with flowing shimmering locks of crimson hair that framed an oval face of astonishing loveliness. Her skin was milky pale, nearly translucent though possessing a quality that reminded him of the soft light that exuded from a perfect full moon on a clear night. Dressed in a red silk gown that hugged her impressive curves, this woman was the embodiment of a modern Venus.

"I am Nosos. Lower your sword," Nosos whispered. "All I wish from you is your love. Come to me, Jean-Pierre. Come and kiss me and I shall give you pleasures beyond the dreams of mortal man."

She paused to spit a ball of black fluid.

Séverin took a step forward, though his face creased in confusion. A smell, like that of disease laden corpses rotting in the harsh summer sunlight, drifted his direction. Also, hadn't this perfect creature just spat a ball of black fluid on the ground? Something was wrong, something was not right, and he stopped, stepping back slightly.

Nosos looked annoyed, but smiled, her jagged brown yellow teeth adding to her beauty.

"Come to me, dear Jean-Pierre. I shall make you forget all your inner pain. One kiss from me and you shall smile forever."

"How do you know my name? And my inner torment?" Séverin asked, still not moving forward.

Something held him back, a soft voice in the back of his mind that caused his feet to remain planted and unmoving in the sandy Earth.

Nosos laughed, a musical sound that resembled that of a drowning man gasping for air.

"How do I know? I am Nosos, I know all! I was ancient when your ancestors were scrawling images of beasts on their cave walls. Come to me! Be my slave and you shall never think of your dead wife and child ever again."

"What did you say?" Séverin whispered, his dour face transforming into open shock.

Nosos laughed again, coughing and spitting with each sound.

"I see their ghosts hanging over you. Weighing down your soul and making you live in darkness. I will love you, provide you with all you need. All you need to do is come forward and embrace me. Let Nosos become your only love."

Séverin stepped forward, spotting the predatory delight in Nosos's yellow and red eyes.

Then he lunged, his rapier lashing out like a bolt of silver lightning.

The needle-sharp point sliced through the perfect breast, causing Nosos to cry out in terror and shock.

She fell backwards, black blood bleeding from the gaping wound, her wails causing the Maestro to wince.

What fell to the ground caused Séverin, despite his years of monster hunting, to stare with open-mouthed horror…

CHAPTER LXX

"Madonna!" Sylvia Dardi cried.

She fired the musket pistol in her extended hand. Her lovely eyes were wide with shock as the creature reeled back, struck by the lead musket ball.

The being before Sylvia's eyes was grotesque, a monstrosity as terrible as any she witnessed in recent days. The creature was about her height with a lean frame and the sallow, grayish, yellow skin of an infected corpse. He appeared garbed as a jester, but that was a horrific deception. The realization for the sheer magnitude of this mockery of mankind caused a wave of nausea to fill her churning stomach.

What Sylvia had mistaken for a red coverall with brown and gray stripes was a deception, a revolting sight that caused her to take a half step back. The red of his apparent costume was the lean muscle that usually lay beneath the skin, hidden by a thin layer of flesh. Here, on this monster, the flesh was flayed away, leaving the crimson tendons open for all to view. The brown and gray stripes were veins and a pseudo exoskeleton resembling that of humanity, but twisted by the mind of a maniac. Worse of all, the flapping jabot, so common with jesters and fools, was not some pale fabric, but that of this creature's own flesh! What she had mistaken for a bizarre jester's cap twitched and writhed independently a top this horror's skull. A sucker shaped mouth with tendrils appeared attached to the side of the baldpate and the body of this creature exuded a viscid pus from its rutted torso. Before Sylvia's horrified eyes, a horn shaped protuberance emerged and appeared to point her direction.

Sinis stood up, the hole in his terrible torso visible, but otherwise he appeared uninjured. He revealed a pair of wicked looking axes.

"Now that is not nice," he said. "Remember, I am the mistress's slave. She will not be happy if you try and hurt me.

Even your pretty face will not save you from her wrath. Now, be a good little handmaiden and submit to the Dark Queen's tender, bloody, embraces."

Disgusted beyond all reason, Sylvia stepped back and swung her heavy cutlass at the repulsive mucus-covered claw. The heavy steel blade sliced the hand off at the wrist, sending hand and axe sailing off to the left of the cave mouth.

Sinis shrieked and stepped back, his abscond eyes seeking and locating his missing limb. Discovering the fallen extremity, Sinis snatched it up and placed the detached hand back on his wrist and sighed. Before Sylvia's unbelieving eyes, the fingers moved, once again flexing and fully in place as a functioning, fully attached, limb.

"Ah, that was refreshing," he sneered. "Did you know I used to cut pieces of myself off while my mistress took her pleasure with her handmaidens and male servants? It has been some time since one of her little sluts resisted and removed a limb or two. Please, do it again. We can play for a time, then when you tire, I shall carry you to the first step in your destiny as a handmaiden to the goddess."

Sinis stepped closer to Sylvia again. Disgusted, she swung the cutlass again, slicing off the reaching arm at the elbow and following with a backswing that severed the opposite leg at the knee. Hearing the horrific creature's laugh, she did not pause. The unwieldy weapon, cleaved through the other arm and leg, sending the limbs skittering across the dark dirt like massive, monstrous insects.

All the while this butchery took place, Sinis giggled and cackled as if the sensation of extreme pain was some form of aphrodisiac. As Sylvia stepped back, she noticed a shifting of the scattered limbs, their twitches appearing to slide them a little closer to their monstrous master.

"Oh, oh! That was wonderful! Thank you! You are even better than René or Angelica!" Sinis said, his voice a moan of ecstasy.

Horrified beyond all measure, Sylvia felt a wave of nausea fill her body. Refusing to be sick, she stepped to the side and moved closer to the vile mockery of mankind. Taking her sword in both hands, she swung out and decapitated the creature. The sighs of delight vanished as the repulsive skull sailed aside, coming to rest near the tree line.

Sinis twitched, his abominable body already pulling itself together in pieces. The detached head, and slug-shaped extension, twitched and quivered, but appeared unable to move any further.

Seeing a method of slowing this repugnant fiend, Sylvia stepped around the convulsing, recreating body. Approaching the head, she thrust the cutlass blade deep into the skull. With a light step, she then carried the disgusting, dripping skull deeper into the woods. Approaching the shores of Lake Avernus, she swung her sword in a hard, fast arc. The heinous head flew from the end of the blade, sailing off into the lake. It struck the water with a soft, plunking sound and vanished from view an instant later.

Returning the cave, she was unsurprised to find Sinis's terrible torso vanished from view. Her father appeared a few seconds later, his face scratched, his clothes in tatters. Yet, as always, he was still smiling and looking quite merry. Spotting the fluid fallen about the area, his face changed to that of concern and confusion.

"Did something happen?" he asked.

Sylvia laughed and shook her head.

"I could not begin to explain without several glasses of wine within my body. Come, we must..."

Her words were cut off by a loud, horrific shriek of agony from within the depths of the cavern.

Without another word, Dardi and Sylvia ran into the dark depths. Their weapons were in hand and both were prepared to face the horrors within...

CHAPTER LXXI

Séverin stared at the howling horror that lay at his feet. Instead of a woman of unearthly and inhuman beauty, he was confronted with a being so repugnant that it took all his iron self-control to keep from becoming violently ill.

Enormously large and bloated, Nosos's shape was closer to that of a titanic burlap sack than that of a human. Her skin was a sickly pale green and covered with a slick, viscous fluid that squished and sloshed with each of her motions. Nosos's nose resembled that of a massive black and red tumor, a cancerous growth rather than a body extremity. Her mouth was a huge, lipless gash and the rotted teeth within were irregularly shaped and appeared barely connected to the visible bloody, bleeding gums.

Séverin realized the reason for his revulsion and understood this screeching terror in an instant. Gazing at the abhorrent Nosos was like staring into the face of disease in one fixed form. This ancient being was a horror, a terror from the ancient depths of the human soul. Disease, the great destroyer of the mighty and the meek—a fear that was embodied in this terrible creature.

Karnstein appeared seconds later, blunderbuss across his shoulder, pistol and saber in his hands. The rents in his clothes and the scratches across his arms and face denoted he had been through some trials since their parting.

From the other direction appeared Dardi and Sylvia, the former looking as battered as Karnstein.

Karnstein immediately made the sign of the cross, his blue eyes widening at the sight of the fallen Nosos.

"*In nomine Patris, et Filii, et Spiritus Sancti. Amen.*"

Dardi and Sylvia followed suit, making the sign, though Sylvia did exclaim, "*Madonna!*" under her breath.

"That is the Nosos? Why is she crawling about like a whipped dog?" Dardi asked, his sword raised and ready.

"We cut off much of her power. Something else hurt her a few moments ago. She screamed and wailed, and has not listed her head except to moan," Séverin explained, not looking away from the frightening figure.

"She has a servant. I doubt it can be killed, but I weakened the creature for a time," Sylvia explained. "I cut off its disgusting skull and threw the nasty object into the lake."

"*Alla Xul Egech Uruku,*" Nosos rasped, her mucus-filled throat barely able to form the word.

"What is she saying?" Séverin asked, looking to Karnstein.

"She's calling on a dark goddess… a birth sister…" the Austrian replied, leaning forward to listen despite his revulsion.

"…*Sarratum Selene Nadandu…*" Nosos continued to mumble.

"*Sister Selene, give me,*" Karnstein translated.

Séverin's eyes widened and he drew a pistol, firing into the face of Nosos. The harsh bark of the gun echoed through the cave, followed by another screech of agony from the ruined face of the monster.

"All of you! Do not let her speak! Fire your guns, use your swords! Franz, exorcise this monster!" Séverin said, his voice a harsh word of command.

Séverin, Sylvia, and Barto Dardi set about the creature, their attacks drowning out the Sumerian invocation by the Austrian exorcist.

A moment later, the silver light appeared before his body and they fell back, watching as the flare of light struck Nosos. A light moan filled the air and they stared down at the infamous dark fate of the Tenebrae.

Nosos was a third or less of her former size, her body dry and as brittle as an ancient mummy. Her yellow and red eyes were rheumy and she stared at them, her jaws moving, but only a dusty cough emerging from her desiccated frame.

"She still lives—or possibly is still undead. Would another of your exorcisms end this demon?" Dardi asked.

Karnstein shook his head.

"She is not a demon. I think all I did was cut her off from a source of dark power. If she receives any other life energy, she shall rise again."

"That shall not happen," Séverin said, not looking away from Nosos. "Go to the cart and bring back the covering. We shall wrap her tight and end this for all time. Franz? Are you prepared to invoke your power as a member of the holy inquisition?"

"If it will help, yes," Karnstein replied. "What are you considering?"

"A method of cutting this demon off from the world for all time," Séverin said.

He explained his plan. It was a very good one...

CHAPTER LXXI

Karnstein closed his eyes and intoned:

"*Anima Christi, sanctifica me. Corpus Christi, salve me. Sanguis Christi, inebria me. Aqua lateris Christi, lava me. Passio Christi, conforta me. O bone Iesu, exaudi me. Intra tua vulnera absconde me. Ne permittas me separari a te. Ab hoste maligno defende me. In hora mortis meae voca me. Et iube me venire ad te, ut cum Sanctis tuis laudem te in saecula saeculorum. Amen.*"

Opening his hands, he picked up the terrible, twisted, Mask of Satan. The face was still hideous, a wide-mouthed demon with a protruding tongue, hooded serpentine eye slits, and wickedly sharp spikes within in the interior. Karnstein, his eyes cold, his face stony, pressed the mask onto the face of the withered, dusty, Nosos. The same coughing cry emerged as he pushed it down into the skull.

Nosos lay chained on the simple wooden bed, each link inscribed with a prayer in Latin. Even a strong man would be hard pressed to squirm free from these bonds, let alone a withered corpse that was neither dead, alive, nor undead.

Then, without looking back, Karnstein opened his right hand. Sylvia, standing at his side, passed him a heavy wooden mallet and made the sign of the cross.

"In the name of Pope Pius VII and the Holy Inquisition, I do name you demon and fiend of the outer darkness. The sentence is eternal punishment," Karnstein said, raised the mallet and struck the mask three times with all the might in his arm.

Dropping the mallet to the ground, he took Sylvia's hand and they left the chamber. Outside, Séverin and Dardi waited, questions visible in their eyes.

"All is complete?" Séverin asked.

"Yes," Karnstein replied.

"It did not have to be you, assisting in there, daughter," Dardi said. "Gâteloup and I would have served willingly."

"Yes, Papa, I had to. My *fidanzato* and I do not require help in our duties," Sylvia replied and gave him a hug. "But thank you nevertheless."

They walked a short distance, stopping before the terrible Black Door that held this area separate from the rest of the prison. With visible reluctance, each headed through the gloom, their bodies quaking as they exited that frightening location.

"Using my position, I requested of King Joseph that he have this wing of the prison sealed off and removed from all records," Séverin stated. "He agreed and, in time, no one alive shall know of the Black Room. Do you know why I reacted so strongly when Nosos was attempting to invoke the dark powers?"

"I assumed you did not wish her to regain her former strength?" Karnstein replied as they strode up the stone steps.

"Yes, that is true. However, there is more. Did you hear the name she stated?" Séverin asked.

"Yes," Sylvia piped in. "Selene—the moon goddess of the Romans. Why?"

"Because," Dardi said from the rear, "Selene is also the name of a city—a terrible dark land known as the City of the Vampires."

"You believe she was trying to beg for power from the city?" Karnstein asked.

Séverin nodded as they exited the stairway into the depths of the prison.

"I do. Not merely because the master or mistress of that primordial state may be one of the Tenebrae. Another fact is quite apparent to those of us who have faced the denizens of Selene."

"Which is?" Sylvia asked, ignoring the soldiers who stared at her in frank appreciation as they headed from the prison.

"The vampires of Selene attack by piercing a victim with their tongue. More we do not know," Dardi explained.

"You two shall return to Paris with me," Séverin said. "I may have a means of finding more from the libraries of the dead Countess Addhema. Sylvia, I shall continue your training. Franz, we shall pursue the new direction we discussed. Then we shall seek Selene and discover a means of preventing another of the Tenebrae from rising in the world!"

Sylvia and Franz exchanged a look, realizing that their paths had already been mapped. Then they smiled, realizing that they would meet their fate together. Their hands squeezed a little tighter while they remained oblivious to the amused looks from the swordmasters.

CHAPTER LXXIII

"…sealed up and shall not bother us again. Also, the rat population is seriously diminished," Johann Spurzheim concluded, closing his small notebook.

"That will not last," Michele Bozzo replied, cutting into his egg with his fork. "Rats, like criminals, multiply without fail."

Spurzheim smiled and returned his journal to his inside pocket.

"It matters not. The *Camorra* is yours, as is the police force. The Cupbearers are gone forever, and the Napoleonic King trusts my word. All is complete."

The infamous master of crime shook his head.

"Not so, my friend. One final point. Giulio Nucci, also known as *Fra Diavolo*, is in hiding near Baronissi. Please capture and hang the scoundrel."

Spurzheim pulled out his notebook and made a notation.

"Forgive me, sir, but are you not *Fra Diavolo*?"

Bozzo finished his eggs and chuckled.

"Not anymore, my friend. You see, I gave the grasping paramour of Nucci a drug that allowed her to induce him to her bidding. I suggested several attacks and she agreed. The powder is nigh impossible to find—a variation of the Black Lotus from the east."

"Why did you use this expensive potion on that fool?" Spurzheim asked, hoping he was not in danger of annoying his patron.

"My plans are not limited to this small kingdom, good Johann. I no longer need to supervise the daily operations of the *Camorra*—my daughter and her husband will serve well enough. I shall move to another location and spread my influence throughout the world. But I shall keep a close eye on Naples and her people," Bozzo explained, rising and waving Lando to his side.

The flat-skulled man handed Spurzheim a heavy purse, laden with gold coins and jewels. Accepting the first of many payments, Spurzheim clicked his heels and bowed.

"I see now. You require the name *Fra Diavolo* to die while you go on. Very clever, sir."

"I agree." Bozzo replied, waving his underling from the room.

All was in readiness now. Naples was merely the first step in a larger plan-one that would result in Michele Bozzo as the most powerful man on Earth!

Afterword

We come to the end of the second of Napoleon's Vampire Hunter's tales, a world that appears to be expanding with each entry. Of course, I owe much of this to my editor/publisher/mentor Jean-Marc Lofficier. Always great to have an expert with an uncanny volume of experience and skill on your side. Thanks again, JM, I wouldn't have a writing career without your guidance and patience.

As mentioned in JM's introduction, Jean-Pierre Séverin comes from the mind of legendary French storyteller Paul Féval. Féval produced three fascinating vampire stories, with Séverin as the protagonist in *The Vampire Countess* (1856). Féval's undead, who emerged over forty years prior to Bram Stoker's *Dracula*, were bizarre, terrible creatures that were frankly far more unsettling than anything before or since. In this tale, I attempted to tell a little more of the life of this amazing character, who, I hope, one day will get his due as one of the first and greatest occult heroes.

Franz Karnstein emerged partially from the family created by Sheridan Le Fanu's *Carmilla* (1871), which pre-dated *Dracula* by 26 years. In that tale Le Fanu hinted at the terrible Karnstein clan and their dark roots—but his focus was really on the hinted sensual relationship between Laura and the undead Carmilla. This story fostered a host of books, anime, manga, and films since that time. The best known are the Hammer Horror Films' Karnstein trilogy, featuring a bevy of insanely lovely ladies and very bizarre characters. Franz's stern, powerfully religious, behavior emerges from the tradition of holy crusaders throughout fiction and history. His skills as an exorcist emerges from a series of legends drawn from the Biblical and Islamic traditions. More, I cannot say, but details shall emerge in time.

When writing the first novel in the series, I did want to include a female protagonist, preferably a heroine who would not merely exist as a "damsel in distress." When growing up, I always disliked Lois Lane for her need to constantly be rescued from harm by Superman in the early comics. The Black Widow, Elektra, Batgirl, and Power Girl, on the other hand...

In any event, Sylvia Dardi fits that tradition. I was partially influenced by Monica Bellucci's character of the same name in the delightful Christophe Gans film, *Le Pacte Des Loups* [*Brotherhood of the Wolf*] (2001). I hadn't planned on her and Franz Karnstein falling in love; I'd had other ideas for his future. But the characters disagreed, and I found them going in directions I hadn't expected, and will be interested in seeing develop. Her training under Séverin should prove interesting; he's a vastly different teacher from her father!

Barto Dardi is based on several swordmasters of the period, bold, exciting adventurers who were dangerous with a blade and lived life to the fullest. I'd planned to design a match for Séverin, but found myself writing someone who looked and behaved like character actor Nick Cravat. Cravat earned Hollywood notice as a partner in an acrobatic duo with legendary Oscar-winning actor Burt Lancaster. In their early swashbuckler films, they managed to include some of their acrobatic stunts to give the audience an additional thrill. Funny detail about Nick Cravat: he always played his parts silent because his thick Brooklyn accent would not fit the historical settings.

Nosos is a true Greek mythological figure, one of the Dark Fates known as the *Tenebrae* or the *Keres*. These creatures were the embodiments of horror—bringing baleful ends such as violent death, hate, and, of course, disease. Few details of these creatures are part of the historical record. Their mythological images show terrible women with dark wings, claws, and fangs. Being a person who spent an inordinate amount of time viewing Italian. French, etc., horror films, I chose a different route. Influenced by Nikolai Gogol's *Viy*, Dario Argento's *Three Mothers* trilogy, and woodcuts of the Black Death, a different version of Nosos appeared.

Her "vampires" came to me after discovering a series of lamprey close-ups on Facebook. Truly Lovecraftian-styled creatures, their toothy gullets magnified are the stuff of nightmares. The use of the tongue as an assaulting weapon came from Féval's *Vampire City* (1867). This was the third of his vampire novels, one which used real-life Gothic author Ann Radcliffe in a proto-*Buffy the Vampire Slayer* role.

Sinis's name comes from the tales of Theseus as he confronted six labors in his quest to find his father. Sinis was a robber who tied captives between two bent trees, resulting in the victim being torn to pieces once he released the trees. Theseus killed that wicked man by that same method and fathered a son with his daughter, Perigune. The image of Sinis on the cover, drawn by renowned Polish artist Mariusz Gandzel, was perfect—a truly chilling image of evil.

Hertz Ende a.k.a. Sinis was a product of my reading many early books on criminal history. Conmen like Ende abounded through Europe—false Satanists who were more interested in money than magic. Few are remembered to this day, but historians like Colin Wilson did devote some time discussing a few of them in various articles and books.

Michele Bozzo, a.k.a. *Fra Diavolo*, a.k.a. Colonel Bozzo-Corona, is probably Féval's greatest achievement. The mastermind behind a worldwide criminal enterprise known as The Black Coats, this character was far ahead of his time. Professor Moriarty and other criminal geniuses all emerged out of the tradition created in this series. I encourage anyone who haven't read these books to look them up; you won't be sorry.

Francesca Policeni née Bozzo was a secondary character in Féval's *Black Coats*. Her husband was mentioned as one of the gang's leaders, but no other details about him emerged in the books. They were the parents of the Colonel's lovely—and important—granddaughter (also named Francesca, or Fanchette), but little else. Our Francesca's details and behavior came from characteristics of Fanchette and my youthful crush on a young Sophia Loren. The fact that I placed her in a knife fight with Sylvia Dardi does go to show that the mind of a writer is a unique place to visit.

Johann Spurzheim is another Féval creation, who appeared as the main antagonist in *The Companions of The Silence*; he is the elderly police chief of Naples. He is a terrifying man, despite being quite decrepit, and as evil as the criminals he was meant to arrest.

Finally, the Vampire City of Selene is also a Féval creation, in the previously mentioned *Vampire City*. A terrifying location, as well as a monstrous vampire lord, Otto Goetzi, make this tale an incredible ride for the reader.

As to the future of Napoleon's Vampire Hunters, I have some thoughts as to their further adventures. I have a feeling we shall see more of Séverin, Karnstein and Dardi soon.

Frank Schildiner

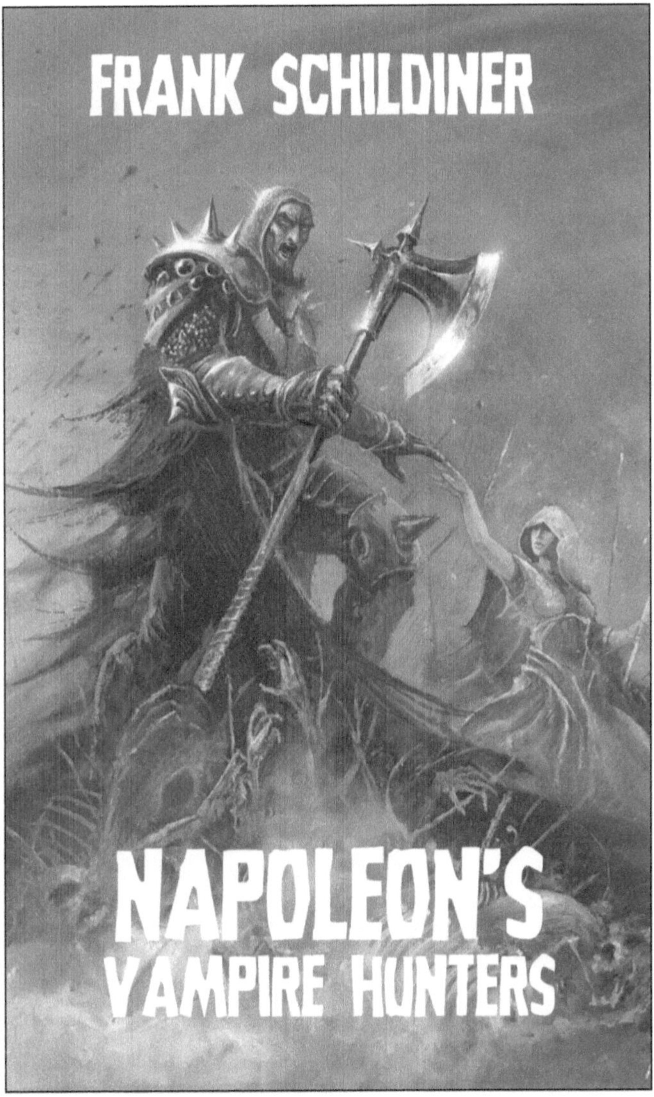
FRANK SCHILDINER
NAPOLEON'S
VAMPIRE HUNTERS

FRENCH HORROR COLLECTION

Cyprien Bérard. *The Vampire Lord Ruthwen*
Aloysius Bertrand. *Gaspard de la Nuit*
Jules Claretie. *Obsession*
Harry Dickson. *The Heir of Dracula*
Harry Dickson. *Harry Dickson vs The Spider*
Jules Dornay. *Lord Ruthven Begins*
Alexandre Dumas. *The Return of Lord Ruthven*
Renée Dunan. *Baal*
Paul Féval. *Knightshade*
Paul Féval. *Revenants*
Paul Féval. *Vampire City*
Paul Féval. *The Vampire Countess*
Paul Féval. *The Wandering Jew's Daughter*
Paul Féval, *fils. Felifax, the Tiger-Man*
Charles-Marie Flor O'Squarr. *Phantoms*
G.L. Gick. *Harry Dickson and the Werewolf of Rutherford Grange*
Léon Gozlan. *The Vampire of the Val-de-Grâce*
Paul Lacroix. *Danse Macabre*
Etienne-Léon de Lamothe-Langon. *The Virgin Vampire*
Maurice Level. *The Gates of Hell*
Maurice Limat. *Mephista*
Jean-Marc & Randy Lofficier. *The Vampire Almanac* (2 volumes)
Marie Nizet. *Captain Vampire*
C. Nodier, A. Béraud & Toussaint-Merle, V. Hugo, P. Foucher & P. Meurice. *Frankenstein & The Hunchback of Notre-Dame*
J. Polidori, C. Nodier, E. Scribe. *Lord Ruthven the Vampire*
P.-A. Ponson du Terrail. *The Vampire and the Devil's Son*
P.-A. Ponson du Terrail. *The Immortal Woman*
Jean Richepin. *The Crazy Corner*
Frank Schildiner: *The Quest of Frankenstein*